W9-BTZ-200

AMERICAN FICTION:
New Readings

AMERICAN FICTION:
New Readings

edited by
Richard Gray

VISION
and
BARNES & NOBLE

Vision Press Limited
Fulham Wharf
Townmead Road
London SW6 2SB

and

Barnes & Noble Books
81 Adams Drive
Totowa, NJ 07512

ISBN (UK) 0 85478 065 3
ISBN (US) 0 389 20370 X

Printed and bound in Great Britain by
Unwin Brothers Ltd.,
Old Woking, Surrey.
Phototypeset by Galleon Photosetting,
Ipswich, Suffolk.
MCMLXXXIII

Contents

Introduction

by RICHARD GRAY

This is a collection of original essays on American fiction. All
of the essays were written by people who have been active in
the field of American studies for some time and have an
enthusiastic and committed interest in the particular authors
they have written about. No one set of critical principles
characterizes every essay: the approaches range from what
now tends to be referred to as traditionalist—but which itself
encompasses a variety of methods including the impression-
istic, the New Critical, the moral and the historical—to what
can perhaps best be described as the structuralist and post-
structuralist. What the essays do have in common, however,
are two controlling aims: to introduce some of the more
important American prose writers' to readers unacquainted
with them, and to offer to those who already have some
knowledge of American fiction the possibility of fresh perspectives, new ways of reading familiar texts. In some situations, it
may be, these two aims would be at odds or at least difficult to
slot into each other, but in the American context they are in
certain very essential ways complementary. For the tradition
of American writing (as critics and the writers themselves
never tire of telling us) is a tradition of the new, of radical
innovation and frequently eccentric experiment: and in a sense
the most useful task that any commentator can perform is to
make us aware of that newness—to recover for all readers,
regardless of their previous knowledge of American literature,
something of the strangeness, the sheer idiosyncrasy or even
oddity, of the text.

Perhaps it would be worth developing this point a little
further, or rather these two points: the nature of American
writing and the response it requires from the reader. To
simplify (as one inevitably must in a brief introduction), the

actual nature of American writing was anticipated by Alexis de Tocqueville in his *Democracy in America*, which was first published in two volumes in 1835 and 1840—that is to say, between the first of James Fenimore Cooper's Leatherstocking tales and the last. 'In democracies', Tocqueville observed, 'men never stay still; . . . there is almost always something unexpected, something . . . provisional about their lives.' More important, he argued, 'each man is for ever driven back upon himself alone'; for whereas 'aristocracy brings everyone together, linking peasant to King in one long chain', one carefully articulated, hierarchical framework, 'democracy breaks the chain and separates each link.' As a result, people 'become accustomed to thinking of themselves in isolation, and imagine that their entire fate is in their own hands'. The literary implications of this were, as Tocqueville saw, enormous; for by definition order, established forms and precedents, became things to be despised, while irregularity and experiment—or what Tocqueville himself referred to as the 'bizarre, incorrect, overburdened, and loose'—became qualities to be sought for and cherished. At the same time, Tocqueville pointed out, the writer in the infant democracy of America, would feel neither willing nor able to turn to 'legends, . . . traditions, and memories of distant times' for his subjects; instead, he would have to explore and articulate his own private being, which would be 'sufficiently exposed for him to perceive something' but 'sufficiently veiled to leave a great deal in impenetrable shade' and so allow room for imaginative manoeuvre. The familiar forms and plots would be lost to him, in fact, but one thing patiently awaited his contemplation: which was, to quote Tocqueville's own ringing words,

> Human destiny, man himself, freed from time and place, and brought face to face with nature and with God, with his passions, his doubts, his unexpected good fortune, and his incomprehensible miseries. . . .[1]

This would be enough to supply an endless variety of narratives and an almost infinite number of structuring principles, shapes peculiar to each work—enough, in short, to create what I referred to just now as a tradition of the new.

Some of the terms and assumptions of Tocqueville's argument

would almost certainly be questioned by many contemporary observers of America and critics of American literature, including several of the contributors to this volume. There is, for example, the point that Tocqueville took very little note of the dialectical nature of literary development, the way that any writing, including American writing, grows out of an inter-action between the old and the new, rather than a simple rejection of one in favour of the other, and the point that he paid little attention to differences of region. And there is the further point that he took as a matter of indisputable fact many things that many now would regard as a matter of language. The notion of the self is an obvious example of this: something which, it is now often insisted, has its basis in a particular system of communication rather than in anything that can properly be called reality. Such things may seem and indeed are important, raising as they do certain quite basic questions, but they do not, I think, affect the essential thrust of Tocqueville's argument; they enrich and complicate it without undermining it and in the event he emerges bloody but unbowed. Thus the fact that things were not quite as simple as Tocqueville suggested, that no American writer could or can ignore Europe, does not invalidate his discovery of a movement away from collective mythologies and inclusive tendencies towards the disintegrative and divisive. Equally, the fact that America is a place of many regions did not and does not fragment the notion of a specifically American identity to the point of non-existence; it simply means that the American nation is one like most others, made up of separate and often conflicting groups. Finally, and perhaps most crucially, the idea that 'the self' may be a matter of idiom rather than fact, epistemology rather than ontology, does not seriously affect the claim that the American writer pursues self-discovery and self-expression. To speak tautologically for a moment, a writer writes: which is to say that he always deals, in the first instance, with epistemology and idiom, matters of perception and expression. In more local terms, he always deals with the language system of his own culture; and, as far as the American writer is concerned at least, 'the self' is so ingrained in that system that even if he tries to dissociate himself from it he is, in a sense, only confirming its importance. Something that the American linguist Benjamin

Lee Whorf said is perhaps worth quoting here. 'We dissect nature', Whorf argued, 'along lines laid down by our native language',

> . . . the world is presented in a kaleidoscopic flux of impressions which has to be organized in our minds—and this means largely by the linguistic systems in our minds. We cut nature up, organize into concepts, and ascribe significances as we do, largely because we are parties to an agreement to organize it in this way—an agreement that holds throughout our speech community and is codified in the patterns of our language. The agreement is, of course, an implicit and unstated one, BUT ITS TERMS ARE ABSOLUTELY OBLIGATORY: we cannot talk at all except by subscribing to the organization and classification of data to which the agreement subscribes.[2]

Without necessarily accepting the authoritarian implications of this, we can see how it restores the concept of the self to a central place in American writing, even for those who question its validity, its basis in empirical reality—and how, too, it confirms the seminal paradox that Tocqueville helped to uncover of an experimental tradition.

But if Tocqueville was right about the nature of American literature—and I believe he was—what consequences does this have for our response to it? The main consequence, surely, is that in reading an American book the world is freshly seen and fully discovered by the reader as it was once, presumably, by the writer: the text restores and renews things for us because, in the act of resurrecting his own habits of perception, the American author resurrects ours too. The point is made over and over again by American writers of otherwise very different persuasions: that their aim is to establish an original connection with the universe for them and for us, to release things from their greasy contexts and unravel new, more personal and more accurate ways of seeing and naming. There is an element here of what the Russian formalist critic, Victor Shklovsky, termed 'defamiliarization'. 'As perception becomes blunted by habit,' Shklovsky argued, 'it becomes automatic'; as a result, 'we see the object as though it were hidden in a sack. We know what it is by its configuration, but we see only its silhouette.' Gradually, habitualization devours everything: 'objects, clothes, furniture, one's wife, and the fear of war'. We begin to lose our sense of things—and, it might be added (although Shklovsky does not say so himself), our sense of ourselves, our own separate identities, as well. As Shklovsky sees it, it is the purpose of art to counter all this, to reverse the desensitizing process; art, he insists,

> exists to help us recover the sensation of life, it exists to enable us to feel things, to make the stone stony. The aim of art is to give a sensation of the object as something seen, not something recognised. The technique of art is to make things unfamiliar. . . .

It is not difficult to see how Shklovsky's remarks apply with particular force to American writing. After all, it was Emerson, a founding father of American literature, who said something very similar in one of his essays. 'All around us', he declared, 'what powers are wrapped up under the coarse mattings of custom, and all wonder prevented . . . the wise man wonders at the usual.' 'Make the aged eye sun-clear', pleads Emerson elsewhere in a poem; and his plea, for what he once described as 'the power to fix the momentary eminency of an object', has been repeated in different forms by most American writers over the past century and a half.

It is worth emphasizing that this act of recovery, of washing the eyes and the imagination clean, is not regarded—by American writers, at least—as a once-and-for-all procedure. For each time the reader returns to an American book he is called on to see it in a new way, from a fresh perspective, perhaps, or with different intonations and inflections; he or she is called on to reimagine and reinvent in the process of becoming acquainted, or reacquainted, with things. The most immediate cause of this is the famous open-endedness of American narratives: their refusal, for instance, to round things off neatly or provide a convenient summation of the lives and fates of the characters. As a result, the reader is forced to hypothesize—to choose, it may be, between alternative interpretations, resolve doubts and equivocations, or simply fill in gaps; he is compelled, in fact, into an act of collaboration or co-production with the writer. 'Small erections may be finished by their first architects', declared Melville in *Moby Dick* (that most seminal of American novels), 'grand ones, true ones, ever leave the copestone to posterity.

God keep me from ever completing anything.' And the reason he neither would nor could complete anything, Melville knew, was not merely his limited supplies of 'Time, Strength, Cash, and Patience'. It was something much more positive—his belief (and his characteristically American belief, at that) in the individual self and the uniqueness of personal experience; and, beyond this, it was his commitment to the idea that each reading is essentially an act of creation, in a way a fresh making of the text.

Which brings us back to the two purposes of this book: to offer an introduction to some readers and another perspective on the familiar to others. Not every American writer has agreed with Melville's reasons for refusing to complete anything (although, as a matter of fact, most have), but every American writer worth looking at and talking about has agreed with the refusal itself; they have shared, in effect, in his efforts not merely to make it new for the author himself but to offer to the reader the possibility of making it new as well. As a result, every venture into an American book becomes, in a very important sense, a new beginning, a fresh start, no matter how many times that book may have been read before and no matter how much, or little, may be known about it beforehand. Obviously, the more that is brought to any story, in terms of previous experience and knowledge, the richer and more satisfying any reading of it is likely to be. But it is this simple and central belief in art as process rather than product that makes it possible for collections such as this one to pursue what might, in other contexts, seem like irreconcilable aims and that, more importantly, makes American fiction itself such a constant surprise—a means of renewal and (the phrase is inescapable) a source of inspiration and wonder.

One final point needs to be made about this collection. There is one essay that is different from all the others, in that it concentrates on a single novel and has already been published as part of a book: Brian Way's piece on *The Great Gatsby*, which is taken from his *Fitzgerald and the Art of Social Fiction* published by Edward Arnold in 1980. Brian Way was asked to write an essay on Fitzgerald, which he readily agreed to do, but, sadly, he died only a short while afterwards. His widow, Josephine Way, and his publishers have generously agreed to allow part of his book to appear here in place of an original essay. More important, Mrs. Way has kindly allowed this book to be dedicated to the memory of her husband. Brian Way was liked and admired by very many with an interest in American writing; and it is on behalf of all these people that this collection of essays is offered as a small tribute, with respect and affection.

NOTES

1. Alexis de Tocqueville, *De la Democratie en Amérique* (1835–40; Paris, 1961 edition), Vol. II, p. 81. See also pp. 66, 106, 231. My translation.
2. This extensive quotation from *Language, Thought, and Reality: Selected Writings of Benjamin Lee Whorf*, edited by John B. Carroll (Cambridge, Mass., 1956), p. 213, is reproduced by permission of the M.I.T. Press. Copyright 1956 by the Massachusetts Institute of Technology.
3. Viktor Shklovsky, 'Art as Device', in *On the Theory of Prose* (Moscow-Leningrad, 1925), p. 12. I am indebted to Dr. Leon Burnett of the Department of Literature, University of Essex, for providing me with a literal translation and advice.

1

James Fenimore Cooper: Historical Novelist

by CHARLES SWANN

1

I want to use *The Leatherstocking Novels* to argue that Cooper's central achievement was to confront the apparently exiguous materials of American history in a brilliantly successful attempt to find ways of discovering and defining its special qualities. To concentrate on these novels is, of course, to ignore the extra-ordinarily wide and fine range of Cooper's fiction and non-fiction. But to deal with most of these works is unfortunately to be too often reduced to plot-summary, as they largely remain unjustifiably unread. And *The Leatherstocking Novels* can fairly be taken as representative not because they are always necessarily his best work (though they are significantly the most famous), but because they all declare the fact that Cooper's mode of understanding the world was radically historical and because they also show Cooper's repeated obsession with political justice. These definitions and evaluations of (American) history were not easy, as the tensions, ambivalencies and ambiguities of the novels repeatedly declare—but these were his constant concerns.

This is to argue against the commonly held set of opinions implied by Harry Henderson's statement in *Versions of the Past*:

> The differences between the complex tensions and microcosmic society of *The Pioneers* and the ritualized and mythicized

15

wilderness of *The Deerslayer*, composed twenty years later—the change which D. H. Lawrence called a '*decrescendo* of reality and a crescendo of beauty' prohibits any attempt to find meaningful generalizations for the special quality of Cooper's historical imagination throughout the whole canon. (p. 73)

I do not want to suggest that Cooper repeats himself; I do want to argue that his literary career should be seen as a coherent whole and that to see *The Leatherstocking Novels* as moving from domestic historical realism to ahistorical myth is incorrect. If there is a shift in the portrayal of Natty, it is from moral authority (however politically powerless) to complicity in the guilt of violent dispossession. It is not a shift from sociological picture to an icon of Christian saint or warrior. It is a movement from the moral symbolic selectivity embodied by his use of the gun or the spear in *The Pioneers* to the virtuoso slaughter of two Indians with a single bullet in *The Deerslayer*. It is hard to see that the society of *The Pioneers* is, in any significant sense, more microcosmic than that of *The Deerslayer*— indeed, the opposite is easier to argue. The suggestion that *The Deerslayer* is more 'mythic' than the earlier work (and the implication that thus 'complex tensions' are somehow resolved) needs to be questioned—and rebutted. All *The Leatherstocking Novels* are concerned with similar problems, such as expropriation and the problem of the relationships between law and justice in periods of historical change—and all are set firmly in a secular, historical framework. The appeal of mythic structure is certainly felt (perhaps most notably in *The Pathfinder*), but it is felt and presented only to be examined and rejected.

The history which Cooper takes as his subject has no simple definition. The conventional comparison with Scott (so tempting to one kind of literary historian ignorant of much of even the history of the British historical novel) should rather be seen as a contrast. Cooper is far more interested in ideas—indeed, his fiction can be described as a fiction of ideas (or rather concepts). But he is not a novelist of ideas in the way, for example, a Thomas Mann is, for his fiction of concepts does not explore the meaning and validity of those concepts through sophisticated debate and extensive analysis but rather by the repetition of key terms in various contexts which are then tested by the frequently violent actions of the narrative—as though an eighteenth-century commitment to generalization is being exposed to the nineteenth-century concern to historicize both concepts and experience. Scott almost always presents history as an evolutionary process, one in which his wavering hero finally settles for the winning side—and the reader knows where he should be. Scott's determining historical moment can be represented by the 'Glorious Revolution', a comparatively simple, unambiguous and peaceful transfer of symbolic power (where the only problem is nomenclature: 1688 was neither glorious nor a revolution). In Cooper's political language, it represents the triumph of an aristocracy. (His view, in this if little else, is remarkably similar to Disraeli's: both point to Venice as a corrupt oligarchy masquerading as a democracy.) The triumph of the bourgeois hero is celebrated by Scott (with sentimental nostalgia the most that can be felt for alternative ways of life): it is merely recognized by Cooper.

Cooper recognizes that historical structures are not unitary as his narrative patterns repeatedly show. His view of history is one of paradoxes and contradictions, absences and silences, for his revolution is the American Revolution—and his fictional treatment of this reveals how problematic he found this event, as the most cursory readings of, for example, *The Spy*, *Lionel Lincoln*, and *Wyandotté* show. Cooper was fascinated by the relationships between appearances and reality, fascinated by the information given and concealed by masks. It is exactly at the moment of revolution that identity may need to be disguised: it is after a revolution that it may be tactless to ask too many questions of who did what during the turmoil, and there is the opportunity to reshape one's identity. Cooper's ambivalent attitude to the event that created his identity as American writer was hardly unique. But it is significant that he never wrote a Leatherstocking novel set in the Revolutionary period despite the clear commercial temptations—and the omission is the more obvious as the novels are all situated in or related to crucial moments of American history. In *The Pioneers* hardly anyone explicitly refers back to the Revolution. (One function of M. Le Quoi as emigré from the French Revolution is to displace overt anxiety about revolution with his role as comic foreigner and with his restoration at the end of the novel.) Yet the difference between the old royalist, the senile *Major*

Effingham, and the new man, *Judge* Temple, together with the fact that Effingham's son, link between past and future, royalism and republicanism, is missing, points suggestively to the felt problems of the transfer of power and the ways in which these changes could be 'legitimated'. Perhaps the most crucial implied judgement on the Revolution is the ambiguous description of how Temple acquires (and exercises) his power and money: he moves from the part of city businessman to the roles of landed gentleman, city founder and lawmaker.

2

What is clear is that Cooper presents us with a view of history as tragic division—a view which subverts any official optimistic version of the American story. In no Leatherstocking novel is land ownership as conventionally understood given anything like a full endorsement. The problem of the relationships between power and legitimate authority constantly recurs and is not resolved, and this is as true of what has mistakenly been called the nostalgic *Pioneers* as of the 'mythic' *Deerslayer*. Nor is there any other form of reconciliation. When a 'happy ending' is provided, it is very much a subordinate part of the total fictional pattern—and it is enacted through a physical and/or ideological recoil from the frontier and thus is a refusal of the very problems and tensions that the location of the novel had insisted on, that had generated the plot. That happy ending is, of course, usually emblematized by marriage (though, significantly, not cross-class marriage, that device so often used by English novelists of the mid-nineteenth century as a way of making a utopian gesture towards social unity, towards a future without conflict). But these marriages cannot be dismissed as merely a sign of the ways in which Cooper was bound by the conventions of romantic fiction. Rather they indicate one part of the ideological divison within the narrative—a split enacted in so many ways and perhaps most significantly (though not exclusively) by the figure of Natty himself. However incisively critical his comments about 'civilization' (*alias* the march of history, *aka* 'progress'), his actions, save in the case of the purely symbolic killings in *The Pioneers*, serve, in all the other novels almost without exception, to advance the changes he so justly criticizes both for their means and their ends. It is as though the most he can do as moral authority is to provide critical moral footnotes to a tragic, relentless history which he helps, consciously or unconsciously, on its way. Thus in *The Prairie* he guides his white middle-class heroes and heroines through a world they do not understand to safety, but he is reduced to having to tell Paul Hover to 'forget anything you may have heard from me which is nevertheless true' (Ch. XXIII). (This is further ironized: Natty and his dependents only escape because of Indian hospitality and because of Ishmael's just judgements when they are in his power. And where do we leave Hover and Middleton but in the State *legislature?*)

This tension is also apparent on the structural level. Cooper's commitment to narrative forces him to expose the contradictions even within what was clearly intended as a unified ideological fiction. Thus, in *Home as Found* (a novel in which Washington and Natty Bumppo are set down as the only two really great men of the time), the Effinghams may make their points about their class position, their culture, their property rights, and a marriage occurs which reinforces these themes through an inheritance plot that verges on the incestuous, but it is left to the shiftless Bragg to go west to grow up (or down) with the country. The Effinghams do not remain to live the values they have asserted, but retreat to Europe, American cosmopolitans, whose United States property seems to exist merely to support their tourism, their tired aestheticism. As one character says (in a rather different context), 'if the spirit of Leatherstocking has any concern with the matter, he is a mocking spirit.'

This is on the visit to the Speaking Rocks: local legend has it that there is no echo at all, and that the sounds come from the spirit of Leatherstocking who repeats everything said 'in mockery of the invasion of the woods'. The references back to Leatherstocking suggest a discomfort with the achievements of the present: the patronizingly generous obituary pronounced over the place where Natty's hut once stood fails to include the fact that Natty burnt the hut in despair at the ways in which Judge Temple's laws had been manipulated and misused. Thus Eve Effingham:

> There . . . stood the hut of Natty Bumppo, . . . a man who had the simplicity of a woodsman, the heroism of a savage, the faith of

19

a Christian, and the feelings of a poet. A better than he, after his fashion, seldom lived. (Ch. XIV)

Thus Natty in *The Pioneers* standing amid the smoking embers:

What would ye with an old and helpless man? . . . You've brought in the troubles and divilties of the law, where no man was ever known to disturb another. . . . What more would ye have? For I am here—one too many. (Ch. XXXII)

3

The Pioneers carries its investigations of legality beyond the question of mere misuse of the law into an investigation of the (moral) validity (and relevance) of Temple's laws themselves. Even when allowance is made for the historical stage which the community has reached, Templeton is presented as a society brought into being by a man who seems, among other things, to be willing to ignore the separation of powers. His laws are too often loosely symbolic declarations of his power (or the power he desires) rather than relevant to the conditions and needs of the community he should be representing—to say nothing of their relationship (or lack of one) to any substantial concept of justice. At the same time, he confuses and exploits the distinctions between private and public that should be inherent in his role as *judge*. Natty cannot understand the distinction:

'I must be governed by the law—'
'Talk not to me of law, Marmaduke Temple,' interrupted the hunter.
'Did the beast of the forest mind your laws when it was thirsty and hungering for the blood of your own child!' . . .
'My private feelings must not enter into—' (Ch. XXXIII)

If this passage is read in isolation, it may seem that only sympathy is due to Natty, that the right is with the Judge. But we need to remember that this exchange occurs when Natty has just heard that he is to be imprisoned until he pays a fine which he cannot hope to pay unless he is allowed out to earn the money. It is as irrational as imprisoning debtors (and Natty can hardly be expected to intuit that Temple in his private role plans to pay the fine). The general point is returned to at the beginning of Chapter XXXV:

'[I]t would sound ill indeed to report that a judge had extended favor to a convicted criminal because he had saved the life of his child.'

'I see . . . the difficulty of your situation . . .' cried the daughter; 'but in appreciating the offense of poor Natty, I cannot separate the minister of the law from the man. . . . I know Natty to be innocent, and, thinking so, I must think all wrong who oppress him.'

'His judge among the number! Thy father, Elizabeth! . . . [T]ry to remember that the laws alone remove us from the condition of the savages; that he has been criminal, and that his judge was thy father.'

Again, at first sight, Temple's position looks, if tough-minded, irreproachable. But as the dialogue continues, we can see (unless our eyes are misted by tears brought on by an appeal to fatherhood) that Temple's argument is not entirely coherent, that he exploits Elizabeth's personal love and loyalty.

This is hardly the only time that Temple's position needs examination. His opening shot with a scatter-gun loaded with buck-shot manages to wound the hidden heir. This is not merely evidence of his unfitness to live in and have a claim on the life of the woods, but his obsessive desire to pretend that the deer is his comes, it may seem, oddly from someone committed to the gospel of profitable use. (There is, we discover, already venison on his table, where 'the object seemed to be profusion . . . obtained entirely at the expense of order and elegance'.) His desire to maintain that claim before his dependants reveals not only that he is willing to bribe (Cooper's word) the black, but his ambivalent position on slavery. Aggy's legal master, owing to the Judge's religious scruples, is Richard Jones—but 'when any dispute between his lawful and his real master occurred' the black is trapped into silence. Here, as elsewhere, Temple is a figure of power—and law is merely a sign of that power.

The epigraph to Chapter XXIII (the seine-fishing episode) is a carefully chosen quotation from *Pericles*: 'Help, masters, help; here's a fish hangs in the net, like a poor man's right in the law.' The full weight of this is only felt when Natty is in court. But there is a further irony in the whole question of the law relating to seine-fishing which makes the symbolic moral contrast between Natty's spearing of a single fish and the almost erotic pleasure in the profusion of the slaughter (which Temple and Oliver, however temporarily, both share) the stronger. The Judge tells his audience in the inn that 'there is an act prohibiting the drawing of seines, at any other than the proper season' (Ch. XIV). But in Chapter XXIII, he informs Elizabeth that it 'is only in the spring and autumn, that, for a few days' the fish are to 'be found around the points within the reach of a seine'—and Cooper has told us that 'the season had now arrived when the bass fisheries were allowed by the provisions of the law that Judge Temple had procured.' The ironic attack on Temple's law-making could hardly be clearer or more forcible: he has helped to pass a law forbidding seine-fishing during the time of year when seine-fishing is impossible (and permitting it at, presumably, the time the fish are spawning). It is an interesting law in that it cannot be broken. The 'crime' of killing a deer out of season is a less clear-cut case of redundancy but it is still worth consideration. Natty breaks the letter of the law—but does he break its (nominal) intention which is presumably to preserve the deer? He kills a *buck*, not a doe, as the text emphasizes, and it is hard to see that this can have any serious effect on the natural order at that time of year. Natty earlier in the novel makes the point that nobody who knows would kill a doe with a fawn. But since coupling takes place in autumn, there is no reason for protecting bucks in the early summer.

Judge Temple, if conservation not declaration of ownership was his intention, might have spent his time better when law-making. But he takes possessive individualism to an extreme with his repeated desire (never argued but simply announced) that there should be personal ownership in game—and this is to make a very radical claim for the extent of ownership. As the ninth edition of *The Encyclopedia Britannica* points out:

> By the very nature of the case, wild animals cannot be made the subject of that kind of ownership which is generally signified by the term property. The substantial basis of the law of property is physical possession, the actual power of dealing with things as we see fit, and we can have no such power over animals in a state of nature. (Vol. X, p. 61)

22

Ownership and possession are points that Cooper radically and generally interrogates and extends far beyond the question of rights to game. For example, in the opening to Chapter VII, he writes 'the Europeans, or, to use a more significant term, the Christians, dispossessed the original owners of the soil'— and this is to be connected to 'Indian John's' recovery of a sense of his own identity only at the moment of death as he repudiates what white cultural control has done to him and his people.

I have been trying to suggest that *The Pioneers* is not so much about a clash between natural and civil law, between Natty and the Judge, as it is an examination of the quality of the civil law that is 'enforced' in Templeton. That criticism is not made only from the point of view of Natty's principles—in which case it might well have turned out to be an ahistorical debate—but by the fiction as a whole. It is, finally, a hostile criticism. This is not to suggest that Cooper rejects civil law in the name of a romantic concept of man in the state of nature— if only because Natty himself is shown as responsible to and responsible for that society. But, to put it crudely, the Judge (and his society) are shown to be intellectually and morally flawed. This is not a religious but a political indictment. The laws that Temple both makes and enforces are shown to have little to do with justice (that key word that resounds through all *The Leatherstocking Novels*) but much to do with a kind of bourgeois attempt to legitimate ownership—and to extend the powers that go with (land) ownership and social status, to give the semblance of authority to power. Cooper recognizes that there will be inevitable tragi-comic tensions as an inevitable historical change occurs, as an agrarian order displaces an earlier order (or disorder). He at the same time experiments with the idea of a happy ending to this history with the notion of the perfect heir (and heiress). Edwards/Effingham could, perhaps, be free of the guilts and claims of the past. But Cooper contrasts the theory of the perfect heir (Edwards/ Effingham is in various ways legitimated by Natty, by Indian John, by his royalist grandfather who first got the land from the Indians, and as Elizabeth Temple's husband—thus, incidentally, redeeming and removing the Temple name) with the narrative which questions that theory, and the narrative settings which show him coming away from any position of potential synthesis and closer and closer to the Judge's world and world-view (including, significantly, similar lapses from his and the Judge's own standards).

Cooper gives a useful definition of his idea of the proper function and justification of civil law at the opening of *The American Democrat*. It comes from the beginning of the section 'On Government':

> Man is known to exist in no part of the world, without certain rules for the regulation of his intercourse with those around him. It is a first necessity of his weakness, that laws, founded on the immutable principles of natural justice, should be framed in order to protect the feeble against the violence of the strong; the honest from the schemes of the dishonest; the temperate and industrious from the waste and indolence of the dissolute and idle.

It gives the basis for the critical comment on the laws we see in *The Pioneers*. Any 'creation' of a new America has failed: any dream of a government of laws and not of men has vanished. Natty states correctly that might makes right here as in the old country. Near the end of the novel, he looks forward to a day when 'justice shall be the law, and not power.' He expresses himself in religious terms—but it points to a political failure and a political possibility. The laws have not been based on natural justice. The feeble have not been protected. Far from the honest being guarded from the schemes of the dishonest, the law has been used by the dishonest as a mask for their attempts to gain illicit knowledge in aid of their dreams of illicit wealth (as the misuse of the search warrant shows). And though the values of temperance are praised by Temple, waste and indolence abound in his community, unchecked by his laws.

The novel ends with a magnificent irony:

> This was the last that they ever saw of the Leatherstocking, whose rapid movements preceded the pursuit which Judge Temple both ordered and conducted. He had gone far towards the setting sun—the foremost in that band of pioneers who are opening the way for the march of the nation across the continent.

Natty goes west, at once a representative of the past and the future, to create in spite of himself a world he despises. But the narrative refuses Natty the moral authority that might be gained from the desperate integrity of his flight (a freedom Temple is unwilling to allow him). He cannot even claim historical priority for Hiram Doolittle, the unscrupulous jack-of-all-trades, has preceded him in stepping westward.

4

The examination of historical priorities and the problem of the definitions of history continue in the other novels—perhaps most ambitiously in *The Deerslayer*. *The Last of the Mohicans*, however, is not far behind. It contains two histories within the narrative. One is the ironically placed history the French and English 'waged for the possession of a country that neither was destined to retain'—two countries which, despite their differences, '*united* to rob' the original 'possessors . . . of their native *right*' to name their land (Ch. 1: my emphases). The way in which the power to name men and natural objects is seen as a significant index of imperialism or of respect for the other is something to which Cooper constantly returns—from Indian John in *The Pioneers* to the question of the proper name of the lake in *The Deerslayer*. The other history is the larger, more tragic theme indicated by the title of the book, which transcends the struggles of French and English yet is an unintended product of those conflicts. It is at the point at which Cooper begins to concentrate on this theme that he rebukes history as conventionally written:

> 'The Massacre of William Henry' . . . is now becoming obscured by time; and thousands, who know that Montcalm died like a hero on the plains of Abraham, have yet to learn how much he was deficient in that moral courage without which no man can be truly great. . . . [A]s history, like love, is so apt to surround her heroes with an atmosphere of imaginary brightness, it is probable that Louis de Saint Véran will be viewed by posterity only as the gallant defender of his country, while his cruel apathy on the shores of the Oswego and of the Horican will be forgotten. Deeply regretting this weakness on the part of a sister muse, we shall at once retire from her sacred precincts, within the proper limits of our own humble vocation. (Ch. XVIII)

Historical fiction in the variety of its voices, and the clash of values that the variety of points of view dramatizes, can produce if not a just narrative, then the materials for right judgement. It is historiography which is ideological; which, Cooper argues, is the product of the mythicizing imagination that creates heroes and villains and presents character as one-dimensional—which 'forgets' the incident that mars the ideological unity. Of course Cooper does not retire from competition with Clio: the repeated emphases on the violence and brutality of frontier warfare and the problems of right action in such circumstances indicate as much. The 'narrative of 1757' (to use the subtitle), with its insistence that the cultural harmony and reconciliation that could have been embodied by marriage between Cora and Uncas is not immoral but historically impossible, reinforces the point. Indeed, Cooper's presentation of the interpretative artist as a figure preaching a comically irrelevant harmony extends the claim for his narrative to criticize historiography—and one kind of art.

The Prairie completes the related historical process enacted in the first three Leatherstocking novels, giving the obituary of Natty against the background of the Louisiana Purchase, the act that guaranteed that the States would become a continental power—but did not guarantee the quality of that 'civilization'. The Indians have even more incomprehensibly than usual had their rights to their lands sold over their heads. It is no wonder that Cooper should choose to have Natty die: his historical role has been fulfilled—all unconscious though he may be of the implications of that role, though he is repeatedly shown as conscious of his diminished status. The only moment when he is granted any real dignity is at the moment of his death. Any suggestion that Natty's first appearance is any sort of representation of the god Terminus and is thus to be invested with some kind of mythic grandeur is not only contradicted by the narrative but by the clear implication that his first appearance is (unconsciously) deceptive and theatrical:

> The figure was colossal, the attitude musing and melancholy . . .
> But embedded as it was in its setting of *garish* light, it was
> impossible to distinguish its just proportions or true character.

The image is, almost literally, cut down to size:

> In the meantime the hues of the heavens had often changed. In
> place of the brightness which had dazzled the eye, a gray and

26

more sober light had succeeded, and as the setting lost its brilliancy, the proportions of the *fanciful form* became less *exaggerated*, and finally distinct. (Ch. 1: my emphases)

And towards the end of the novel this image is recalled as another silhouette is seen against another sunset sky while Abiram White waits for his death—to be cut down in his turn:

The sun was near dipping into the plains beyond, and its last rays lighted the naked branches of the willow. He [Ishmael] saw the ragged outline of the whole drawn against the glowing heavens, and he even traced the still upright form of the being he had left to his misery. (Ch. XXXII)

The images are of diminution, destruction, and death. Ishmael Bush and Natty are crucial to historical progress—but their moment on the historical stage is at once crucial and very brief. The narrative writes them out of history. Yet, oddly, it is Ishmael the outcast who exercises power, a kind of law, and a very good approximation to justice. At the crucial moment, when everyone is sent their various ways, Natty is completely powerless. Ishmael has the power and uses it justly. Indeed, of all the judge figures in Cooper's fiction, he is among the best, if only because he is clearer about the rules he operates under and the limitations of his role (as Ch. XXXI makes clear). That authority may ignore the wider spheres that Natty raises for debate. But Natty is only in a position to raise general questions of justice for *debate*. He has no power—or, rather, his effective power is as servant to a white culture which hardly deserves either his moral wisdom or his knowledge of nature. The whites survive only because of the refusal of the Indians to exercise their full power. Hard Heart's values of hospitality and generosity are destructive of the existence of the culture he embodies. When Natty tells Middleton that he has no son but Hard Heart, he proclaims where moral authority lies, but it is clear that power resides elsewhere.

The Pathfinder is, notoriously, the story of Natty in love. It is, inevitably, a story of failure. As I have suggested, it is in this novel that Cooper comes closest to (Christian) myth. The Adamic references are indices enough of that interest, but the way in which the Adamic reference is first assigned to Natty and then reassigned to Jasper suggests that it is only as metaphor that this carries any significance. (And the references are rather to Milton's epic reworking of the story than to the Bible.) If the same role can be assigned to two such differing characters, then myth is being avoided—if toyed with. When Cooper selects the terms to evaluate Natty, he first describes him as an egalitarian and then chooses as his central quality that crucial if problematic value: justice. The values are secular and, in the widest sense of the word, political and thus concerned with history. For one question *The Pathfinder* asks is whether the values that Natty embodies can be carried on to another generation. *The Last of the Mohicans* answered that question in the most general terms when Chingachgook and Natty are left to mourn more than just the loss of a son and a friend, when Tamenund pronounces the obituary of a whole culture. *The Pathfinder* answers the question in a more limited fashion but equally strongly in the negative. This is shown not merely by the fact that Natty does not marry Mabel, but also by the fact that his surrogate son, Jasper, does not build a hut in the woods for her. Mabel, representing as she does a kind of class culture, has to be removed from the great lakes to become the wife of a successful city merchant who will transform nature as it were by remote mercantile control. The furs that Natty sends resemble a feudal tribute to a mercantile civilization.

Mabel returns to the area many years later, after the Revolution. Cooper tactfully reminds us of the origin of the series, for the reference is very clearly to the time just before the beginning of *The Pioneers*. A year later in *The Deerslayer*, he concluded *The Leatherstocking Novels* with a story of Natty's beginnings.

5

The case I have been trying to make faces its hardest test with *The Deerslayer*. The other *Leatherstocking Novels* can without difficulty be related to some larger secular theme or determining historical moment. But *The Deerslayer* can seem to be at once a more general and a more private fiction, dealing with a young man's movement to maturity. Yet the fact that it is not tied to any one significant historical event enables Cooper to

28

make his most radical statement about the nature of American historical experience and about the need to historicize any rendering of experience. This is to argue against received opinion, for it seems to have been fairly commonly agreed from D. H. Lawrence on that *The Deerslayer* is the most 'mythic' of *The Leatherstocking Novels* or, at least, it is in this fiction that Natty approaches closest to mythic status. This, as I have suggested earlier, seems to me to be a profoundly mistaken reading. That Cooper is tempted by myth may be accurate enough, but the novel takes history (and the problem of the definition of history) as its subject. Here, as elsewhere, the circularity of nature is contrasted with the difficult linearity of history—and it is clear that history displaces the natural as the Whites displace the Indians.

The writer can imagine a mythic, pre-historical world with his reference to 'the long succession of unknown ages in which America and all it contained existed apart in a mysterious solitude, a world by itself, equally without a familiar history and without an origin that the annals of man can reach' (Ch. IX). But this cannot be material for narrative. It is an unknown, unrecoverable past, and what the novel records is the irruption of history into this world. We cannot see its origin, only its ending. The whites may recoil from the lake at the end of the novel, but this is only a temporary retreat. Neither the Indians nor nature can regain dominance, and Cooper's repeated emphases that this is a real lake which he has visited services as a reminder that the lake is now known and possessed, that it is only an act of the imagination which can temporarily re-create it as wholly natural.

There has been much debate about the structure of *The Deerslayer*. Dekker, in his very useful book, draws attention to one formulation of the problem:

> Why does Cooper pay so much attention to the lesser unities and so little to the crucial unity of action? It does not seem to be the case . . . that observance of the unities of time and place forced him to neglect unity of action. On the contrary, there is ample evidence to show that he quite deliberately crowded as many incidents as possible into the space of a few days.

He suggests an answer:

So far as Deerslayer is concerned, the action of this novel, by crowding the trials of an average lifetime into a few days, does initiate him into manhood in the fullest possible sense: he has already lived through whatever lies before him as a Christian warrior. It is as a novel of initiation, if at all, that the crowded, episodic form of *The Deerslayer* can be explained and justified. (Pp. 188, 189)

But this does not entirely solve the problem, as Dekker seems to realize. The solution, I would suggest, lies in considering the action of the novel as a whole rather than focusing one's attention on Natty. The novel opens with a reasoned and generalizing statement about the paradoxical nature of American historical experience and American perception of that history:

> On the human imagination events produce the effects of time. Thus, he who has travelled far and seen much is apt to imagine that he has lived long, and the history that most abounds in important incidents soonest assumes the aspect of antiquity. In no other way can we account for the venerable air that is already gathering around American annals. When the mind reverts to the earliest days of colonial history, the period seems remote and obscure, the thousand changes that thicken along the links of recollections throwing back the origin of the nation to a day so distant as seemingly to reach the mists of time; yet, four lives of ordinary duration would suffice to transmit, from mouth to mouth, in the form of tradition, all that civilized man has achieved within the limits of the republic. . . . Thus, what seems venerable by an accumulation of changes is reduced to familiarity when we come seriously to consider it solely in connection with time. (Ch. 1)

Dekker quotes much of this but relates it to personal time rather than to public history—which is surely where its principal significance lies. It is obviously remarkably similar to the opening of *The Pioneers*, but it has one crucial difference: the language is carefully neutral. Cooper implies that his readers take it for granted that America has a history but that they need to be reminded how brief it is. He faces the problem that American history is so short—and inverts that formulation. Given the criteria for history that Cooper sets up (intensity, number of important incidents and degree of change), then

America has its unique, notable history. Thus the chaotic and crowded action of the novel is mimetic of American history. The 'deliberate crowding of incidents' that (rightly) troubles Dekker is caused by Cooper's intention to make the actions of all the characters (not just Natty) parallel and illuminate the patterns and achievements of American history. The plot and action of the novel provide a continual tension that shifts back and forth between the generalized public perspective and the private levels of experience.

Dekker is undoubtedly right to connect the opening of the novel to Judith's statement when she proposes to Deerslayer:

> You are not the acquaintance of a week, but it appears to me as if I had known you for years. So much, and so much that is important, has taken place within that short time, that the sorrows and dangers, and escapes of a whole life have been crowded into a few days; and they who have suffered and acted together in such scenes, ought not to feel like strangers. (Ch. XXXII)

> This is . . . a view of human experience which the author himself endorses. . . . So far as Deerslayer is concerned, the action of this novel, by crowding the trials of an average lifetime into a few days, does initiate him into manhood in the fullest possible sense: he has already lived through whatever lies before him as a Christian warrior. (P. 189)

But he fails to see how the endorsement is qualified. Judith may wish that the experiences of 'a whole life' had just been lived through, but this is, however excusably, self-deception. And it might have occurred to Dekker that one outcome of the proposal scene is that Natty refuses initiation into manhood 'in the fullest *possible* sense'. The concentration of incident within the plot does not mean that the characters lack antecedents. They almost without exception bring their pasts to and into the novel—just as American history has European antecedents (which are also determinants). Cooper has a very sceptical attitude towards the idea of a revolutionary rupture with the past, towards new beginnings. It is stressed throughout the novel that identity is revealed and created by a character's personal history, as it is shown that it is more than possible that the determining incidents in a character's biography may have occurred before the narrative begins. So, too, the determining forces of American history may not be within America's control. America's may not be a redemptive history nor Natty's a redemptive role.

In Hutter, for example, we are given a kind of black joke as answer to the question a de Crèvecoeur had optimistically asked and answered over half a century earlier, 'What is this American, this new man?' with its implication that Europe can be left behind. Here is the immigrant who has come to the woods to make a new life. However, there is no real break with his past—except that legal scalping has replaced piracy. The scenes with his chest are among the best in the novel, with the chest as a brilliant symbol of the ways in which the past lives on into the present, at once valuable and dangerous in its concrete mystery. In the first, Natty and Judith excavate, as it were, only through the public level—through Hutter's plunder in a search for something that the Indians will find 'worth' Hutter's and Harry's lives. The scene brings together a complex of questions about class, identity and cultural values.

After Hutter's terrible death, the second level is exposed as Judith re-opens the chest in an attempt to discover 'who we really are' (Ch. XXIV). The tragic irony is that she manages to piece together enough from fragments of clothing, documents and letters to discover that she has never known who she is and never will know. One does not have to be a Freudian to note the way in which her discovery that Hutter was not her biological father is felt as a liberation into nothingness. (Indeed, given the class as well as the moral implications, one had better not be.) Her mother has mutilated the documents to remove all names that might enable Judith to discover an identity. This systematic defacement of the texts is particularly noticeable in a novel in which the problems and significances of naming are such central themes, and in which Hetty's trust in the authority of the Biblical text is sympathetically but critically examined. She can trust that it has a single meaning while Deerslayer has to tell her that reliance on its message would be for an uncertain life in the woods. She cannot understand how that text's authority can be refused or ignored, and becomes anxious when asked about the gaps between words and acts.

Dislocated from any relationship to the past other than that provided by personal memory, Judith is necessarily left with 'the helplessness of a future that seemed to contain no resting place' (Ch. XXIV). All that she feels is left to her is a choice between living up to her reputation as scarlet woman (shades of Hester Prynne!) and the utopian dream of marriage with Natty—which would redeem her from the trap of her personal past which she only too clearly sees may have to become her future. Judith's recognition that the sheer intensity and number of experiences that she and Natty have shared means that they *know* each other is, unfortunately, true. She forgets just how much they know of each other. Cooper is arguing through Judith that it is up to these characters to take these incidents and transform them into something coherent and meaningful. But just as American history is flawed and unable to fulfil its promise, so is Judith unable to succeed because her history is already flawed before she meets Deerslayer—which is not to suggest that he suggests unflawed promise.

If Hutter is unable to escape from his un-American past, Hurry Harry is the embodiment of young America. He has no relationship to the past—or rather that relationship is established and defined by his alliance with Hutter: an alliance defined by their willingness to pursue profit with the blessing of legality as they go scalping. Hurry is prophetic of an unscrupulous future. Dekker has complained that he is not sufficiently mythic. But this is only a valid criticism if it is accepted that Natty is a mythic figure—either saint as Bewley would have him or Christian warrior as Dekker suggests. But while the presentation of Natty occasionally borders on myth, Cooper always pulls his fiction back into relationship with history. In so far as *The Deerslayer* is about the education of its hero, there is no doubt about the most important thing he learns: he learns how to kill. Much has been made of the famous Chapter VII and the discrimination and chivalry involved in Natty's first killing. But this pastoral killing does not stand as representative of Natty's whole education into frontier life. Natty begins as *Deer*slayer: he ends as Hawkeye—a name conferred on him by his first victim. The novel is, oddly, named after the name he has lost. We need to remember the instinctual throwing of the tomahawk and, more

33

importantly, Natty's last recorded killing in the book where he shoots two Indians with a single bullet. All that is demonstrated here is skill—and his is the first shot which initiates a massacre in which Hetty, at once innocent Christian and victim, perishes by an anonymous shot. The redcoats have arrived, precursors of the cavalry riding over the hill in the nick of time, but the redcoats show themselves more savage than the redskins:

> the shrieks, groans, and denunciations that usually accompany the use of the bayonet followed. That terrible weapon was glutted in vengeance. The scene that succeeded was one of those, of which so many have occurred in our own times, in which neither age nor sex forms an exemption to the lot of a savage warfare. (Ch. XXX)

The passage is the more powerful in its silent refusal to enter into detail or commentary. The reader is only invited to remember that vengeance is not a Christian virtue, to ask how vengeance can be a relevant concept here, to recall that youth and old age are only to be found among the Indians, and to recall that in so far as ruthless massacre goes the present is at least as guilty as the past. American history—Cooper's readers' history—has not escaped from the guilt of repetition.

Natty (to use Dekker's vocabulary) may be a whole man: he is most certainly not perfect. In one terrifying speech he describes the rifle innocently named Killdeer as *the one perfect object*. It is ironic that Deerslayer should initially interpret the chess-pieces found in the chest as signs that Hutter is an idolater, when it is he who (virtually) turns the gun into an object of worship—and doubly ironic when it is remembered that Killdeer belonged to Hutter. It has, Natty claims, all the value of a creature and none of its failings: 'Hist *may* be, and *should* be precious to you, but Killdeer *will* have the love and veneration of your whole people.' These are my emphases and have been made to indicate how radical a criticism Chingachgook makes of Natty's values: 'One rifle like another. . . . All kill; all wood and iron. Wife dear to heart; rifle good to shoot' (Ch. XXV).

Natty is no Christian saint or warrior. He is far too committed to history for either of these roles. The most that can be claimed for him (and it is the most that Cooper does claim) is that he has or should have the status of a national hero—which is to invite questions about the nature of heroism and the nature of the nation. Significantly, Cooper excludes any Christian reference in his claim that Natty belongs to a history of American heroism when he shows

> a generosity that would have rendered a Roman illustrious throughout all time—but which, in the career of one so simple and humble, would have been forever lost to the world, but for this unpretending legend. (Ch. VII)

Morality and the pressures of actuality co-exist uneasily, however. When Natty demonstrates his skill with Killdeer, killing the eagle, he certainly errs morally—and his recognition of his error is significantly phrased, recalling as it does the earlier novels' concern with the difficult relationships between power and its manifestations:

> We've done an unthoughtful thing in taking life with an object no better than vanity! . . . I haven't larnt the first duty yet. . . . What a thing is power . . . and what a thing it is to have it and not know how to use it! (Ch. XXVI)

Natty, as much as any other character, is defined by the pressures of a public history. It is only possible to accept Dekker's description of the novel as one of initiation if that definition is widened and deepened. It deals with the initiation of Natty into a world of flux and change, just as it deals with the initiation of America into a knowable if problematic history. At first Deerslayer is presented as a man who celebrates a nature that 'the hand of man had never yet defaced or deformed' and claiming that ' 'tis an edication of itself. . . Not a tree disturbed even by redskin hand, . . . but everything left in the ordering of the Lord, to live and die according to His own designs and laws' (Ch. II). By the end of the book, this vision of nature can no longer be sustained, and Hawkeye is seen as a man who acts with and through society. As I pointed out earlier, the novel began with a generalized statement against which the events of the novel are to be placed. It ends similarly with an emphasis on the secular nature of Natty's achievement:

> The war that then had its rise was stirring and bloody. . . . As for the Deerslayer, under the sobriquet of Hawkeye, he made his fame spread far and near, until the crack of his rifle became as terrible to the ears of the Mongos as the thunders of the Manitou. His services were soon required by the officers of the crown. (Ch. XXXII)

The fifteen years that pass before Natty returns to the lake may seem designed to give Nature a chance to recover its dominance:

> The storms of winter had long since unroofed the house, and decay had eaten into the logs. All the fastenings were untouched, but the seasons rioted in the place, as if in mockery at the attempt to exclude them. The palisades were rotting, as were the piles, and it was evident that a few more recurrences of winter, a few more gales and tempests, would sweep all into the lake and blot the building from the face of that magnificent solitude. (Ch. XXXII)

But it is war that brings man back to the lake, and man has left his 'signs' behind him if only in the form of 'bones bleaching in the rains of summer'. Now it is only the author who perceives the beauties of nature. For Natty and Chingachgook the place has value because of its historical associations, because of their memories. Nature cannot regain undisputed control, because the characters see the place not as 'edication of itself' but as a part of their own pasts. Their memories give human significance to the place.

Frank Kermode, in an essay in *Continuities* commenting on Eliade's theory of myth, writes:

> Myths take place in a quite different order of time—*in illo tempore*, as Eliade says. *Then* occurred the events decisive as to the way things are; and the only way to get at *illud tempus* is by ritual re-enactment. But here and now, *in hoc tempore*, we are certain only of the dismal linearity of time, the impossibility of re-enactment. Our fictions, as distinct from myths, have a Judaeo-Christian linearity too—beginnings, middles and ends in time.

If this definition is accepted, it can be seen that the end of the novel leads decisively away from any kind of mythic definition. Perhaps we tremble on the edge of *illud tempus* at that

36

marvellous moment when Deerslayer knots Judith's ribbon to the stock of Killdeer. But we are returned to history, to a recognition of the 'impossibility of re-enactment' as Chingachgook, Uncas and Hawkeye leave the lake for 'new adventures'.

I am particularly indebted to the following: Marius Bewley, *The Eccentric Design* (London: Chatto and Windus, 1959); George Dekker, *James Fenimore Cooper, Novelist* (London: Routledge and Kegan Paul, 1967); David Howard, 'James Fenimore Cooper's Leatherstocking Tales', in David Howard, John Lucas, John Goode, *Tradition and Tolerance in Nineteenth Century Fiction* (London: Routledge and Kegan Paul, 1966); Harry Henderson, *Versions of the Past* (New York: Oxford University Press, 1974); J. P. McWilliams, *Political Justice in a Republic: James Fenimore Cooper's America* (Berkeley: University of California Press, 1972); E. Fussell, *Frontier: American Literature and the American West* (Princeton: Princeton University Press, 1965).

2

Nathaniel Hawthorne: 'A Watchman All-heeding and Unheeded'

by JOSEPH ALLARD

1

Every reader of Hawthorne is struck by a number of ambiguities and divisions in his work, and his life, that seem to reflect problematic gulfs between spirit and intellect and between private and public selves. It seems strange that the same pen that produced the genial and gregarious sketches also wrought the deeply philosophic and sometimes profoundly gloomy tales; that the same man who cloistered himself in his mother's attic in Salem for twelve years experienced a happy marriage and family life and successfully held such public posts as customs officer and consul. There was in Hawthorne a deep sense of alienation, the feeling that he was an observer rather than a participant, a watchman. He was a moral philosopher who perceived truth in a metaphysical realm of altered consciousness, one who could fancy a greater reality in reflections in water, mirrors, or polished armour, or through senses affected by moonlight and the weird flickering of an anthracite fire. He was, at the same time, sympathetic to his fellows. His own accounts of himself in his Notebooks, and the reports of his friends and family, suggest that he could be bright and charming in society. In his walking tours of the 1830s and '40s he never lacked company when he sought it; his sympathy and strongly held democratic sense and bearing must have been obvious, and he could, it seems, achieve an easy intimacy with strangers. One cannot doubt his honesty in 'The Custom-House' sketch when he reports his relief at 'decapitation' partly inspired by a fear that he might otherwise have been trapped there for life, because of his competence and ability to get along with others.

The gulf in Hawthorne, the 'problem' so many readers have perceived, is the result of the balanced co-existence of deep detachment and sympathy; the sympathy, however, effected by the detachment, is curiously analytic in nature. It was necessary for him to range back and forth between the private and the public realms. His twelve year apprenticeship in isolation genuinely frightened him, I think, and accounts for his understanding and criticism of characters like Wakefield. The following fifteen years, until he sailed for England in 1853, showed a regular shifting back and forth between the solitary writing desk and a variety of social experiences.

Because of his severe and fiery self-censorship during his early productive years all his works, save *Fanshawe*, could be considered 'mature'. There is little sense in the surviving early work of striving to find a voice. The voice we hear, however, like the man, is divided. It is also, in several of its manifestations, original. There are obvious, but not very significant, echoes of Spenser, Bunyan, Milton and the Gothic novelists, but taken over all Hawthorne stands as one of a small number of literary innovators. The spur to innovation, beyond unique genius, was provided by time and place. He was the first great American writer of prose fiction. There was no particular national tradition of literature; and contemporary English influences were less important in the first half of the nineteenth century than they were to become later. As Matthiessen suggests 'though the major drift of fiction had set in towards realism, the term had not yet been applied to the novel in English. Hawthorne was therefore taking advantage of the unsettled standards of taste to make a plea for the assumptions that came to him from his past, and for what could not be expressed by the "direct effort", for the freeing of the inner life through the mode of symbolizing.'[1]

Hawthorne's tendency was toward emblem and allegory, toward the discovery of 'types'. It was a tendency that had deep roots in his New England Puritan heritage and in the English literary models of Spenser and Bunyan, whom he had read from childhood. The protestant intellectual in the seventeenth century sought cosmic correspondences for even the most trivial earthly event. The American Puritan sense of history was controlled by the belief that the colonizing experiment and experience was not only *like* the exodus of the tribes of Israel, but was miraculously and theologically linked to it. New England was a New Israel: a City on the Hill, a New Jerusalem that had been blessed by God and that held all promise for the future. God manifested his anger or pleasure in direct signs and portents which the Elect could literally see, respond to, and comment upon. The reflex could produce anxiety when times were hard, but the general drift of development in New England throughout the eighteenth century was toward material success. The notion became secularized during the provincial eighteenth century but hardly weakened; for belief in Divine 'providences' was replaced by a more general but equally forceful feeling that God's blessing was to be found in personal economic success and social 'progress'. Social attitudes in the early nineteenth century, during Hawthorne's youth and early manhood, were blindly cheerful, blandly optimistic. The triumphs of the Revolution, the War of 1812, and continued economic growth could be seen as proof that America was, indeed, God's chosen land.

Hawthorne was repelled, intellectually and temperamentally, by the prevailing optimism of his period. He felt impelled to challenge, through his art, the bland self-righteousness of his fellows; any notion of progress in the areas of importance to the writer—the human spirit and heart—was, he believed, nonsense. Implicit in so much of his work, this idea is central to 'Earth's Holocaust'.[2] Having reached a stage of progress beyond 'what the wisest and wittiest men of former ages had ever dreamed of', mankind met, we are told, on 'one of the broadest prairies of the West' to burn all the trumperies of civilization. The orgy of incineration consumes the civilized trappings of life ranging from church fittings, to liquor, to literature. The jubilant crowd of reformers feels itself on the verge of perfection, on the margin of the millenium: but one 'dark-complexioned' onlooker whose 'eyes glowed with a redder light than that of the bonfire' suggests a flaw in the plan, and speaks, in a sense, for Hawthorne. The 'dark visaged stranger' observes that one thing of most importance has escaped the purifying flames:

> 'And what might that be?' eagerly demanded the Last Murderer.
> 'What but the human heart itself! . . . And, unless they hit upon some method of purifying that foul cavern, forth from it will re-issue all the shapes of wrong and misery—the same old shapes, or worse ones—which they have taken such a vast deal of trouble to consume to ashes.' (403)

He speaks 'in a sense' for Hawthorne, but Hawthorne keeps the last word for himself. The devil incarnate may rejoice that the reformers will fail in their task. The author, however, chooses to draw his own moral from the devil's words:

> How sad a truth—if true it were—that Man's age-long endeavour for perfection had served only to render him the mockery of the Evil Principle, from the fatal circumstance of an error at the very root of the matter! The Heart—the Heart—there was the little, yet boundless sphere, wherein existed the original wrong, of which the crime and misery of this outward world were merely types. Purify that inner sphere; and the many shapes of evil . . . will turn to shadowy phantoms, and vanish of their own accord. But, if we go no deeper than the Intellect, and strive, with merely that feeble instrument, to discern and rectify what is wrong, our whole accomplishment will be a dream. . . . (403–4)

The mechanism of Hawthorne's use of typology was drawn whole from his Puritan forebears, but it was turned inside-out. He accepted a division of man between the intellect and human nature, as his ancestors had, but reached quite different conclusions. Nature for the Puritan was most typically a wilderness: the province of Satan, inhabited by savages and beasts. It was a place to be conquered or avoided. The natural parts of man, carnal appetite, sensuality, and so on, were to be regarded with suspicion and to be kept in check by the operations of Reason, Understanding, and the Law; of these operations those of the Intellect were of first rank importance.

For Hawthorne, however, nature was ambiguous, and intellect was suspect. The ideal resolution for Hawthorne was one in which mind and heart were in balance. Intellect in itself was, he felt, cold and destructive. At its worst it could lead to that unpardonable sin, the intentional and cold-blooded violation of the human heart: this, of course, is the sin of his most evil villains Ethan Brand and Roger Chillingworth. It could also encourage people to give too much play to intellect at the expense of spirit: in this category are the scientists like Rappaccini, Baglioni in 'Rappaccini's Daughter' and Aylmer in 'The Birthmark', artists like Owen Warland in 'The Artist of the Beautiful' and, potentially, Holgrave in *The House of the Seven Gables*. Finally, and more subtly, it could lead to a kind of emotional paralysis of dehumanization—the kind that is illustrated by Roderick Elliston in 'Egotism; Or, the Bosom Serpent', Gervayse Hastings in 'The Christmas Banquet' and, not least, Arthur Dimmesdale. Each denies human sympathy, or sacrifices the private for the public, or will not respond to grief. Theirs is the deep egotism that is a sub-category of pride. Like Elliston, and perhaps Dimmesdale, there might be hope for them, but any salvation must come from within. Salvation, in Hawthorne, is normally achieved through sympathy, but sympathy at its deepest is a state or condition that one must actively pursue; it can be offered to someone, but not forced.

Sympathy, Hawthorne felt, is one of the crowning attributes of the realm of the heart. But what produces so much ambiguity in his treatment of the heart, and so many qualifications in the narratives, is his sense that the heart is the source of much evil, if also the potential source of ultimate good. There is, for instance, no question in *The Scarlet Letter* that Hester and Arthur's sin of passion, of the heart, is anything other than a sin. Nor is there any question that it is their sin that lies at the root of much of the suffering in the book. At the same time, theirs is a less serious sin than Chillingworth's because it is of nature and has its own (natural, if not social) consecration. Hawthorne left statements about his own notion of the heart in two documents written in 1842. The first was a letter to Sophia in which he tried to explain his own reserve:

> I am glad to think that God sees through my heart; and if any angel has power to penetrate into it, he is welcome to know

everything that is there. Yes; and so may any mortal, who is capable of full sympathy, and therefore worthy to come into my depths. But he must find his own way there. I can neither guide him nor enlighten him. It is this involuntary reserve, I suppose, that has given objectivity to my writings. And when people think I am pouring myself out in a tale or essay, I am merely telling what is common to human nature, not what is peculiar to myself. I sympathize with them—not they with me.[3]

What is common to human nature, Hawthorne believed, is within the province of the human heart. That area certainly and unavoidably contains evil and, of necessity, must be the devil's from time to time: but it also holds out the possibility for sympathy in its broadest and most constructive sense. It is sympathy that can strike the balance between mind and heart; that can forgive wrongs done by others; that can understand and accept that all people are evil in some measure. When activated by grief or repentance it can lead to salvation. At its highest, sympathy is akin to the platonic or christian notions of Love.

Shortly after writing the letter to Sophia, Hawthorne sketched this outline for an allegory in his Notebooks:

> The human heart is to be allegorized as a cavern; at the entrance there is sunshine, and flowers growing about it. You step within, but a short distance, and begin to find yourself surrounded with a terrible gloom, and monsters of divers kinds; it seems like Hell itself. You are bewildered, and wander long without hope. At last a light strikes upon you. You press towards it, and find yourself in a region that seems, in some sort, to reproduce the flowers and sunny beauty of the entrance, but all perfect. These are the depths of the heart, or of human nature, bright and peaceful; the gloom and terror may lie deep; but deeper still is this eternal beauty.[4]

Taken together, these notions of sympathy and of the heart must make one conclude that Hawthorne was hardly the thorough pessimist that some people suppose. This almost mystical perception of perfection at the very foundation of existence is Spenserian, finally, and could help account for his early sympathy with the Transcendental Brook Farm experiment, and his inability, or disinclination, to warm very much to Melville.

According to Hawthorne's own cosmology, then, the sin

and misery of the outward world are of less intrinsic interest than the woeful workings of the inner being. External events are seen as 'types' of the original wrong in the human creature. When he wrote on such subjects as sin, guilt, and suffering he was reversing, in a sense, the usual practice of contemporary novelists; the external was for him a specific route to a symbolically generalizable internal. At its best his work manages to function on external and internal levels simultaneously: but when he fails to strike the correct balance, the effects falter.

2

The bulk of Hawthorne's production falls into one of four categories: the listing allegory, the sketch, the tale, or the romance. Although there are many similarities in style, tone, and point-of-view which make the borders of the forms overlap in a number of ways, the four are distinct. The listing allegories begin, like the sketches, as genial observations, but shift quickly to the realm of fantasy. The sketches tend to reveal the public and sunny side of Hawthorne's nature and experience; some are rather like friendly conversations, while others achieve the sort of distance he needed to broach moral questions. In the tale and the romance he strove for more profound utterance; his sense of the power of type, emblem, and symbol to communicate a deep moral gives them a particular quality of originality. *The Scarlet Letter* stands mid-way, as it were, between tale and romance, having more in common with the earlier tales, than the longer works to follow. The later romances, which attempt to tread the border between the novel and the morality tale (or, to use Hawthorne's own terms, between the tale and the sketch), are his least successful works.

The listing allegories are perhaps the least memorable of his works. 'The Hall of Fantasy', 'A Virtuoso's Collection', and pieces like them are in no way intended to have much of a link with daily life. They are exercises of the fancy in which Hawthorne wrings as much as possible out of a particular, clever idea, but without a profound moral purpose. They are usually light and well-written, sometimes amusing. 'The Celestial Railroad' is a brilliant little parody of Bunyan, and a mildly satiric comment on nineteenth-century American mores. 'Earth's Holocaust' (which I discussed earlier) develops an idea that has a number of germs in the Notebooks but, even though its concluding sentiments may help towards an understanding of Hawthorne, the piece is not unified by the sort of firm but complex moral structure that is basic to the best sketches and tales. On the whole the allegories are rather mechanical accretions of detail.

Although the sketches are often derived from Hawthorne's experiences as an observer of social life, and may be drawn from the Notebooks, they are often invested with a sense of distance. They become small instructional moralities. 'The Old Apple-Dealer'[5] is a good example. The American Notebooks contain a description of an old apple-dealer observed on Salem railroad station.[6] The portrait is closely observed and objective. It does not attempt to delve beneath the surface of a rather pathetic old man; and it closes with the comment 'I should like, if I could, to follow him home, and see his domestic life—all that I know of him, thus far, being merely his outward image, as shown to the world' (p. 226). 'The Old Apple-Dealer' sketch takes the descriptive details almost *verbatim* from the Notebook entry with only slight changes of order. The introduction, however, raises the piece to the level of the imaginative and the moral: 'The Lover of the moral picturesque may sometimes find what he seeks in a character, which is, nevertheless, of too negative a description to be seized upon, and represented to the imaginative vision by word-painting.' He continues characteristically 'As an instance, I remember an old man . . .' (p. 439). The opening paragraph ends with what might be taken as a summary of the method Hawthorne used to bridge the distance between the external world, and his notion of moralizing fiction in the sketches: 'It is a strange witchcraft, whereby this faded and featureless old apple-dealer has gained a settlement in my memory!' The rather straightforward and detailed description of a particular apple-dealer from the Notebooks is internalized in the sketch, and becomes an instance of more generalized humanity about which the author can moralize. By the end the old man has been turned into a type, 'the representative of that melancholy class who, by some sad witchcraft, are doomed never to share in the world's exulting progress'. Hawthorne has shifted from being simply a neutral observer in the Notebooks to being 'a student of human life' who uses the old man to make the final and infinitely broad suggestion that, were he able to read the core of the man's being or even 'a tithe of what is written there, it would be a volume of deeper and more comprehensive import than all that the wisest mortals have given to the world; for the soundless depths of the human soul, and of eternity, have an opening through your breast' (p. 446).

In many ways, Hawthorne was at his best as a miniaturist; for he achieved his most enduring effects in the tales rather than in the romances, saving, of course, *The Scarlet Letter*. The tales have something in common with the allegories and the sketches, but are generally more fully felt and considered than the sketches, and more coherent than the allegories. In a letter to George Hilliard in 1841 he apologized for the failure to produce a new story for *The Token*. The reasons for failure, he said, were the labour, atmosphere, and odd social pressure at Brook Farm:

> You cannot think how exceedingly I regret the necessity of disappointing you; but what could be done? An engagement to write a story must in its nature be conditional; because stories grow like vegetables, and are not manufactured like a pine table. My former stories all sprung up of their own accord, out of a quiet life.[7]

With enough quiet time for reflection his tales developed like plants. Very few are drawn even in part from the Notebooks, although the occasional sentence might contain a seed that would later sprout and grow.

The best tales are shrouded in mystery, with a dreamlike and tentative atmosphere, heavy with authorial intrusions and qualifications. They are moralities which delve as deeply as possible into the intricacies of the heart; and they are essentially ambiguous because of the ambiguities of that region. Many are set in the past, but seldom very specifically: they occur 'very long ago' or sometime 'in the reign of James II' or 'in those strange old times'. Hawthorne often claims to have heard the story somewhere else, to be merely the relator, not the creator. The 'Legends of the Province House' sequence is presented as smoking room chat. 'The Wedding-Knell' is the narrator's grandmother's favourite tale. 'Rappaccini's Daughter' is said to be a translation from the works of M. de l'Aubépine. The story of Hester Prynne was the Surveyor Pue's, which Hawthorne happened to find one day in the custom house attic. And so on. Such dislocations of time and source are used to achieve a distance from the imagined event and to bring him closer to the reader as confidante and moralizing observer.

Hawthorne's desire, in tale after tale, was to tell at least some of the truth about human experience: experience, however, in his own sense of the priority of inner life to outer. That his stories are dim and dreamy, that his characters, even at their best, seem somehow watery and insubstantial, is the result of his belief that the story of *real* life is the story of the heart; that the best way to deal with such concerns, perhaps the only way, was through emblematizing. Characters in the tales are presented as breathing flesh and blood human beings and as 'types' simultaneously. The actions which they play out are types or emblems of real (that is, internal) life. The places where they act are both geographical places like early Boston or Salem, and emblematized landscapes which act as backdrops to the more important, morally critical action. Fantasy, allegory and the supernatural are such a large part of Hawthorne's practice because without them, it would be so much more difficult to achieve moral and symbolic reverberations. Many commentators have complained that Hawthorne's characters lack blood (Melville amongst them), that they do not convince often enough of their human reality. This criticism is to miss the point of Hawthorne's method. His characters reside on the border between fictional humanity—of the kind one finds in a realist novel—and allegorical type—of the kind one meets with in, say, Spenser or Bunyan. Some of the most effective tales are types or emblems in their own right.

The step from tale to romance was successfully taken after Hawthorne was removed from his office in the custom house. He was already a master of short fiction, and had established a healthy reputation as a writer on the basis of the two major collections of tales and sketches. With a growing family to support he decided to attempt a longer piece, which would further establish his reputation, and would stand to bring in more income than short stories. The product of this effort was

The Scarlet Letter, arguably the first great American long fiction. It is Hawthorne's best work and, in many ways, his last successful one. It drew together most of the concerns that had occupied his thoughts and feelings and fiction during the preceding quarter of a century.

The Scarlet Letter shares with many of Hawthorne's tales the qualities necessary to give moral and intellectual energy to a partly emblematized story; to lift, with the help of the activated symbol, the veil that is ever present, ever shrouding us one from another; to lead us on a journey to the centre of 'the dark wilderness' of the human heart; and to suggest, however tentatively, a manner not just of survival, but of salvation. The romance is set in the Puritan past that was so important to Hawthorne. It has, unlike the later romances, an extremely tight, highly organized structure. Moreover, it manages to present characters that, while operating as types, allegorical emblems, are also entirely credible as human beings—and who are revealed to us, for the most part, at those moments of confrontation and choice that have the deepest moral significance for them.

The Scarlet Letter is not unlike a series of tales, in each of which Hawthorne investigates another aspect of the workings of sin and guilt upon the human spirit. The most powerful moments in the romance are ones that Hawthorne had treated in only slightly differing ways in earlier tales. The Chillingworth motif has its genesis in 'Ethan Brand'. The trappings of the wilderness, and the notion that certain sympathetic energies are to be found there, both recur in the sketches. The sin, guilt and pain of Hester appear in tales as early as 'The Hollow of the Three Hills', while, of course, Hester herself is to be found in germ in 'Endicott and the Red Cross'. The weak-willed Arthur Dimmesdale is, in a sense, an inverted variation of the Reverend Hooper, with qualities of Goodman Brown, Roderick Elliston, and Reuben Bourne. Only Pearl is new—based, one suspects from the Notebooks, on little Una Hawthorne. In a real sense *The Scarlet Letter* is a series of twice-told tales, involving the same characters who are shown to us at a number of significant moments in their lives. What binds them so tightly together are the workings of sin and guilt. It is worth emphasizing the fact that the sin which activates the romance,

and for which all the principals suffer, was committed before
the romance begins: the sin between Hester and Dimmerdale
is, in effect, mostly significant in terms of its more intangible,
internalized consequences.

The Scarlet Letter's impact is profound; its atmosphere is
consistently dark and brooding. It was a master-stroke on
Hawthorne's publisher's part to combine *The Scarlet Letter* with
'The Custom House' sketch, for the result is that we are given,
within a single volume, both sides of Hawthorne at his best.
Hawthorne was well aware that the romance was focused in
the way I have just described; and his own view about the
success of the book was that it had more to do with the sketch
than with the romance. As he wrote to his publisher, Fields,
early in 1850:

> I found it impossible to relieve the shadows of the story with so
> much light as I would gladly have thrown in. Keeping so close
> to its point as the tale does, and diversified not otherwise than
> by turning different sides of the same dark idea to the reader's
> eye, it will weary very many people, and disgust some.[8]

The Scarlet Letter represents the summit of Hawthorne's
achievement, in that the best work of the preceding twenty-
five years leads up to it, and in that it stands as a fulfilment of
that work. It also represents the summit in the sense that he
never achieved such artistic success again, for the later
romances showed more and more flaws. The decline began in
The House of the Seven Gables. Hawthorne consciously set out to
combine in one work what had been held separate in *The
Scarlet Letter*: the sunny, genial side of his writing in the sketch,
and the powerfully gloomy side. The tension and profundity of
Hawthorne at his most serious will not, however, admit sun-
shine. The source of Hawthorne's power is a carefully maintained balance between narrative and symbol, often giving
pre-eminence, at least initially, to symbol. In *The House of the
Seven Gables*, to achieve daylight effects, he begins with narrative, then attempts to introduce symbol and emblem; the
result is a discomfiting sense of authorial intrusion, of manipulation and contrivance. The structure of the book is good,
focusing the action, as it does, upon and within the house; and
the narrative point-of-view which removes narrator from action

is, as in *The Scarlet Letter*, successful. Both tone and characterization, however, are not consistent. What is terrifying in *The Scarlet Letter* is that each main character is logical both as person and type: there is no brightness because the subject does not allow it. The artificial injection of light into *The House of the Seven Gables* forces Hawthorne to renege on his basic, tragic assumptions about life and history; rather than confront problems that one knows Hawthorne could deal with, he slides around them. One simple example is the conversion of Holgrave; another is the happy and inept ending. Neither is consistent with the problems that are potential in the plot.

The Blithedale Romance is even less successful. In it, Hawthorne sacrifices three of the qualities that make his best tales and romances work: a tight and focused structure, a third-person narrator, and a profound sense of history. The placement of Miles Coverdale as first-person narrator is, finally, awkward and unconvincing. His own deep self-consciousness, and Hawthorne's, raises more embarrassing problems than it solves. Coverdale is treated by Hawthorne with some irony, but one's sense is that the narrator is undercut even further than Hawthorne intended. And the romance is really two stories, that of Coverdale and that of Zenobia and the others: this lack of coherence robs what ought to have been effective passages of most of their power.

The final completed romance, *The Marble Faun*, is interesting because of its place in the development of American letters, and its international theme, but it is an utter failure as a credible or coherent fiction. One can see clearly enough what Hawthorne was attempting to achieve in the Miriam-Donatello relationship, but because Miriam and Donatello (to say nothing of Kenyon and Hilda) never persuade us to suspend our disbelief, the potential for symbolic significance is never realized. Other trappings of the book, the aesthetic observations in particular, are offensive; artistic judgements, most of which were probably Sophia Hawthorne's anyway, are sometimes contradictory, and often absurd.

3

In the best of his fiction, Hawthorne's point-of-view is consistent, precise, subtle, and peculiar to him. One of his shorter pieces, 'Sights from a Steeple', sums it up quite effectively. In it, Hawthorne reflects upon the perspectives and sights possible from the steeple of a church that is situated across the street from his own 'chamber under the eaves'. 'How various are the situations of the people covered by the roofs beneath me', he declares,

> and how diversified are the events at this moment befalling them! The new-born, the aged, the dying, the strong in life, the most recent dead, are in the chambers of these many mansions. . . . In some of the houses over which my eyes roam so coldly, guilt is entering into hearts that are still tenanted by a debased and trodden virtue,—guilt is on the very edge of commission, and the impending deed might be averted; guilt is done, and the criminal wonders if it be irrevocable. There are broad thoughts struggling in my mind, and, were I able to give them distinctness, they would make their way into eloquence.[9]

Both Hawthorne's detachment, his distance from his fellows, and his power to project himself, to achieve the kind of sympathy that does not preclude analysis, are emphasized in this passage—and, together with these things, his need to make 'broad thoughts' distinct, to deploy generalizations about human nature, the workings of sin, guilt, and remorse, in terms of specific and memorable emblematic types.

The self-consciousness that marks out a passage like this one is also characteristic of Hawthorne's usual narrative voice and viewpoint. For Hawthorne was nothing if not aware of himself, his own burdens and opinions, his capacity for analysis—and, not least, his particular strengths as a writer. He had, he knew, the ability to bring a moment of significance in the inner life into clear focus: his characters are led to a point of crisis in troubled anticipation (to 'the very edge of commission', as he puts it in 'Sights from a Steeple'), and then led away from it suffering acute pain and guilt, feelings that are 'irrevocable' in the sense that they serve to shape life thereafter. And he also had, as he knew, the ability to construct a series of bridges between narrator, character, and reader, based on the perception that this movement towards and away from a moment of crisis is one that we all of us share, just as we all share, in varying degrees, the impulse toward self-analysis. It may be that, as Hawthorne admitted, his writings are marked by an 'inveterate love of allegory'. But the allegory is there so that thoughts struggling in all our minds can 'make their way into eloquence'—so that, in fact, the self-exploration that was habitual with Hawthorne could and still can become an exploration of humanity.

NOTES

1. F. O. Matthiessen, *American Renaissance* (New York, 1941), p. 268.
2. 'Earth's Holocaust', *Graham's Lady's and Gentleman's Magazine*, XXV (May, 1844), pp. 193–200. Collected in *Mosses from an Old Manse*, 1846; my references throughout are to The Centenary Edition of the Works of Nathaniel Hawthorne. *Mosses from an Old Manse*, Centenary Edition, Vol. X (Columbus, Ohio: Ohio State University Press, 1974), pp. 381–404.
3. Letter to Sophia Peabody, 27 February 1842. Cited in Arlin Turner, *Nathaniel Hawthorne: A Biography* (New York, 1980), pp. 124–25.
4. Nathaniel Hawthorne, *American Notebooks*, Centenary Edition, Vol. VIII, p. 237.
5. 'The Old Apple-Dealer', *Sargents New Monthly Magazine of Literature, Fashion, and the Fine Arts*, I (January 1843), pp. 21–4; collected in *Mosses from an Old Manse*, Centenary Edition, Vol. X, pp. 439–46.
6. The entry is for January 1842. Nathaniel Hawthorne, *American Notebooks*, Centenary Edition, Vol. VIII, pp. 222–26.
7. Cited by J. Donald Crowley in his historical comment about *Twice-Told Tales*; Twice-Told Tales, Centenary Edition, Vol. IX, p. 519.
8. Letter to Fields, 20 January 1850. Cited in Turner, *Hawthorne*, p. 193.
9. 'Sights from a Steeple', *The Token*, Boston, 1831, pp. 41–51; collected in *Twice-Told Tales*, 1837, pp. 273–82; *Twice-Told Tales*, Centenary Edition, Vol. IX, pp. 191–98.

3

Edgar Allan Poe, the Will, and Horror Fiction

by ALLAN GARDNER SMITH

Poe's obsession with the idea of the 'will' is inescapable. His protagonists act out their deepest desires, yet seem to be victims of those desires, which return upon them with redoubled force as guilt. The will seems to be separate from the self, expressive of needs beyond anything articulable as personality or coherent psychology, yet more fully resuming the identity of the first-person narrators than all the self-descriptions they produce. This is especially true of the tales Poe published around 1839: 'Ligeia' (1838), 'The Fall of the House of Usher' (1839), 'William Wilson' (1839), 'The Man of the Crowd' (1840).[1] In these tales the will behaves with absolute autonomy, murderously sweeping aside impediments to the satisfaction of desire, even to the point of suicide. It is desire that the notion of 'will' reifies into a separable faculty, able to take over the self and overcome its rational or culturally determined objections. But this desire is neither one of the neo-classical passions (envy, love, jealousy, etc.) nor is it constitutive of a socially determined psychological coherence of the sort advanced by the nineteenth-century English novel. 'Will' stands in as a shield or disguise for the fragmentary, discontinuous, subversive desires of the non-self (what is not allowed as *the* self), and hence evades and subverts the particular set of repressions of Poe's society. Instead of an imposition of control through

53

psychological coherence, and the associated adequation of all action and setting to the developmental design, we see a fierce imposition of formal coherence ('unity') which insists upon the short form as sufficient to the fragmentary impulse. The full psychology and coherent personality had been co-opted by the mercantile economics of the Allans: a man's word would be his bond only if his personality had coherence, was itself a product of his economic place, a monument to integrity erected paradoxically upon the foundation of *risk* in venture capitalism. Poe's position as adopted son of the Allans repeats this pattern: to be acceptable must be to adopt the shape of personality preferred by John Allan in denial of his own sense of origin and needs—the need, for example, to write.

In escaping from the monumental self of economic responsibility and fiscal integrity Poe turned to the weakest point in that model's construction, the question of desire, motive, 'will'. At exactly this time the idea of will was brought under scrutiny by American theorists of psychology. Thomas Upham turned from his massive *Elements of Mental Philosophy* of 1831 to produce the dark mirror of optimistic 'sane' psychology in his *Outlines of Imperfect and Disordered Mental Action* (1840). In 1839 Henry Tappan gave 340 pages to an argument over freedom of the will in his *Review of Edward's Inquiry into the Freedom of the Will*, and followed this by a full statement of his own reasoning in *The Doctrine of the Will, Determined by an Appeal to Consciousness* (1840). Jeremiah Day had anticipated him in 1838 with *An Inquiry Respecting the Self-Determining Power of the Will, or, Contingent Volition*. And writers not concerned explicitly with the problem of the will in their titles, nevertheless accorded it lengthy treatment; Leicester Sawyer, in his *Critical Exposition of Mental Philosophy* (1839), and Samuel Schmucker, in his *Elements of a New System of Mental Philosophy* (1842), both have significant statements on the issue.[2] Sawyer thought that although the mind could not make choices that contradicted all its feelings, it could choose in favour of some and against others. Schmucker argued that motives do not act with irresistible force upon the will, and therefore it is free, but failed to explain what it was free to do, if not to follow motives.[3] Jeremiah Day argued against the idea that the will could act without motives, or against its strongest motive, but held that the self could aim to control future volition by 'placing ourselves in such circumstances, and bringing into view such considerations, as will tend to incline our wills, in the direction in which we wish'.[4] In such company, of course, we might imagine Poe to be in the situation that Hawthorne was described as being in once at a literary dinner, that of 'a rogue in the company of detectives'.[5] But Poe could exploit the confusion that the idea of determinism sowed among his contemporaries and appreciate the way that their need to defend establishment interests could lead to significant reformulations of the nature of mind, of which Henry Tappan's *Doctrine* is exemplary. Tappan elevated the will to a new significance, tracing its involvement with many other functions. In reasoning, he thought the will provides the necessary act of attention, and has the functions of abstracting, generalizing, and directing memory. As the power of combining the materials and principles supplied by observation and reflection, it is involved in acts of creative imagination. In the grotesque, especially, it acts arbitrarily in the subversion of logic, truth, beauty, and reality. Tappan also decided that the idea of possession depends upon the will, from the sense of having things in one's power; in fact the will *is* the person, or personality, able to inspire or suppress passions.[6] Behind most of these arguments rested the unexamined assumption that the way in which the will might resist desire, of which 'the very existence involves the probability of action', is a mystery consonant with the will being the 'point of union, the position of contact, with the Divine Mind' (Upham).[7] From a different starting point, it may be remembered, Coleridge had reached a similar conclusion, finding the very basis of identity in a divine act of will:

> The spirit (originally the identity of object and subject) must in some sense dissolve this identity, in order to be conscious of it. . . . But this implies an act, and it follows therefore that intelligence or self-consciousness is impossible, except by and in a will. The self-conscious spirit therefore is a will.[8]

In transcendental philosophy, then, as in its 'commonsense' opposite, the will remained an inspiring mystery, whether as the foundation of all knowledge in an act of freedom or the reservation of an area marked off from philosophical (or

Calvinist) determinism. But it was necessarily posited as a vacuum, a void. In the first place, the doctrines of faculty psychology had been rejected by this time, the mind being seen rather as indivisible and the faculties merely its various complete states. So the stress on the faculty of will constitutes a distinct *re*-reification of an action or state of the mind: willing. Secondly, the assertion of an ability to resist desire without either dependence upon some stronger desire (which would reopen the question of determinism) or dependence upon logic and reason (which would elevate rationalism above faith) was an assertion of a numinous emptiness, labelled freedom. In attempting to fix the coping stone of their theory the naïve realists reinstituted mystery and openness at the very centre, just as the transcendentalists enthusiastically insisted upon it.

'Ligeia' begins with a quotation ascribed to the neo-Platonist Joseph Glanvill (though not in fact written by him):

> And the will therein lieth, which dieth not. Who knoweth the mysteries of the will, with its vigor? For God is but a great will pervading all things by nature of its intentness. Man doth not yield himself to the angels, nor unto death utterly, save only through the weakness of his feeble will.[9]

We would be rash to argue from this that Poe was himself a neo-Platonist, just as Barton Levi St. Armand was unwise to assume that Poe was gnostic, from the evidence of gnosticism in 'Eureka' and 'The Fall of the House of Usher'.[10] But Poe's parodic text clearly signals his interest in this aspect of mind that his contemporaries found most mysterious and inaccessible, the 'will', and its relation to the conscious self on the one hand, and to the subconscious 'angelic' or 'demonic' desires on the other.

Most readers of Poe suppose that his fiction dramatizes splits within the construct of the self, but find themselves in a quandary when trying to establish *which* aspects of the self are allegorically represented. In 'The Fall of the House of Usher', for example, is Roderick Usher representative of mind, and his sister a version of emotion and the body?[11] A less bodily creature than Lady Madeline would be difficult to imagine, and Roderick himself seems the victim of an emotion (an inexplicable fear of fear itself) which is most fully expressed in music and painting (traditionally vehicles of deeper impulses than the intellectual) and which is perhaps induced by the influence (on the body) of the miasmic vapours of the tarn. In 'Ligeia' however we may be sure that Poe intends to represent a particular aspect of the mind, by his insistence in the 'Glanvill' passage that the will is an ultimate mystery, something which is repeated by Ligeia herself:

> O God! O Divine Father!—shall these things be undeviatingly so?—shall this Conqueror be not once conquered? Are we not part and parcel in Thee? Who—who knoweth the mysteries of the will with its vigor? Man doth not yield himself to the angels, *nor unto death utterly*, save only through the weakness of his feeble will.

The narrator testifies to 'that gigantic volition' which caused in Ligeia an *intensity* in thought, action or speech. He observes the curious contrast between this 'fierce spirit' and the 'external placidity' of her demeanour, the 'fierce energy' of her words and the 'almost magical melody, modulation, distinctness, and placidity of her very low voice'. 'Of all the women I have ever known,' he observes, 'the outwardly calm, the ever-placid Ligeia, was the most violently a prey to the tumultuous vultures of stern passion.' This exemplar of the will is an exemplar of repression, a human volcano developing ever greater force through denial of that force's expression. No wonder that the terrified narrator performs obeisance to her memory and experiences her return from the dead (alive in death as dead in life). And what is her will, so powerfully expressed? Nothing but the will to survive, the intensity 'of her wild desire for life,—for life—*but* for life', which the narrator attempts to interpret, without much confidence, as love for himself:

> That she loved me I should not have doubted; and I might have been easily aware that, in a bosom such as hers, love would have reigned no ordinary passion, [it was] a passionate devotion [which] amounted to idolatry.

In her 'more than womanly abandonment to a love, alas! all unmerited' he recognizes the principle of her 'longing with so wildly earnest a desire for life', while denying the ascription of

57

it to love in the repeated phrase, '*but* for life'. It is, then, the
will that Ligeia most fully represents, and the narrator, cor-
respondingly, is presented as almost will-less, her pupil in life,
her devotee in death. His enslavement to opium provides a
physiological version of his psychological vacuum; as an
opium addict he has, of course, no will but the desire for the
drug, and in so far as he demonstrates will after Ligeia's death
it is in his preparation for her necromantic return, in the body
of Rowena. Poe later felt that he should have reduced the
supernatural implication of this climax, saying 'I should have
insinuated that the *will* did not perfect its intention. . . .'[12] The
will, separated from the self, has become an independent
entity, with a vampire's appetite for life.

'William Wilson' (as the name suggests) also presents the
experience of an overpowering will, but narrated from an
opposite perspective. Wilson's double incarnates his rejected
conscience and perhaps also his rational self, whereas Wilson
himself demonstrates limitless desire and indomitable will,
even to the extent of suicide.[13] In this story the personified will
expresses a less problematic relation to desire than that in
Ligeia; its repressions are entirely projected upon the other
Wilson, for whose 'elevated character', 'majestic wisdom' and
'apparent omnipresence and omnipotence' Wilson feels a deep
awe only to be overcome by the influence of wine, which produces at last a 'stern and desperate resolution' to 'submit no
longer to be enslaved'. The other Wilson is finally (and fittingly,
for Lacanians) killed in a struggle which turns out to be self-
murder perceived in a mirror. The extreme conventionality of
Wilson's wrong-doings (card-sharping, dissipation, adultery)
suggests that neither the *frisson* of crime nor the rather more
moral subject of its punishment is Poe's goal in this tale but
rather the dissociation of will and its constraints—conscience,
which incorporates moral precept and religious sanction, and
rationality, or enlightened self-interest and fear of retribution.

The intensification of will in these stories, and its separation
as an independent entity, is by no means unique to Poe but
appears in many fictions of his period. In Washington Allston's
Monaldi (1822) for example, the picture Monaldi paints of
Satan and his acolyte Maldura shows the same division as
'William Wilson'.

It was the appalling beauty of the King of Hell. The frightful discord vibrated through my whole frame, and I turned for relief to the figure below; for at his feet knelt one who appeared to belong to our race of earth. But I had turned from the first only to witness in this second object its withering fascination. It was a man apparently in the prime of life, but pale and emaciated, as if prematurely wasted by his unholy devotion, yet still devoted—with outstretched hands, and eyes upraised to their idol, fixed with a vehemence that seemed almost to startle them from their sockets. The agony of his eye, contrasting with the prostrate, reckless worship, but too well told his tale: I beheld the mortal conflict between conscience and the will— the visible struggle of a soul in the toils of sin.[14]

What differs, of course, is the nature of the moralized recuperation, which occurs as closure in Allston's *Monaldi* but not in 'Wilson'. Both describe what Rudoph Otto calls the 'daemonic will', the urgency and energy of dread felt in numinous states of mind when the daunting and the fascinating combine in a harmony of contrasts: 'the daemonic-divine object may appear to the mind as an object of horror and dread, but at the same time it is no less something that allures with a potent charm.' This is the possibility also of the profane, when mere unlawfulness becomes impiety, sin, or sacrilege, as 'the character of numinous unworthiness or disvalue goes on to be transferred to and centred in moral delinquency'.[15] The neo-Platonic theurgy intimated in Glanvill's supposed claim of possible immortality achieved through an act of will, a deliberate refusal of death, depends upon the cultivation and concentration of a purified will, freed from contamination and developed through stoical self-denial.[16] The macabre will expressed in the ending of 'Ligeia', on the contrary, is the mental force of goetic magic, as is amply suggested by the narrator's insistence upon black magic trappings in the pentagonal chamber of the ruined (and therefore desacralized) abbey to which he brings Rowena. If the will might be the point of union with the divine, it might equally be portrayed as the point of union with the satanic. It is then developed as the notion of possession, an overpowering desire to do evil which is frequently represented in the fiction of this period as the drive to murder a beloved (as in *Monaldi*, or

Richard Henry Dana's *Paul Felton*) or less than beloved (as in 'Ligeia') wife. In later horror fiction this separation of the satanic will from the self has proved particularly resonant, whether as the result of demonism (from *Dracula* to *The Exorcist*), or science (as in Stevenson's *Dr. Jekyll and Mr. Hyde*). Poe was particularly interested in the philosophical and scientific, or pseudo-scientific, aspects of the concept. He returned to the problem of the will in two further tales, 'The Imp of the Perverse' and 'The Facts in the Case of M. Valdemar' (1843–44).[17] 'The Imp of the Perverse' begins with an essay on the will which is both more complex and more parodic than the device of 'William Wilson'. The narrator observes that most metaphysics, and especially phrenology, have been invented *a priori*. It would have been wiser, however, to classify 'upon the basis of what man usually or occasionally did, and was always doing, rather than upon the basis of what we took it for granted the Deity intended him to do'. Such induction *a posteriori* would have brought phrenology— and presumably other 'sciences' of mind—to admit that perverseness constitutes 'an innate and primitive principle of human action'. The overwhelming tendency to do wrong for the wrong's sake cannot be further analysed into ulterior motives but is a radical, elementary and primitive impulse. Nor can it be explained as some sort of malfunction of the phrenologist's principle of combativeness, because that principle has our well-being as its essence. The propensity to perverseness, on the contrary, does not consider our well-being: 'the desire to be well is not only not aroused, but a strongly antagonistical sentiment exists.' Poe demonstrates his satirical or parodic intention by reflecting the complacency of common-sensers back upon themselves; in their own phrase he maintains that 'an appeal to one's own heart is, after all, the best reply to the sophistry just mentioned.' The essay is satirical, but also serious, with the same looping logic as its apparently absurd examples and its meta-example, the confession that this philosophical exercise is conducted only as an explanation for the folly of an insane murderer, that is, his folly not in murdering, but in giving himself up to the police. Poe undoubtedly knew that the 'moral sense' so beloved of common sense psychology, the 'lawgiver' as Benjamin Rush called it, was supposed to originate in the will, as it could only then escape a necessary relationship with expediency or passion.[18] So the idea that—far from it being impossible to act against our own interests if these are fully considered—we 'always occasionally' do so, having a propensity to the perverse, strikes a low blow to the weak point of orthodox psychology.

'Valdemar' explores 'scientific' pretensions to knowledge of the will. Mesmerism, which Poe knew about chiefly through reading Townshend's *Facts in Mesmerism* (Boston, 1840), depended heavily upon a mystical notion of the will as being relatively strong or weak, and hence productive of magnetic influence or dependency. A letter from Poe to James Russell Lowell suggests that he did actually share some of the mesmeric tenets, for in it he wrote of 'a matter unrecognised by our organs—recognised occasionally, perhaps, by the sleep-walker directly—without organs—through the mesmeric medium'.[19] The fundamental significance of 'will' in these beliefs is shown by Townshend's assertion that 'it is plain that such motions as occur in the mesmeric medium, and are thence transferred to a human body, are primarily produced by mind—in other words, by will.'[20] But Poe made of it a characteristically black farce, in which Valdemar's decomposed body is held together with the magnetic will, experienced as torture by the dead man, who longs only for release into putrefaction.

Surely a pattern emerges in these fictions: the extreme exertion of will becomes demonic and results in the institution of horror, decay and putrefaction, the kingdom of the Conqueror Worm apprehended by Ligeia. Here we must return to the assertion that the 'will' is a way of disguising what is really at issue, desire. The will provides a cloak for desire, which is thereby dramatized as inexplicably different from the rational, responsible, self. In the clothing of madness, the inadmissible desire is thrust away from the self as an autonomous, uncontrollable will, free to prey on the other in a vampiric way, or to indulge in profane explorations of death, or to annihilate all resistance to infantile regression. The supreme 'will' can overcome all the intransigence of the materialistic, commercial repressions of Poe's historical experience, and reinstitute the longed-for 'oneness' he lost as a child. But as in 'punishment

61

dreams'[21] the intrinsic violence of desire, its spontaneous assumption of the annihilation of all otherness, and 'rageful recognition of the world's capacity to resist and survive' the desire, is insinuated into the fantasy as horror. If desire is itself a product of repression, as Freudian theories suggest, then desire itself is guilty. But its suppression may actually increase the feeling of guilt. To articulate forbidden desire in a disguised form (in Poe's writing there is almost certainly an Oedipal longing and aggression against the agents of repression) is to intensify guilt without achieving the satisfaction of release.[22] The 'will' is asserted against the 'Conqueror Worm', but the Worm is the hero of the tragedy.

NOTES

1. *The Complete Works of Edgar Allan Poe*, edited by James A. Harrison, 17 vols. (New York: Crowell & Co., 1902). To avoid unnecessary footnotes I have not given page references within the tales. Vol. II, pp. 248–69, Vol. III, pp. 273–99, Vol. III, pp. 299–325, Vol. IV, pp. 134–46.
2. Thomas Upham, *Elements of Mental Philosophy* (Boston: Wells, 1831); *Outlines of Imperfect and Disordered Mental Action* (New York: Harpers, 1840). Henry Tappan, *Review of President Edward's Inquiry Into the Freedom of the Will* (New York: 1839); *The Doctrine of the Will, Determined by an Appeal to Consciousness* (New York: Wiley & Putnam, 1840). Jeremiah Day, *An Inquiry Respecting the Self-Determining Power of the Will, or, Contingent Volition* (New Haven: Herrick, 1838). Leicester Sawyer, *A Critical Exposition of Mental Philosophy* (New Haven: Durrie & Peck, 1839). Samuel Schmucker, *Elements of a New System of Mental Philosophy on the Basis of Consciousness and Common Sense* (New York: Harpers, 1842).
3. Schmucker, *Philosophy*, p. 119.
4. Day, *Inquiry*, p. 128.
5. Poe is of course more literally the thief, of the censor's notions, which he inverts. See T. Martin, 'The Imagination at Play', *Kenyon Review* XXVIII, 194–209.
6. Tappan, *Doctrine*, pp. 125–27, 133, 183–84, 243.
7. Upham, *Elements*, Vol. 3, p. 26.
8. Samuel Taylor Coleridge, *Biographia Literaria* (1817; London, J. M. Dent edition, 1965), Thesis VII, p. 153.
9. 'Ligeia', *Works*, Vol. II. Like other critics, I have been unable to trace the passage in Glanvill, but it is quite characteristic of his style.
10. Barton Levi St. Armand, 'Usher Unveiled: Poe and the Metaphysics of Gnosticism', *Poe Studies* V, No. 1 (June, 1972), pp. 1–8.

11. Daniel Hoffman is one of the more persuasive advocates of such views: 'If Roderick Usher represents the *moi intérieur* of the rational, daylight self of the narrator, what does Madeline represent but the dreaded because beloved muse-figure of that inner self'—*Poe, Poe, Poe, Poe, Poe, Poe, Poe* (London: Robson Books, 1973), p. 303.

12. Letter to Philip Cooke in *Letters of Edgar Allan Poe*, edited by John Ostrom (Cambridge, Mass.: Harvard University Press, 1948), p. 118.

13. 'William Wilson' in *Works*, Vol. III, pp. 229–325. The mirror phase is the first encounter with self as other, as later the self will be constructed through the responses of others. See J. Lacan, *The Language of the Self*, translated by A. Wilden (Baltimore: Johns Hopkins University Press, 1968).

14. Washington Allston, *Monaldi*, p. 16, in *Lectures on Art & Monaldi* (Gainsville, Fla.: Scholars Facsimiles & Reprints, 1967), p. 16.

15. Rudolph Otto, *The Idea of the Holy*, translated by J. W. Harvey (London: Oxford University Press, 1968).

16. See, for example, Cornelius Agrippa, *Occult Philosophy* (1651), translated by J. F., I, i, III, XI.

17. Richard Henry Dana, 'Paul Felton' in *Poems and Prose Writings* (New York: Baker and Scribner, 1850); 'Imp of the Perverse' and 'The Facts in the Case of M. Valdemar' in *Tales 1843–1844*, edited by T. O. Mabbott (Cambridge, Mass.: Relknapp, 1978), pp. 1217–228, 1228–244.

18. Benjamin Rush, *Selected Writings*, edited by D. Runes (New York, 1947), p. 181.

19. *Letters*, I, p. 137.

20. Chauncy Townshend, *Facts in Mesmerism* (Boston, 1840), p. 430.

21. See, for example, Sigmund Freud, *The Interpretaton of Dreams* (London: Penguin Books, 1976), Vol. IV, pp. 710ff.

22. See, for a suggestive discussion of these matters in another context Leo Bersani, *A Future for Astyanax* (Boston and Toronto: Little, Brown & Co., 1976), pp. 6–13.

4

Herman Melville: Prophetic Mariner

by HAROLD BEAVER

Melville was a major moral and political commentator of his age. Take three of his most celebrated tales: *Bartleby*, *Benito Cereno*, and *Billy Budd*. Though differing in structure and narrative technique, they share a single concern. Each centres on innocence of some kind. Each innocent confronts an alien and unimaginable version of himself. Each is trapped in a claustrophobic, black-and-white world. In *Bartleby* it is the world of Wall Street (between one white wall and one black) controlled by the smuggest, easy-going form of Christianity. In *Benito Cereno* it is that of racial war, instigated by the whites, but dominated now by the most unscrupulous form of black vindictiveness. In *Billy Budd* it is that of a British man-of-war, undermined by the most devious form of sexual depravity.

Yet the precise nature of Melville's commentary is never easy to judge. For innocence is symbiotically linked to its adversary: as Bartleby is linked to the anonymous attorney; the American to the Spanish captain; the Spanish captain to Babo, his slave; and the master-at-arms aboard the *Bellipotent* to its peacemaker, Billy Budd. A point of vantage, or discrimination, belongs to neither. A middleman is needed. But in *Bartleby* there is no such middleman; that is the problem. In *Benito Cereno* he is the self-indulgent intruder, the North American; in *Billy Budd*, the fatal father figure, Captain Vere.

All points of view for Melville after *Moby-Dick* became partial and limited. Thus the need for the readers' constant, watchful discrimination, a kind of double decoding. As Amasa Delano unriddles the mystery of the *San Dominick*, we have to riddle out his text. Though *Billy Budd* is presented as an '*inside narrative*', we have still to discern the inside of that '*inside*'; for at its touchiest psychological moments, the text is riddled with blanks.

What for us becomes a problem of reading was for Melville a problem of writing. Billy Budd (that handsome foundling, the illiterate with a stutter) is literally an inscrutable and uninscribed blank. So is Bartleby the scrivener who gives up scrivening; so was Moby Dick, the White Whale himself. *Benito Cereno* proceeds from the grey murk of its opening to its final court-room revelation. But revelation of what? All texts for Melville, be they official histories or eyewitness testimonies or myths, were lopsided and capable of being critically undermined. These tales were necessarily commandeered by the lawyer and two naval commanders (Amasa Delano and Vere) since their polar opposites, their obsessive doppelgangers (Bartleby, Babo, Budd), remain voids at the centre of the circling exposition in the power of whiteness (the scrivener), or of blackness (the African), or of sexuality (the adolescent sailor).

In his awareness of such shifting perspectives Melville seems peculiarly modern. Yet he fits uncomfortably into the history of modernism. He is too early for one thing—both too magnificent and too odd, too rhetorical, too verbose, and somehow uncouth—to be treated on anything but his own terms. He is American, of course, and in that context the paradigms proliferate: in his relation to Hawthorne, for example, or romance, or autobiography, or sea fiction, or the Calvinist insistence on the 'Great Art of Telling the Truth'.[1] The only non-American to whose works he is constantly referred, or even assimilated, is that Polish expatriate, Joseph Conrad. (And Conrad, incidentally, could stand neither *Typee*, nor *Omoo*, nor *Moby-Dick*!) When a larger thesis is presented, such as by David Lodge in *The Modes of Modern Writing*, or by Gabriel Josipovici in *The World and the Book*, or by William H. Gass, or by George Steiner in his ascent of the Tower of Babel,

Melville is usually ignored.[2] Josipovici, for example, in his 'study of modern fiction' treats Chaucer and Rabelais and Hawthorne among forerunners, but not Melville. This used to puzzle me. Somehow that leviathan among authors had been consigned to Americanists, to specialists, to a grandiose but isolated cul-de-sac of his own, where (like that skeleton in the 'Bower in the Arsacides') he was ministered to by a priesthood who

> kept up an unextinguished aromatic flame, so that the mystic head again sent forth its vapory spout; while . . . the terrific lower jaw vibrated over all the devotees, like the hair-hung sword that so affrighted Damocles.[3]

For the truth is that our contemporary grasp of Melville is partly dependent on our earlier apprenticeship to Baudelaire, say, or Nietzsche, or Mallarmé, or Joyce, even—as it may sometimes happen—if we have actually read none of those authors at first-hand. And if we are more perceptive, more dumbfounding even, than our predecessors half a century ago, it must be because we are their heirs. We do not *use* Joyce to decipher Melville; we simply cannot help reading *Moby-Dick* in the light of *Ulysses*, or even at times of *Finnegans Wake*. But the more recent advent of Derrida and Lacan and Gilles Deleuze is bound to put us on our guard. If *L'Ecriture et la Différence* or *Le Séminaire sur la Lettre Volée*—if the vocabulary of 'le supplément' or 'la dissémination'—now seem the natural watchwords for tracing Melville's discourse, perhaps our earlier concern with myths and symbols was equally partial.[4]

I am all for putting ourselves on our guard. Fashion can corset imagination in the oddest ways. But Melville, like Dante, or Blake, or Sterne, or Joyce (to produce a list of miscellaneous supporters, some of whom at least Melville had read), is, I believe, a large enough author to outlive all our concerns. It is not so much a question of whether he anticipated them as of whether he can accommodate them. His intentions are rarely discernible. His drafts or working notes (bar the uncompleted manuscript of *Billy Budd*) are mostly lost. His famous letters, written in the heat of composition, tell only a partial story. It is the texts themselves in their extraordinary verbal intricacy and hallucinatory cunning—part tall tales, part Yankee cabbala, part *Ancient Mariner*—that continue to exfoliate their meanings. Melville himself, in a famous metaphor evoking his personal growth, felt that (in writing *Moby-Dick*) he had 'now come to the inmost leaf of the bulb, and that shortly the flower must fall to the mould'[5]; but we refuse to grant him such finality. We prefer to read his texts, in Roland Barthes's phrase, as onions, 'as constructions of layers (or levels, or systems), whose body contains finally no heart, no kernel, no secret, no irreducible principle, nothing except the infinity of their own envelopes—which envelop nothing other than the unity of their own surfaces'.[6] Such spiralling readings, like the unravellings on cutting into a whale's blubber, can never be wholly premeditated. The reader of *Moby-Dick*, who is summoned physically to his task by its opening ('Call me Ishmael'), is kept to that task by the very sketchy and uncompleted nature of the project:

> For small erections may be finished by their first architects; grand ones, true ones, ever leave the copestone to posterity. (241)

We come not to dismantle, but to be dismantled, and so keep the meanings in perpetual and ever more amazing circulation.

Melville, who had followed in the wake of Darwin to the Galapagos Islands and had written his greatest text before the publication of *The Origin of Species*, can neither be classified as a modernist exactly, nor as a post-modernist, nor as a post-structuralist. Though he does seem to anticipate Nietzsche increasingly, as he progresses from *Mardi* to *The Confidence-Man*, there remains too wide a gulf between the mid-Victorian period and our own. (In his search for the origin of all myths, it is to his German contemporary, Wilhelm von Humboldt, if anyone, that he might most usefully be compared.) Yet of all nineteenth-century authors he remains an outstanding candidate for one of our own cant terms: Barthes's distinction between the *scriptible*, or writerly, and the *lisible*, or merely readable. 'Why is the writerly our value?' asked Barthes in *S/Z*. Then answered:

> Because the goal of literary work (of literature as work) is to make the reader no longer a consumer, but a producer of the text. Our literature is characterized by the pitiless divorce

which the literary institution maintains between the producer of the text and its user, between its owner and its customer, between its author and its reader.[7]

Melville, as we have seen, leaves 'the copestone to posterity': that is, demands further generations of readers to complete the structure, to grope for the aspiring meaning, to impose a copestone. Or as he confided in *The Confidence-Man*, in defending himself from the merely *lisible* texts of consistently 'real life':

> Experience is the only guide here; but as no one man can be coextensive with *what is*, it may be unwise in every case to rest upon it. When the duck-billed beaver of Australia was first brought stuffed to England, the naturalists, appealing to their classifications, maintained that there was, in reality, no such creature; the bill in the specimen must needs be, in some way, artificially stuck on.

Or, taking the argument a step further:

> It is with fiction as with religion: it should present another world, and yet one to which we feel the tie.[8]

That other world, whether from fictional or metaphysical necessity, as like as not was the world of myth, as H. Bruce Franklin brilliantly exposed in *The Wake of the Gods* (1963). *Osiris* might be an alternative title for *Moby-Dick* as surreptitious predecessor of *Ulysses*. Like another Osiris, Ahab is dismembered 'in mid winter' by a leviathan/fish. Like Osiris, he revives as the sun revives. Dead 'for three days and nights', Ahab becomes literally a priest-king-god intent on 'supernatural revenge'. As Joyce drew on the oldest European narrative tradition, Melville drew on Egyptian mythology as the authentic source (he considered) of Hebrew mythology and so ultimately of the myth of Christ. It also structured and located his text. As H. Bruce Franklin commented:

> The Season-on-the-Line forms the chronological and geographical centre of *Moby-Dick*. At that time and place the whale for the first and last times dismembers Ahab. One Season-on-the-Line passes between these two; precisely at this time, Christmas Day, the twice-maimed Ahab begins his fiery hunt. Although Ahab's second injury comes shortly before the Season-on-the-Line, all three injuries coincide with the various dates given for the

dismemberment of Osiris, sometime between the autumnal equinox and the winter solstice.[9]

The modernist text, to escape the confines of consistent 'realism', returns to myth.

Not only to myth, but literally *mythos*, in the sense of speech or talk. Melville quite consciously was weaving a web of words. His are texts, in the basic, etymological sense, stretched on a linguistic loom. Treadles and shuttles, 'the warp and woof' of jungle tendrils (as in the 'Bower of the Arsacides') are a constantly recurring theme. The title of the very opening chapter, 'Loomings', punningly contains a 'loom', at which 'those stage managers, the Fates' are no doubt busily at work. *Moby-Dick* amazingly, but appropriately, opens with a section on 'Etymology', supplied by various dictionaries, giving the name in thirteen different languages (dead and alive, western and exotic, from Hebrew to Erromangoan) for 'whale'. The 'whale', it turns out, in Swedish and Danish 'is named for roundness or rolling'; for *hvalt* means 'arched or vaulted'. Such root-meanings become almost a principle of composition concealed in the text's cellars and vaults. 'Roll' is the very first verb used of the whale ('where he rolled his island bulk') just as it is the last repeated verb of the almost completed text, after the wreck 600 pages later, when 'the grey shroud of the sea rolled on as it rolled five thousand years ago' (685).

That appropriately jokey chapter 'Cetology' (as full of the spurious scholarship of the imagination as any later *apparatus criticus* by a Borges or Nabokov) first defines the whale as '*a spouting fish with a horizontal tail*', and then categorizes whales, according to magnitude, into 'three primary BOOKS (sub-divisible into CHAPTERS)' (231):

    I.   The FOLIO WHALE;
    II.   the OCTAVO WHALE;
    III.   the DUODECIMO WHALE.

For *The Whale* remained the working title, even by the time Melville signed the contract with Harpers in September 1851. (It was his brother, Allan, who suggested the change.) And if the whale is a whale is a whale, it is also a book (entitled *The Whale*), a self-conscious verbal artefact, moving laterally through its root meanings. For the whole world, like the whale, is round and rolling and arched and vaulted; and the whole *Whale*, as book, is a world to be read with etymological spectacles to trace the overlapping pattern of puns and opposing ranges of double meaning. (As there is a chapter entitled 'Moby Dick' inside *Moby-Dick*, so there is a White Whale inside *The Whale*.) How those whales slip in and out of their homonyms! The whale turning to a pastoral *vale*, or dirge-like *wail*, or metaphysical *veil*, half-heard in *ale*, that turns to a *wall*. The reader should be alert to such oral shifts as he skims the text. For as the text performs, it insists on our reciprocal and ever vigilant performance. Unlike the act of whaling itself, in the literary *Whale* it is the unriddling of the circuit alone that matters; it is always the chase, the hunt, and never the capture.

For all his heroic stature we have little to learn, as readers, from Ahab who insists on confrontation, face to face, mask to guarded mask; who is enclosed by a single pun in his despair:

> How can the prisoner reach outside except by thrusting through the wall? To me, the white whale is that wall, shoved near to me. (262)

Language should open worlds, not close them. This is partly what Robert Shulman, twenty years ago, called 'The Serious Functions of Melville's Phallic Jokes', heard even in those giant 'erections' which he left to the erotic and literary needs of posterity. There is a hint here of what Barthes called the *plaisir*, or *jouissance*, or bliss of the text. As Shulman more soberly put it: Melville's dislike of closed aesthetic systems is intimately

> related to his rejection of the respectable social order, including its economic, political and religious systems. Primal sexual energy is intrinsically subversive of conventional order and of respectable systems. . . . His enormous phallic imagery also embodies Melville's belief that the sources of artistic and sexual creation are closely related.[10]

Sexual energy apart, in his controlled and ceaselessly patrolled use of language, Melville anticipates that vast late nineteenth-century project which Mallarmé called 'the Orphic explanation of the earth': that is, the project of picturing the whole world (of whales and whalers) not merely *in* language but *as* language. The phallic and bibliographical jokes of 'Cetology' restore the whale (as *'spouting fish'*) back to its etymological roots as a narrative performance. That void, ten chapters on, of 'The Whiteness of the Whale' is also the whiteness of (the FOLIO, the OCTAVO, the DUODECIMO) text. It suggests a speculative absence of the kind that haunts contemporary, French-inspired readings of *all* texts: an infinite regress of meaning among circling signs of all semiological systems. Or as Melville himself expressed it in a dizzying series of oxymorons:

> Or is it, that as in essence whiteness is not so much a color as the visible absence of color, and at the same time the concrete of all colors; is it for these reasons that there is such a dumb blankness, full of meaning, in a wide landscape of snows, a colorless, all-color of atheism from which we shrink? (295–96)

At that point we reach the very edge of the textual abyss, the etymological *vor-text*, or vortex, to which the voyage of the *Pequod* (name of an extinct tribe of Massachusetts Indians) inevitably drives.

The nature of the journey, then, is from the start self-consciously verbal and etymological and textual, as Edgar A. Dryden argued in *Melville's Thematics of Form* (1968). It is in the fiction of Melville, not Hawthorne, that 'the acutely self-conscious artist is given his most radical and important role.' *Moby-Dick*, as he writes, is 'persistently calling attention to itself as fiction. Ishmael's narrative strategy . . . is grounded in a supreme fiction.' That is, he retreats into a fictive world by 'choosing the role of teller rather than actor' (masked by a pseudonym); by turning from those voluminous whales to whales as volumes; by swimming, not through seas, but 'libraries'. 'His relationship to other people is that of a story-teller to his audience, in touch with them through his words but removed from their meaningless masquerade.'[11]

Ishmael's words feed on words and provoke more words. One mode, as in Joyce, is parody. A curious and, at first sight, rather otiose-seeming chapter like 'The Blacksmith' turns out to play an ironic counterpoint to Longfellow's 'The Village Blacksmith': the one enfeebled by gin, a suicidal widower, bereft of his children, staggering at last off to sea; the other seated smugly at church among his boys:

> He hears the parson pray and preach,
>   He hears his daughter's voice
> Singing in the village choir;
>   And it makes his heart rejoice.

If it is only this awareness of local and contemporary parody that can make sense of such an awkward chapter, what about Melville's use of his many whaling books, of Shakespeare and, above all, of the Bible? The roguish list of 'Extracts' (supplied by a sub-sub-librarian) that precedes the main text makes something of the style, if not the nature, of this parody clear. For if the Osiris myth structures the narrative, the biblical parodies (from Moses's rod and the back parts of God to long-haired, hermaphroditical Jesus-freaks) everywhere inform that structure. *Moby-Dick*'s ultimate and recurring source for parody is the book of *Revelation*, with its dire threat of Armageddon. The whole of *Revelation*, it becomes clear, underscores Melville's design, turning the biblical apocalypse to 'leviathanic revelations'.

This insistent and universal parody commits the text, both openly and surreptitiously, to (what has more recently been labelled) intertextuality. His book is not only the culmination, the summa, of all pre-Melvillean whaling literature, it exhausts that literature with its speculative irony. For it is in the context of whaling (among the 'meanest mariners, and renegades and castaways' (212), as Ishmael calls them) that, from the very first chapter, we must conceive Cato's suicidal self-control, *and* Ovid's *Metamorphoses, and* Pythagorean abstention from beans, as well as more recent travels to the vaults of Saccara along the Nile, or Bayard Taylor's 'pedestrian trip' closer home to 'Rockaway Beach', or, for that matter, Washington Irving's *Knickerbocker History of New York*. Such interlardings, such surreptitious quotations and parodies, such literary retrievals and ripostes (whose ultimate models, no doubt, were Montaigne and Bayle and Burton and Browne) have become a commonplace of Melville criticism. Yet the diversity and rapidity of such literary play still amazes. The scholarly footnotes, as with Miltonic and Joycean commentaries, continue to proliferate.

Melville insists on a way of reading, a way of double exposure, a way of juxtaposition and hieroglyphical compression. For an alternative text is both there and not there. It is both glimpsed and superseded and superimposed. The very act of writing conceals yet further writing. Only a multiple text can respond to the complex simultaneity inherent in all things. Only a multiple reading can respond to the multiple incoherences of a text, the flux and reflux of whose contradictory movements is held in a kind of constant oscillation; whose visible embodiment is a rocking whaleboat; whose most typical trope, the oxymoron (such as 'the coffin life-buoy' of the 'Epilogue'). If Ishmael, in the end, is 'buoyed up by that coffin', the simultaneity of *The Whale* again and again finds its most obvious expression in the pun. Literally we must learn to 'read about whales through their own spectacles'. We must read, as it were, through eyes situated on either side of our head:

> True, both his eyes, in themselves, must simultaneously act; but is his brain so much more comprehensive, combining, and subtle than man's, that he can at the same moment of time attentively examine two distinct prospects, one on one side of him, and the other in an exactly opposite direction? If he can, then is it as marvellous a thing in him, as if a man were able simultaneously to go through the demonstrations of two distinct problems in Euclid. (437–38)

If reading evokes this two-, or three-, or four-ply quality, so too, of course, does writing. It is the very essence of the Sperm Whale's tail:

> The entire member seems a dense webbed bed of welded sinews; but cut into it, and you find that three distinct strata compose it:—upper, middle, and lower. The fibres in the upper and lower layers are long and horizontal; those of the middle one, very short, and running crosswise between the outside layers. This triune structure, as much as anything else, imparts power to the tail. (483)

Such is the very nature of this tale, or cross-webbed text. Furthermore such texts, by juggling their constituents, proliferate or extend themselves with a wholly verbal autonomy. Take the Nantucket chapters of *Moby-Dick*, for example, where Melville, at the time of writing, had never been. The subtext was Obed Macy's *History of Nantucket*; but the text needs only a map and a single image ('a mere hillock, and elbow of sand; all beach, without a background' (157)) in order to compose a Gordian Knot of self-contradictions drawn from Canada to Rome, from Lapland to the Eddystone Lighthouse. Or take the Try Pots, recommended as 'one of the best kept hotels in all Nantucket' (159). The subtext there seems to be the opening chapter of *Hosea* ('Go, take unto thee a wife of whoredoms and children of whoredoms'), transforming the landlord to one 'Hosea Hussey' and introducing Mrs. Hussey 'under a dull red lamp' as literally a hussy (the biblical 'adultress') wearing a necklace of polished vertebrae. So the Old Testament is linked to an avatar of Kali (black goddess of death with her necklace of skulls) and to an elaborate colour coding of red, purple and yellow, that almost alone evokes a narrative out of the constituent textual and subtextual elements. When Melville's head was flush, every shake of the kaleidoscope could produce new narrative patterns, new chapters that he intercalated into his ever-burgeoning text. Ultimately, like all symbolic ventures, it appears almost autonomous.

Almost, but not quite. Even Régis Durand, in his recent *Melville: Signes et Métaphores* (1980), holds off from treating *Moby-Dick* wholly as a metafiction: that is, as debating the function of signs, undermining its own signs, and mocking all available codes. This is no post-modernist text, he insists.[12] Melville's texts, at least before *The Confidence-Man*, are always concerned *with* something, the memory *of* something, the memory of some original violence which has been postponed, or the inscription of that violence (like Ahab's stump, or scar, like the scars on male sperm whales' backs) which has been deferred. That original scene, like Bartleby's mysterious origin, is shrouded in rumour. For Melville's texts work on us rather like rumours: simultaneously presenting a distortion (of something) and a production (of something else) in an indistinguishable amalgam. The need (for both reader and writer in their various ways) is to sort, to sift this circulation of signs, these rumours (about whales, about Bartleby), these emblems (like the doubloon), these living hieroglyphs (like Queequeg). Such is the bliss of this quest, this chase, this adventure for its own sake.

For Melville's work is all puzzles. The puzzle of *Typee* is: are they, or are they not, cannibals? The puzzle of *Moby-Dick* is: what, and where, is the White Whale? The puzzle of *The Confidence-Man* is: is he one, or is he many? There may well be an interpreter, either as narrator or protagonist, attempting to unpuzzle the strange case of the lethargic slave-ship (*Benito Cereno*), say, or of the anorexic scrivener (*Bartleby*). Invariably it is a matter of scrutiny and interpretation of signs.

But not all such enigmas, by their very nature, are capable of resolution. They present a crux. They demand some kind of insistent, searching penetration. Which is what Ishmael offers. *His* is the fluid, wayward, spiralling discourse, repeatedly ravelling and unravelling its enquiry, as if spooled on some never-ending shuttle. But there are also obsessional crypto-graphers, like Ahab, who follow their one fixed code with an unflinching if baffled will, as if

> some certain significance lurks in all things, else all things are little worth, and the round world itself but an empty cipher, except to sell by the cartload, as they do hills about Boston, to fill up some morass in the Milky Way. (540)

Whatever significance lurks in these *signifiés*, the task is not merely to search out the interplay of the referents, but to redouble the confusion of the *signifiants* with synonymous and homonymous branchings and intertwinings so that nothing is ever reduced to a single interpretation, a single authoritative stance.

Only one thing is sure: 'on errands of life' (as *Bartleby* concludes), 'these letters speed to death.' The inevitable para-dox, throughout Melville's *oeuvre*, is that of death-in-life. This very paper (pulped in the sexual violence of female labour, according to *The Tartarus of Maids*) is destined to be defaced of every trace. All ends, as it began, in an open whirl, in the blank indeterminacy (of white whale or pallid scrivener) that determines the ceaseless circulation of signs.

This Proteus-like instability of the text is reflected in the unceasing, yet hesitant, metamorphoses of the whale, as of the text itself. For as the jungle laces and interlaces ('Life folded Death; Death trellised Life' (561)), so the text reinvents itself from moment to moment, chapter to chapter, by acts of deconstruction (those anatomical examinations of the Blanket, the Tail, the Fountain, the Cassock, the Nut of the whale) which constitute further stages of construction; by a deployment of symbols which becomes a further enjoyment of the text. For Melville's ultimate aspiration, at least in these decades, was some transcendent ecstasy, beyond life and death, in trance.

But that search Melville finally abandoned in *The Confidence-Man*. The novelist, he concluded, was an impostor. On reading *Essays in Criticism* he mightily approved Matthew Arnold's quotation from Maurice de Guerin ('The literary career seems to me unreal, both in its essence and in the rewards which one seeks from it, and therefore fatally marred by a secret absurdity'), marginally commenting:

> This is the first verbal statement of a truth which everyone who thinks in these days must have felt.[13]

The Confidence-Man in its inconsistency, incoherence, incongruity presents the novel itself as a self-conscious artefact whose intrusive author manipulates his readers with a series of further incongruous arguments. For what is a novel but 'masquerade'? What is an author but the wiliest of confidence men? Among literary signs the so-called 'natural' and fictive are either indistinguishable or interchangeable. Here all the world is a stage; every actor in drag; every action some kind of transformation. So in *The Confidence-Man* fictions as often as not are told at second or third hand; or further fictions told within fictions. While again and again the narrator intrudes with further digressions or discusses technical matters to underscore the unreality of the narration. But since 'reality' (presumably inhabited by both the narrator and his readers) is similarly presented as a stagey world of disguises and transformations, nothing natural or supernatural, social or artistic, is preserved from the all-devouring circle of fiction. As Edgar A. Dryden put it:

> Plagued by suspicions but led on by such conventional literary clues as puns, complex patterns of imagery, and suggestive allusions to important people, events, and products of human history, the reader is tempted time and again to try to bring to the surface the meaning and order which seem to lie concealed behind the action and words of the novel's characters. But . . .

each newly discovered clue, each new operative pattern or allusion, leads not beneath the verbal surface but across it to another mystery or, more often, to an example which subverts the implications of the original pattern.[14]

The very circularity of this procedure is reflected in the first of the author's critical intrusions, with its palindrome-like title: 'Worth the consideration of those to whom it may prove worth considering'. The fatal presence of the confidence-man not merely defrauds his victims of their cash but of the very confidence in their own beliefs, their own language, their own roles. That is the paradox: in this protean world-as-art, it is the conscious actors alone who achieve the illusion of 'truth'.

For there is no transcendent, or divine, Truth beyond this play of fictions. (The cosmopolitan, amid yet further echoes from *Revelation*, finally puts out the solar lamp and brings the novel to its apocalyptic close.) There is no waiting for Godot, in Beckett's contemporary formulation. There is no supreme, exemplary paradigm, no permanent code or map, as Wellingborough Redburn had discovered as he checked his father's guidebook against his own experience of Liverpool:

> Yes, the thing that had guided the father, could not guide the son. . . . And, Wellingborough, as your father's guide-book is no guide for you, neither would yours (could you afford to buy a modern one today) be a true guide to those who come after you. Guide-books, Wellingborough, are the least reliable in all literature; and nearly all literature, in one sense, is made up of guide-books.[15]

Nearly all literature! Melville, in the eight short years after 1849, was to add considerably to the saving remnant. As he confided to Hawthorne in 1851:

> And perhaps, after all, there is *no* secret. We incline to think that the Problem of the Universe is like the Freemason's mighty secret, so terrible to all children. It turns out, at last, to consist in a triangle, a mallet, and an apron,—nothing more![16]

While writing *Moby-Dick* he was still worrying away at the world (or whale) as 'a riddle to unfold', a mystery destined to 'be unsolved to the last' (593), as indeterminate as the colour white which Melville challenged Champollion himself to read. ('I but put that brow before you. Read it if you can.' (455).)

But what if Queequeg's living hieroglyphs and the whale's 'pyramidical white hump' (281) and Ahab's 'Egyptian chest' (284) were a circular language after all? *Pierre*, word by word, seems to anticipate Barthes. Melville, like Ahab, continued to strip layer from a little lower layer until that pyramidical vastness of riddling meaning was

> found to consist of nothing but surface stratified on surface. To its axis, the world being nothing but superinduced superficies. By vast pains we mine into the pyramid; by horrible gropings we come to the central room; with joy we espy the sarcophagus; but we lift the lid—and no body is there!—appallingly vacant as vast is the soul of a man![17]

So the world—and the text—become uncentred. No longer an apricot with its core or pit or stone, nor onion even (in Barthes's image), but a kind of unpetalling lettuce. Those 'superinduced superficies' hint at an Einsteinian universe whose centre is now nowhere, whose circumference everywhere, and where all possible paths along which radiation can travel are curved paths 'so that they are infinite in the sense of returning infinitely upon themselves, though finite in the sense of being confined within a determinate volume'.[18] Such is a post-modern work of art. For Melville at last removed the transcendent mystery even from 'the soul of a man'. This sense of the self's inherent instability, of its ability to adopt any role or mask, to become anything precisely because in itself it was nothing, came more and more to dominate Melville's thought, until in *The Confidence-Man* (as we have seen) there is a sense that the unique status of the 'self'—a belief in its stable and independent existence, its transcendent godlikeness—was the ultimate illusion.

Such a Melville already sounds suspiciously like Nietzsche with his emphasis on the illusory nature of understanding, on the possibility of reversing the privileged axes of good and evil, on the subjection of the self to the ceaseless circulation of meanings. Such a Melville, in fact, emerges more a post-structuralist than a mere modernist; and his hieroglyphic indeterminancy principle ('Read it if you can') may finally be translated from the terms of *The Confidence-Man: His Masquerade* to those of Derrida's *Grammatology*.[19]

NOTES

1. Herman Melville, 'Hawthorne and His Mosses', *The Literary World*, 17 and 24 August 1850.

2. David Lodge, *The Modes of Modern Writing: Metaphor, Metonymy, and the Typology of Modern Literature* (London, 1977); Gabriel Josipovici, *The World and the Book: A Study of Modern Fiction* (London, 1971); William H. Gass, *Fiction and the Figures of Life* (1972; Boston, 1978 edition) and *The World Within the Word* (New York, 1978); George Steiner, *After Babel: Aspects of Language and Translation* (New York, 1975).

3. Herman Melville, *Moby-Dick; or, The Whale* (1851; London, Penguin Books, 1972 edition), p. 560. Further references in the text will be to the Penguin edition.

4. Jacques Derrida, *L'Ecriture et la Différence* (Paris, 1967), translated by Alan Bass, *Writing and Difference* (Chicago, 1978), and *La Dissémination* (Paris, 1972); Jacques Lacan, 'Seminar on the Purloined Letter', *Yale French Studies* 48 (1973), 38–72.

5. Letter to Nathaniel Hawthorne (1 June 1851), in *The Letters of Herman Melville*, edited by Merrell R. Davis and William H. Gilman (New Haven, 1960), p. 130.

6. Roland Barthes, 'Style and its Image', in *Literary Style: A Symposium* (London, 1971).

7. Roland Barthes, *S/Z*, translated by Richard Miller (New York, 1974), p. 4.

8. Herman Melville, *The Confidence-Man: His Masquerade* (1857; Indianapolis, Bobbs-Merrill, 1967 edition), pp. 95 and 260.

9. H. Bruce Franklin, *The Wake of the Gods: Melville's Mythology* (Stanford, 1963), pp. 83–4.

10. Robert Shulman, 'The Serious Functions of Melville's Phallic Jokes', *American Literature* 33 (1961).

11. Edgar A. Dryden, *Melville's Thematics of Form: The Great Art of Telling the Truth* (Baltimore, 1968), pp. 21, 83, 85 and 113.

12. Régis Durand, *Melville: Signes et Métaphores* (Lausanne, 1980), pp. 20 and 117.

13. Merton M. Sealts, *Melville's Reading: A Check-List of Books Owned and Borrowed* (Cambridge, Mass., 1950).

14. Edgar A. Dryden, *Melville's Thematics of Form*, pp. 151–52.

15. Herman Melville, *Redburn: His First Voyage* (1849; London, Penguin Books, 1976 edition), p. 224.

16. Letter to Nathaniel Hawthorne (16 April 1851), p. 125.

17. Herman Melville, *Pierre; or, The Ambiguities* (1852; Evanston and Chicago, Newberry Library, 1971 edition), pp. 284–85.

18. R. G. Collingwood, *The Idea of Nature* (London, 1945), pp. 153–54.

19. Jacques Derrida, *De la Grammatologie* (Paris, 1967), translated by Gayatri Spivak, *Of Grammatology* (Baltimore, 1976).

An earlier version of this essay appeared in the *Dutch Quarterly Review*.

5

Kingdom and Exile: Mark Twain's Hannibal Books

by RICHARD GRAY

It was not until he wrote *The Adventures of Huckleberry Finn* that Mark Twain came to successful creative terms with the most significant part of his own life. 'My books are simply autobiographies',[1] Twain declared once. True of every American writer, perhaps, the declaration seems especially true coming from him: partly because he relied so much on fact (the dividing line between journalism and fiction virtually disappears in books like *The Innocents Abroad* (1869) and *Roughing It* (1872)) and partly because even those of Twain's works that were undeniably the product of strenuous imaginative labour can be read as attempts to resolve his inner divisions and create some sense of continuity between his present and his past. The inner divisions and the discontinuity were, in fact, inseparable. For nearly all Twain's best fictional work has to do with what Henry Nash Smith christened 'the matter of Hannibal'[2]: that is, the author's experiences as a child in a small town in the slave-owning state of Missouri and (even if only by extension and implication) his years as a steamboat pilot on the Mississippi River. This was not simply a matter of that nostalgia for the good old days before the Civil War that Twain certainly shared with many Americans—those who

80

felt, along with Henry James, that civil conflict had made 'the good American . . . a more critical person than his complacent and confident grandfather' because he had 'eaten of the tree of knowledge'.[3] Nor was it simply another instance of the Romantic idealization of youth: although Twain did firmly believe that, youth being 'the only thing that was worth giving to the race', to look back on one's childhood was to give oneself 'a cloudy sense of having been a prince, once, in some enchanted far off land, and of being in exile now and desolate'.[4] It was rather, and more simply, that Twain recognized (in however intuitive or unwilling a fashion) that his years in the South had shaped his being for good and ill and provided him with what he most loved and hated; so to explore those years was to explore the often equivocal nature of his own vision — to understand them was to begin at least to understand himself.

Not that Twain ever began drawing on the matter of Hannibal in anything like a deliberate or self-conscious way: he was not that kind of writer. He often said, in fact, that he was only interested in writing a book if it would write itself. Like Poe's claim that he composed 'The Raven' from back to front this was, of course, something of a fabrication, but it did point to a deeper truth: that he wrote best when he allowed his imagination free rein, in a relatively impulsive and unpremeditated manner. As if by way of illustrating this, Twain's first significant venture into his Southern past began as a series of articles for the *Atlantic Monthly*, undertaken—at least, according to his own account of it—at the suggestion of a friend. 'Old Times on the Mississippi', which describes Twain's experiences as a steamboat pilot, appeared in the magazine in 1875. They were well received, and Twain was reasonably pleased with them: nevertheless, he turned to writing other things, among them *The Adventures of Tom Sawyer* and part of *Huckleberry Finn*, before using them as the basis for a book. In adding to the essays when he did come to write the book, Twain used his favourite motif of a journey, in this case one taken by himself up the Mississippi River from New Orleans to St. Paul, in order to see how things had changed since his childhood and steamboating days. Further padding was supplied by passages taken from the manuscript of *Huckleberry Finn*, material left over from *A Tramp Abroad*, and long passages quoted, with disarming frankness, from travel books by other writers. The result, now called *Life on the Mississippi*, finally saw the light of day in 1883.

Given the way *Life on the Mississippi* was composed—which was haphazard even by Twain's own standards—it is not surprising that the chapters originally prepared for the *Atlantic Monthly*—that is, Chapters IV–XVII—are easily the most deeply felt and fascinating. Their fascination stems, at least in part, from the fact that they represent Twain's first serious attempt to map the geography of his spiritual home. The map that emerges, however, is a far from clear one. The famous description of what, in Twain's own opinion, he gained and lost by becoming a steamboat pilot illustrates this. In becoming a pilot, Twain explains, he learned to read 'the face of the water' as though it were 'a wonderful book'—a book, he adds, 'that was a dead language to the uneducated passenger, but which told its mind to me without reserve'. Twain's attitude towards books and things literary remained fiercely ambivalent throughout his life (Huck Finn, for example, the hero of Twain's best book, invariably associates books with 'study' and 'Sunday school'); so it is hardly surprising to find that this painfully acquired mastery of the alphabet of the Mississippi River is not regarded as an unmixed blessing. 'I had made a valuable acquisition', Twain admits,

> But I had lost something, too, I had lost something which could never be restored to me while I lived. All the grace, the beauty, the poetry had gone out of the majestic river. . . . All the value any feature of it had for me now was the amount of usefulness it could furnish toward compassing the safe piloting of a steamboat.[5]

In effect, Twain argues, an attitude founded on a kind of innocence and illiteracy was replaced once he became a pilot by a more knowledgeable, and in a sense more useful, but sadly disillusioned one.

Several points need to be made about this distinction. In the first place, as a distinction of fact it is not strictly true. As one critic has pointed out,[6] Twain did not lose the ability to appreciate the 'grace' and 'beauty' of the Mississippi and its environs—*Life on the Mississippi* is, after all, full of rather florid passages describing that grace and beauty; all he did lose was the belief that the simply aesthetic stance, and the vocabulary the aesthete deploys, could do justice to the empirical realities of the river. In the second place, as an imaginative distinction, a way of defining possible attitudes or structures of feeling, it is painfully inadequate. Twain presents his education as a process whereby one form of myopia, one set of preconceptions, simply replaces another. The vision of the romantic dreamer, who sees the river in terms of an embarassingly conventional landscape painting, is displaced by that of the gruff, commonsensical realist, who thinks of it as no more than a tool, something to be used and exploited. And finally, as a small piece of mythmaking, what Twain says here provides him with a frame for the entire book and a way of relating his own personal history to the history of his region. For in distinguishing between the South of his Childhood and steamboating days and the South of his adult years—the South, in particular, that he had seen on his trip from New Orleans to St. Paul—Twain falls back on the tired and ultimately unsatisfactory contrast he establishes here between (to put it crudely) the romance of the past and the realism of the present.

In making this connection, however implicit, between the personal and the public, and describing the contrast between the old world of the riverside South and the new, Twain is—it cannot escape any reader who notices the contrast in the first place—uncertain, his sympathies fiercely divided. There are, of course, frequent criticisms of the 'romantic juvenilities' of the Old South, and of poor Sir Walter Scott in particular, who is blamed for encouraging Southerners to fall in love with the 'grotesque "chivalry" doings' and 'windy humbuggeries' of the past. There are constant and approving references, too, to 'the genuine and wholesome civilization of the nineteenth century' and to the way Twain's homeplace seems to have become an integral part of that civilization since the Civil War, 'evidencing progress, energy, and prosperity'. Yet, time and again, there is also a profound nostalgia, a sense of loss noticeable in Twain's descriptions of the world that is gone or the few, lingering traces of it that remain. Describing the changes that have occurred in the riverside towns since his own steamboating days, for instance, Twain ruefully admits, 'a glory that once was [has] dissolved and vanished away.' And his actual descriptions of the old steamboats themselves, and the period when they reigned supreme on the Mississippi, convey an irrepressible joy, involvement and affection—feelings that are utterly lacking whenever Twain turns his gaze to the 'quiet, orderly' river traffic and men of 'sedate business aspect' associated with the needs and demands of a more 'wholesome and practical'[7] age. No attempt is made to resolve this contradiction: the glamour of the past is dismissed at one moment and then recalled with elegiac regret the next, the pragmatism and progressivism of the present is welcomed sometimes and at others coolly regretted. Even if one were made, however, it is difficult to see how it could be successful; for at this stage of his career, at least, Twain lacked the language to accommodate and reconcile his two attitudes to the past. All he could do was offer what can only be described as a verbal equivalent of double vision.

Inadequacy of language is also a characteristic of *The Adventures of Tom Sawyer*—which was published in 1876— although here that inadequacy takes a rather different form. According to contemporary accounts, Twain began the book 'with certain of his boyish recollections in mind' and gradually wove together three quite separate narrative strands: the 'love story' of Tom and Becky Thatcher (which, among other things, parodies the rituals of adult courtship), the story of the rivalry between Tom and his brother Sid (which inverts the many Sunday school stories popular at the time about the Bad Boy who ends up in trouble and the Good Boy whose maturity is crowned with success), and the melodramatic tale of Injun Joe (which illustrates Twain's love of popular literature, the 'dime novel' and the 'court-room drama'). From the beginning, however, Twain seems to have been doubtful about the exact nature and age of his audience. Would it appeal primarily to children or to adults? Quite simply, he was not sure, although he did try to assume an appearance of certainty when the book was completed. 'It is *not* a boy's book at all', he insisted in a letter to William Dean Howells, 'It will only be read by adults. It is only written for adults.' Howells was unconvinced. 'Treat it explicitly *as* a boy's story', he insisted; Twain's wife, Livy, agreed; and so, in the Preface to *Tom Sawyer*, the author hedges his bets. The book, he declares, 'is intended mainly for the entertainment of boys and girls'. Nevertheless, he goes on,

> I hope it will not be shunned by men and women on that account, for part of my plan has been to try pleasantly to remind adults of what they once were. . . .[8]

The uncertainty of purpose and perspective implicit in these opening remarks is uncomfortably obvious when one turns to the story. Certain elements of *Tom Sawyer* certainly do seem to identify it with the best kind of children's literature, in that they involve the dramatization of common childhood fantasies or the carthartic exploration of childhood nightmares. Tom Sawyer himself, for example, discovers hidden treasure. He becomes 'a glittering hero . . . —the pet of the old, the envy of the young', when he identifies Dr. Robinson's murderer. And he enjoys the delicious pleasure of feeling sadly wronged, apparently dying, and then returning in secret to hear penitent adults lament their treatment of him and admit that 'he wasn't *bad*, so to say—only mischeevous.'[9] Injun Joe really belongs to this area of the book, too, in that he is not so much a fictional character as a bogey-man, designed to give protagonist and reader alike an almost voyeuristic thrill of terror; it is notice able, for instance, that he is nearly always seen from a hidden point of vantage, so that the threat that he offers is in effect framed and contained. But while all this serves to confirm the opening claim in the Preface, certain other aspects of the story seem to assume a more adult and sophisticated audience, looking back on the past—their own past, the author's past, and the past of a nation—from a distanced, sometimes amused and sometimes regretful, standpoint. The parodic element in Tom and Becky's courtship, for example, presupposes an adult audience that can appreciate the nature of the parody. This is also true of the inversion of popular sentiment and genteel literary convention implicit in the contrast between Tom and Sid. Quite apart from that, there is the simple fact that Twain as narrator tends to maintain a Thackerayan distance between himself and the reader, on the one hand,

and, on the other, Tom Sawyer, Huck Finn, their friends and enemies, and the unsophisticated folk of St. Petersburg.

This last point is the most important one. At times, as when for instance Twain is describing Tom and Huck's adventures on Jackson's Island, the language has the kind of power and immediacy that implies direct involvement. For the most part, however, it creates a sense of distance between character and reader because the narrator is clearly a person of some sophistication, maturity, and refinement, who is trying to make us aware of this through his vocabulary. In *Tom Sawyer*, people do not spit, they 'expectorate'; they do not wear clothes, but 'accoutrements'; breezes are 'zephyrs', and buildings are 'edifices'. There is a measure of self-directed irony contained in such genteel diction, of course, but that irony acts as no more than a qualification: Twain may be slightly embarrassed and uncomfortable about the contrast between simple characters and sophisticated narrator, but that contrast remains and is even insisted upon. We are constantly being reminded, in fact, that he and we are no longer a part of the 'kingdom' of the child or, for that matter, of a small, 'simple-hearted' community like that of St. Petersburg, Missouri. Along with explicit statements to that effect, this message comes to us via the narrator's constant tendency to step back from the action to elicit a moral of some sort, and his placing of all the characters on a stage, as it were, with a 'curtain of charity' and footlights between them and us. As in *Life on the Mississippi*, Twain may be drawn back now and then into the world of his childhood, 'a Delectable Land, dreamy, reposeful, and inviting', where 'there was cheer in every face, and a spring in every step'[10]: but for much of the book he seems intent on emphasizing the fact that both he and the world have changed—and not entirely, he intimates, for the worse.

In this connection, it may not be entirely irrelevant that Twain's earliest reminiscences about his boyhood, which provided the bginnings of *Tom Sawyer*, coincided with the first year of his marriage to Livy. Whatever else may be said about their relationship, it seems fairly clear now that he used his wife as a civilizing agent, the embodiment of his conscience, the more respectable side of himself. 'You will break up all my irregularities when we are married', he wrote to her shortly before the wedding, 'and *civilize* me, and make of me a model husband and an adornment to society—won't you . . .?'[11] Quite apart from offering a parody of his own courtship, therefore, the story of Tom Sawyer and his friends seems to have acted as a kind of safety-valve, a way of releasing rebellious feelings and indulging in evidently unrealizable dreams of freedom before committing himself to orthodoxy, respectability, and success. The three narrative strands of the book tend to confirm this cathartic pattern. As far as the love story goes, Tom eventually assumes the conventional male protective role with Becky, by accepting a punishment which should by rights have been hers. As far as the contrast between Tom and Sid is concerned, Tom, it gradually emerges, is the *really* good boy—any of his more dangerously subversive appetites having apparently been satisfied by the time out on Jackson's Island. And as for the tale of Injun Joe: Tom, it emerges, is not an outlaw at all but the very embodiment of social justice. Like his creator Tom ends up, in fact, by accepting the disciplines of the social norm. Injun Joe, who seemed for a moment to be a projection of Tom's darker self, is killed; the integrity and sanctity of the community is confirmed; and Tom is even ready, it seems, to offer brief lectures on the advantages of respectability. Here again, as in his account of his education as a steamboat pilot and the contrast between Old South and New, Twain tries, really, to resolve his inner divisions and in particular his ambivalent attitude towards the stuff of his earlier years, by imposing on his material the notions of personal development and social betterment—in a word, the myth of progress.

Only one character in *Tom Sawyer* stands outside of this pattern of rebellion, release, and moral improvement; and that, of course, is Huckleberry Finn. When Huck first appears in the book, he is seen from the outside, and almost with disapproval. Gradually, however, he is given his own voice, allowed to speak for himself and his own, profoundly anti-social values: so that, by the end, he is even beginning to hold his own in debate with the newly respectable Tom. The ground is prepared, in effect, for *The Adventures of Huckleberry Finn* (1885), Twain's greatest work, in which he moved even more fully back into the past—not merely remembering steamboat days or even childhood now, but speaking in and from the person of a child. The full significance of this movement seems to have been lost on Twain at first; for when he began *Huckleberry Finn* in 1876 it is fairly clear that he saw it simply as a sequel to *Tom Sawyer*. Several narrative threads were carried over and in the opening pages at least, although Huck was now permitted to be the narrator, much of the comedy was as uncomplicated as it had been in the earlier book. It took nearly a year, in fact, for Twain to realize that things were heading in a direction other than the one he had originally intended—and that, in particular, Huck and Jim, under the pressure of their relationship and the problem of Jim's slavery, were growing into complex and even difficult characters, requiring more than just a series of set comic routines. When he did realize it, his response was characteristic: he put the manuscript aside, leaving Huck and Jim on a suitably apocalyptic note with their raft smashed up by a riverboat, and turned to the writing of other things.

Critics are divided as to exactly how long it was before Twain returned to the Huck Finn manuscript. One thing is certain, however: when he did, his entire attitude to the project had changed. More specifically, he now seemed ready to embark on a more serious kind of comedy which would explore the conflict between (to use his own later description) 'a sound heart and a deformed conscience'[12]: between, in other words, Huck's own personal impulses which prompt him to help Jim as a friend and a suffering individual and those notions of right and wrong, inherited from society, which tell him that Jim, like everyone, is no more than a commodity, to be assigned some predetermined role or function—some part that he is required to play whether he likes it or not. In addition, Twain seemed to recognize that the best way in which he could dramatize this conflict was in terms that he had had to hand for years now but which he had never really effectively exploited: in terms, that is, of his Southern background, the years on or near the Mississippi. In *Huckleberry Finn*, and especially in the chapters written after Twain returned to the manuscript, we are confronted with two radically different ways of looking at the world, two utterly opposed structures of thought and feeling; and Twain seems instinctively to have recognized that he could project both those visions, give flesh and blood to the two structures, without straying very far from his own past.

As far as Twain's portrait of society, the system that had deformed Huck's conscience, is concerned, Twain seems to have been helped by his reading. In between writing the first and second parts of the manuscript, Twain had been involved in the preparation of a collection of comic tales and sketches: which had required him, among other things, to read or re-read the work of a group of writers known as the Southwestern humorists—people like Augustus Baldwin Longstreet and George Washington Harris, who specialized in satirical portraits of life in the Old South. As several commentators have pointed out, this almost certainly encouraged Twain in his formulation of a new plan for the Huck Finn story; it could be, he saw, a series of comic but harshly critical scenes from old Southern provincial life along the lines of Longstreet's *Georgia Scenes* (1835) and Harris's *Sut Lovingood* (1867). Too much should not be made of this particular influence, however. Even in the earlier chapters, written before Twain had renewed his interest in the Southwestern humorists, there are strong touches of satire: Pap Finn, for instance, is essentially a satirically conceived figure, a classic, comic portrait of the 'poor white'—in his fear of the unknown, his habitual drunkenness followed by equally habitual bouts of repentance, his inverted Calvinism, his violence, and his bigotry. Quite apart from that, no Southwestern humorist had ever attempted a portrait of Southern life anywhere near as rich and detailed as the one that gradually emerged in *Huckleberry Finn*—or, for that matter, achieved a perspective that even begins to approach Twain's in the clarity of its focus or the incisiveness of its judgements.

The comprehensiveness of Twain's vision of the Old South is perhaps the first thing that strikes the reader. In the course of the book, we are offered an account of every level of ante-bellum society: from planters with aristocratic pretensions, like the Grangerfords, through plain farmers like the Phelps family who own a little land and, at the most, only two or three slaves, to the poor whites of Bricksville and, below them even, the blacks. With each additional detail, too, we understand more about the system that seeks to control Huck's mind and Jim's body; that tries to contain reality by controlling every possible form of language, thought, and behaviour—in short, by imposing its own fictive version of things. In this sense, the 'style' that Huck so innocently admires when he observes it in, for example, the Grangerfords infects every aspect of life: it dictates the words people use, the clothes they wear, the opinions they form. It is the essence of Twain's criticism, in fact, that the patterns ordained by this—or, indeed, by any— culture are at once intricate, interconnected, and inclusive: the Grangerfords are controlled by the same inexorable laws whether they are making a fine speech, writing sentimental poems, killing their enemies in the name of 'the feud', or enslaving their fellow human beings. Florid words, fine clothes, and the exploitation of others all issue, Twain insists, from the same false consciousness: a consciousness which manages to be at once sentimental and crudely opportunistic—justifying its economic base, and the major historical crime on which that base was built, in terms of an absurdly romantic myth of gentility.

If characters like the Grangerfords are a paradoxical mixture of the genteel and the utilitarian, and in being this recall the false opposites on which a book like *Life on the Mississippi* is founded, then Huck Finn himself suggests the other side of the coin, a more hopeful possibility. For his power as a hero stems directly from the fact that, in creating him, Twain managed to harness together the two sides of him which might be described, albeit crudely, as the romantic and the realistic. Huck is a focus for all Twain's nostalgia, all his yearnings for childhood, the lost days of his youth, the days before the Civil War and the Fall; and he is also, quite clearly, an embodiment of his creator's more progressive feelings, the belief in human development and perfectibility—he suggests hope for the future as well as dreams of the past. Among other things, this is indicated by Huck's language, in that it is precisely Huck's attention to empirical detail that gives his observations such colour and immediacy. His words do not deny things as they are, they acknowledge them and derive their beauty from that acknowledgement; his eloquence depends on patient observation, in fact, a fierce sense of the particular. And it is even more apparent, perhaps, from Huck's judgements and actions. For, like many subsequent American heroes, Huck is easily the most honourable and, indeed, chivalric character in his world simply because he sticks closest to the facts. To be more precise, it is Huck's realistic awareness of other people and objects, his understanding of their separateness and individuality that allows him to assume, without being priggish, a certain nobility; he sees Jim as someone in his own right, commanding respect and requiring sympathy, and it is this that makes him behave like a perfect gentle knight.

It has often been observed that the last few chapters of *Huckleberry Finn* represent a decline or, to use Hemingway's term, a betrayal in the sense that Huck is pushed to one side of the action, Tom Sawyer is permitted to play his familiar games, and the issue of Jim's slavery is reduced to the level of farce. For all Huck's occasional protests at Tom's behaviour, or his famous final cry of defiance, the comedy loses its edge, the moral problems are minimized, and the familiar divisions and contradictions in Twain's writing begin to reappear. There are many possible reasons for this, but one that should not be overlooked is that Twain was perhaps beginning to have doubts about the effectiveness and viability of his hero. 'I have always preached', Twain declared once.

> If the humour came of its own accord and uninvited I have allowed it a place in my sermon, but I was not writing the sermon for the sake of the humour.[13]

This, while not strictly speaking true, does point to a powerful impulse in his writing, which led him quite often to search for remedies for the ills he diagnosed, to offer his readers guidance, or to find models of belief and behaviour which he felt were relevant to his times. And it might well have been this, among other things, that prompted him to turn away from the figure of Huck Finn towards a rather different kind of hero: Hank Morgan, the narrator and protagonist of *A Connecticut Yankee in King Arthur's Court* (1889). Like Huck, Hank is a vernacular hero with a strong commitment to facts. Unlike him, however, he is a down-to-earth, self-made man; he is very much a part of the new, urban-industrial world that Twain knew was growing up all around him; and he has a programmatic, reforming side to his character. In devising Hank, in short, Twain seems to have been trying to meet a criticism of Huck that someone with a more didactic approach to literature might have offered—someone like himself at times, in fact— the criticism that for all his virtues, Huck was too much of a loner and a mythic figure to provide an imitable model, and too much a part of the vanished agrarian past to offer hope to those trapped in the Gilded Age.

The basic plot device in *Connecticut Yankee* is simple. Hank Morgan, a 'Yankee of Yankees' and an accomplished engineer, finds himself carried back into the world of King Arthur, where his knowledge of technology enables him to gain power and import 'the civilization of the nineteenth century'.[14] The stage is set by this device for a contrast between sound sense, liberal principles, and progress on the one hand and on the other the nonsense, barbarism, and romanticism of a society incapable of distinguishing between reality and illusion. What seems to have been intended, in effect, was a revised, updated version of the contrast between Huck Finn and the Old South, with sixth-century England acting as the Old South's doppel- ganger (the gentlemen are now knights, the poor whites peasants, the slaves serfs, and so on). As so often happened with Twain, however, intention and achievement turned out to be two quite different things. Arthurian England certainly emerges as a shadowy version of Twain's childhood home- place, and Hank certainly assumes the mantle of progressive hero. The book in which they meet and conflict, however, is not so much a development of *Huckleberry Finn* as a revised version of *Life on the Mississippi*. For in attempting to make his hero more 'relevant', Twain divorced him completely from that world of the past, the world of prelapsarian innocence, that held such sway over his imagination. The power of the character of Huck Finn, it is perhaps worth repeating, issues directly from the fact that Huck is at once a progressive and a regressive figure for his creator; both an expression of Twain's belief in perfectibility and a gathering-point for all his deepest feelings about childhood. And in the absence of this synthesizing figure the familiar divisions reappear, the old 'either-or' distinctions: between past and future, romance and realism, the beautiful and the useful.

This is as much to say that Twain is as ambivalent about the Arthurian kingdom as he had been in his earlier books about the kingdom of Tom Sawyer or that Mississippi River on which the riverboat pilot had reigned once as 'absolute monarch'. As I have just suggested, the 'lost land' to which Hank Morgan finds himself returned is, in fact, a thinly disguised version of Twain's own 'lost land'[15] of childhood memory; and, as such, it exercises a profound pull on the author's imagination and, eventually, on the narrator's and reader's as well. Certainly, there is plenty of criticism of the backwardness, cruelty, and romantic silliness of early medieval England, just as there had been in *Life on the Mississippi* of the Old South and its legacy; and occasionally the parallels as well as the criticisms are made quite explicit—as when, for example, Hank compares the false consciousness of the peasants (who, it seems, are ready to turn 'their . . . hands against their own class in the interest of the common oppressor') to that of the poor whites during the Civil War (who, we are told, fought 'to prevent the destruction of that very institution that degraded them'). The name of poor Sir Walter Scott is even dragged out once again as a means of belabouring romanticism in general. But these deliberate criticisms and conscious parallels are more than countered by those moments in the book when author and narrator alike appear to be thoroughly seduced, their imaginations captured by a world where—to borrow a phrase quoted at the beginning of this essay—they have had the cloudy sense of being a prince. Even in Chapter I, as Hank moves 'as one in a dream' into the world of Camelot, there is an unmistakable sense of moving back into the author's past: there is the same mixture of poverty and glamour as we find in the portraits of the riverboat towns in *Life on the Mississippi*, the same 'soft, reposeful, summer landscape, as lovely as a dream and as lonesome as Sunday'. And later passages serve merely to strengthen this tendency, to underline this suggestion; the haunting passage at the beginning of the twelfth chapter, for instance, which describes Hank and his aide setting off on a journey, moving 'like spirits',[16] dreaming along 'through glades in a mist of green light', finds its echo in Twain's descriptions of the countryside surrounding the Quarles plantation where, as a boy, he spent long, idyllic summers.

93

If Hank's kingdom is seen at once as barbaric and romantic, a closed society and a vanished virgin land, it is not surprising that uncertainty and ambivalence comes to characterize Hank himself. This ambivalence takes two forms really. When, as in for example many of the earlier chapters, Twain is fairly distanced from Hank and can see him objectively, as a spokesman for reform, a progressive hero; then Hank is sometimes celebrated, praised for his technological innovations and his liberal politics, and sometimes regarded with profound distrust—for he is, after all, introducing irreversible historical change, guaranteeing that the lost land will be forever lost. But when, as in the closing chapters, Twain begins to identify with Hank and his experiences and use him as a mouthpiece; then, in such cases, Hank tends to become as full of pessimism, doubt and self-contradiction as his creator—pessimism as to the possibility of progress, doubt as regards the value of what he is doing, and self-contradiction when it comes to describing the lost world of Camelot. By the end of the book, Hank Morgan has been returned to the nineteenth century; he is in exile with, as he puts it, 'an abyss of thirteen centuries between me and my home and my friends'.[17] And as he lies dying, dreaming that he has returned to his lost land, trying to pretend that it is the strange new world of technology and progress that is the dream, he offers a poignant reflection of the author's own predicament—caught once again between present and past.

After *A Connecticut Yankee*, Twain made several more attempts to deal with the experiences of his childhood and his life on the Mississippi, but only one of these attempts ranks as a notable achievement. This is *The Tragedy of Pudd'nhead Wilson*, published in 1894, which explores the themes that obsessed Twain by means of a story of exchanged identities: a black slave woman substitutes her master's son for her own, while the two are still in the cradle. The woman herself, Roxana, has only a small amount of Negro blood, and is to all appearances white. She, and her son, are only black by convention, a socially accepted fiction, just as her fellow-slaves are only slaves, and inferior, according to a fiction; and in effect, Twain suggests, she is merely replacing one fiction for another when she makes the exchange. Her own son, now known as Tom Driscoll,

consequently grows up to become a member of the privileged
class, wearing the clothes and playing the role of gentleman;
while his secret 'twin', the real Tom Driscoll grows up to
become a 'nigger', with the language and characteristics
which were thought by apologists for slavery—and perhaps
are still thought by some racists—to be the prerogatives or
rather the disabilities of a particular race. 'Training is everything',[18] we are told at one point in the book; and this process
whereby a 'black' man is turned into a 'white' man, and a
'white' man is turned into a 'black' man, would certainly seem
to bear this assertion out. From a bare summary of the plot, it
might also be inferred that in *Pudd'nhead Wilson* Twain recovered
the moral pungency and imaginative confidence of *Huckleberry
Finn*, with Roxana assuming the function that had been
assumed in the earlier book by Huck. After all, it could be
argued, she too challenges the 'style', the fictions and role-
playing, of the society in which she finds herself; more
specifically, she does this just as Huck does, by helping a
particular person escape from the horror of slavery.

As so often in Twain's work, however, there is something of a
gap between intention and accomplishment: between what
seems to be the case—and what the author may well have been
aiming for—and what, in fact, *is*, in terms of the readings made
available by the text. The small town in which Roxana lives, for
example, called Dawson's Landing, is perceived with quite as
much ambivalence as King Arthur's Camelot. It is a slave-
owning community, Twain admits; its inhabitants are, in many
ways, unattractive, particularly when they act as a mob; and its
leading citizens are, in their own way, as deluded, romantic,
and theatrical as the Grangerfords. But there is no escaping the
idyllic nature of the opening description of the town, with its
'snug little collection' of houses manifesting, we are told, 'con-
tentment and peace',[19] or the way in which Twain's criticisms
are continually blunted by a sense of nostalgic yearning. One
eminent critic of the book, F. R. Leavis, has even gone so far as
to claim that the author 'unmistakably admires' the town's
leading citizens and sees the town itself as an example of 'an
expanding and ripening civilization'.[20] This seems to me to be a
misreading: but it does help to indicate, I think, the muted
nature of Twain's approach here—the extent to which, that is,

the irony or satire can soften into affection and the moral perspective is consequently blurred.

Quite apart from this problem of Twain's approach to Dawson's Landing and its more privileged inhabitants, there are the further confusions created by his treatment of Roxana and her child and by his choice of narrative point-of-view. Unlike Huck, Roxana does not tell her own story: she is presented from the outside by a third-person narrator who seems to possess much of the gentility of the narrator of *Tom Sawyer* and some of the ironic pessimism of the character who gives this book its title. And the terms in which she is presented to us seem precisely calculated to appeal to the prejudices that Twain elsewhere attacks. 'Only one sixteenth of her was black,' we are informed,

> and that sixteenth did not show. She was majestic of form and stature, her attitudes were imposing and statuesque, and her gestures and movements distinguished by a noble and stately grace.[21]

More important, perhaps, Roxana herself seems to share many of these prejudices. When she exchanges the babies, for instance, she defends it to herself by claiming that it is not an act of rebellion but part of the Calvinist scheme of things; and when her son Tom turns out to be vicious and a coward she rebukes him by insisting that 'it's de nigger' in him that has made him that way—'Thirty-one parts o' you is white,' she declares, 'en on'y one part nigger, en dat po' little one part is yo' *soul*.'[22] If Roxana is a rebel or an outsider, in fact, she is a profoundly uncertain and compromised one, more like Hank Morgan than Huckleberry Finn.

And then there is Tom Driscoll: in a sense, he exposes the inner divisions of the book more clearly than any other character. The 'degenerate remnant of a noble line', Pudd'nhead Wilson (the nearest thing we have to a spokesman for the author) calls him long before he knows about the exchange, and in a profoundly unnerving sense this is true. All the other 'aristocrats' in Dawson's Landing are merely silly, whereas Tom is *evil*: he steals, he sells his mother down the river, and he kills his adoptive father. So, in a sinister way, the hidden message of the book seems to be, not 'white and black are alike', but 'never give someone ideas above his station'. Which is not to say that Twain ever intended this message—merely that he is caught, by this time, in the trap of his own inner divisions and determinism. 'Training is everything', and if blacks have been trained as a race to be inferior, then, according to Twain's own philosophy of the prison-house, they are to all intents and purposes just that. There is no escape; the fate assigned to Roxana's son at birth is finally his at the end of the narrative when he is sold as a slave down the river. The belief in an Adamic figure like Huck, who can weave past, present, and future together in one significant pattern is replaced here by an inexorable series of opposites, a set of inner divisions as painful as they are inescapable—and, more simply and sadly, by the feeling expressed in the epigraph to the Conclusion: 'It was wonderful to find America, but it would have been more wonderful to miss it.'[23]

'He was a youth to the end of his days,' William Dean Howells once said of Twain,

> the heart of a boy with the head of a sage; the heart of a good boy, or a bad boy, but always a wilful boy, and wilfulest to show himself out at every time for just the boy he was.[24]

In saying this, Howells was, as he probably knew, pointing to the well-spring of Twain's inspiration. For, in the first place, it is precisely the 'boyishness' of Twain's work (produced, it need hardly be said, at the cost of considerable sweat and calculation) that gives it its power and appeal: its imaginative energy, its emotional exuberance, and that sense of open-endedness and release that makes his writing, at its best, at once characteristically American and utterly individualistic. And, in the second, it is just as precisely Twain's obsession with his actual lost youth and years of early manhood in the South before the Civil War that provided him with an appropriate landscape and a potential map of the world: a source of ideas, that is to say, a compelling setting and subject, and a possible means of placing himself and interpreting experience. As I have tried to indicate, it was only occasionally that Twain took full imaginative possession of this landscape or achieved

anything approaching a coherent map. But this should not be
allowed to detract from his achievement or prevent us from
acknowledging the splendour and variety of his narratives—
which are, as it happens, quite as intriguing in their divisions,
their labyrinthine twists and turns, as they are in their
occasional moments of synthesis. Which is all by way of saying
that, while Twain wrote only one undeniably major work, all
of his writings provide a fascinating insight into one particular
but representative American, in his mixture of hope and
nostalgia, his optimism and occasional doubt, his practicality
and his romanticism. Taken as a whole, they can be read as
one long imaginative autobiography, one great book to which
Walt Whitman's remark in *Leaves of Grass* could act as a
preface: '. . . this is no book/ Who touches this touches a
man.'[25]

NOTES

1. Cited in Dixon Wecter, *Sam Clemens of Hannibal* (Boston, 1952), p. 67.
2. Henry Nash Smith, *Mark Twain: The Development of a Winter* (Cambridge, Mass., 1962).
3. Henry James, *Hawthorne* (1879; Ithaca, 1956 edition), p. 114.
4. *The Autobiography of Mark Twain* edited by Charles Neider (New York, 1959), p. 121; *Mark Twain—Howells Letters* edited by H. N. Smith and W. M. Gibson (Cambridge, Mass., 1960), Vol. II, p. 665.
5. *Life on the Mississippi* (1883; New York, New American Library, 1961 edition), pp. 67–8.
6. Tony Tanner, *The Reign of Wonder* (Cambridge, 1965), p. 120.
7. *Life on the Mississippi*, pp. 142, 144, 237, 266, 331.
8. Preface to *The Adventures of Tom Sawyer* (1876; London, Pan Books, 1968 edition), p. 23. See also, *Mark Twain—Howells Letters*, I, pp. 91, 110; Walter Blair, *Mark Twain and Huck Finn* (Berkeley, 1960), p. 51.
9. *Tom Sawyer*, pp. 101, 140.
10. Ibid., p. 29.
11. On this relationship see, in particular, Justin Kaplan, *Mr. Clemens and Mark Twain: A Biography*, pp. 76–93, and Clara Clemens, *My Father Mark Twain* (New York, 1931), pp. 13–23.
12. See Kaplan, *Mr. Clemens and Mark Twain*, p. 198; also Walter Blair, *Mark Twain and Huck Finn* (Berkeley, 1960).
13. Autobiography, p. 273.
14. *A Connecticut Yankee in King Arthur's Court* (1889; London, Collett, 1957 edition), p. 59.

15. Twain referred to Arthurian England as Hank Morgan's 'lost land' in his Notebooks: see H. N. Smith, *Mark Twain*, p. 156.
16. *Connecticut Yankee*, pp. 8, 71, 227–28. Cf. *Autobiography*, pp. 12–13.
17. *Connecticut Yankee*, p. 342.
18. *The Tragedy of Pudd'nhead Wilson* (1894; New York, New American Library, 1964 edition), p. 46.
19. Ibid., pp. 21–22.
20. 'Pudd'nhead Wilson' in *Anna Karenina and Other Essays* (London, 1967), pp. 126, 130.
21. *Pudd'nhead Wilson*, p. 29.
22. Ibid., p. 109.
23. Ibid., p. 166.
24. Cited in Andrew Sinclair, Introduction to *The Adventures of Tom Sawyer* and *The Adventures of Huckleberry Finn* (London, Pan Books, 1968), p. 9.
25. 'So Long!' in *Leaves of Grass*.

6

The Transatlantic Romance of Henry James

by ROBERT CLARK

It is a 'brilliant day in May, in the year 1868'.[1] A connoisseur of commodities, Christopher Newman (happy, handsome and rich and therefore in want of a wife) is in Paris because he wants 'to possess, in a word, the best article in the market' (44). He left the Union Army penniless three and a bit years ago. Since then he has amassed, by a process he calls 'work', enough money to spend the rest of his life in dilettante cultural acquisition. Generically American, he believes culture can only be had in Europe, so here he is with a project that is remarkably like the one Andrew Carnegie will draw up in December of the same year.

> Thirty-three and an income of 50,000$ per annum. By this time two years I can arrange all my business to secure at least 50,000$ per annum—Beyond this never earn—make no effort to increase fortune, but spend surplus each year for benevolent purposes. . . . settle in Oxford and get a thorough education making the acquaintance of literary men. This will take three years active work. . . . man must have an idol—the amassing of wealth is one of the worst species of idolatry—no idol more debasing than the worship of money.[2]

Although two years younger than Christopher Newman, and although usually considered a fast operator, Carnegie had taken much longer to amass his fortune. Born in 1835, he was bobbin-boy in a cotton mill at the age of 14, dealing in railroad shares before his twentieth birthday, and a millionaire broker in rails and bonds by his thirtieth. The optimum time for 'making it' in the mid-nineteenth century seems to have been nearer to fifteen years than to three. (Henry James's grand-father, William, had taken nearer forty, arriving penniless in 1789 and dying in 1832 'worth' three millions.[3])

Andrew Carnegie did not manage to give up amassing wealth as quickly as he had planned, although he did manage to set aside more time for reading and collecting cultural artefacts. He finally succeeded in quitting some thirty years later than promised when he sold out to a bigger shark than himself, J. Pierpont Morgan. This was in 1901, twelve years after he published *The Gospel of Wealth*, a work which explains how good comes to all when individuals devote their lives to self-interested accumulation, provided that when they die they give it all back to the people from whom they have taken it. Thanks to the application of this gospel, the Andrew Carnegie Foundation is now a thriving philanthropic concern.

Making enough in order to stop making it and then using it to buy the 'priceless' was a central dream of the late nineteenth-century capitalist. As a dream it was predicated on the impossibility of satisfaction. Unique commodities could be bought and displayed like trophies from the hunt, but sooner or later they were tossed into museums like so much bric-à-brac.[4] Dismembering and re-membering the cultural corpse of the Old World, the New World hunter moved on, yearning always for the refusal of the ultimately unpurchasable, and always deprived of that which could never be bought: friend-ship, love, Orson Welles's metaphor, 'Rosebud', named best the unnamable, that which the hunter had not, and believed that money could provide—something lost in the origins of the hunt, an impelling absence never to be filled.

As the urge was projective, so it fell to the children to complete the desire, rejecting the vulgar acquisition of lucre (they now had enough of it) and instead going after lucre's sublimated currency, the language of learning, the veneer of social approval, righteous possession. William James was fortunate in his son Henry, and in his grandsons Henry and William, for—aspects of William's philosophy apart—their product was as priceless as the grandfather's product had been the inverse. The child with whom we are concerned, the novelist Henry, gives us a portrait of the process of laundering one's fortune in the very act of turning his back on it. In *The American*, the new money of America is rejected by the European aristocracy that had created the grandfather's poverty, thereby secretly proving that the grandson has so thoroughly repossessed European culture that he is able to deny the parvenu in himself. To achieve this end, a traditional nineteenth-century realist plot is deployed: Newman, the upwardly mobile man of talent and fresh banknotes essays to marry Cintré, the aristocrat of declining means. Were he to succeed, the iconography of power (titles, tiaras, accents) would re-wed the transformed economic base; the élite, in Pareto's sense, would have been recycled. But although he was later to remark that the Bellegardes would have leapt at his fine young American, James breaks the genre, keeping money and culture apart.[5] His desire is the reverse of democratic; rather he views Newman with the same kind of fascination as Flaubert showed for Emma Bovary, enticed and aghast at the energetic devotion to commodities and to the self-image. When the New Man describes his desire for Claire, she is reduced to a description which might well have come from a mail-order catalogue for Western brides:

> If you only knew how exactly you are what I coveted! . . . You have been holding your head for a week past just as I wanted my wife to hold hers. You say just the things I wanted her to say. You walk about the room as I want her to walk. You have just the taste in dress I want her to have. In short, you come up to the mark; and, I can tell you, my mark was high. (184)

Newman should perhaps have looked in a Cook's brochure. He does not have a sex-object in view; like James's later millionaire, Adam Verver in *The Golden Bowl*, he has a European culture object.[6] Where the contemporary tourists flood the Old World in search of their pre-packed commodity image (ruins and peasants), and where the millionaire seeks his manuscripts, canvases and marbles, Newman seeks the living flesh, the real thing. But, as James was later to make clear, the real thing is never more than an idea whose reality is in the mind. It therefore cheats those who believe it can be literally and materially had.

If there is a way to cultural possession in James's world it is by a seduction essentially 'female', an ensnaring that is never clear, not by a masculine grasping or penetrating. The first cause of the sexualization of culture lies in the Jamesian family romance, which, according to Leon Edel, is constituted by a dominant mother, the image of an ineffectual and openly mocked father, and a concealed acute rivalry between two brothers.[7] In *The American* we can observe how the hero's quest for marriage is frustrated by the wiles of an aristocratic father-murdering mother in conspiracy with an older brother. The hero threatens a denunciation (adding, in the later revised version, the mother's adultery for good measure), but the threat is empty because, whilst to prove the mother's iniquity may justify the son's iniquitous desires, the unmasking carries the same penalty for denouncer and denounced alike. James wishes to reject the masculine in the New Man, as he wishes to reject the commerce, money and all that seems without the patination of established position. He wishes to associate himself with the intricate, labyrinthine, aristocratic and 'feminine'; the text dramatizes this split but wants to proliferate it rather than to make it clear. The hero's rejection by the maternal (because original) culture thus roots the family romance in the transatlantic romance, confers eroticism upon international relations, and opens up an endless potential for encoding signification. For as long as one remains physically impotent (a metaphor for political and economic impotence as well) one is capable of aesthetic intercourse, so runs the Jamesian paradigm.

Risking the pun, the specific device that brings this home to the New Man is an inverted Occam's razor of semantic distinctions. The Bellegardes guard their beauty by multiplying words, *commanding* Claire not to marry when they had promised not to *persuade* her against the match. The distinction is devious and dishonourable, as Valentin and the young Marquise agree, but in a sense it is no more than Newman's just deserts for he had come to Europe to master precisely this kind of sophisticated cultural play. So had his author, and the text of *The American* is an early sign of his mastery in the art of a sensuously educated social life, especially in irony. One joy of the ballroom scene in which Newman makes the acquaintance of the Parisian nobility is our hero's sense of achievement in handling the *double entendre* and the barbed shaft; but the joy of reading is the ironic discrepancy which James establishes between Newman's sense and our own. We know that Newman is making a fool of himself; Newman doesn't. We are inside society; he is outside. The pleasure is that of class distinction, so it is important to note that no previous American author had been adept at this technique. James's mastery then tells us more than that this author had befriended Turgenev and attended Flaubert's salons; it tells us that a new historical phase has arrived in the United States, one that produces not only New Men but a coterie of readers who can exchange a knowing glance about the vulgarity of the upstarts. James's representation is of course first split and then recombined, for in the actuality of Paris James was excluded from high society, but in relation to the wider world of Yankee tourism, James was the resident, the insider, so he could play snob and social connoisseur while sympathizing with the victim. As his art developed, he would sympathize less and discriminate more, damming his New World energies behind more and more elaborate banks of semantic differentiation until their flow was a meandering yet never entirely stifled stream. By repression of the basic, the economic, the 'vulgar', he would advance the status of his work as a commodity whose purity is measured by its distance from utility. His work would not be moralizing, didactic, nor naïvely mimetic. It would aspire to be 'a perfect work' expressing 'a direct impression of life'; its morality would consist in aestheticizing experience, its ethics would be its aesthetics.[8] Thus was James able to produce a morality of refined experience that made the art of living and the art of fiction into one and the same endeavour.

James, in this sense, was in the *avant-garde*. Critics protested at his lack of plot, at his tendency to analyse and discourse, at the vagueness of it all. They wanted only a moralistic mimesis.[9] But James's contemporary popularity was less with the critics and readers of the vulgar kind than with people like himself, whose contact with the commercial world was not direct and gross but indirect, mediated by half-yearly interest payments on stocks and bonds. Having never 'made money' and never 'worked' (not even in the Newman/Carnegie sense of speculating on the market, watering stock, embezzling this, defrauding that), James's readers devoted their lives to an art of consumption, a correct way of dressing, of speaking, of eating, of appearing. And, like Henry James Sr., they had left the United States because maintaining the *bon ton* was cheaper in the original accent:

> looking upon our four stout boys, who have no playroom within doors, and import shocking bad manners from the street, . . . we gravely ponder whether it would not be better to go abroad for a few years with them . . . and get a better sensuous education than they are likely to get here.

So wrote Henry's father to Emerson in a letter which the son would make famous by changing the *likelihood* expressed in the last line to an absolute *impossibility*: in the son's eyes the reasons were not that the family could not afford a large enough house to insulate the boys from vulgarity (oh the pathos of 'who *have* no playroom'!), but that America did not possess the culture necessary for a proper sensuous education.[10] The father's motives, however, at least in part, were more material, as were those of many similar emigrants who found themselves cornered by a fixed income at a time of massive immigration, industrialization and urbanization. Unable to keep up with the calculus of rapid economic growth, they decided that the better fitted to survive were beyond the pale and left for the Old World. Scarcely had the old rich emigrated, however, than they found the new rich on package tours inundating Europe with what James righteously described as their 'unhappy poverty of voice, of speech, and of physiognomy'.[11] There are some amusing anecdotes of European responses to these new barbarians, but it was the American expatriates who found them most offensive.

This is perhaps nowhere clearer (though it is also obscured in a manner I shall touch upon) than in 'Daisy Miller', a story which represents the hostility of the expatriates to young girls who do not agree with their concept of proper behaviour. It is important to note that the story's significance was read by contemporary reviewers as embracing not just the Americans abroad but also those at home: it was attacked or praised depending upon whether the reader sided with the upper classes of Boston and New York or with the provincial girls of Schenectady.[12] The nuances of Daisy's dialect may be lost on the modern ear, but in the 1870s her beginning sentences with 'I guess' and her enthusiasm about 'going in cars' signalled her status as *nouveau riche* even before she indicated her willingness to go about unchaperoned with a man. Perhaps the snobbish extreme of the contemporary response may be best instanced by the friend's opinion that James takes up in his later Preface to the novella—that he had done 'too much honour' to a very vulgar class of person in making Daisy such an interesting character.[13] Such a remark speaks precisely the tension provoked in an established and self-esteeming social class by the appearance on the scene of less disciplined energies.

It is around this tension that James elaborates his 'Americano-European legend', opposing America, new money, vitality and naïvety to Europe, established money, propriety, experience and culture. The dyadic opposition extends to include so many terms that it can be endlessly elaborated, endlessly re-read, whether in terms of the ego and the id, of sexual repression versus sexual licence, of national stereotypes, or of social classes. It achieves this polyvalence because it is essentially a mythical opposition constructed to stabilize, displace and seemingly resolve the contradictions of history. (One brief instance of this procedure has already been seen: James's translation of his father's reasons for taking his children to Europe is a way of representing a local economic problem in terms of the eternal lack of culture in the United States.) When Mrs. Walker ostracizes Daisy Miller, she does so in the name of civilized European values, just as when Madame de Bellegarde rejects Christopher Newman she rejects not just an individual but the essential American type. But these symbolic discriminations are in many ways false—Mrs. Walker, the expatriate American, has less right to speak for European values than the looked down on Giovanelli; the Bellegardes are more representative of the Gothic novel than of France on the eve of working-class uprising; and Monsieur Nioche, the bankrupt merchant, is more of a reduced Père

Goriot than a valid representative of the thrusting bourgeoisie of the Empire. When one analyses James's symbolic oppositions, one finds that the marginal is made central (the Bellegardes, Nioche, the Americans who live abroad) and the central is made marginal (thus one discovers the wealthy bourgeoisie reappearing as Kapp, the brewer's son from Alsace, a frontier region, and the Italian aristocracy in 'Daisy Miller' reduced from Don Giovani to Giovanelli and left to haunt the Pincio, hungry for American love). The mythic opposition effaces the established, mannered upper class in the United States and obscures the rise of the new rich and new poor in Europe. One land becomes eternally new, energetic, capitalist, free of history and encumbering cultural institutions; the other land becomes eternally old, perhaps vitiating, historied, furnishing to the artist and person of taste a domain for sensuous experience. The opposition of Europe and America, which in the time of Cooper and Hawthorne had been an alibi for continental expansion (because by describing Europe as 'feudal' and 'despotic', 'asylum America' was justified in expanding 'the area of freedom'), becomes in James's time a way of expressing the growth of class discrimination without destroying the myth of American democratic egalitarianism.[14] It also becomes an alibi for the devotion of an entire class of readers to the pleasures of consumption, something which American Protestantism had been actively proscribing for nearly three hundred years. Thus, what Edith Wharton recognized as a struggle between old America and new America is mapped onto another landscape: Boston versus Schenectady is symbolized as Geneva versus Rome, an imperial transfer that allows Americans to appear to be defending European values which have in effect been constituted by projecting onto Europe what America disowns in itself.

Since the mythical strategy of misrecognition is evidently prior to James's work, he may be thought to be reinscribing it ironically, using it as a mere armature around which to wind his more sophisticated, more critical meanings. Probably James would have argued as much himself, for when taxed with the social truthfulness of his types he invariably denied that types had been in his mind, even though when sketching his fictions he invariably began with just such types. Varying his 'Americano-European legend' was a way of proliferating what in each phase of writing could only be held to be a hypothesis about national identities, and yet thereby of making the mythical hypothesis appear to have transtextual substance. In accordance with James's refusal to defend the 'truth' of his fiction, in George Eliot's sense, his syntax aims at the characteristic elegance of tentative suggestion which contemporary reviewers disliked, holding out a way in which the world might be seen, and even interrogating its validity in the act of offering it, pausing, hovering, redefining itself, before moving to a barely possible close. This way of writing establishes a convention that in order to do the object justice one must catch the myriad aspects it presents to a participant observer's eye, much as an Impressionist imitates not the object-in-itself but the retinal effect, or as the Cubist represents in the same plane temporally discrete perceptions. These contemporary parallels are pertinent as they instance the late nineteenth-century shifts from realism to relativism, and from a transparent mimesis to a foregrounding of the techniques that mark out the aesthetic object as a distinct commodity, but they mask an important peculiarity of James's work: what he represents is not the perception of an object-in-itself but the perception of a fiction. This order of distinction is the subject of 'The Real Thing' in which the idea of aristocracy is represented as having the reality of a neo-Platonic essence, one that is more perfectly revealed in the artistic representation than in any concrete particular. The same might be said of the 'Americano-European legend', for although it evidently motivates mass tourism and the acquisition policy of millionaires, it can be maintained that its most perfect existence is in the minds of the *cognoscenti*, those expatriates who, being originally outsiders, can savour the quality of European life with the greatest refinement. James's characters are ranked according to their ability to give such fictions a refined material form, but it is always clear that they first choose the idea and then make it into a practice.

James thus implicitly recognizes that ideology precedes and constructs social relations, but rather than materialize ideology he dematerializes society, according it only the function of bearer to the immaculate idea. This is of course in keeping with his artistic ideology that the purpose of writing is to end in the perfect work. It is also in keeping with the general ideology of a mass production/mass consumption society which, whilst being grossly materialist, pretends that the purchase of each new object takes the consumer nearer to a condition of immaterial refinement. Possessions in such a society are not valued by use or exchange, but by their magical power to assure the possessors of their style and status. From *The American* to *The Golden Bowl*, James's fictions consistently represent fetishistic commodity relations between people, but the extent to which this representation offers a critique remains uncertain. James's aesthetic of the perfect work is so in accord with the values of his characters that any irony he might imply is muted by the desire not to disturb the process of consumption. Furthermore, although James's inspiration comes from the world and he believes that the purpose of art is to represent life, his belief that he is finally representing an idea that achieves its highest realization in his work leads to the conviction that his work is autonomous and has no responsibility for how it is received. If, then, his work should be accused of reinscribing at a higher level fictions which it abhors at the lower, James's answer would be, as it was about 'Daisy Miller', that his work is 'pure poetry'.[15]

In the case of 'The Real Thing', the poetic suggestion is that 'aristocracy' exists primarily as an ideal way of living, not as part of an ideology that constructs power relations between rulers and subjects. The pathetic failure of the Monarchs to be monarchs results from their taking literally what should be taken essentially. (Is it not always the fate of the impoverished to believe that culture is material, not ideal?) James, however, does not ironize his artist-narrator who earns a living representing aristocracy, unless, that is, we are supposed to look down on him because he does it for the *Cheapside* and assume therefore that the future Monarchs who wreck themselves trying to imitate his 'royal romance' will be too cheap to be worth our concern. Miss Churm, the working-class woman who is able to be all things to the artist because she has 'no stamp' of her own is also presented without authorial irony, perhaps because she is truly *insignificant*: her personality is an absence to the bourgeois gaze because expressed in a different class semiotic. She is therefore able to give the right 'impression' because no one is concerned with the real thing. Like more recent photographic models whose origin in the lower classes has given them the ability to see with acute precision the mannerisms of bourgeois style, and who are therefore able to mask their own fragility in the guise of high-style sensuality, Miss Churm is only too happy to be paid to project the image that keeps her own kind in servitude. Since, according to James, 'impressions are experience', the impression she and the artist create will inevitably determine the experience of others.[16]

The impressionist method of dematerializing the real by splitting off the ideological and treating it as merely aesthetic had already provided James with his narrative method in 'Daisy Miller'. There Winterbourne begins by deciding that Daisy is 'only a pretty American flirt', but, having decided that, he cannot decide how to behave towards her and leads the reader through a path of uncertain discriminations up to the point where he decides that she really is beyond the pale, then doubts his own decision. Such oscillation leaves the reader trying to decide which impressions to trust, and how to respond to the type who is the supposed origin. It therefore obscures the more important question why Daisy is to be judged a flirt for wanting to go about unchaperoned with men, when Winterbourne, who is happy to propose a midnight row on the lake, is not to be judged by the same standards. In other words, whilst the reader watches the play of impressions, the ideology of Mrs. Costello and Mrs. Walker is effectively reinscribed. Women should not have the same rights as men. The splitting of the sexes anchors all the other splits in the text, convincing us of a world where the superior and the inferior require man to train and exercise his art of discrimination.

The story of Isabel Archer, however, further embroiders the essential failure of impressionism to provide a basis for exercising such discriminations. Isabel is so taken in by her own idea of Osmond—an image composed not so much of 'what he said and did but rather what he withheld', an image based on her assumption that he is no 'type' but a specimen apart'[17]— that she is incapable of heeding the warnings of the more discriminating Ralph. She has voyaged in search of an unquantifiable experience, and, finding it, desires to be possessed. She cannot desire to possess it for she is essentially receptive, incapable of productive or transforming action. She is also forced to want an absence, because absences best allow the narcissistic imagination to believe that the object of fantasy is actually constituted by the qualities the perceiver invests it with. For her, Osmond's importance is as a cultural fetish, a sign that she has passed into a world where all things appear priceless because they have no system outside themselves in which to measure their cost. Her fate thus exemplifies the paradox that at the historical moment when discrimination becomes most central in the relation of individuals to their world (because they are now choosing from a seemingly endless range of experiences), all knowledge is reduced to a provisional notation in a sliding scale of values, and all basis for making discriminations therefore becomes relative. What the reader is left with as a point of security is the grosser fictions: the myth of aristocracy, of refinement, of America and Europe, of the impressionist art of living. Deployed one upon the other in a constantly shifting *rondo*, these myths delight the mind by taking it ever further from the troubling world of production and history.

One sees around the edges of these myths at odd moments: the opening paragraph of *The Portrait of a Lady*, for example, where the garden at Gardencourt is repeatedly described as 'perfect' (a vulgar insistence that betrays the tautologous absolutism of James's world), or when Isabel is described as perceiving Osmond as 'thinking about art and beauty and history'.[18] Here again it is the fetishist who speaks, for such words are brand names for processes which Henry James knows to be far more demanding of human effort than Osmond is capable of. But this other Henry James is well hidden behind the Isabel who treasures above all the 'picture that has been made real',[19] a reduced image of the human condition that has been mapped back onto the world and made to appear as a totality. Her vision cannot be ironized by James because it is he who furnishes the environment of *Guide Bleu* vignettes and cliché cameos that have all the elaborate triteness of illustrations on Osmond's porcelain, an environment whose chief requirement is that it should give the impression that an absence of labour and history makes for beauty and art. Consider for example:

> The scene had an extraordinary charm. The air was almost solemnly still, and the large expanse of the landscape with its gardenlike culture and nobleness of outline, its teeming valley and delicately-fretted hills, its peculiarly human-looking touches of habitation, lay there in splendid harmony and classic grace.[20]

Here the populous Italian valley becomes a beautiful garden by reducing the homes of the labourers to peculiar 'touches' (dabs of paint?), by deleting the 'teeming' animals whose produce supports the life of the inhabitants, and by converting the hills into skilled cabinet work. Isabel's mistaking such cheapside impressions for experience is sufficient explanation for the failure of James's most intensely drawn heroine to do more than marry a seedy if fastidious collector of *objets d'art*.

Later James turns a more knowing eye upon the business of furnishing a refined situation, most splendidly, perhaps, at the end of *The Golden Bowl* where the Prince and the Ververs are described as trying to approximate to the condition of the possessions which possess them:

> Mrs Verver and the Prince had fairly 'placed' themselves, however unwittingly, as high expressions of the kind of human furniture required, aesthetically, by such a scene. The fusion of their presence with the decorative elements, their contribution to the triumph of selection, was complete and admirable; though, to a lingering view, a view more penetrating than the occasion really demanded, they also might have figured as concrete attestations of a rare power of purchase.[21]

James's critical economic comment is only slipped in after it has been censored by the suggestion that such observation is impolite—'more penetrating than the occasion really de-manded'. The impersonal construction reveals the extent to which James's discourse is in agreement with the surrender of intellectual and moral responsibility to 'situations', 'things', 'society', the great capitalist reifications that seem responsible for the hidden but palpable imperatives. Given that Gilbert Osmond is in the habit of 'consulting his taste'[22] as if his taste were an external and monitory entity rather than a subordinate aspect of his personality, the fate of the Prince and Princess at the end of *The Golden Bowl* must seem an entirely typical one for the Jamesian character. Having been produced in a discourse that regales itself on impersonal formulations, they achieve their most intense existence when they come into phase with the formalist commodity logic of their lives. They exist in the end to decorate the stage set of their possessions.

They are not alone in this. In a society determined by mass production, all experience falls under the belief that style is the thing, just as it falls under the spell of the serial versus the unique. In order to possess the correct tone one must understand the contemporary typology and then disdain what is commonly available. One must search for the unique experience, the priceless impression, the incomparable quantity. But once one has found it one also finds that it too falls back into the serial, because the discrimination of the serial from the unique is a function of the consumer's way of seeing the world. The unique is, in effect, something which can only be had in the first fugitive moment of possession, for once possessed it soon relapses into the series and goes unnoticed.

When this logic is applied to the activity of writing the tendency is to leave the story 'open', because, after ending the labour of production, the work itself, perfect commodity and unique impression of life as it may be, falls back into the 'series' novel and into the series 'Henry James'. Its uniqueness is a consistently fragile affair. Far better then to make the plot a flirtation with possession, beginning with the quest for, or the sight of, the prey, and then to protract the narrative until such point as it is about to regress towards the type. The reader is then offered a brief holiday from routine, a holiday that refines consumption, and then closes the book before the tawdry resumes its sway.

NOTES

1. Henry James, *The American*, edited by James W. Tuttleton (New York: W. W. Norton, 1978), p. 17. Page numbers to future citations are given parenthetically in the text.
2. Quoted Burton J Hendrick, *The Life of Andrew Carnegie* (New York: Doubleday, Duran and Co., 1932), I, p. 147. For a general history see

Matthew Josephson, *The Robber Barons: The Great American Capitalists, 1861–1901* (London: Eyre and Spottiswoode, 1962).

3. See Leon Edel, *The Life of Henry James* (London: Penguin Books, 1977).
4. Josephson, *The Robber Barons*, pp. 360–64.
5. James's concern at the implausibility of *The American* is expressed in his 1907 Preface. See *The Art of the Novel: Critical Prefaces*, edited by R. P. Blackmur (New York: Charles Scribner's Sons, 1962), pp. 20–39. Royal A. Gettman, in his 'Henry James's Revision of *The American*', *American Literature* 16 (1945), 279–95, details James's efforts to remove the more obvious absurdities.
6. As so beautifully expressed by Maggie to Prince Amerigo: 'You're at any rate part of his collection . . . one of the things that can only be got over here. You're a rarity, an object of beauty, an object of price. . . . You're what they call a *morceau de musée*' (London: Penguin Books, 1972), p. 35.
7. Edel, *Life*, I, pp. 43–57. This is not, one must emphasize, how it was, but how James consistently represents it as having been.
8. Henry James, 'The Art of Fiction', in *Selected Literary Criticism*, edited by Morris Shapira (London: Penguin Books, 1968), pp. 96, 83. James's opposition to 'art for art's sake' is discussed by Wellek, *A History of Modern Criticism: 1750–1950* (London: Jonathan Cape, 1966), IV, pp. 218–19. James's importance is that for him it is not just art, but life that is for art's sake.
9. See the Introduction to *Henry James: The Critical Heritage*, edited by Roger Gard (London: Routledge and Kegan Paul, 1968), pp. 1–18.
10. The point is made by Edel, *Life*, I, p. 100. On the cheapness of European travel, see Allison Lockwood, *Passionate Pilgrims: The American Traveller in Great Britain, 1800–1914* (New York: Cornwall, 1981), pp. 283–330.
11. Quoted Isabel Ross, *The Expatriates* (New York: Crowell, 1970), p. 207.
12. See William T. Stafford, *James's 'Daisy Miller': The Story, The Play and The Critics* (New York: Charles Scribner's Sons, 1963). The behaviour typified by Daisy Miller was so recurrent as to receive mention in the Paris Guide of 1867. See Eric Hobsbawm, *The Age of Capital: 1848–1875* (London: Weidenfeld, 1975), p. 274.
13. James, *The Art of the Novel*, p. 269.
14. I have explored the logic of these transformations more fully in my *History, Ideology and Myth in United States Fiction, 1823–1852* forthcoming with Macmillan.
15. *The Art of the Novel*, p. 269.
16. 'The Art of Fiction', p. 86.
17. Henry James, *The Portrait of a Lady* (London: Penguin Books, 1963), p. 261.
18. Ibid., p. 263.
19. Ibid., p. 54.
20. Ibid., p. 264. On *Guide Bleu* prose see Roland Barthes, *Mythologies*, translated by Annette Lavers (London: Jonathan Cape, 1972), pp. 74–7.
21. Henry James, *The Golden Bowl* (London: Penguin Books, 1966), p. 541.
22. *The Portrait of a Lady*, p. 262.

7

Theodore Dreiser: Outsider/Insider

by JIM PHILIP

'There stirs in Dreiser's books a new American quality . . . it is an authentic attempt to make something artistic out of the chaotic materials that lie around us in American life.'[1] Challenge and anxiety underlie Randolph Bourne's words. We can perceive the experience of that crucial generation of American intellectuals, active in the early years of the century, who were the first to seek conscious articulation of those major transformations of the national life that had been proceeding for the previous three decades. The combined effects of industrialization and urbanization, the closing of the frontier and the increasing tide of immigration from Western and Central Europe had all played their part in creating a new society, but one whose structures and implications were still largely ignored by the 'official' organs of American culture and education. As another commentator was to put it, to grow up at the turn of the century was to grow up 'in a sort of orgy of lofty examples, moralized poems, national anthems and baccalaureate sermons',[2] but to become aware at the same time of an 'unbridgeable chasm between literate and illiterate America'.[3] To open this new world to view, and to make possible fresh initiatives in literature and social criticism was the task undertaken by Bourne himself, and by other such notable figures of the period as H. L. Mencken, Van Wyck

Brooks and Waldo Frank. However we cannot read far into the works of any of these without realizing that, each in their separate ways, they pay homage to one further and symptomatic figure, that of Theodore Dreiser. As these writers were the first to recognize, what made Dreiser's writing of special interest was not simply his attempt to engage the novel in the 'chaotic materials' of city life, but also the fact that he was himself so obviously the product of the very forces he was describing. The son of a German immigrant, he was brought up amidst increasingly limited economic circumstances, and in the relative cultural desert of the Midwest. His formal education beyond school age consisted of one year's study at the University of Indiana. Like his elder brothers and sisters he experienced from an early age the lure of the cities, and was to undergo several years of menial labour in Chicago before obtaining the first newspaper job that was to lead eventually, and by no means directly, to his successful journalistic and literary career.

The case can readily be made, then, for the historical importance of Dreiser's fiction. Momentous changes in American life are being recorded, by a man who underwent them, and in modes that are formed by the pressure of direct experience rather than the requirements of genteel culture. More contentious, however, is the matter of Dreiser's success or failure in the mastery of his new materials, of his ability to forge them into an art that convinces both by the breadth and the depth of its approach. Few American writers have met with such a mixed critical response, and it would be fair to say that at the heart of the debates lies the problem of Dreiser's own various levels of intention. In one respect it is clear that his purpose was simply to document and describe, to give some permanence to his continuous, contrasting but at the same time fleeting impressions of city life, rather in the manner of the 'Ashcan' school of painters whose achievements he so much admired. He was also, however, a persistent seeker of explanations, of general laws and principles that would give some coherence to the frantic and changeable life he saw around him. And it would be fair to say also that there are many moments in his novels in which the text moves close to personal confession, and in which we feel the immediacy of direct and participatory emotions.

116

Many of the predominant critical reactions can be seen to centre themselves around one or other of these issues. Perhaps the most famous attack on Dreiser's writing is that conducted by Lionel Trilling in his essay of 1945 called 'Reality in America'. Complaining of the dense, descriptive, material textures of Dreiser's novels, and of those who have admired them as a kind of American truth, he claims that

> his books have the awkwardness, the chaos, the heaviness which we associate with 'reality'. In the American metaphysic reality is always material reality, hard, resistant, unformed, impenetrable and unpleasant. And that mind is alone felt to be trustworthy which most resembles this reality by most nearly reproducing the sensations it affords.[4]

Thus Dreiser's whole project is dismissed as an inadequate expression, indeed a deliberate denigration, of that liberal spirit, that humane and organizing intelligence, that Trilling locates in the contrasting figure of Henry James. Later criticism has done much to reduce the effect of these polemics by pointing to other elements in the writing. From the academy have come valiant attempts to give coherence to Dreiser's shifting philosophical positions, and to trace the effects of these on his fiction. Moreover there has been a consistent recognition, most interestingly from other creative writers, of Dreiser's open emotional presence in his own books, and of the continuity and relevance of the feelings evoked. Thus John Berryman has spoken of 'the bright, vague longing or aspiration or *yearning* that every reader will probably recognize as Dreiser's central or characteristic emotion'.[5] Such approaches have been useful, but it can fairly be claimed that, in their various partialities, they have somewhat distorted the actual experience of reading Dreiser's texts, of encountering his various and often contradictory presences, and the way in which these effect both the detail and the overall plotting of his works. The following account of his major novels is undertaken in the belief that the most useful task the critic can perform is that not of evading, but of revealing and exploring the elements of disjunction and struggle within them.

Dreiser told his biographer, Dorothy Dudley, that *Sister Carrie*, his first novel, was written in 1899 instinctively and without planning, as if 'there was something mystic about it, as if I were being used like a medium.'[6] As the pent up thoughts and feelings are released they cast a dramatic light on even the most apparently casual moments in the book. The following is an account of 'Hannah and Hogg's Adams Street place', that 'gorgeous' saloon in Chicago, where Hurstwood, one of the major characters, is employed as manager.

To one not inclined to drink, and gifted with a more serious turn of mind, such a bubbling, chattering, glittering chamber must ever seem an anomaly, a strange commentary on nature and life. Here come the moths in endless procession to bask in the light of the flame. Such conversation as one may hear would not warrant a commendation of the scene upon intellectual grounds. It seems plain that schemers would choose more sequestered quarters to arrange their plans, that politicians would not gather here in company to discuss anything save formalities where the sharp-eared may hear, and it would scarcely be justified on the score of thirst, for the majority of those who frequent these more gorgeous places have no craving for liquor. Nevertheless, the fact that here men gather, here chatter, here love to pass and rub elbows, must be explained upon some grounds. It must be that a strange bundle of passions and vague desires gives rise to such a curious social institution or it would not be.

Drouet, for one, was lured as much by his longing for pleasure as by his desire to shine among his betters. The many friends he met here dropped in because they craved, without perhaps consciously analyzing it, the company, the glow, the atmosphere, which they found. One might take it after all as an augur of the better social order, for the things which they satisfied here, though sensory, were not evil. No evil could come out of the contemplation of an expensively decorated chamber. The worst effect such a thing could have would be perhaps to stir up in the material minded an ambition to arrange their lives upon a similarly splendid basis. In the last analysis, that would scarcely be called the fault of the decorations, but rather of the innate trend of the mind. That such a scene might stir the less expensively dressed to emulate the more expensively dressed could scarcely be laid at the door of anything save the false ambition of the minds of those so affected. Remove the element so thoroughly and solely complained of, liquor, and there would not be one to gainsay the qualities of beauty and enthusiasm

118

which would remain. The pleased eye with which our modern restaurants of fashion are looked upon is proof positive of this assertion.

Yet here is the fact of the lighted, chamber: the dressy, greedy company; the small, self-interested palaver; the disorganized, aimless, wandering mental action which it represents—the love of light and show and finery which, to one outside, under the serene light of the eternal stars, must seem a strange and shiny thing. Under the stars and sweeping night winds, what a lamp-flower it must bloom—a strange, glittering night-flower, odour-yielding, insect-drawing, insect-infested rose of pleasure.

The passage well reveals those various levels of intention that have already been indicated. So far as description is concerned, Dreiser's fascination with the new spectacular settings of American city life is evident. In phrases such as 'the bubbling, chattering, glittering chamber' he seeks in an original manner to convey the combined sensory bombardments of light, sound and movement. Too often his repetitions, his strings of words, his inharmonies of phrase, have been dismissed as a kind of literary *gaucherie*. What a passage like this makes clear is that part of his awkwardness should surely be recognized as a creative attempt to evoke the sensations of a dense urban world in forms appropriate to it. However, description is not the only purpose here, and it is not long before we find Dreiser presenting himself in the role of disinterested and scientific observer. He sets out to discover the truth about this 'curious social institution', and the 'bundle of passions and vague desires' that gives rise to it. It is this determination which produces what can only be described as a hopelessly reductive analysis. We are to imagine the saloons of Chicago populated by characters like Drouet in whom the dominant obsession has become that of associating themselves with the trappings of wealth, and the special codes of those who possess and display it. They 'crave' for this experience and are drawn to its contexts with the same chemical automatism that draws the moth to light. We have evidence, then, of the way in which Dreiser's ideas, his 'laws', can work against any full and complex registration of human presence.

119

But we must be grateful that here, as elsewhere, it is not the simplistic analyst who is in full control of the text. Despite Dreiser's attempts at distance, we cannot help noticing his closeness to the material and the way in which it works as a nexus of dynamic and contradictory emotions. We note, for instance, his eagerness to display a relaxed familiarity with the world that he describes, to present himself as one who has explored and enjoyed 'the better social order'. When he speaks of the 'pleased eye with which our modern restaurants of fashion are looked upon' the pleasure is that of the participant, the assured insider. But if such an emotional tone is present, it is one that cannot wholly suppress the persistent and disturbed voice of the outsider. It is in fact this figure who is allowed the final comments on the scene, and we can see that his 'outsideness' is registered in different ways. It is, first of all, an experience of pain and deprivation—the 'rose of pleasure' invites but eludes him. But while voicing his own compulsions he also condemns the very world to which he is attracted. The ephemerality, the selfishness within the saloon are contrasted with 'the serene light of the eternal stars' under which he stands. The possibility remains that in his separation he may act as the preserver of more lasting, more constructive values. The journey from outside to inside was, of course, one that Dreiser had traversed in his own life, and one that, as we shall see, remained the groundwork of his fiction. But what the present passage reveals is his remaining uncertainty as to what has been gained and what has been lost in the process. The sense of material satisfaction is countered by the reminders of a spiritual hunger that has not been satisfied. He parades his own inclusion while at the same time acknowledging the moral limitations that have accompanied it. At this fundamental level, then, the text can be read as an intense and worried autobiography, an expression of contradictions that the act of writing is intended to resolve, but patently does not.

The tensions that have been outlined here between reductive explanation and complex expression are in fact recurrent in Dreiser's fiction. An examination of the overall plotting of *Sister Carrie* will show how these affect not simply the details of his writing, but also its larger construction. At one level the book is an attempt to convince himself and his readers of the inevitability of an intensely competitive system; this is grounded in certain basic facts of human nature, in that instinctive and universal longing for wealth, status and pleasure newly stimulated by an America in the process of compounding its own riches. In the main Carrie is used as the vehicle for this argument. She comes to Chicago from a poor country background to stay in the first instance in the working-class home of her married sister. Depressed by the degrading conditions of life and work at this social level she agrees to become the mistress of Drouet, a travelling salesman she encounters on her first entry to the city. Though it contains a certain amount of affection this relationship is really based on compatible self-interests. Drouet introduces her to Hurstwood who, as a saloon manager, represents a higher level of success and assurance. By the combined effects of her attraction to him and his trickery of her, she is lured into fleeing with him to New York, after he has left his wife and stolen money from his employers. In New York his attempts to re-establish himself founder, but Carrie, forced by need into developing her latent talents as an actress, achieves increasing success on the popular stage. Eventually she rejects the declining and apathetic Hurstwood in favour of her own career. What Dreiser suggests is that Carrie's progress is essentially a self-interested one. At each important juncture of her life she is motivated primarily by a new image of herself that becomes attainable. She is led into her association with Drouet by the fine clothes, the 'lace-collar', the 'soft new shoes' that speak to her invitingly from the windows of the big stores. She pictures to herself the life of status and ease that she would enjoy as Hurstwood's wife. And it is the imagined pleasures and gestures of fame that spur her on in her acting career.

Yet, in tracing in characteristic detail this sequence of events, Dreiser cannot entirely exclude from his text those moments in which Carrie has thoughts and feelings of a different kind. Consider, for instance, the following:

> Her old father, in his flour-dusted miller's suit sometimes returned to her in memory-revived by a face in a window. A shoemaker pegging at his last, a blastman seen through a narrow window in some basement where iron was being melted, . . . —these took her back in fancy to the details of the mill. She

felt, though she seldom expressed them, sad thoughts upon this score. Her sympathies were ever with that underworld of toil from which she had so recently sprung and which she best understood.[8]

Here, despite her immersion in the immediate and pressing contexts of desire, Carrie reaches out for the past; despite her self-concern, she is troubled by moral denials of her family and class. But the essential point to make about this wider consciousness is that it exists in the passive and delayed forms of regret. A sympathy can be extended to the 'underworld of toil', but only after this world has been escaped. Carrie has a moral awareness, then, a sense of duty, of loyalty, of wider human commitment, but it is one that is always too late, always out of time, and can never become a fully active principle.

The intensity of such moments when they occur suggests that, despite his frequent pleas for a sympathetic understanding of Carrie, Dreiser felt an underlying frustration and despair at the very character he had created. It is this frustration that breaks out in his sudden introduction, late on in the story, of a further and enigmatic figure, that of Robert Ames. A young electrical engineer from the Midwest, Ames impresses Carrie by his detachment, his intelligence and his idealism. It is not long before we find him addressing her in the following forthright terms:

> You can't become self-interested, selfish and luxurious, without having these sympathies and longings disappear, and then you will sit there and wonder what has become of them. You can't remain tender and sympathetic, and desire to serve the world, without having it show in your face and your art. If you want to do most, do good. Serve the many. Be kind and humanitarian. Then you can't help but be great.[9]

Ames's presence in the book is really that of a voice, rather than a fully developed character, but it is clear that that voice is a totally disruptive one so far as the whole fiction, and in particular the construction of Carrie's life, are concerned. He asserts the existence of an altruistic motive and the possibilities of transforming it into action. He has a vision of an American future very different from the materialist and

122

competitive present. We have the dramatic evidence, then, of Dreiser's inability to accept his own conclusions. Ames speaks for a part of himself that he has been unable wholly to suppress. Indeed, with this episode Carrie's story is brought to a hasty and unsatisfactory ending. She is simply abandoned as a character who has not carried the full freight of his own experience, and, because of the constraints within which she has been created, can never do so.

Repressed elements of human concern and protest are also evident in Dreiser's handling of the sub-theme of the novel, that is to say, the fall of Hurstwood. The mere fact that he chose to include this element suggests his anxiety about the new society, about its inability to yield any position of security free of the threat of failure and exclusion. At times he argues for the acceptance of this as a further and inevitable fact of nature. Thus he states that

> a man's fortune, or material progress, is very much the same as his bodily growth. Either he is growing stronger, healthier, wiser, as the youth approaching manhood; or he is growing weaker, older, less incisive mentally, as the man approaching old age. There are no other states.[10]

However, the actual account of Hurstwood's last months displays a direct emotional involvement in his experience of isolation and depression, his stubborn refusal to surrender the last shreds of human dignity. Implicit, though never stated, is a strong accusation against a society that can do nothing with its own casualties except ignore them.

Sister Carrie was enthusiastically accepted for publication by Frank Norris, then working as an editor for the publishing firm of Henry Doubleday. But when the publisher himself read it, he was, partly under the influence of his wife, disturbed by its distance from any conventional presentation of the role of women. He decided virtually to suppress it by producing, with no promotion, an edition of only 1,000 copies. The short term effects of this were to throw Dreiser into the worst depression of his whole life, and the long term effects were the postponement for ten years of his further efforts as a novelist. During the intervening period he created a successful career for himself as an editor of popular New York magazines, rising by

1907 to become one of the chief executives of the Butterick's Publishing Company. When he was finally ousted from this position after a series of personality battles, one of the first tasks that he committed himself to was the writing of a long work that would reflect his new knowledge and experience of the American business world at its higher levels. In order to give his writing a fuller authenticity he decided to base it upon the real life history of a particular individual, Charles Tyson Yerkes. Yerkes was a financial manipulator who made his first fortune in Philadelphia in the 1870s before being imprisoned for embezzlement. He then moved to Chicago to undertake a battle for control of the city's street railways. When he failed to secure long-term franchises he transferred his operations to London, challenging J. P. Morgan for control of the underground system. Dreiser's original plan was to present this whole history in one book, but it emerged eventually as the three novels, *The Financier* (1912), *The Titan* (1914) and *The Stoic* (1948). Of these the first is undoubtedly the most interesting as it embodies Dreiser's initial and formative responses to his chosen world.

In *The Financier* the documentary element is precise and painstaking. It is clearly one of Dreiser's intentions to expose what he considers to be some of the worst features of the age he has lived through; the concentration of enormous power in the hands of few individuals, the penetration of the political and legal systems by financial interests. However, it must be admitted that these more constructive purposes are consistently undermined by processes of reduction and sensationalization. His awareness of the intensity of commercial struggle leads him at times into the Darwinian presentation of a social world in which nothing can be observed but the preying of the strong upon the weak. Moreover, there is the added conviction that at the heart of this world, at its centres of manipulation, there exist human individuals of a peculiarly ruthless and wilful type. It is in these terms that he presents Frank Cowperwood, his fictional version of Yerkes:

> Again, it was so very evident, in so many ways, that force was the answer—great mental and physical force. Why, these giants of commerce and money could do as they pleased in this life, and did. He had already had ample local evidence of it in more

than one direction. Worse—the little guardians of so-called law and morality . . . so loud in their denunciation of evil in humble places, were cowards all when it came to corruption in high ones. They did not dare to utter a feeble squeak until some giant had accidentally fallen and they could do so without danger to themselves. Then, O Heavens, the palaver! . . . It made him smile. Such hypocrisy! Such cant! Still, so the world was organized, and it was not for him to set it right. . . . The thing for him to do was to get rich and hold his own. . . . Force would do that. Quickness of wit. And he had these. 'I satisfy myself', was his motto. . . .[11]

Cowperwood, then, is a figure supremely, one might almost say absurdly, adapted to his environment. His 'great mental and physical force' ensure that he is not subject to those moments of exhaustion and confusion that beset others in the competitive battle. His confident dismissal of all morality as 'hypocrisy' and 'cant' ensures that he can pursue without scruple his goal of self-satisfaction. His 'quickness of wit' ensures that he can be faster than others to perceive both opportunities and dangers. To be sure he cannot entirely evade the accidents of chance (his temporary downfall is brought about as a consequence of the great Chicago fire), but these are to be welcomed as the unpredictable elements in the game that he plays with life. What the passage reveals is that the construction of this character has its roots not only in theory, but also in fantasy and wish-fulfilment. Cowperwood survives and prospers because of the absence within him of those elements of anxiety, self-doubt and wider questioning to which, as we have seen, Dreiser was himself so prone. To the writer troubled by the status of his own morality, his amoral hero was a source of fascination and allurement. To read the Cowperwood books, then, is to feel oneself drawn in two directions, towards two contradictory versions of American experience. One is aware first of all of a novelist concerned to open the hidden centres of power to wider view, to make them available to analysis and change; but one is aware also of a Dreiser so overawed by the atmosphere of competition that he has encountered that he can see nothing else, and do nothing else but participate vicariously in the endurance and the triumphs of his Superhero.

The Financier helped to establish Dreiser as a national figure. Perhaps, in his very ambivalence, he had exactly caught the mood of the public at large. More recent opinion, however, has often demoted the writing of this period, and sought instead to present *An American Tragedy* (1925) as the fullest achievement of his art. Here Dreiser turns away from the more lavish worlds of success to consider, as he himself was to put it, 'the tribes and shoals of the incomplete, the botched, the semi-articulate—all hungry and helpless'.[12] We first encounter Clyde Griffiths, whose story this novel recounts, as he is forced to participate unwillingly in the ineffectual missionary work of his parents on the streets of Kansas City. Seeking more acceptable social status amidst the contexts of wealth he secures a job as a bell-hop in the Green-Davidson, one of the best hotels in town. When working in a Chicago club two years later he meets by accident his uncle who is a prosperous manufacturer of collars in Lycurgus, New York. Clyde solicits from him the promise of a job and moves to the town. Here he finds himself in an ambiguous social position, not fully accepted either by his relations, or by the working people of whom he is put in charge. Out of his sense of isolation he develops a relationship with Roberta Alden, a factory girl, but his attentions are later won away by a young socialite who displays an interest in him. When Roberta's pregnancy threatens his rise to respectability he turns against her. Desperation leads him into an ill-planned attempt at murder by drowning, but Roberta's actual death is the product of accident as much as deliberate purpose. Clyde is caught, tried, convicted and eventually dies in the electric chair.

Strong claims have been made for the greater realism of this book, in its handling both of the overall social environment and of particular individuals. It is certainly true that Dreiser displays a sharp eye for the detailed stratifications of an increasingly class-organized and class-conscious society. In Lycurgus Clyde comes to learn the many gradations that exist between the immigrant workers at the bottom and the families of established wealth at the top. It is true also that he does manage to present his story from a number of different viewpoints, showing how Clyde is viewed and used by others, ranging from Sondra Finchley, the vain rich girl, to Mason, the district attorney who sees his prosecution as an aid to his own political career. However, the problems of the book lie, once again, in the construction of its central figure, and it would be fair to say that in many respects Clyde is as one-dimensional a figure as was Frank Cowperwood. It is as if the writer, now more fully assured of his own success and status, can turn at last to the confession of all those experiences of anxiety, panic and isolation that have accompanied his own long journey. Clyde, in this sense, is the expression of a nightmare, of all those things that might have been were it not for the lucky coincidence of personal effort and exterior chance. Having arrived in Lycurgus, Clyde reflects on his experience in the following terms:

> For, after all, was he not a Griffiths, a full cousin as well as a full nephew to the two very important men who lived here, and now working for them in some capacity at least? And must not that spell a future of some sort, better than any he had known as yet? For consider who the Griffiths were here, as opposed to 'who' the Griffiths were in Kansas City. . . . The enormous difference! A thing to be as carefully concealed as possible. At the same time, he was immediately reduced again, for supposing the Griffiths here . . . should now investigate his parents and his past? Heavens! . . . If they should guess! If they should sense!
>
> Oh, the devil—who was he anyway? And what did he really amount to? . . .
>
> A little disgusted and depressed he turned to retrace his steps, for all at once he felt himself very much a nobody.[13]

We note the way in which his desire to rise is thoroughly undermined by a compulsive self-denigration, a fear that the 'nobody' he really is will always betray the 'somebody' he aspires to be. Though he is close physically to the world of his rich relations, there is a sense that he can never become fully a part of it, that the marks of his past poverty and desperation exist upon him as a distinguishing brand. The predominant emotions, then, are those of resentment, shading to self-pity and apathy. In his actual history Clyde lives out to its bitter end the personal disintegration threatened here. He involves himself furtively with Roberta, although he knows the social dangers of doing so. When the facts of her pregnancy emerge his attempts to rescue the situation are weakened by an 'ever-haunting fear of inability to cope'. In a schizophrenic manner he watches the rising within him of a criminal impulse that he can neither resist nor fully live out. At his trial he listens to the conflicting versions of his story, having himself abandoned any hope of personal identity or dignity. The novel retells, then, in a revealing manner Dreiser's perennial plot of the journey from outside to inside, but it does so in wholly negative terms. The fears, the horrors are all there, accurately and instinctively expressed, but Clyde has none of that determined drive of Dreiser's other characters, and none of that unsatisfied moral doubt which is, as we have seen, such an essential part of his own total response.

From what has been said it should be clear that at the heart of Dreiser's extensive fiction there lies the recurrent problem of the creation of a character adequate to embody the full and complex freight of his own past and his own social experience. That width of lived encounter emerges through the books, but it does so in incomplete, fragmentary and diverted forms. In the light of this it would seem worthwhile to recommend for fresh attention one of his more neglected books, *The 'Genius'*. When this novel first appeared in 1916 it met with opposition from the New York Society for the Suppression of Vice, who forced its publisher into withdrawing it from sale. A public campaign and legal action failed to alter the situation and it was not until 1923 that it was reissued. At the time the immediate notoriety of the book worked against any full critical assessment of it, and it has still not been given the respect it deserves. Like all semi-autobiographical novels it works partly to reveal and partly to disguise the author's own life. The text is used at times to provide fictional solutions to actual problems, but at others to explore those problems in considerable depth. But what is most remarkable about it is that, in the story of the artist, Eugene Witla, Dreiser comes closest to telling the whole tale, to creating a character through whom many and various currents of feeling are allowed full play. Towards the end of the book we find him in a New York hospital where his wife Angela is about to undergo a dangerous caesarian operation.

> They wheeled her out after a few moments and on to the elevator which led to the floor above. Her face was slightly

covered while she was being so transferred, . . . and the nurse said that a very slight temporary opiate had been administered. . . . He walked far down the dim-lit length of the hall before him, wondering, and looked out on a space where was nothing but snow. In the distance a long lighted train was winding about a high trestle like a golden serpent. There were automobiles honking and pedestrians laboring along in the snow. What a tangle life was, he thought. What a pity. Here a little while ago, he wanted Angela to die, and now,—God Almighty, that was her voice groaning! He would be punished for his evil thoughts—yes, he would. . . . What a tragedy his career was! What a failure! Hot tears welled up into his eyes, his lower lip trembled, not for himself, but for Angela. He was so sorry all at once. He shut it all back. No, by God, he wouldn't cry! . . . It was for Angela his pain was, and tears would not help her now.[14]

Behind this moment of self-appraisal there lies a tortuous history. It is his long engagement and marriage to Angela, a farmer's daughter from the Midwest whom he met in his home town when he was 19, that have provided the element of continuity in his personal relationships. But his wider experience of city life has led to affairs with other women: with a young model during his art-school days in Chicago; with an aspiring and career-minded singer during his attempts to establish himself in New York as an artist; and, following his marriage, with a bored middle-class wife who takes him up during his period of separation and breakdown. The present crisis has been brought about by his recent infatuation with Suzanne Dale, a young New York heiress with whom his successful advertising career has brought him into contact. Out of jealousy and possessive rage Angela chooses to become pregnant despite the risks to her own life. Compulsive sexuality, extreme fantasy and a certain ruthlessness have thus all had their part to play in his relationships with women, but, as the passage makes clear, these have not gone unchallenged. As he realizes the distortions to which Angela has been driven, and his own part in them, his reaction is one of guilt, self-accusation and irrepressible sympathy. The past, with its legacy of honest commitment as well as error, cannot be excluded from the present.

Dreiser wants us to see that this unresolved personal moment takes place in the context of an unresolved social experience. In his bewilderment Eugene looks out of the window to where 'a long lighted train was winding about a high trestle like a golden serpent.' It is an apt image of that powerful but not unquestioned influence that the city has had upon his life. He has had his moments of success, of power, when as advertising executive and manager he has learnt what it means 'to stand up firm, square to the world and make people obey'. But throughout his life his wholehearted participation in this world has been undermined by other perspectives and other influences. Returning with Angela to her father's farm he has encountered the survival of an older America of craftsman labour. During his period of breakdown he has spent time in the carpentry shop of a railroad company, where the cynicism, the guardedness but also the underlying fellowship of working people becomes evident to him. Above all he has felt the need, despite external pressures, to define himself in the individual and expressive role of the artist.

Eugene's artistic ambitions in fact develop through different stages as his life evolves, but there is the consistent element of protest, of the need to assert a range of values that the surrounding culture denies. To begin with it is sensual expression that fascinates him as opposed to the repressive contexts of his childhood. In response to the city, however, his art takes on new qualities. Dreiser based this aspect of Eugene's life on the work of Everett Shinn, an acquaintance of his, and one of the 'Ashcan' School.[15] Like his real life model, Eugene paints scenes of metropolitan life that are remarkable for their attention to individual lives amidst the massive environments and the anonymous crowds. He is pleased when one reviewer of his exhibition declares that he has 'the ability to indict life with its own grossness, to charge it prophetically with its own meanness and cruelty in order that mayhap it may heal itself; the ability to see wherein is beauty—even in shame and pathos and degradation'.[16] The irony is, however, that this humanitarian art becomes the fashionable plaything of a consumer class. Uncertain of how to progress, and uncertain whether there is any real role for the artist in his society, Eugene falls into his period of depression and apathy. When he 'returns' as a successful businessman he mocks the poverty and marginality that he sees as the inevitable lot of the artist critic; but it is a mockery that has its roots in the undeniable and unsatisfied need to be the agent of some 'noble and superhuman purpose'.[17]

In the story of Eugene's life, then, Dreiser gives us his fullest and most complex account of the journey from outside to inside. What is revealed in passages like the one above is that the resultant condition is one of continuing ambivalence and instability. Eugene is at once both insider and outsider. His drives towards immediate pleasure in fact generate an active acknowledgement of the past; his pursuit of solitary power in fact generates an awareness of other lives and a need to devote himself to some larger social project. Given these ultimate recognitions, it is not surprising to discover that Dreiser had great difficulty in finishing his book, and changed the ending several times. The conclusion as we have it is wholly mythical. Eugene returns to success as an artist, but his art is now no longer marginal, and penetrates and conditions the very centres of power. 'At Washington in two of the great public buildings and in three state capitals were tall glowing panels also of his energetic dreaming.'[18] Angela has died, but has been replaced by 'little Angela', for whom he cares with an unwavering loyalty. As he searches the universe it seems to him no longer 'a space where was nothing but snow', but rather the scene of evolutionary advance from which 'great art dreams welled up into his soul.'[19] At all levels, then, facts of disjunction have been replaced by myths of connection. In his personal life, in his social life, and in his ontological life, Eugene's divisions have been resolved in a transforming harmony. The reader may be moved to mock such evident devices, but our reaction should perhaps be different. We can allow and even respect the dreamings of a man who struggled so long and so hard to convey the full terms of his own experience, and offer it as characteristic of his generation.

NOTES

1. Randolph Bourne, 'The Art of Theodore Dreiser', in *The Stature of Theodore Dreiser*, edited by Alfred Kazin and Karl Shapiro (Bloomington: Indiana University Press, 1965), p. 95.
2. Van Wyck Brooks, *The Early Years, A Selection from His Works, 1908–1921*, edited by C. Sprague (New York: Harper and Row, 1968), p. 88.
3. Van Wyck Brooks, *The Early Years*, p. 87.
4. Lionel Trilling, 'Reality in America', in Kazin and Shapiro, *The Stature of Theodore Dreiser*, p. 139.
5. John Berryman, 'Dreiser's Imagination' in Kazin and Shapiro, *The Stature of Theodore Dreiser*, p. 151.
6. Theodore Dreiser, quoted in Kazin and Shapiro, *The Stature of Theodore Dreiser*, p. 175.
7. Theodore Dreiser, *Sister Carrie* (London: Penguin Books, 1981), p. 46. The extensive quotations from *Sister Carrie* are reprinted by permission of Viking Penguin, Inc.
8. Theodore Dreiser, *Sister Carrie*, p. 145.
9. Theodore Dreiser, *Sister Carrie*, p. 486.
10. Theodore Dreiser, *Sister Carrie*, p. 338.
11. Theodore Dreiser, *The Financier* (New York: New American Library, 1967), p. 121.
12. Theodore Dreiser, quoted in Kazin and Shapiro, *The Stature of Theodore Dreiser*, p. 206.
13. Theodore Dreiser, *An American Tragedy* (New York: New American Library, 1964), p. 189.
14. Theodore Dreiser, *The 'Genius'* (New York: Boni & Liveright, 1923), p. 718.
15. See particularly Joseph J. Kwiat, 'Dreiser's The "Genius" and Everett Shinn, The "Ashcan" Painter', *P.M.L.A.*, Vol. LXVII, No. 2, March 1952, 15–31.
16. Theodore Dreiser, *The 'Genius'*, p. 237.
17. Theodore Dreiser, *The 'Genius'*, p. 238.
18. Theodore Dreiser, *The 'Genius'*, p. 732.
19. Theodore Dreiser, *The 'Genius'*, p. 736.

8

Willa Cather

by HERBIE BUTTERFIELD

It was not until her last novel that Willa Cather's Virginia birthplace and early childhood home received anything other than peripheral mention in her fiction. Yet despite its absence from the foreground, its influence upon her was all along profound and pervasive, if in nothing so much as the loss and leaving of it. For this writer who sounds a constant note of homesickness, whose principal act is that of commemoration, Virginia was the first home to be sick for, the first past to be remembered.

She was born, the eldest of seven children, on 7 December 1873, in hill country near the West Virginia border, where for several generations ancestors on both sides had lived in modest prosperity. Here in a large three-storey house she spent her first nine and a half years, a country child helping with the sheep and watching in the mill. Then in April 1883 her father followed his brother and parents to the West, to Webster County, Nebraska: to 'the Divide', the high, bare plateau between the Republican and the Little Blue rivers, for which she was later to express such intense, haunted yearning. The next year the family moved into the railroad town of Red Cloud, the model for all the small towns in her Nebraska novels and stories, a place from which it was of course necessary for the lively young woman eventually to escape, but also one which she regularly revisited for long stays until well into her fifties.

Between 1890 and 1895 she attended the University of Nebraska in Lincoln, studying Latin and English, establishing a taste for the heroic and the high romantic, and devoting an increasingly large part of her time to literary and theatrical criticism for the *Nebraska State Journal*. Thereafter she lived for ten years in Pittsburgh, working first as a journalist, then as a schoolteacher, before finally reaching the Mecca of New York, to spend six years as an editor of McClure's magazine. She had travelled to England and France on holiday in 1902, and she returned to London twice on assignments; but ultimately of deeper consequence was a journey to the American South-West in 1912 that gave her a new perspective on both European and modern industrial civilization. She had also published a volume of poems in 1903, of short stories in 1905, and a first novel, *Alexander's Bridge*, in 1912. But it was not until her fortieth year that, with the writing of *O Pioneers!*, she knew herself to have discovered her mind's proper country, what she called 'the thing by which our feet find the road home on a dark night'.

O Pioneers! is a song of praise both to the prairie land of her later childhood and to the ideal pioneer. 'One January day, thirty years ago', the novel begins, with the straightforward efficiency characteristic of all Cather's first sentences.[1] We are back in the 1880s, with John Bergson pitted against a relentless round of blizzards, drought, fever, mischance, and family sorrow. He dies in his prime, broken in body, but leaving in his daughter, Alexandra, an indomitable spirit. Alexandra possesses neither high intelligence nor vivid imagination; but what she does have are courage, tenacity, foresight, and above all a deep-rooted love of the land. If her practical success lies in the pioneer feat of converting 'The Wild Land' of Part One into the 'Neighboring Fields' of Part Two, her spiritual triumph lies rather in the possibility that 'for the first time . . . since that land emerged from the waters of geological ages, a human face was set toward it with love and yearning.' She is not in conflict with nature, but at one with it, her heart 'hiding down there, somewhere, with the quail and the plover', keeping time with the 'ordered march' of the cosmos. She has a ready sympathy for the holy fool, Ivar, who 'had lived for three years in the clay bank, without defiling the face of nature any more than the coyote . . . had done'. And her dreams of desire are less for a human lover than for some kind of god, fertile and vegetative, 'yellow like the sunlight' with 'the smell of ripe cornfields about him'. She survives banality and catastrophe: the mean-spirited antagonism of the brothers next to her in age, Lou and Oscar; and the tragedy that befalls the youngest, Emil, in whom she had placed such hope, but who is murdered with his beloved, Marie Shabata, by Marie's husband, Frank. She survives, to visit Frank in prison, compassionate, forgiving, unblaming even; and to find in Carl Lindstrum a partner likewise enchanted with the freedom of the frontier, likewise haunted by memories of the 'wild old beast' before it was tamed into plenitude, and able to share with her the sacred, simple knowledge that 'we come and go, but the land is always here.'

The same heroic presences, of pioneer girl and changing land, inspire *My Ántonia* (1918). The story is told by Jim Burden, arriving in Nebraska from Virginia at the same time and age as had Cather, an autobiographical persona in part therefore and a reminder that virtually all the figures in her mature fiction were modelled closely on people of her acquaintance. She was an interpreter rather than an inventor, a memorialist rather than a fabulist. Jim tells his story in a rambling, apparently artless manner, an effect of course only of superbly skilled craft.[2] Though Jim's story, it is largely Ántonia's; though, again, Ántonia's story is at times displaced by her friend Lena Lingard's story or by Tiny Soderball's. The whole is a web of stories, of anecdotes, tales, life-histories, a loose-knit aesthetically comfortable fabric.

Jim and Ántonia Shimerda grow up close to one another on the scarcely broken prairie, he with his grandparents in an atmosphere of decent, capacious Protestantism ('The prayers of all good people are good'), the Shimerdas in a sod-house, struggling against all things strange—language, foodstuffs, climate—and eventually, in the case of old Mr. Shimerda, giving up the struggle. Gentle, devout Catholic though he is, homesickness and helplessness overwhelm him, and in the frozen depths of his first Nebraska winter he takes his own life. His grave is at the cross-roads, where

under a new moon or the clear evening star, the dusty roads
used to look like soft grey rivers flowing past it. . . . In all that
country it was the spot most dear to me.

The material of such tragedy will not, however, be what Jim
recalls, but instead a marvellous freedom ('I had the feeling
that the world was left behind me, that we had got over the
edge of it, and were outside man's jurisdiction'), and a pervasive movement:

> More than anything else I felt motion in the landscape; in the
> fresh, easy-blowing morning wind, and in the earth itself, as if
> the shaggy grass were a sort of loose hide, and underneath it
> herds of wild buffalo were galloping, galloping. . . .

After a time in the very different, small town air of Black
Hawk, their paths diverge. Jim goes on to University and to
the linked delights of mental and emotional awakening, whilst
Ántonia follows the rougher road through seduction, desertion,
and a childbirth, unconsorted and unaided, encouraged only
by the union of her European peasant blood and American
pioneer spirit. So it is that some twenty years later Jim,
now a New York lawyer, returns to seek out Ántonia, now
Ántonia Cusack, farmer's wife and mother of a cheerful,
sprawling family. She is still part stocky peasant, part sturdy
pioneer, the memory of her father who 'never goes out of my
life' linking her Bohemian past to her Nebraska present 'where
I know every stack and tree, and where all the ground is
friendly'. But she is also more than peasant or pioneer, more
than human even; an image, a flow, a source.

> Ántonia had always been one to leave images in the mind that
> did not fade—that grew stronger with time. . . . She lent herself
> to immemorial human attitudes which we recognize by instinct
> as universal and true. . . . She was a rich mine of life, like the
> founders of early races.

Like *O Pioneers!*, but still more resoundingly, *My Ántonia* is a
song of praise, to the pioneer generation, to the earth, with its
'solemn magic that comes out of those fields at nightfall'; but,
it must be noticed, also increasingly to the past, where the
good things reside: 'Whatever we had missed, we possessed
together the precious, the incommunicable past.'

In between these two Nebraska novels she had published her longest work, *The Song of the Lark* (1915), the culminating expression of her youthful fascination with the figure of the artist and with the world of music, in particular opera. It is a cumbersome, over-extended book that follows Thea Kronberg from her childhood in Moonstone, Colorado, through her years of musical study in Chicago, New York, and Germany, to the present time of her world-wide fame. In many respects Thea is a musical version of Alexandra and Ántonia, the Western girl of exceptional character triumphing over adversity. Her adversaries, though, are not recalcitrant soil and furious weather, but her fellow townspeople, her family even, those who, characteristically conformist, respectable, philistine, and Protestant, are either suspicious of the young girl's distinctiveness or deaf to her musical gift. In contrast, Thea's true friends and helpers have in common only that for one reason or another they do not fit that respectable mould. There is Wunsch, the melancholy, alcoholic piano teacher who tells Thea that 'there is only one thing—desire. . . . It brought Columbus across the sea in a little boat'[3]; Spanish Johnny, the bar room guitarist from the enticing Mexican section of town; Dr. Archie, who finances Thea's studies in Germany; and Ray Kennedy, the railroad worker whose life insurance in Thea's favour upon his death lays the foundations of her musical career. He it is who tells Thea of the ancient Indian civilizations and first gives her a sense of the continuity of human endeavour. Years later, in a cañon in Arizona, amongst the remnants of that Indian world, she is seized with, on the one hand, the necessary tragic perception of the 'inevitable hardness of human life' and, on the other hand, with equally necessary wonder at the 'glorious striving of human art'. An eagle wheeling and mounting above the cañon becomes an emblem of desire, linking long ago and now.

> O eagle of eagles! . . . It had come all the way; when men lived in caves, it was there. A vanished race; but along the trails, in the stream, under the spreading cactus, there still glittered in the sun the bits of their frail clay vessels, fragments of their desire.

It is then that her own resolve is stiffened, to climb towards the peaks of her art. Once before as a child she had been similarly stirred by the marks of human effort. Up in Wyoming on the Laramie Plain she had seen 'deep furrows, cut in the earth by heavy wagon-wheels, and now grown over with dry, whitish grass', signature of those who had striven across a continent. Then too the eagles had soared high above, and she had 'told herself she would never, never forget it. The spirit of human courage seemed to live up there with the eagles', the spirit that joins Thea, the singer, across time with ancient craftsman and yesterday's frontiersman.

Ironically, the book which won her the Pulitzer Prize in 1922 and established her popular reputation, is perhaps the least successful of her novels. *One of Ours*, which is set in Nebraska and France at the time of the First World War, had its origins in the death at the front in May 1918 of a favourite cousin, who here lives and dies again as Claude Wheeler. Cather's 'research' for the novel included conversation with numerous soldiers and a trip to France specially taken in 1920; and that the novel is unsatisfying has less to do with any failure to convince on the realistic level, than with a seeming lack of coherent general design, a sense that the novel emerges mainly from an unfocused disgruntlement on Cather's part with the latterday Middle West and the post-war world. For this Nebraska of Claude's generation is no longer the world of Alexandra and Ántonia, but, repressed and repressive, closer to Anderson's Winesburg or Lewis's Gopher Prairie. The prohibitive spirit is abroad, and mechanization is everywhere, 'machines to do the work and machines to entertain people'; the old crafts are dying, the old rhythms fading, the old West has gone. To escape the ubiquitous, oncoming ugliness Claude enlists in the army, seeking in France a beauty and in war service a purpose that are not to be found in Frankfort, Nebraska. What he finds of course is death, but a death that at least, a jaundiced Cather implies, saves him from the disillusionment of those who survive.

One of Ours is a long novel, tediously long; but before it was published Cather had begun the book that in contrast strikingly exemplifies her concept of the 'novel démeublé', the novel emptied of clutter, 'bare for the play of emotions great and little'. In *A Lost Lady* the heavy discontent of *One of Ours* is transmuted into the lightness of melancholy, the grace of elegy, and the vitality of complex portraiture. Marian Forrester, the lady of the title, becomes lost in several senses, including the literal sense of being last heard of in Buenos Aires; but above all is she lost to Niel Herbert, the teenage boy growing into manhood, from whose partly comprehending viewpoint the story is unfolded. She is also, importantly, a *lady*, the wife of Sweet Water's patrician, Captain Forrester, the railroad builder and type of the old heroic West, who is twenty-five years older than her. It is as much as anything else the combination of her elevated social position with her personal approachability that renders her for the young Niel the romantic embodiment of the feminine ideal; she is above, yet not out of reach. Despite her affection and care for the old Captain in his ageing disability, her story will be one of deceits and infidelities, couplings with gross or vicious men, and of a general coarsening of sensibility and a moral deterioration. Necessarily she must be the source of Niel's disillusionment, of his awakening from youthful enchantment. But the novel would be altogether less if it were not with the clear memory of an exceptional, splendidly passionate nature that she had left us. Her life and its meaning are inextricably interwoven with the meaning of the old West and its decline. The Captain has been a man of vision ('We dreamed the railroads across the mountains, just as I dreamed my place on the Sweet Water'), of enduring strength ('like an old tree walking'), and of an honour which compelled him to impoverish himself rather than fail his obligations. After his death his place at table is for a time taken by Ivy Peters, spiteful and destructive, who

> by draining the marsh . . . had obliterated a few acres of something he hated, though he could not name it, and had asserted his power over the people who had loved those unproductive meadows for their idleness and silvery beauty.

Ivy it was who as one of Niel's boyhood gang had shattered the idyllic mood of the novel's early pages when methodically he slit the eyes of a captured woodpecker before releasing it. His adult success as an unprincipled lawyer and as Mrs. Forrester's lover signals 'the end of an era, the sunset of the pioneer'. For Niel the real lostness of the lady stems from the fact 'that she was not willing to immolate herself . . . and die with the pioneer period to which she belonged; that she preferred life on any terms'. Niel is a scrupulous and discriminating person, but not an especially vigorous one; and the irony must remain that it is in Marian Forrester's very love of life, in her undiscriminating vitality, that all along her appeal has lain.

Though its setting is quite different—a University town within sight of Lake Michigan—Cather's next novel, *The Professor's House* (1925), is similarly suffused with the elegiac mood and with the feeling of estrangement from the present. An historian, whose life's work is a massive study of the *Spanish Adventurers in North America*, Professor St. Peter has lived and worked for years in an ugly, inconvenient house whose 'walled-in garden has been the comfort of his life'. His two daughters having married and left, he has recently built his wife a well-appointed new home, but himself still clings to his beloved study, which has always doubled as a sewing-room, at the top of the otherwise now empty family home. He is mildly but comprehensively disaffected, from his family, from his University and colleagues, from the contemporary world generally, which he finds largely mercenary and utilitarian. For him the truths are ancient; there is nothing new under the sun; no advance beyond what art and religion permanently rehearse:

> The human mind . . . has always been made more interesting by dwelling on the old riddles, even if it makes nothing of them. Science hasn't given us any new amazements. . . . Art and religion (they are the same thing, in the end, of course) have given man the only happiness he has ever had.

More and more does he come to inhabit the past: his childhood, the childhood of his daughters, his University in earlier days before it had succumbed to 'the aim to "show results" that was undermining and vulgarizing education', the Spanish-American past of his intellectual project. Above all does his mind dwell upon one especially brilliant student, the resonantly named Tom Outland, a physicist with a genius for aeronautics, whose ready mind and generous character had been the inspiration of St. Peter's middle years. 'Tom Outland's Story' forms a long parenthesis, quite independent of the rest of the narrative. Its position in the novel is beautifully described by Cather herself as being like that of a seascape glimpsed through the window of a Dutch interior painting. His story is of his awed fascination with the ancient Indian cliff city he had discovered while working on the railroad in New Mexico, until

> for me the Mesa was no longer an adventure but a religious emotion. I had read of filial piety in the Latin poets, and I knew that was what I felt for this place.

Tom had been killed in the war, leaving his reverence for that lost Indian world and his disinterested inventive ability to combine for St. Peter as an image of purity, indelible but associated only with the past and the West. Gradually St. Peter has fallen into a habit of melancholy, dreaming of the South-West's 'long, rugged untarnished vistas dear to the American heart', and contemplating 'eternal solitude with gratefulness'. One summer evening this veiled death-wish is almost granted, when, drifting in a contented reverie, he is saved from asphyxiation by the fumes of his gas-stove only by the intervention of the old sewing-woman Augusta, a devout Catholic, emblem of traditional propriety, remnant of a simple integrity amidst complicated disintegration. Her 'corrective, remedial influence' wordlessly encourages, if not exactly his will to live, at least his recognition of his duty to do so. It is a moral decision, but hardly one taken with enthusiasm; his enthusiasm, like Willa Cather's lives among the things of memory.

Both St. Peter, in the importance he attaches to religion, and Augusta play their parts in the movement of religion, particularly Roman Catholicism, towards the centre of Cather's stage. She had been received into the Protestant Episcopal church with her parents in 1922, but so prominent did Catholicism become in her novels of this period that she has regularly been mistaken for a Catholic convert. *My Mortal Enemy* (1926) has affinities with *A Lost Lady*; it too is 'démeublé' and it too features an attractive, exceptional woman who disillusions and educates a youthful narrator. Myra Henshawe was brought up by her great uncle, an Irish-American rough diamond, who had made a fortune, lived high, but kept his faith, to such an extent that when Myra married outside the church, he disinherited her and willed his huge mansion for a convent. All that is many years before we first meet Myra, in her prime in New York, 'compelling, passionate, overmastering something'. She entrances the 15-year-old narrator, Nellie, and the spell is not broken until, overhearing a row between Myra and her husband, she experiences the force of Myra's fury as 'evil', and later sees about her scornful mouth the curl and twist of a snake. It is in the second part, however, that the novel's power lies. Ten years later, in a shabby boarding-house on the West Coast, Myra is now an embittered invalid, tended loyally by her husband. Her circumstances are pathetic, but her character registers a vital, complex triumph. She has no kindness, no charity, and for her devoted husband only hatred; but in the absence of such sweeter virtues, we are to see in her a savage strength and passion which give her affinities both with the great poets she loves and who for her 'shine into all the dark corners of the world', and with the primitive springs of religion. 'I wonder whether some of the saints of the early Church weren't a good deal like her', muses her priest. She dies a set-piece death, on a cliff facing out to the Pacific, at the last defying the faith to which she had returned by leaving instructions that her body be cremated and her ashes buried 'in some lonely and unfrequented place in the mountains, or in the sea'. 'She was a wild, lovely creature' is her husband's epitaph, by which he elevates her to the diverse company of Cather's heroic dead and gone: Indian cliff-dwellers, Spanish explorers, early Christian saints, romantic artists, immigrant pioneers, and the barons of individual enterprise.

Descendants and heirs of Indian, Spaniard, and saint populate her next novel, *Death Comes for the Archbishop* (1927). It is a marvellous book, full of warmth and space, episodic in form, epic in range, in its barest outline the story of Bishop Jean Latour's organization of his New Mexico diocese in the years following his appointment in 1851, in its broadest sweep a rhapsodic celebration of that whole, huge land. The Bishop and his vicar, Father Joseph Vaillant, besides being lifelong friends from their seminary days, complement each other perfectly. Latour is high-born, scholarly, contemplative, a man 'of courtesy toward himself, toward his beasts, toward the juniper tree, before which he knelt, and the God whom he was addressing'. Vaillant is of humbler parentage, 'homely', full of practical energy, 'truly spiritual' though 'passionately attached to many of the things of this world'. Each has a deep love of France, and of all things French enriched by custom and lore ('There are nearly a thousand years of history in this soup', says Vaillant, an excellent, highly particular cook[4]), but it must be the novel's burden that eventually their hearts will be given to the land of their mission.

It is a land peopled by those who love and reverence it, Indian and Mexican alike, an idyllic relationship threatened now chiefly by the Americans seeping in from Texas, who have no respect, no awe. The world of Anglo-Saxon names is redeemed only by Kit Carson, archetypal frontiersman moulded in an earlier age, portrayed here as 'reflective, a little melancholy', and possessed of 'standards, loyalties, a code which is not easily put into words, but which is easily felt'.[5] In contrast to the Americans, the Mexicans, whether lofty patrician or corrupt, worldly priest, are marked out by a fierce attachment to the land. Don Manuel Chavez 'loved the natural beauties of his country with a passion, and he hated the Americans who were blind to them.' Father Martinez reminds Latour that the earth under his feet is a good deal nearer than Rome:

> Our religion grew out of the soil, and has its own roots. We pay a filial respect to the person of the Holy Father, but Rome has no authority here.

As for the Indians, they are not so much attached to the land, rooted in it, as intermingled with it, indistinguishable from it.

> Just as it was the white man's way to assert himself in any landscape, to change it . . . . it was the Indian's way to pass through a country without disturbing anything.

The Bishop senses in the Indians something untranslatably foreign, but in their veneration for the ancient, in their accommodation with nature, in their fusion of earth and spirit, they are inseparable from that which at length he can neither live nor die without. Having returned to France on retirement, he finds himself yearning constantly for the air that 'one can breathe . . . only on the bright edges of the world, on the great grass plains or the sage-brush desert.' And so once again he turns about.

> That air would disappear from the whole earth in time perhaps, but long after his day. He did not know just when it had become so necessary to him, but he had come back to die in exile for the sake of it.

The 'sage-brush desert' may be the country of his diocese, but the 'great grass plains' are of course the country of Cather's childhood, the 'bright edges of the world' she had once walked upon and which she knew in her lifetime to have 'disappeared'. This epic of the South West is also elegy.

Willa Cather's father died in 1928, her mother three years later, after a long period of severe incapacity, when she was often attended by her daughter. It was during this time of illness and death that, founded on two visits to the city of Quebec, *Shadows on the Rock* was composed, to be published in 1931. It shares much with *Death Comes for the Archbishop*—the episodic structure, the highly pictorial quality, the general theme of Roman Catholicism in the New World and of the gradual transference of prior allegiances from historical France to continental America. There is, however, a major difference in perspective. In *Death Comes for the Archbishop*, the eye and mind travel, jog-trot on pony-back, countless miles across the South-Western expanses; in the later novel they bear down and fix in the year 1697 on the single point of the rock of Quebec, a settlement of slate-roofed, spire-topped cliff-dwellings, clambering down to the riverside. It is of course an hierarchic world, dominated by two noblemen: Bishop Laval in his Palace, 'stubborn, high-handed, tyrannical', but in his self-sacrificing austerity an exemplary shepherd of his flock; and, in constant feud with him, the governor, Count Frontenac, in his chateau, a man of both responsible conscience and independent instinct, who

> belonged to the old order; he cherished those beneath him and rendered his duty to those above him, but flattered nobody, not the king himself.[6]

He is a good protector, especially of the novel's two centres of consciousness, his apothecary and physician, the widowed

Auclair, and Auclair's daughter Cécile, who keeps house for her father and attempts to maintain the spirit of her dying mother's wish 'that the proprieties . . . be observed, all the little shades of feeling which make the common fine'. Frontenac's is the traditional authority, Mme. Auclair's the traditional wisdom. It is a story of tradition, then, of the handing on of old world wisdom, purged as far as possible of the old world horrors and brutalities that darken or bloody so many of the retrospective episodes. The rock of Quebec is to be both repository of ancient graces and refuge from ancient cruelties. But if it is a story of tradition and handing on, it is also a story of transfer and handing over; and upon Frontenac's death, his place as guardian of the Auclairs' fortunes is taken, not by the next aristocratic French governor, but by Pierre Charron, new world archetype, who smells of 'tobacco and the pine-woods and the fresh snow', and whom Cécile will marry. He

> had not the authority of a parchment and a seal. But he had authority, and a power which came from knowledge of the country and its people.

Auclair, who had so often pined for France, at length feels 'indeed fortunate to spend his old age here where nothing changed'. Though ostensibly in early eighteenth-century Quebec, 'here where nothing changed' is of course really once again that permanent pioneer moment Cather had extrapolated from her childhood and enshrined in her memory.

After her parents' deaths Cather's physical ties with Nebraska were broken, and she seemed to feel no need to return to a place that was now but a grave of the past. But she could have paid it no finer homage than the volume of three long stories, *Obscure Destinies*, that appeared in 1932. 'Neighbour Rosicky' is a tribute to a pioneer farmer, a kindred spirit of Ántonia's, who, having tried cities and found them deathly, has settled here in the West, 'to see the sun rise and set and to plant things and watch them grow'. Here at the point of death, with his extraordinary affinity for all living things, he transmits to his daughter-in-law, as she holds his 'warm brown' hand, 'some direct and untranslatable message'. He is buried amongst his friends in the graveyard than which 'nothing could be more undeathlike . . . this little square of long grass

which the wind for ever stirred.' To his doctor, the narrator,
his life seemed 'complete and beautiful'. 'Old Mother Harris'
is similarly saluted. In the background of her daughter's
household, not always heeded, not enough appreciated, Grandmother Harris gently dispenses wisdom or firmly teaches duty
to her grandchildren, until she too in the tranquil fullness of her
time goes to her death. The third story is a memorial to 'Two
Friends', a cattleman and a banker who long years ago, of a
summer evening, would take arm-chairs and sit outside the
bank, talking off and on about this and that, while the young
narrator lolled about, half-listening. They were 'nights of full
liberty and perfect idleness', of witnessing 'the strong, rich,
overflowing silence between two friends that was as full and
satisfying as the moonlight', until politics came between the
two, shattered the mystery of friendship, and wasted, as the
story concludes, 'one of the truths we want to keep.' *Obscure
Destinies* is a gathering of such quiet truths for the keeping.

Cather wrote one more nostalgic story about Nebraska,
'The Best Years', her last completed work,[7] and a novel, *Lucy
Gayheart* (1935), whose heroine, Lucy, in her musical ability
and her need to escape the small town for Chicago, has
initially something in common with Thea Kronborg in *The
Song of the Lark*. It is a pathetic tale of star-crossed lovers, of
rejection, retaliation, guilt, and penance. The deaths in
separate drowning accidents of Lucy and the famous singer
she loves are prefigured in the heroine's earlier

> discovery about life, a revelation of love as a tragic force, not a
> melting mood, of passion that drowns like black water.

But the passion, the force, and therefore the tragedy, are not
here; it is a strangely weightless book, or light-weight precisely,
very much a footnote to the great prairie and pioneer romances.
That world's perfectly sufficient epitaph Cather had already
composed in *Obscure Destinies*.

After her Greenwich Village home had been demolished in
1927, Cather stayed on in New York, but was often, especially
in the humid summers, to be found elsewhere, in New Mexico,
in California visiting her brothers, in upstate New Hampshire.
But the spot she particularly loved was Grand Manan, a
rocky, forested Island in the Bay of Fundy off the coast of

Nuvia Scutia, where she acquired a cottage. This enchanted retreat she celebrated in the story 'Before Breakfast',[8] where, for the tired businessman, Henry Grenfell, watching from the cliff-top a girl swimming amongst the cold waves, the history of human striving falls into proper place. It was very much as to a sanctuary that she went to Grand Manan, for, as she moved into her sixties, she was increasingly out of sympathy with most aspects of the contemporary world, antagonistic on individualist grounds to the politics of the New Deal, and disdainful of the young urban-based intelligentsia.[9] She quoted Sarah Orne Jewett approvingly:

> Country friends, she used to say, were the wisest of all, because they could never be fooled about fundamentals.

It was in such a spirit of alienation from the city-bred young that in 1936 she put together a selection of essays, addressed as the title stoutly declares, to those *Not Under Forty*. 'The world broke in two in 1922 or thereabouts', she announced in the preface, and 'it is for the backward, and by one of their number that these sketches were written.'

There was, though, one further task for her imagination—perhaps indeed a backward one—and that was to recreate the world of her earliest memories. This in 1937 she set out to do, despite being now considerably impeded by a manual disability, which for long periods made it physically impossible for her to write. It took her three years, but by December 1940 *Sapphira and the Slave Girl* was completed and published. The story takes place in the ante-bellum South, in 1856, two decades before Cather's birth, but the surroundings, the buildings and the landscape, are those of her childhood recalled. This is Southern border country, and just as Cather's relatives had been divided in their allegiances during the Civil War, so here the Colberts are divided, between Sapphira who comes from a slave-owning family and her husband, who does not. Slavery, the sexual abuse of slaves, and escape from slavery are central to the narrative. Our rational sentiments necessarily espouse the cause of the slave-girl, Nancy, and her libertarian well-wishers, over against her jealous, scheming, egomaniacal mistress, the invalid Sapphira, at the same time as Sapphira's imperious character and the stoic courage with which she

147

faces her death tempt out the admiring emotions we feel for all intractable old warhorses. The epilogue, which sees Nancy return from Canada twenty-five years later, is narrated in the first person by a little girl, 'something over five years old'. If we permit ourselves to associate that little girl directly with Willa Cather, it may help us to explain the somewhat detached, long-focused feel about the novel, one by an old person looking back and out through the eyes of her own distant self and recounting events, even then remote and legendary to her. For *Sapphira and the Slave Girl* is not an historical novel, with the past reawoken into presence, so much as a novel that takes place a very long time ago, in a world far gone.

Willa Cather died on 24 April 1947, at the age of 73. She had lived beyond her three score years and ten, but her vital writing life spanned less than two decades, roughly the second and third of the century, from the time when she discovered her own imaginative territory to the time when, with her parents' deaths, she lost touch with the actual ground of that territory. Nevertheless, during that relatively short time, she produced a body of work that, with the exception of her prize-winning, reputation-founding, sales-boosting *One of Ours*, was as consistently fine, as powerful and as resonant, as any other American fiction-writer's of this century. In her outlook she may be described as, variously, aristocratic, preservative, elegiac, primitivist, ceremonious, libertarian, individualistic; which is perhaps to say that she was a Southern Protestant, raised on the evanescent Western frontier, who became enthralled by the Spanish-Catholic and Indian West beyond. From this kaleidoscopic viewpoint, in a prose that was regularly lucid, firm, elegant, and self-confidently modest, she both venerated a particular, ephemeral past and affirmed common, permanent values. To conclude in the large terms that she requires and deserves: she was romantic, yes, and classicist; a poet in prose and a master of prose; what she was not, unlike so many of her contemporaries, was realist; what she was not, unlike so many of her successors, was fantasist; her art was greater than either's, that of imaginative truth.

Willa Cather

NOTES

1. Without exception her novels begin either with the immediate introduction of the main character or that character's closest associate (e.g. 'Claude Wheeler opened his eyes' or 'I first met Myra Henshawe'), or with an immediate situation in time (exact as in 'One afternoon late in October of the year 1697', broad as in 'Thirty or forty years ago, on one of those gray little towns') or in place (as in 'In Haverford on the Platte . . .'). The brief quotations from Cather's fiction in this essay are taken from the English editions published by Hamish Hamilton and Virago Press.
2. The manner is in some respects reminiscent of Ford's *The Good Soldier*, which had been published three years previously. Ford regarded Cather as 'one of the greatest novelists of the present day'.
3. His name in German means 'desire'.
4. In his enjoyment of good food and his insistence on its careful, loving preparation Vaillant here represents his author.
5. Even so, Kit Carson too betrays his code in the last chapter, when 'misguidedly', tragically playing his leading part in the destruction of the Navajos' agriculture.
6. In her portrait of Frontenac, Cather relied considerably on one of her favourite romantic writers, the historian, Parkman.
7. To be found in *The Old Beauty and Others*, posthumously published in 1948, and also in *Five Stories* (New York: Vintage, 1956).
8. See *The Old Beauty and Others*.
9. However, one of the great joys of her declining years was her intimate friendship with the Menuhin family, particularly with the younger members.

9

Fitzgerald and the Art of Social Fiction: *The Great Gatsby*

by BRIAN WAY

The power of a great novel often depends, more than anything else, upon the firmness and suitability of its underlying structure.[1] 'On this hard fine floor', Henry James wrote in his Preface to *The Awkward Age*, 'the element of execution feels it may more or less confidently *dance*.' A novelist cannot hope to compensate by mere 'treatment' for 'the loose foundation or the vague scheme'. He can best avoid this kind of weakness by making his work express as far as possible the necessities of dramatic form.

> The dramatist has verily to *build*, is committed to architecture, to construction at any cost; to driving in deep his vertical supports and laying across and firmly fixing his horizontal, his resting pieces.[2]

If a novel is to have this secure basis, it should be written, like a play, in scenes; and each scene should have a definite shape and a precise location—those qualities we associate with theatrical performance.

The most striking formal characteristic of *The Great Gatsby* is its scenic construction, and Scott Fitzgerald himself spoke of it as a 'dramatic' novel. In this respect, it shows extraordinarily

150

close affinities with the theory and practice of James's later fiction. James's vivid account of the little diagram he drew in order to explain the structure of *The Awkward Age* to his publisher, corresponds exactly with what we find in *Gatsby*:

> I drew on a sheet of paper . . . the neat figure of a circle consisting of a number of small rounds disposed at equal distance about a central object. The central object was my situation, my subject in itself, to which the thing would owe its title, and the small rounds represented so many distinct lamps, as I liked to call them, the function of each of which would be to light with all due intensity one of its aspects. . . . Each of my 'lamps' would be the light of a single 'social occasion', in the history and intercourse of the characters concerned, and would bring out to the full the latent colour of the scene in question and cause it to illuminate, to the last drop, its bearing on my theme.[3]

The 'central object' of *The Great Gatsby* is clearly Gatsby himself, and the chapters of the novel are in the main a series of dramatic scenes, each illuminating some new aspect of his character and situation. The scenes are invariably 'social occasions'; often they are parties, in that special sense which is so fundamental to Fitzgerald's understanding of the 1920s. Chapter I is built around the dinner party at the Buchanans' at which Nick Carraway discovers the subtle charm and the inner corruption of Daisy and of the American rich—the woman and the class which Gatsby has made the object of his dreams. Chapter II presents the 'foul dust' that floats in the wake of his dreams. It opens with a poetic and atmospheric evocation of the valley of ashes, but its main source of energy is once again dramatic—the raucous Prohibition-style party in Myrtle Wilson's apartment. In Chapter III, Nick visits one of Gatsby's own parties for the first time, and begins to understand the equivocal nature of the latter's creative powers—his capacity to mix the beautiful with the vulgar, the magical with the absurd. Chapter IV functions like an act in two scenes, each revealing a contrasted aspect of Gatsby's identity: the lunch in New York, at which Nick meets Meyer Wolfsheim and has a glimpse of Gatsby's underworld connections; and the tea during which Jordan Baker tells him the story of Gatsby's wartime affair with Daisy. The dramatic focus of

Chapter V is the tea party at Nick's house, when Gatsby and Daisy are reunited; and in Chapter VI Nick attends a second party at Gatsby's, at which Daisy herself is present. Chapter VII, like Chapter IV, is an act in two scenes: the lunch party at the Buchanans' where Tom realizes for the first time that Daisy and Gatsby are lovers; and the abortive cocktail party at the Plaza Hotel in New York, where Tom not only ends the affair, but succeeds in destroying Gatsby's 'platonic conception' of himself. Only in the last two chapters does Fitzgerald largely abandon the dramatic method, and, even here, some of the most vivid moments depend on effects which are scenic in character—Mr. Gatz's arrival at Gatsby's house, Nick's second meeting with Meyer Wolfsheim in New York, and Gatsby's funeral.

Nick Carraway is a key element in the success of this scheme, indeed he is no less vital to the structure of *The Great Gatsby* than to its tone and meaning. He is both stage manager and chorus, re-creating situations in all their actuality, and at the same time commenting upon them. Sometimes he even devises the action—contrives the circumstances by which the actors are brought together on the stage: it is he who arranges the reunion of Gatsby and Daisy. Nick has a further value from the structural point of view: through him, Fitzgerald is able to maintain a kind of flexibility which James considered impossible in the dramatic mode of fiction. James believed that, in order to benefit fully from the firmness of dramatic construction, the novelist was compelled to relinquish the privilege of 'going behind' the action so as to analyse and comment upon it.[4] But, thanks to Nick Carraway, Fitzgerald has the best of both worlds: he moves from the dramatic concentration of 'the scenic thing' to the rich texture of narrative without the smallest effect of incoherency or inconsistency.

*   *   *

The evolution of Gatsby's dream is the history of his involvement with a social class, the American rich. The turbulent imaginings of his adolescence first take shape in the scheme of self-advancement which he draws up in imitation of Benjamin Franklin and Horatio Alger. At this time, he has a plan to make himself rich, but no clear mental picture of what wealth

and success would be like. This gap is partially filled when
Dan Cody's yacht anchors off the Lake Superior shore, and
Gatsby meets Cody himself. At once Cody, the Western
tycoon, who is spending his money in the flamboyant style of
the Gilded Age, becomes Gatsby's image of the wealthy and
successful man. He changes his name from Jimmy Gatz to Jay
Gatsby in an attempt to embrace this new conception in all its
aspects. Cody's swagger is the basis of his own social style,
and, like the former, he sees the acquisition of wealth as
essentially an activity of the frontier—if not the actual geographical and historical frontier, then the no-man's-land
between business and criminality.

As well as an image of himself, however, Gatsby needs an
image of something beyond him to which he can aspire, and
this final stage in his imaginative development is completed
when he meets Daisy during the War and becomes her lover.
When he kissed her for the first time, he 'wed forever his
ineffable vision to her perishable flesh': from that moment, she
was the substance of his dream, and 'the incarnation was
complete.' In his eyes, she is intensely desirable both as a
woman and as the symbol of a way of life:

> Gatsby was overwhelmingly aware of the youth and mystery
> which wealth imprisons and preserves, of the freshness of many
> clothes, and of Daisy, gleaming like silver, safe and proud above
> the hot struggles of the poor.[5]

Daisy's charm involves a subtle fusion of two powerful sources
of attraction, sex and money: one might say that, in her,
money becomes sexually desirable. This quality is concentrated in her voice, the one facet of her beauty which can never
fall short of Gatsby's dream. As Nick Carraway reflects, when
he leaves them alone together for the first time after their five
year separation, 'I think that voice held him most, with its
fluctuating, feverish warmth, because it couldn't be over-
dreamed—that voice was a deathless song.'[6] Nick's tone
surrounds the metaphor of song with an aura of high romance,
but it is Gatsby himself who uncovers the secret of those
elusive cadences, when he remarks with impressive simplicity
that 'her voice is full of money.' Many American novelists,
including Henry James, Edith Wharton and Theodore Dreiser,

were well aware that a beautiful woman may contain within herself all the beguiling characteristics of a social class, but no one apart from Fitzgerald has ever found so felicitous an image for the interior music of wealth.

Gatsby is incapable of seeing the American rich in any other way, but Fitzgerald, through Nick Carraway, makes us equally aware of their shortcomings from the very beginning of the novel. His introductory portraits of Daisy and Tom Buchanan are sketched in with delicate irony. Nick is half dazzled by their wealth, and yet knows that their lives are pervaded by an atmosphere of rootlessness and futility. Since their marriage, they have 'drifted here and there unrestfully wherever people played polo and were rich together'—a year in France, a season or two on Chicago's North Shore, and now a summer on Long Island. Tom's discontent seems an expression, in part, of his permanent immaturity. He had been a great football star at Yale, 'a national figure in a way, one of those men who reach such an acute limited excellence at twenty-one that everything afterwards savours of anticlimax.' Nick suspects that he will 'drift on forever seeking, a little wistfully, for the dramatic turbulence of some irrecoverable football game'.[7]

These weaknesses are serious enough, but worse is to follow, and when Nick accepts Daisy's invitation to dinner he quickly learns the full extent of the Buchanans' corruption. Their failure is presented as the failure of a civilization, of a way of life. Nick Carraway imagines that he will find among the sophisticated Eastern rich the high point of American civilization. The expanse of the Buchanans' lawns, the graciousness of their house, the formality of dinner, the poised, confident social tone give all the outward signs that a high civilization has been achieved. Nick contrasts the occasion with parties in the Middle West, where people hurry from one phase of the evening to the next in a state of 'continually disappointed anticipation' or in 'sheer nervous dread of the moment itself'. 'You make me feel uncivilized,' he says to Daisy, 'can't you talk about crops or something.' At once he is ludicrously disillusioned by Tom, who is provoked by Nick's remark into an incoherent account of a book he has just read which 'proves' that 'civilization—oh, science and art, and all that' is threatened by the rise of the coloured races. To our sense of the restlessness and futility of their lives is now added an element of brutality and arrogance. A telephone call from Tom's mistress, and a tense whispered quarrel with Daisy offstage on which Jordan Baker eavesdrops shamelessly, conclude the scene. The rottenness of these people is conveyed with a fine sense of comedy.

Nick's disappointment has already been prefigured poetically in his first glimpse of the Buchanan household:

> A breeze blew through the room, blew curtains in at one end and out the other like pale flags, twisting them up toward the frosted wedding-cake of the ceiling, and then rippled over the wine-coloured rug, making a shadow on it as wind does on the sea.
>
> The only completely stationary object in the room was an enormous couch on which two young women were buoyed up as though upon an anchored balloon. They were both in white, and their dresses were rippling and fluttering as if they had just been blown back in after a short flight around the house.[8]

The house, the draperies, the young women themselves, seem positively airborne upon Nick's romantic sense of expectation, until Tom enters: 'Then there was a boom as Tom Buchanan shut the rear windows and the caught wind died out about the room, and the curtains, and the rugs and the two young women ballooned slowly to the floor.'[9] Tom brings everything quite literally down to earth. There is no more impressive instance of how much Fitzgerald's fiction gains from his sense of the specifically poetic possibilities of the novel. And we are dealing here with dramatic poetry, not the large abstractions of symbol and myth. In a way which is both subtler and more flexible, the local effects of language are finely adapted to the immediate demands of the scene, the moment.

The element of physical brutality in Tom Buchanan's character is insisted upon from the beginning. An arrogant stare; a manner which is both supercilious and aggressive; 'a great pack of muscle shifting when his shoulder moved under his thin coat'—these are the details of his appearance which catch our attention. His brutality is constantly breaking through the veneer of his surface gentility, just as the movements of his 'cruel body' show under the 'effeminate swank' of his riding clothes. At that first dinner Daisy displays a finger he has bruised in some domestic tussle; he breaks Myrtle Wilson's nose with a singularly efficient application of force; and he takes a vindictive pleasure at the end in setting Wilson on Gatsby.

Tom's style of physical dominance, his capacity for exerting leverage, are not expressions merely of his individual strength but of the power of a class. Fitzgerald does not make the mistake of imagining that because the rich are corrupt, they must necessarily be weak. That fallacy was to be a part of the sentimentality of the 1930s—as we see in *The Grapes of Wrath*, where the rich appear as impotent, scared little men hiding behind barbed wire and hired guns. Tom Buchanan is a far truer representative: he draws on the sense of self-assurance his money and position give him as directly as he draws upon his bank account. The consciousness that, in contrast to himself, Gatsby is 'Mr. Nobody from nowhere', gives him a decisive psychological advantage in their struggle over Daisy.

The rich have subtler styles of dominance than the brute power of Tom's money or of his pampered athletic body. One of these appears in the behaviour of Jordan Baker when Nick first sees her stretched out at full length on the sofa in the Buchanans' drawing room. She takes no apparent notice of his entrance, but maintains a pose of complete self-absorption as if she were balancing some object on her chin. Far from resenting her discourtesy, Nick feels almost obliged to apologize for having interrupted her. After he and Daisy have chatted for a few moments, Daisy introduces Jordan to him:

> . . . Miss Baker's lips fluttered, she nodded at me almost imperceptibly, and then tipped her head back again—the object she was balancing had obviously tottered a little and given her something of a fright. Again a sort of apology arose to my lips. Almost any exhibition of complete self-sufficiency draws a stunned tribute from me.[10]

This was the quality Fitzgerald had been trying to isolate in the character of Dick Humbird in *This Side of Paradise*. By the time he wrote *The Great Gatsby*, he had learnt enough about the novel of manners to be able to make such subtle notations with complete success. In terms of dramatic conflict, these are the forces which defeat Gatsby, although clearly there are self-destructive potentialities in his own romanticism.

By the end of his first dinner party at the Buchanans', Nick Carraway is already disillusioned with the American rich. He is forced unwillingly to observe the violent contrast between their opportunities—what is implied by the gracious surface of their existence—and the seamy underside which is its reality. In the Buchanans—and in Nick's reactions to them—we see once more how completely the American upper class has failed to become an aristocracy. Nick's disappointment is so sudden and complete that the episode has an effect of comic anti-climax. The chapter ends, however, not with his small disappointment but with Gatsby's first appearance. Gatsby is still totally committed to his dream: he stretches out his arms in a great yearning gesture, across the dark waters of the bay towards the green light at the end of Daisy's dock. He never discovers how he has been betrayed by the class he has idealized, and, for him, the failure of the rich has disastrous consequences.

Gatsby's unique quality is his capacity to dream—

> ... some heightened sensitivity to the promises of life, as if he were related to one of those intricate machines that register earthquakes ten thousand miles away ... an extraordinary gift for hope, a romantic readiness such as I have not found in any other person and which it is not likely I shall ever find again.[11]

His tragedy lies in the impact of reality upon his dreams: neither the circumstances of his own life, nor the pseudo-aristocratic style of the American rich to which he aspires, offer him anything 'commensurate with his capacity for wonder'. Most of the ironies of his situation arise from the balancing of illusion against reality. The clearest, though by no means the most important, of the ways by which Fitzgerald gives poetic substance to this duality is that of creating two settings with strongly contrasted atmospheres. The glittering palaces on Long Island Sound are set against the ash-heaps on the outskirts of New York. Gatsby's dreams are concentrated upon the former; the sordid realities which shatter his illusions and destroy his life lurk among the latter. Among the ashes, in or near Wilson's garage, Tom's rottenness and Daisy's cowardice are fully revealed; while Wilson himself, the ash-grey phantom gliding on Gatsby's track, is a singularly appropriate instrument for murder—there is after all nothing more dangerous than the hatred of the mean-spirited.

The ironic relation between illusion and reality in Gatsby's situation is conveyed most interestingly, however, by the actual language of the novel. Fitzgerald takes some of his own most vicious forms of writing—his journalistic chatter, his false rhetoric, and the cheap style of his poorest magazine fiction— and turns them into something which is artistically satisfying. It is a strange process of transmutation, by which styles that seem fitted only for crude and vulgar sentiments are, para- doxically, made to carry subtle shades of meaning and emotion. The bad writing produced with uncritical facility in the inferior pieces is here employed with conscious and elaborate artistry. An obvious and highly successful example is the list of 'the names of those who came to Gatsby's house that summer' at the beginning of Chapter IV. This is, among other things, a parody of the style of the gossip columns—of the cheap journalistic tone Fitzgerald could slip into all too easily himself. But it is more than a parody, or a mere compilation of those funny names which are a consequence of the diverse origins of Americans. It is a poetic composition (critics have often pointed to a similarity with T. S. Eliot's use of proper names in 'Gerontion') which gives expression to the social chaos of the Jazz Age. The names and scraps of rumour are interwoven to show how people are being hurried indiscriminately together in the frenetic pursuit of money and pleasure—the wealthy, the criminal, the disreputable, the pretentious, the showy and frivolous, the rootless and the abandoned—even the respectable. The whiff of violence is in the air, and the presence of disaster is never far away. This is the foul dust that floated in the wake of Gatsby's dreams— the motley crowd that flock to the glittering and lavish enter- tainments he conceives at West Egg.

Fitzgerald takes this kind of writing farthest in his treat- ment of Gatsby's love for Daisy. Gatsby's taste in language is as flashy and overblown as his taste in cars or clothes: when he talks about his feelings to Nick Carraway, the words he uses retain echoes from many cheap and vulgar styles.

Fitzgerald is able to catch these inflections in Gatsby's voice, and yet give to the paltry phrases vibrations they never had before.

*   *   *

Gatsby's feelings for Daisy, the moment he tries to define them, become the banal stereotypes of romantic magazine fiction, and so it is fitting that the language he uses should be vitiated by worn-out images and sentimental clichés. Fitzgerald indeed states this quite explicitly in the scene in which Gatsby drives Nick Carraway to New York, and tells him the story of his life. Gatsby recounts the autobiography he would like to have had—the wealthy family in the Middle West; the Oxford education; the grand tour—

> 'After that I lived like a young rajah in all the capitals of Europe—Paris, Venice, Rome—collecting jewels, chiefly rubies, hunting big game, painting a little, things for myself only, and trying to forget something very sad that had happened to me long ago.'
> With an effort I managed to restrain my incredulous laughter. The very phrases were worn so threadbare that they evoked no image except that of a turbaned 'character' leaking sawdust at every pore as he pursued a tiger through the Bois de Boulogne.[12]

The tale concludes with the amazing heroism of Gatsby's war service: 'Every Allied government gave me a decoration—even Montenegro, little Montenegro down on the Adriatic Sea.' 'It was', Nick comments 'like skimming hastily through a dozen magazines.'

Nick has just dismissed him as an extravagant imposter, a liar on the grand scale, when there is an astonishing volte-face: Gatsby produces the Montenegrin medal and a photograph of himself with a cricket bat (superb authenticating touch!) at Oxford. Nick veers to the other extreme—'Then it was all true': he pictures Gatsby, surrounded by tiger skins, in a palace on the Grand Canal, gazing into a chest of rubies to find relief from the 'gnawings of his broken heart'.

It is not 'all true', of course, nor is it all imposture: it is a question of language, a question of images. From one point of view, it is of the essence of Gatsby's greatness that he can make these threadbare phrases and magazine stereotypes the vehicle for his stupendous capacity for wonder and imaginative response, in the same way as much of Fitzgerald's greatness in this novel lies in his ability to transmute a bad style into great art. From another angle, however, it is Gatsby's tragedy that the purest element of truth in his life-story should be conveyed in the most false and sentimental of his words: 'trying to forget something very sad that had happened to me long ago'. The fusion of wonder and vulgarity is caught with superlative tact again and again in the novel.

We find an illuminating parallel to Gatsby's case in the greatest of all novels about the romantic sensibility—*Madame Bovary*. It is interesting to note that *Madame Bovary* had been much in Fitzgerald's mind during the period when he was writing *The Great Gatsby*. In an article which was syndicated to a number of newspapers, he listed what he considered to be the ten greatest novels ever written, and among these *Nostromo*, *Vanity Fair*, and *Madame Bovary* are singled out for special emphasis.[13] When he wrote to Maxwell Perkins about last minute revisions he was making to the text of *Gatsby*, he warned him that the proof 'will be one of the most expensive affairs since *Madame Bovary*'.[14] Flaubert's heroine shows the same capacity for wonder, the same restriction to banal images, and the same failure to find speech that can match the intensity of her feelings, as Gatsby does.

*   *   *

Emma Bovary is condemned to express herself in the enfeebled phrases of early nineteenth-century sentimental fiction, just as Gatsby uses the debased coinage of the magazines. In their predicament, both Fitzgerald and Flaubert show an awareness not only of the problems of the romantic sensibility, but, more specifically, of the agonies of the romantic artist—a sense that the artist himself is foredoomed to defeat whenever he tries to put his inexpressible visions into words. It has always been recognized that *The Great Gatsby* gives a wonderfully intimate picture of American manners in the 1920s, and that it is a profound exploration of the nature of American civilization, but no one has fully grasped the extent to which it is the great modern novel of romantic experience. In the entire history of the novel, only Flaubert has gone as deeply into the dangers and despairs of romanticism, and only Stendhal has seen as much of the comedy.

Gatsby himself is not an artist, however—unless one regards his parties as in some sense works of art—and he is certainly not aware that the language he uses is vulgar and ridiculous. For him, the most destructive aspect of romantic experience lies in a somewhat different direction: he finds that attaining a desired object brings a sense of loss rather than fulfilment. Once his dream loses its general and ideal quality and becomes localized within the confines of actuality, his life seems emptier and poorer. On the afternoon when Daisy first visits his house, they pause at a window to look out across the waters of the Sound, and Gatsby tells her that, but for the rain and mist which obscure the view, they would be able to see the end of her dock where the green light burns every night. Daisy takes his words as a movement of tenderness, and puts her arm through his, but Gatsby is far away—lost in what he has just said. His sense that the green light is no longer the central image in a great dream but only a green light at the end of a dock, is momentarily stronger than his response to Daisy herself touching him with her hand: 'His count of enchanted objects had diminished by one.'

This feeling is made still more explicit in the conversation in which Gatsby tells Nick how he first kissed Daisy. Gatsby has made a decisive choice—from this point onwards all his capacity for wonder is concentrated upon her. Even if she were far more remarkable than she is, she could not possibly measure up to such fabulous expectations, and the affair must inevitably end in some personal disaster for Gatsby. It is only because of their five-year separation that the catastrophe is delayed for so long—in Daisy's absence, Gatsby is able to dream and idealize once more without having to subject his visions to the test of actuality. Once he is reunited with her, ruin comes almost immediately: her personal weaknesses and the inadequacies of the way of life she represents only serve to aggravate the self-destructive tendencies of Gatsby's own romanticism. This passage also raises once again, in a most interesting way, the question of language and the romantic sensibility. Nick Carraway, in the paragraph which follows it, comments explicitly on the way Gatsby talks, and on the difficulties he himself experiences in finding words for what Gatsby is trying to say:

> Through all he said, even through his appalling sentimentality, I was reminded of something—an elusive rhythm, a fragment of lost words that I had heard somewhere a long time ago. For a moment a phrase tried to take shape in my mouth and my lips parted like a dumb man's, as though there was more struggling upon them than a wisp of startled air. But they made no sound, and what I had almost remembered was incommunicable forever.[15]

The sober precision of Nick's account of his own difficulties with language makes a marvellous contrast with the turgid unrestraint, the 'appalling sentimentality', of the images which evoke Gatsby's first kiss. This seems to me to be the clearest evidence in the novel that the ironic use of bad writing in *The Great Gatsby* is the result of conscious artistry on Fitzgerald's part.

Gatsby's ruin is accomplished in a single afternoon, in the stifling hotel room in New York where he and Tom struggle for possession of Daisy, with Nick and Jordan as unwilling bystanders. The ease of Tom's victory shows the extent to which Gatsby's identity is an insubstantial fabric of illusions. There is no occasion on which Tom appears to greater disadvantage: his homilies on the sanctity of family life are as absurd as they are hypocritical; his manner towards Gatsby is crassly snobbish, towards Daisy disgustingly maudlin. He does not have the least conception of what exists between Gatsby and Daisy, nor the smallest understanding of the former's complex inner life, and yet he blunders, as unerringly as if he knew exactly what he was doing, into the area where Gatsby is most vulnerable. Through his crude accusations, he presents Gatsby, as if in a distorting mirror, with a picture of himself which is unfamiliar and yet horribly real. Tom forces him to realize that he does not necessarily appear to others in the forms which he assumes in his own magnificent conception of himself: to settled respectable people, perhaps even to a 'nice girl' like Daisy, he is simply a vulgar *arriviste*, a bootlegger, a cheap swindler, the associate of crooks and gambling operators like Meyer Wolfsheim. Gatsby cannot survive this attack, clumsy as it is. The identity he has constructed for himself out of dreams and illusions, banal images and sentimental clichés, is so fragile that it disintegrates at a touch: ' "Jay Gatsby" had broken up like glass against Tom's hard malice, and the long secret extravaganza was played out.'[16]

After this, his dream of Daisy too begins to recede: while he watches her bedroom window all night from the grounds of her house, she seems to be moving steadily away from him; and when she fails to telephone him the next day, he is at last compelled to relinquish 'the old warm world' which he has inhabited for so long. In these final moments of his life, he is forced to contemplate 'a new world, material without being real', a world in which the loss of his dream changes the very quality of his perceptions. The common objects which surround him—sky, leaves, grass and flowers—come to seem unfamiliar, frightening, grotesque.

The core of Gatsby's tragedy is not only that he lived by dreams, but that the woman and the class and the way of life of which he dreamed—that life of the rich which the novel so ruthlessly exposes—fell so far short of the scope of his imagination. Daisy is a trivial, callous, cowardly woman who may dream a little herself but who will not let her dreams, or such unpleasant realities as running over Myrtle Wilson, disturb her comfort. That Gatsby should have dreamt of her, given his marvellous parties for her, is the special edge to his fate. Fitzgerald shows Gatsby watching over Daisy from the grounds of her house, on the night of the accident, imagining that she might still come to him, and that he is protecting her from her brutal husband. Meanwhile, Tom and Daisy are sitting comfortably in their kitchen over fried chicken and bottled ale, coming to a working arrangement for their future lives. There is a banal and shabby intimacy about their marriage, it is a realistic, if worthless, practical arrangement that suits their shallow personalities. Outside, in the night, stands Gatsby, the man of tremendous and unconquerable illusions, 'watching over nothing'.

By the close of the novel, Fitzgerald has completed his immensely difficult task of convincing us that Gatsby's capacity for illusion is poignant and heroic, in spite of the banality of his aspirations and the worthlessness of the objects of his dreams. The poignancy is conveyed through one incident in particular— that of the car which drives up to Gatsby's house one night long after he is dead. 'Probably it was some final guest, who had been away at the ends of the earth and didn't know that the party was over.' The heroic quality is there in his vigil in the garden, in the scale of his entertainments, the determination behind his criminality.

In the closing paragraphs of the novel there is a sudden enlargement of the theme—a vision of America as the continent of lost innocence and lost illusions. The Dutch sailors who first came to Long Island had an unspoilt continent before them, something 'commensurate with their capacity for wonder'. Gatsby's greatness was to have retained a sense of wonder as deep as the sailors' on that first landfall. His tragedy was to have had, not a continent to wonder at, but only the green light at the end of Daisy's dock, and the triviality of Daisy herself. The evolution of such triviality was his particular tragedy, and the tragedy of America.

NOTES

1. This essay is taken from Brian Way, *Fitzgerald and the Art of Social Fiction* (London: Edward Arnold, 1980). Copyright the estate of Brian Way, 1980.

2. Henry James, *The Art of the Novel*, edited by R. P. Blackmur (New York, 1934), p. 109.

3. Ibid., p. 110.   4. Ibid., pp. 110–11.

5. P. 243. The extensive quotations from *The Great Gatsby* in this essay are reprinted with permission of The Bodley Head from THE BODLEY HEAD SCOTT FITZGERALD, Vol. 1. Permission has also been received from Charles Scribner's Sons.

6. Ibid., p. 201.

7. Ibid., p. 129.   10. Ibid., pp. 131–32.

8. Ibid., p. 131.   11. Ibid., p. 126.

9. Ibid.   12. Ibid., p. 176.

13. Arthur Mizener, *The Far Side of Paradise* (Boston, 1951), p. 336.

14. *The Letters of F. Scott Fitzgerald*, edited by Andrew Turnbull (London: Bodley Head, 1964), p. 172.

15. *Gatsby*, p. 213.   16. Ibid., p. 242.

10

From Oxford: The Novels of William Faulkner

by RICHARD GRAY

William Faulkner was born, brought up, and spent most of his life in the American South, a region which he claimed he could simultaneously love and hate—and which, he declared in later years, 'I will still defend . . . even if I hate it.'[1] Just what he felt he might be defending was not always clear. 'In the South,' Faulkner said once in an interview, 'there is still a common acceptance of the world, a common view of life, a common morality.' Unfortunately, he did not go on to say what he thought that morality was. Or, again, in *Intruder in the Dust* Gavin Stevens declaims (on behalf of Southerners faced with the possibility of enforced desegregation),

> We are defending not actually our politics or beliefs or even our way of life, but simply our homogeneity. . . . only from homogeneity comes anything of a people or for a people of durable and lasting value.[3]

That still left the question unanswered, however. If, as Faulkner appeared to believe, a region or community is 'the indigenous dream of any given collection of men having something in common, be it only geography and climate',[4] then what exactly was the dream that had given his own homeplace identity? And in what ways, more specifically, was he himself not only from but of the South?

165

Tell me about the South [says Shreve in *Absalom, Absalom!*]
*What's it like there. What do they do there. Why
do they live there. Why do they live at all.*[5]

In a sense, Faulkner never stopped 'telling', since the Yoknapatawpha novels as a whole constitute an imaginative
recovery of the South, an attempt to know it as a region. These
novels not only tell, however, they show: much of their power
derives from the fact that, in drawing us a map of his imaginary
county, Faulkner is also charting his own spiritual geography.
The dreams and obsessions which so startle and fascinate
Shreve are his, the novelist's, and not just an aspect of
described behaviour. They profoundly affect his fiction, feed-
ing into the substance of each narrative: so that when, for
instance, Quentin Compson is described in *Absalom, Absalom!*
as 'a barracks filled with stubborn backlooking ghosts'[6] the
reader feels that the description could equally well apply to the
story itself—and to Faulkner, the master storyteller, as well as
Quentin, his apprentice.

What are the dreams and obsessions that help shape the
novels in this way? What intrigues Shreve, the Canadian, and
compels Gavin Stevens to see the South as a homogeneous
place? Perhaps the first thing that strikes anyone new to the
South, Southern writing, or indeed to Faulkner, is simply that:
the sense of place which hovers behind the remarks of Shreve,
Stevens, and their creator—because that sense is so strong,
obvious even to the outsider, and in certain ways quite unusual,
even strange. As one fairly minor Southern writer has put it,
'More than any other people of the world, the Southerners have
that where-do-you-come-from sense'[7]; and, with a few qualifications, one would have to agree. The environment seems to
be as much a part of the Southern character as any moral,
emotional, or intellectual quality is: so much so, in fact, that
W. J. Cash in *The Mind of the South* comes close to making the
environment—and the sultry, stormy climate that goes with
it—actively responsible for the character. One need not go as
far as this, however, in order to see that for Southerners a sense
of belonging to what Faulkner called a 'little postage stamp of
native soil'[8] is absolutely essential, if only because (to quote
another Southern writer, Eudora Welty) *'feelings* are bound up

in place. . . . It is by knowing where you started that you grow able to judge where you are.'[9]

To some extent, this sense of place is a widespread characteristic, to be found—if one looks only at the literature of the past hundred years—in writers as otherwise different as Hardy and Joyce, Yeats and Lawrence. And yet there is a difference, I think, between the notion of place that characterizes most Southern books, including Faulkner's, and the notion of place as it reveals itself in other writing. In English fiction, for instance in a novel like *Tess of the D'Urbervilles*, the place, wherever it may be, seems to be already established and identified, a prepared landscape structured by countless previous activities and perceptions; it is there, the impression is, for the writer to record and for the characters to enter and be defined by. In Southern writing, by comparison, there is a far more conscious, more open and deliberate sense of the landscape being structured: tamed by the particular eye that confronts it, given shape and substance by the particular imagination that comes to grapple with it in the text. So, in *Absalom, Absalom!* the landscape of Sutpen's Hundred is made by the major characters and narrators, imaginatively and sometimes also literally; each of them creates a place that gives their inner lives geographical location, a local habitation and a name. Equally, the people Faulkner describes in the inter-chapters of *Requiem for a Nun* seem to will Jefferson into being: in order, like the girl who scratches her name on a window-pane in the town jail, to leave some 'fragile and indelible' evidence of themselves on the physical universe—something that says, '*Listen, stranger: this was myself: this was I.*'[10]

Character, narrator, and also the author: in scenes like the one, say, that opens *Light in August*, a sense of place seems to be created by the seeing eye of the writer—as he observes the land over which Lena Grove travels and gradually attaches to it the notions of ceremony and permanence. Like the setting on the banks of the Mississippi River in John Crowe Ransom's poem, 'Antique Harvesters', what appeared at first anonymous and meagre assumes a heroic significance. The calculated and, to some extent, 'high profile' language is partly responsible for this: the mules pulling the wagon on which Lena rides, for instance, are said to 'plod in steady and unflagging hypnosis'

167

while Lena herself is compared to 'something moving forever and without progress across an urn.' But just as important is the emphasis Faulkner puts on the active perception and, in effect, reinvention of this scene. Watching the wagon, we are told,

> . . . the eye loses it as sight and sense drowsily merge and blend, like the road itself, with all the peaceful and monotonous changes between darkness and day, like already measured thread being rewound onto a spool. So that at last, as though out of some trivial and unimportant region beyond even distance, the sound of it seems to come slow and terrific and without meaning as though it were a ghost travelling a half mile ahead of its own shape.[11]

Here, as elsewhere in his landscapes, Faulkner seems to be inhabiting a space that would otherwise be empty: clearing a wilderness, in his own way, and filling 'a kind of vacuum'—as Shreve describes the South, at one point, in *Absalom, Absalom!*—with solidity and spiritual presence.

Of course, this difference as far as the sense of place is concerned between Faulkner and someone like Hardy is partly a matter of impression and degree. Ultimately, Hardy is just as much making a landscape by writing about it as Faulkner is. But in Hardy's work, I think, the language refers us to something that is supposed to be objectively there, more or less in its entirety, its essential patterns established and requiring only a frame: in the Yoknapatawpha novels the writer is very much more his own explorer and topographer. Place is far more ambiguous and fluid because, like the settings in many of Wallace Stevens's poems, it is clearly and indeed sometimes ostentatiously (thanks to the obtrusively figurative, oratorical idiom) the product of an interchange between language and environment, the mind and its surroundings. It is constantly created and then re-created out of a feeling of personal need.

This is also the case with that sense of the past for which Southern writers, and again most notably Faulkner, are famous. Southern literature is, as Allen Tate put it once, 'a literature conscious of the past in the present'.[13] At first sight, that may not make it seem very different from other literature: an awareness of history is not, after all, a Southern monopoly—nor was it a Southerner who said that those who forget the past are condemned to repeat it all the time. Here, however, as with the sense of place, there is a difference between Southern and most other writing, because in Southern books memories are nurtured in a way that can only be described as heroic; yesterday is much more of a living and even obtrusive presence, much more available to recreation and change. Just as, in a way, many earlier Southerners tried to involve themselves with a tradition by consciously imitating the manners and habits of an inherited aristocracy—by living as one of them, William Byrd of Westover, put it, 'like . . . the patriarchs'[14]—so modern Southern writers have tried actively to reconstruct the past, to make a tolerable inheritance for themselves. Even more important, they have made the actual attempt to do this one of their leading subjects.

Not that every involvement with the past in the Yoknapatawpha novels takes this deliberate form: Old 'Colonel' Bayard Sartoris is introduced to us, in *Flags in the Dust*, as a man haunted whether he likes it or not, while some of the characters in *Sanctuary* and *Light in August* appear to behave like sleepwalkers, so tied to another time that they can hardly begin to function. For such people, the phrase associated with Joe Christmas in *Light in August* might serve as an appropriate epitaph—'Memory believes before knowing remembers'[15]—since they rarely seem aware that their minds have been shaped by ghosts. These characters are counterpointed, however, by others who are consciously trying to recollect and reinterpret the past: like the Southern boys described by Gavin Stevens in *Intruder in the Dust*, for whom 'yesterday won't be over until tomorrow'[16] and who feel, consequently, that it can be changed—not merely remembered but reinvented.

It is an indication, perhaps, of just how deeply embedded in Faulkner's work this idea of actively recovering the past is that it is adumbrated in his very first novel. At the centre of *Soldier's Pay* is Donald Mahon, a living corpse, badly wounded in the First World War, who has been cut off from his past by the loss of memory. He appears to be in a state of suspension, waiting for something as one of the characters observes,

> Something he has begun, but not completed, something he has carried over from his former life that he does not remember consciously.[17]

Just what that something is eventually becomes clear: towards the end of the novel Mahon remembers in detail the day on which he was wounded, and then he dies. His past has been reimagined, apparently, and since it has he can have a present; the story has been recovered, re-told, and can now be ended.

A comparable but infinitely more complicated process occurs in *Absalom, Absalom!* where character after character appears to be reinventing the past in order to create a sense of identity. A narrative that links yesterday to today is something that people like Quentin Compson and Shreve clearly yearn for, as they work together,

> creating . . . out of the rag-tag and bob-ends of old tales and talking, people who perhaps had never existed at all anywhere, who, shadows, were shadows not of flesh and blood which had lived and died but shadows in turn of what were . . . shades too, quiet as the visible murmur of their vaporizing breath.[18]

With the past as with place, the reality seems to be a kind of vacuum which the observer must populate with his own imagined inhabitants; or, if not that exactly, it is at any rate an uncharted territory containing a few clues, one or two hints and guesses, to tease even the least curious or speculative of minds. The speculations, as several critics have pointed out,[19] are the author's and reader's as well as the characters': Faulkner throws himself furiously into the process of reconstructing the Sutpen story, and the reader is so required to fill in the gaps, compare versions, and discover inconsistencies that he too becomes a historian and storyteller, actively engaged in reimagining the past. Nor is this process confined to the one novel. 'I am telling the same story over and over,' Faulkner admitted once, 'which is myself and the world.'[20] The entire Yoknapatawpha series—with its recurring characters, its repetition and revision of familiar stories, and its gradual accumulation of incident—ends up by offering us a microcosm of history in which 'nothing ever happens once and is finished'[21] either for the author or for the reader.

Quite often, one consequence of emphasizing and exploring past experience is a radical sense of human limitations. People, seen in terms of what they have done rather than what they might do, seem no longer free and perfectible but deeply flawed, weighed down by the burden of inherited failure. This, it seems, is what has happened in Southern thought and writing: a preoccupation with the past (and, of course, the fact that the South has had to suffer failure, defeat, and humiliation) has encouraged Southerners to believe that, to quote one of them, 'evil . . . is the common lot of the race.'[22] More particularly, it has prompted Southern authors to replace the Adamic hero of American legend with characters who dramatize, express, or explore the idea that 'Man is conceived in sin and born in corruption and he passeth from the stink of the didie to the stench of the shroud.'[23] Of course, outside of the American context this would not be a remarkable notion (the South did not, after all, invent the idea of Original Sin) were it not for the fact that it is usually associated with one thing in particular—the potent, if often shadowy, figure of the black. For the black brings with him, whether as slave, half-breed, or more simply as a member of an oppressed race, an unnerving reminder of inherited guilt. To the white Southerner he becomes, simply by being there on the scene, an emblem of sin, the reminder of a crime committed not so very long ago by some mythic, communal ancestor.

To the white Southerner, that is, and to the white Southern writer: it is worth emphasizing that writers like Faulkner have had some experience of the guilt they are talking about in their books. That guilt is part of their structure of thought and feeling as Southerners of a particular race, and so it invariably becomes ingrained in the texture of their work. When they come to explore evil, in fact, that exploration becomes a peculiarly self-conscious activity: which is to say self-aware, self-dramatizing, and self-critical. This comes out, I think, in a book like *Go Down, Moses*: when for instance, one of the characters Roth Edmonds feels that he can no longer sleep in the same bed as Henry Beauchamp, the black boy who has been his closest friend and constant companion up until then. There is no specific reason why Roth feels this, Faulkner tells us. It is just that

> one day the old curse of his fathers, the old haughty ancestral pride based not on any value but on an accident of

171

geography, stemmed not from courage and honour but from wrong and shame, descended to him.[24]

In effect, Roth inherits the racial bias and guilt of his ancestors and re-enacts their Original Sin. The fact that he and Henry are related, since they share the same (white) great-great-great grandfather simply compounds the sin: Roth is denying his 'brother' in a double sense, Faulkner implies, and repressing his humanity in a way that must remind the reader of both Thomas and Henry Sutpen. One could go on discussing the further reverberations of this episode: the way in which, for instance, it illustrates Faulkner's tendency to dwell on miscegenation rather than slavery as the repressed myth of the Southern past. What I want to emphasize here, however, is that the power of this incident depends on the fact that it echoes a feeling provoked by the entire narrative. The idea of the black as the bearer of a curse is at once a preoccupation of the various characters, something that helps to give them a definable identity, and part of the mythological framework of the novel in which they appear. We are invited to observe and examine the sense of doom, and we are also made to share it. And this, quite simply, is because it is an obsession of the *writer's*, not just a facet of the behaviour he describes. It is something which, having inherited, he cannot ignore or suppress—and which he is now inviting us to explore.

Self-conscious: it may be an inadequate term, but it is perhaps the best, shorthand way of referring to a certain quality or set of qualities that Faulkner shares with many Southerners, especially Southern writers. The deliberate construction of a landscape, a sense of place; an urgent, dramatized recreation of the past; and the rediscovery, and the very personal and self-critical exploration, of an inherited name for evil—these can all be absorbed into the idea of self-consciousness, as long as that idea is interpreted in a fairly generous fashion. It is perhaps significant, too, that Southern history and literature constantly present us with people who are self-conscious in a more straightforward sense, and whose self-consciousness leads them into a concern with manners, ritual, and self-dramatization. Life, under the pressure of this concern, is transformed into a kind of heroic art or, less grandly, into a carefully controlled game. One thinks, in Southern history, of the sheer theatricality of so many local heroes—in fairly recent times, people like Cotton Ed Smith, Pitchfork Ben Tillman, and Huey Long. Or one thinks of that love of rhetoric, gorgeously contrived, self-aggrandizing speech, which has long been a regional characteristic. As W. J. Cash remarked, rhetoric flourished in the South,

> far beyond even its American average; it early became a passion—and not only a passion but a primary standard of judgement. . . . The greatest man would be the man who could best wield it.[25]

In Southern literature, this same interest in self-dramatization, ceremony and oratory can be found everywhere—for example, in those characters of Caroline Gordon and Eudora Welty who tend to treat life as a game or dance; in that concern with manners and ritual shown equally by John Crowe Ransom and Allen Tate; and in the abundant, apparently inexhaustible language of a writer like Thomas Wolfe.

To some extent, Faulkner's participation in all this is obvious. Of the great modern American novelists he is easily the most rhetorical and *oral*, and the one most interested in the theatrics of living. He shares with many of his characters a love of language that is nothing less than passionate—a love which is registered, among other things, in his long, labyrinthine or elaborately balanced, sentences; his metaphors that startle the reader with their bravado; his sonorous word melodies, his syntactical fluidity, and his startling juxtapositions of image and sound. Coming from a culture of the spoken word, he and people like Gavin Stevens and V. K. Ratliff (*The Hamlet, The Town, The Mansion*) are always willing to spin out a story or repeat a familiar tale, adding colour with the products of their own verbal wit and inventiveness. Both author and characters seem clearly aware, too, that this inventiveness can be applied to living as well as storytelling: which is perhaps why one of the narrators in *Absalom, Absalom!* remembers the protagonist Thomas Sutpen as a kind of actor or dancer, who willed himself into the part of gentleman. Sutpen, we are told,

> was like John L. Sullivan having taught himself painfully and tediously to do the schottische, having drilled and drilled

173

himself in secret, until he . . . believed it no longer necessary to count the music's beat.[26]

Sutpen has his own design; he is the keystone of his own self-appointed drama. In turn, each of those trying to re-tell his story (including, of course, the reader) is firmly placed as someone attempting to write a new play built around his or her individual consciousness.

What all this tends to leave out of account, however, is the sheer slipperiness of Faulkner's attitude to language and just how far his self-consciousness could take him. Certainly, he was not averse to role-playing in the simple sense or even to playing parts himself—the plain farmer was a favourite one in later life just as 'Count Nocount', the careless bohemian, had been in his youth—and he could be as easily seduced by words as Cash's notional Southerner. Even during the period of his greatest work, from about 1929 until 1936, he was not above committing such verbal atrocities as this, in the apparent belief that he was producing powerful rhetoric:

> Now they could cross Grandlieu Street. There was traffic in it now; to crash and clang of light and bell, trolley and automobile crashed and glared across the intersection, rushing in a light kerb-channelled spindrift of tortured and draggled serpentine and trodden confetti pending the dawn's white wings—spent tinsel dung of Momus' Nile barge clatterfalque.[27]

But most of the time that very self-awareness which prompted him to play roles, or emphasize the theatricality of his characters' behaviour, also made him acutely conscious of the dangers of words and the fictive process—made him suspect, in fact, that they might end up by disguising the subject rather than exposing it. Quite frequently, this distrust of artifice in general and the artificial structures of language in particular is attributed to a woman. 'Women', we are told in Faulkner's first novel, 'know more about words than men ever will. And they know how little they can ever possibly mean.'[28] This is a sentiment echoed by a character in *Mosquitoes* ('They don't care anything about words except as little things to pass the time with'[29]), and either illustrated or expressed by such otherwise diverse figures as Addie Bundren in *As I Lay Dying*, Laverne Schumann in *Pylon*, Charlotte Rittenmeyer in *The*

Wild Palms, and Eula Varner in *The Hamlet* and *The Town*. Even if it is not associated with a woman (occasionally, for instance, Faulkner prefers the silent figure of the sculptor or craftsman), this suspicion that 'words are no good'[30] is invariably there thickening the texture of Faulkner's writing—adding a further dimension of self-consciousness by implicitly questioning the scope and success of his own verbal constructs.

Exactly how this thickening process works can best be indicated by looking briefly at one novel; and perhaps as good an example as any in this respect is offered by *The Sound and the Fury*, the book most intimately related to Faulkner's own experience ('. . . I am Quentin in *The Sound and the Fury*',[31] he once admitted) and the one that remained his favourite throughout his life. At the centre of *The Sound and the Fury* is Caddy Compson. She is its source and inspiration: the book began, Faulkner tells us, with the 'mental picture . . . of the muddy seat of a little girl's drawers in a pear tree where she could see through a window where her grandmother's funeral was taking place'.[32] She is also its subject: 'To me she was the beautiful one,' Faulkner said later,

> she was my heart's darling. That's what I wrote the book about and I used the tools which seemed to me the proper tools to try to tell, try to draw the picture of Caddy.[33]

She could perhaps be seen as the book's ideal audience—that is, if we accept the proposition put forward by a character in *Mosquitoes* that 'every word a writing man writes is put down with the intention of impressing some woman.'[34] It is certainly her story from which Faulkner tries to 'extract some ultimate distillation' by telling it four or five times; and in trying to capture her essence he seems to have experienced an 'emotion definite and physical and yet nebulous'[35] which, at the very least, matches the feelings he attributes to the Compson brothers Quentin and Benjy—in its intensity, that is, its ephemerality, and not least in its sexual connotations.

In short, Caddy Compson is the novel's beginning, middle, and end, the reason why it exists ('I who had never had a sister', he declared, 'and was fated to lose my daughter in infancy, set out to make myself a beautiful and tragic little girl'[36]); and yet she seems somehow to exist apart from it or beyond it, to escape from Faulkner and all the other story-tellers. To some extent, this is because she is the absent presence familiar from many of Faulkner's other novels: a figure like Donald Mahon, say, or Thomas Sutpen who obsesses the other characters but very rarely speaks with his or her own voice. Even more important, though, is the fact that she is female, and so by definition someone who tends to exist for her creator outside the parameters of language: Faulkner has adopted here the archetypal image (for the male imagination, at least) of a woman who is at once mother, sister, daughter, and lover, Eve and Lilith, virgin and whore, to describe what Wallace Stevens once referred to as 'the inconceivable idea of the sun'[37]—that is, the Other, the world outside the Self. And while she is *there* to the extent that she is the focal point, the eventual object of each narrator's meditations, she is *not there* in the sense that she remains elusive, intangible—as transparent as the water, or as invisible as the odours of trees and honeysuckle, with which she is constantly associated. It is as if, just as each narrator tries to focus her in his camera lens, she slips away leaving little more than the memory of her name and image.

Not that Faulkner ever stops trying to bring her into focus—for himself, his narrators, and of course for us. Each section of the book, in fact, represents a different strategy, another attempt to know her. Essentially, the difference in each section is a matter of rhetoric: in the sense that each time the tale is told another language is devised and a different series of relationships between author, narrator, subject and reader. The Jason section, for instance, is marked by a much greater sense of distance than the other sections. Faulkner is clearly out of sympathy with this Compson brother, even if he is amused by him (he once said that Jason was the character of his that he disliked most). Jason, in turn, while clearly obsessed with his sister and her daughter, never claims any intimacy with either of them. And the reader is kept at some remove by the specifically public mode of speech Jason uses, full of swagger, exaggeration, saloon-bar prejudice, and desperate attempts to bolster his image of himself:

Once a bitch always a bitch, what I say . . . .

> I never promise a woman anything nor let her know what
> I'm going to give her. That's the only way to manage them.
> Always keep them guessing. If you can't think of any other
> way to surprise them, give them a bust in the jaw.[38]

By contrast, Faulkner tends to identify with Caddy's oldest
brother, Quentin, to the point where the second section can
become almost impenetrably private. Quentin, for his part,
tries to abolish the distance between Caddy and himself—
although, of course, not being insane he is less successful at this
than Benjy. And he tends sometimes to address the reader like
Jason—or, at least, try to address him—and sometimes like
Benjy to forget him. Whether addressing the reader or not,
however, his language remains intensely claustrophobic:
based not on a logic of the senses as Benjy's is, nor on the
appearance of rational logic as is Jason's, but on a tortuous
and convoluted series of personal associations. The style is
intense and disjointed, ranging between attempts at orderly
narration and uncontrolled stream-of-consciousness: Quentin,
it seems, is always trying to place things within conventional
linguistic structures only to find those structures slide away or
dissolve.

> I found the gasoline in Shreve's room and spread the vest on the
> table, where it would be flat, and opened the gasoline.
> *The first car in town a girl Girl that's what Jason couldn't bear smell of*
> *gasoline making him sick then got madder than ever because a girl Girl*
> *had no sister but Benjamin Benjamin the child of my sorrowful if I'd just*
> *had a mother so I could say Mother Mother*[39]

The disintegration of syntax in passages like this one finds its
analogue, in the second section as a whole, in Quentin's failure
to tell his story in an orderly manner. Quentin cannot quite
subdue the object to the word; equally, he cannot quite
construct a coherent narrative for himself because, in losing
Caddy, he has lost what Henry James would call the 'germ'[40]
of his narrative—the person, that is, who made sense of all the
disparate elements of life for him by providing them with an
emotional centre.

As I have suggested already, Quentin's idiot younger Benjy

is very like Quentin as far as intentions are concerned but quite unlike him in terms of achievement. Benjy, too, wants to ignore the otherness of his sister; for him, however, this leads to very few problems since, according to his own radically limited perception of things, otherness simply does not exist. There is nothing 'out there', as he sees it, everything is merely an extension, an adjunct of his own being. The whole purpose of Benjy's language is, in fact, to deny the irreducible reality and particularity of the objective world and to absorb every experience, each person or thing that confronts him, into a strictly closed and subjective system:

> I opened the gate and they stopped, turning. I was trying to say, and I caught her, trying to say, and she screamed and I was trying to say and trying and the bright shapes began to stop and I tried to get out. I tried to get off of my face, but the bright shapes were going again.[41]

Vocabulary is kept to a minimum; the sentences are simple, declarative, and repetitive; and the presence of an audience of any kind never even begins to be acknowledged. Benjy's 'trying to say' really involves little more than an attempt to simplify by identifying knowing with being—an effort, not to communicate, but to reduce everything to a private code; and, in response to it, the reader is likely to fluctuate between feelings of strangeness or what the formalists call 'defamiliarisation'[42] and a more radical, less pleasurable sense of alienation.

And what of Dilsey, and the final section of the novel? Here, of course, the reader is addressed directly and with consideration, in an attempt to communicate that scrupulously avoids the self-conscious swaggering of Jason's monologue. Caddy, in turn, is recalled with understanding and warmth—but with the acknowledgement that she is a separate person whose separateness needs to be remembered and respected. And Faulkner himself—or, to be more accurate, a third-person narrator who bears a close resemblance to the author[43]— appears for the first time as a distinct voice and a distinctive presence, ready to embrace Dilsey and her point of view even while describing them strictly from the outside. In effect, all the relationships here between author, narrator, subject, and reader are characterized by a combination of sympathy and detachment; while the language carries us into a world where significant contact between quite separate individuals does at least appear to be possible.

> The day dawned bleak and chill, a moving wall of grey light out of the north-east which, instead of dissolving into moisture, seemed to disintegrate into minute and venomous particles, like dust that, when Dilsey opened the door of the cabin and emerged, needled laterally into her flesh, precipitating not so much a moisture as a substance partaking of the quality of thin, not quite congealed oil. She wore a stiff black straw hat perched upon her turban, and a maroon velvet cape with a border of mangy and anonymous fur above a dress of purple silk. . . .[44]

For once, the closed circle of the interior monologue is broken, the sense of the concrete world is firm, the visible outlines of things finely and even harshly etched, the rhythms exact, evocative, and sure. And yet, and yet . . . : here, as in the passage from *Light in August* discussed earlier, the language is intricately figurative, insistently, almost obsessively artificial; and the emphasis throughout is on appearance and impression, on what *seems* to be the case rather than what is. We are still not being told the whole truth, the implication is, there remain limits to what we can know; despite every effort, in fact, even this last section of the novel does not entirely succeed in naming Caddy. So it is not entirely surprising that, like the three Compson brothers, Dilsey (who, as the passage just quoted indicates, tends to dominate this section) is eventually tempted to discard language altogether. In this respect, Quentin's suicide, Benjy's howling, and Jason's moments of impotent, speechless fury find their equivalent in the mindless chant that the Compson's black housekeeper and cook shares with the congregation at the Easter Day service: in ways that are, certainly, very different all four characters place a question mark over their attempts to turn experience into speech by turning aside from words, seeking deliverance and redress in a non-verbal world.

These are only the crudest of distinctions, of course, for there is a great deal more than I have indicated to the rhetoric of *The Sound and the Fury*: but perhaps I have said enough to make the point. At times, Faulkner felt that experience, life 'out there', existed beyond the compass of language: a feeling that would prompt him to claim that all he really liked was '. . . silence. Silence and horses. And trees'.[45] But at other times, he seemed to believe that he could and should try to inscribe his own scratchings on the surface of the earth, that he should at least attempt the impossible and tell Caddy's story, using all the tools—all the different voices and idioms— available to him. As Faulkner himself put it once, 'Sometimes I think of doing what Rimbaud did—yet I will certainly keep on writing as long as I live.'[46] And at all times, no matter what his mood, Faulkner was effectively drawing on his Southern heritage: that self-consciousness, and more specifically that acute sense of both the possibilities and the limits of language, which was part of the 'common view of life' given to him by his region.

It is often said that Faulkner is a modernist writer.[47] In a way, this is undeniable. His is a literature of the edge, marked by a sense of disorientation and experiment, unafraid to explore the fundamentals of expression: as such, it has much in common with, say, the writings of Joyce, Eliot, and Pound, or in other arts with the work of Stravinsky or the post-Impressionists. But it would be wrong to assume that, because of this, Faulkner was not also a literary regionalist or that his regionalism was invariably at odds with his modernism. Sometimes it was, perhaps. More often than not, however, those characteristics which might in another writer be termed specifically modernist were in any case a part of Faulkner's regional inheritance. He did not have to turn to Eliot, for instance, to discover the importance of a tradition: all around him he could find examples of people trying to recreate the past, to forge a valid inheritance for themselves. Nor did he have to refer to Joyce in order to become aware of the fictive process, the difficulties of naming and telling: that awareness was inherent in the Southern preoccupation with artifice, role-playing, and rhetoric. All of this is not to say that Faulkner did not know of writers like Eliot and Joyce, and was not influenced by them. Of course he knew of them—although he was sometimes misleading about the amount he knew—and was affected by them—although perhaps less than is commonly imagined. But it is to say that, for the most part, what Faulkner responded to in those writers, and in modernism generally, were forms of knowledge and speech that he could also find in his regional tradition; what he absorbed from the crisis of his own times tended merely to confirm, comment upon, or develop that dream (to use his own word), that system of inherited argument and metaphor, that was the special gift of the South. 'You know', Faulkner said once in an interview,

> sometimes I think there must be a sort of pollen of ideas floating in the air, which fertilizes similarly minds here and there which have not had direct contact.[48]

For Faulkner, that 'pollen of ideas' was primarily Southern in origin; with its help, he managed to produce fiction that was regional in the best sense—something that could speak from Oxford, Mississippi, and the land he loved and hated to anyone anywhere willing to attend.

NOTES

1. *Faulkner at Nagano*, edited by Robert A. Jelliffe (Tokyo: The Kenkyusha Press, 1956), p. 26.
2. *Lion in the Garden: Interviews with William Faulkner 1926–62*, edited by James B. Meriwether and Michael Millgate (New York: Random House, 1968), p. 72.
3. *Intruder in the Dust* (1948; London, Chatto and Windus, 1949 edition), p. 155. The extensive quotations from Faulkner's work in this essay are reproduced by permission of the Author's Literary Estate, Chatto and Windus Ltd., Curtis Brown, and Random House, Inc.
4. 'An Introduction to *The Sound and the Fury*', edited by James B. Meriwether, *Mississippi Quarterly*, 26 (Summer 1973), 411.
5. *Absalom, Absalom!* (1936; London, Chatto and Windus, 1937 edition), p. 174.
6. Ibid., p. 12.
7. Eugene Walter, *Untidy Pilgrim* (New York, 1954), p. 21.
8. *Lion in the Garden*, p. 255. For Cash's remarks on the Southern environment, see *The Mind of the South* (1941; New York, Vintage Books, 1957 edition), pp. 48–9.
9. 'Place in Fiction', in *Three Papers on Fiction* (Northampton, Mass., 1962), p. 11. For a fuller discussion of the sense of place, see Lewis P. Simpson,

The Dispossessed Garden: Pastoral and History in Southern Literature (Athens, Ga., 1975).

10. *Requiem for a Nun* (1951; London, Chatto and Windus, 1953 edition), p. 231. See also p. 230.
11. *Light in August* (1932; London, Chatto and Windus, 1933 edition), p. 6.
12. P. 361.
13. *Essays of Four Decades* (New York, 1968), p. 545. For a fuller discussion of the sense of the past, see Thomas D. Young, *The Past in the Present: A Thematic Study of Modern Southern Fiction* (Baton Rouge, La., 1981).
14. Letter to Charles Boyle, Earl of Orrery, 5 July 1726, cited in *The London Diary and Other Writings*, edited by Louis B. Wright and Marion Tinling (New York, 1958), p. 37.
15. P. 111.
16. P. 194.
17. *Soldier's Pay* (1926; London, Chatto and Windus, 1930 edition), p. 152.
18. P. 303.
19. See, for example, John T. Irwin, *Doubling and Incest/Repetition and Revenge: A Speculative Reading of Faulkner* (Baltimore, Md., 1975), pp. 20, 157; Estella Schoenberg, *Old Tales and Talking: Quentin Compson in William Faulkner's 'Absalom, Absalom!' and Related Works* (Jackson, Miss., 1977), pp. 135, 140; Joanna V. Creighton, *William Faulkner's Craft of Revision* (Detroit, Mich., 1977), p. 12.
20. Cited in David Minter, *William Faulkner: His Life and Work* (Baltimore, Md., 1980), p. 34.
21. *Absalom, Absalom!*, p. 261.
22. Allen Tate, 'Remarks on the Southern Religion', in *I'll Take My Stand: The South and the Agrarian Tradition* by Twelve Southerners (1930; New York, Harper Torchbooks, 1962 edition), p. 159.
23. Robert Penn Warren, *All the King's Men* (New York, 1942), p. 180. For a fuller discussion of the sense of evil, see C. Van Woodward, *The Burden of Southern History* (Baton Rouge, La., 1966).
24. *Go Down, Moses and Other Stories* (1942; London, Chatto and Windus, 1942 edition), p. 83.
25. *Mind of the South*, p. 53.
26. P. 46.
27. *Pylon* (1935; London, Chatto and Windus, 1935 edition), p. 57.
28. *Soldier's Pay*, p. 252.
29. *Mosquitoes* (1927; London, Chatto and Windus, 1964 edition), p. 96.
30. *As I Lay Dying* (1930; London, Chatto and Windus, 1935 edition), p. 136. Examples of the sculptor or craftsman figure include Gordon in *Mosquitoes* and Cash Bundren in *As I Lay Dying*.
31. Cited in Joseph Blotner, *Faulkner: A Biography* (New York, 1974), p. 1522.
32. *Lion in the Garden*, p. 245.
33. *Faulkner in the University: Class Conferences at the University of Virginia 1957–58*, edited by Frederick L. Gwynn and Joseph L. Blotner (Charlottesville, Va.; University of Virginia Press, 1959), p. 6.
34. P. 208.

35. 'An Introduction to *The Sound and the Fury*', edited by James B. Meriwether, *Southern Review*, 8 (Autumn 1972), 709; 'Introduction to *The Sound and the Fury*', *Mississippi Quarterly*, p. 414.
36. 'Introduction to *The Sound and the Fury*', *Southern Review*, p. 710.
37. *Notes Toward A Supreme Fiction*, 'It Must Be Abstract', poem 1. For a fuller discussion of Caddy, see André Bleikasten, *The Most Splendid Failure: Faulkner's 'The Sound and the Fury'* (Bloomington, Ind., 1976).
38. *The Sound and the Fury* (1929; London, Chatto and Windus, 1931 edition), pp. 179, 192.
39. Ibid., p. 171.
40. See Henry James, *The Art of the Novel*, edited by R. P. Blackmur (New York, 1934), p. 42.
41. *The Sound and the Fury*, p. 64.
42. See the introduction to this volume.
43. The 'implied author', to use Wayne Booth's term in *The Rhetoric of Fiction* (Chicago, 1961).
44. *The Sound and the Fury*, p. 330.
45. *Lion in the Garden*, p. 64.
46. Ibid., p. 71.
47. The tendency to describe Faulkner as a modernist dates back at least as far as 1929. See Winfield Townley Scott's review of *The Sound and the Fury* (Providence *Sunday Journal*, 20 October 1929), in *William Faulkner: The Critical Heritage*, edited by John Bassett (London, 1975). See also Michael Millgate, *The Achievement of William Faulkner* (London, 1965) and Donald M. Kartiganer, *The Fragile Thread: The Meaning of Form in Faulkner's Novels* (Amherst, Mass., 1979) for, respectively, one of the most effective and one of the more recent developments of the same idea.
48. *Lion in the Garden*, pp. 30–1.

11

Ernest Hemingway

by HERBIE BUTTERFIELD

To begin at the beginning of the writing, in the story set first in the first book young Nick Adams witnesses a birth and a death. The birth is exceptionally painful, the Indian woman cut open with a jack-knife by Nick's father and sewn up with fishing line. And the death too is peculiarly dreadful, the husband in the bunk above, listening to the woman in her agony, and cutting his throat.

> 'Why did he kill himself, Daddy?'
> 'I don't know, Nick. He couldn't stand things, I guess.'

Although this is to be the only significant, foreground suicide in all Hemingway's fiction, the terms have been set: 'things' will remain to the last hurtful and terrifying, to be 'stood' with as much dignity and courage as possible: and, of course, of the real world it is eerily prophetic, as, remarkably, all the men in Hemingway's family, doctor-father, famous son, and younger brother, were eventually to die by their own hands.[1] For the moment, though, these things of horror are too much for Nick to dwell on; he must pack them far down in his mind and rest secure in the shelter of God-the-father:

> In the early morning on the lake sitting in the stern of the boat with his father rowing, he felt quite sure that he would never die.

Such are boyhood's good times, not mother and home, but out in the open with father, boating and fishing and hunting, recreating a frontier idyll. So, in the second story, to escape his wife's nervous chatter, Nick's father goes out for a walk.

> He found Nick sitting with his back against a tree, reading.
> 'Your mother wants you to come and see her,' the doctor said.
> 'I want to go with you,' Nick said.
> His father looked down at him.
> 'All right. Come on, then,' his father said.

Soon, when Nick is a little older, in 'The End of Something' and 'The Three-Day Blow', father will be replaced as the companion by Bill, and mother by Marjorie as the girl to be free of. But only the counters have changed, not the game, for, as the title of his next volume of stories, *Men Without Women*, plainly asserts, the best times of all, because the least complicated, the least painful, and the most inwardly tranquil, are had by men or boys together, preferably in some wide space of land or sea, away from the noise and fun and sexuality of cities: Jake, Bill, and Harris fishing at Burguete in *The Sun Also Rises*; the adult Nick and in turn his son in 'Fathers and Sons'; Thomas Hudson and his three sons in *Islands in the Stream*; and from *In Our Time*, further on, in 'Cross-Country Snow' Nick and George skiing in Switzerland one last time before Nick commits himself to the trap of his marriage and fatherhood. 'Once a man's married, he's absolutely bitched' is Bill's whisky wiisdom in 'The Three-Day Blow', bitched by responsibilities, bitched by domesticity, but perhaps most of all bitched by the pain bound in with the love that, some way or other, so easily may be broken or lost. That vaunted hair on the chest originally grew over the thinnest and most sensitive of skins. The major of 'In Another Country', biting back the tears over his dying wife, speaks here most pertinently and poignantly:

> 'A man must not marry. . . . He cannot marry. . . . If he is to lose everything, he should not place himself in a position to lose that. He should not place himself in a position to lose. He should find things he cannot lose.'
> . . . .
> 'But why should he necessarily lose it?'
> 'He'll lose it,' the major said. . . . 'He'll lose it,' he almost shouted.

Yet a man's world, of men without women, though safer from certain kinds of anxiety or threat, is of course only relatively so. A man will lose his wife; but a man will also lose his father, not just in death, but in disillusionment, in de-thronement. Towards the end of *In Our Time* an exemplary father dies, not Nick's, but the jockey, 'My Old Man', with whom, around the race-courses of France and Italy, the young narrator has had such a swell time, and not a mother, not a woman, in sight. When his father falls in a steeplechase and is crushed to death, the son is left to bear not only his grief but also the discovery that his father had been notoriously crooked. More than a life has been lost. As he overhears his father's name being smirched, it 'seems like when they get started, they don't leave a guy nothing.' The stage is set, empty of all save a palpable nothing, for some of the most intense and searing moments of the later fiction.

Indeed, it is from a place now of nothing that, in 'Big Two-Hearted River', the long story that concludes *In Our Time*, Nick starts out, from the site of the burned-out town of Seney in Northern Michigan.

> There was no town, nothing but the rails and the burned-over country. . . . Even the surface had been burned off the ground.

The disaster that has annihilated Seney aptly crowns the world of violence and slaughter, in battle, backstreet, jail, and bullring, revealed in the vignettes that have interleaved the stories of *In Our Time*. Putting that stuff of nightmares behind him, 'everything behind, the need for thinking, the need to write, other needs', Nick heads away from the road for the woods and the river. Far from other human sound, he fishes, pitches his tent, builds a fire, cooks a buckwheat flapjack, brews coffee. 'He was there, in the good place. He was in his home where he had made it.'

It is a familiar American literary moment, this sealing of the solitary compact with nature, marked most famously amongst Hemingway's predecessors by Thoreau, in *Walden* and his other journals and natural histories. Thoreau was a writer who on the face of it would appear to have been unimportant to Hemingway. He is mentioned not at all in the more than 900 pages of *Selected Letters* and elsewhere only once, in *Green Hills of Africa*, where, amidst disparaging comments on other nineteenth-century New Englanders, Hemingway admits that at least

> there is one at that time that is supposed to be really good, Thoreau. I cannot tell you about it because I have not been able to read it. But that means nothing because I cannot read other naturalists unless they are being extremely accurate and not literary.[2]

Some ten years later, according to his biographer, Carlos Baker, he had still got no further than merely intending to read him. However, that he sensed a kinship between himself and Thoreau can be gauged from the fact that in the first draft of 'The Snows of Kilimanjaro' the names he gave to the dying writer, who, simply because he is a writer, is the closest representative in the fiction of Hemingway himself, were the determinedly significant ones of Henry Walden. He soon suppressed the association, but an underlying connection had briefly surfaced.

There were of course immense differences between the times and the lives and personalities of Thoreau and Hemingway. For Thoreau, self-encouragingly, 'the truest account of heaven is the fairest', where Hemingway had early on seen things that permanently disturbed his sleep, so that the dark was full of terrors and empty of God. Conversely, there were compensatory pleasures of the body, of board and bed, that Hemingway joyously rendered, but that Thoreau for whatever reason denied himself; just as, gregarious, amatory, and self-damagingly restless, Hemingway envied Thoreau's capacity for solitude.[3] But at the core, at the still centre, as Hemingway recognized, there was affinity of spirit. In different accents each spoke the language of a radical, isolate individualism that separated them from others, the mass of men leading lives of quiet, or hectic, desperation, and beckoned them towards an unpopulated nature. Each in fundamentally Protestant manner knew that what a man does with his solitariness is the true subject of philosophy. And each to be renewed, to be made whole, went home to nature, to earth and water, to Walden Pond and Big Two-Hearted River.

To be sure, where Thoreau levels a long, steady gaze at

nature, Hemingway, as here with Nick, offers only brief homecomings; where Thoreau evolved into a herbivore, Hemingway remained a predator; and where Thoreau in his narratives has his solitude interrupted by only occasional or chance meetings, Hemingway's fictional world is often densely populated. But the important point is this, that whether the world be as uninhabited as Nick's in 'Big Two-Hearted River', or as crowded as the expatriate caravan of *The Sun Also Rises*, the essential condition of life for Hemingway is solitary, and the interesting, the properly serious business, is the management of that solitude.

Thus, in *The Sun Also Rises*, which was published exactly a year after *In Our Time*, Jake Barnes managerially 'did not care what it was all about. All I wanted to know was how to live in it', the primary characteristic of 'it' being a loneliness that is in fact in the general nature of things, though for Jake it has been given particular immediacy by the war-wound that has deprived him of the possibility of sexual love and comfort. To the problem of how to live in the days there are simple solutions; they can be filled with activity, people, laughter, and one more drink to fend off the night. 'It is awfully easy to be hard-boiled about everything in the daytime, but at night it is another thing.' There, alone, the dark is a place less of pointless yearning than of terror. 'For six months I never slept with the electric light off.' The fear is not of hidden presences, but of emptiness, universal absence, oblivion. It is of course a legacy of the war, for Jake, as it will be for the narrator of the short story, 'Now I Lay Me', who

> had been living for a long time with the knowledge that if I ever shut my eyes in the dark and let myself go, my soul would go out of my body. I had been that way for a long time, ever since I had been blown up at night and felt it go out of me and go off and then come back.

The war as a cause, though, is scarcely important; what matters is the reality of its effect, the knowledge of the fearful loneliness, the 'it' that must be lived in. There are the daytime distractions, which give to the novel such colour and movement; there are the natural world's healing balms (fishing at Burguete, bathing at San Sebastian, re-establishing footholds upon the earth that abideth forever); and for the nominally Catholic Jake there are some very flimsy 'consolations of religion'. But the continuing impression and the final picture (Jake sardonically puncturing Brett's wishful daydream of togetherness) is of a solitariness, that must be borne, coped with, lived in. And this is not just because of Jake's exceptional status, imposed upon him by the misfortunes of war. Other figures, central and peripheral, for whom we feel sympathy, are similarly marked, whether Brett in her loneliness of spirit careless and abandoned, or the Englishman Harris and fat Count Mippipopolous in theirs composed and dignified. Indeed, it is almost a precondition of our sympathy. Only the despised, those outside the circle, those who try too hard or not hard enough, seem not to know of such loneliness.

Jake's enforced apartness from Brett was a state with which in a different form Hemingway himself was recently acquainted, for two months before the novel's publication he and his first wife, Hadley, had separated, soon to divorce; their young son had gone to live with his mother. Though Hemingway was shortly to remarry, loss, separation, and excision remain conspicuous in the fiction of these years. *Men Without Women* (1927) contains the directly autobiographical 'A Canary for One', with its ironically revelatory final sentence: 'We were returning to Paris to set up separate residences.' The emotional alienation of a woman from a man amidst the preparation for an abortion is the subject of 'Hills Like White Elephants', a masterpiece of obliqueness and omission, in which, incidentally, virtually all the awareness of significance rests with the woman and all the clumsy insensitivity and myopic imperceptiveness with the man. Similarly economical in its means, and yet more affecting, is 'In Another Country', in which the Italian major, already importantly disabled by his wound and disbelieving in the efficacy of his treatment, has to endure the further loss of his young wife from pneumonia. The culmination in this context of the sundering of men and women is *A Farewell to Arms* (1929), the war story that after Lieutenant Henry's declaration of 'a separate peace' becomes a love story. In the famous final scene Henry, who has survived a serious injury in battle and escaped an impromptu firing squad, loses his beloved Catherine in the childbirth of a stillborn son. Once more a work of Hemingway's concludes with an image of human solitariness, this time of desolate pathos: 'After a while I went out and left the hospital and walked back to the hotel in the rain.' An American deserter from the Italian army, Henry is islanded in Switzerland, companionless, and now woman-less and childless. In this programme of isolation, this removal of fictive partners and progeny, we may perhaps see a part even for the otherwise eccentric *Torrents of Spring*, which had been published back in 1926 as a parody, rather tedious at this distance, of some of his earliest mentors, chiefly Sherwood Anderson, but also Ford Madox Ford[4] and Gertrude Stein. In being thus lampooned the three older writers are effectively jettisoned as literary parents. In both literary manners and the heart's matters either self-reliance is necessary or solitariness is inevitable.

Hemingway's two studies of human isolation *in extremis*, the one at the cool centre of a void, the other at the stifling moment of death, were composed in the 1930s. The very short 'A Clean, Well-Lighted Place' is the high point of the por-tentously entitled volume, *Winner Take Nothing* (1933). Typically uneventful, it is no more than the story of two waiters in a café late at night waiting for an old man, drunk but impeccably behaved, to go home. The old man has last week tried to kill himself; the younger waiter, with a wife, 'youth, confidence, and a job . . . everything', has no patience with him; his colleague, who lacks 'everything but work', understands why he lingers. Eventually, under pressure, the old man leaves, 'walking unsteadily but with dignity', whereupon the younger waiter is free to hurry home, all eager purpose, and the stage is left to the older. As, very slowly, he shuts up the café, makes his way along the street, stops off absent-mindedly at an otherwise deserted bar, he holds all the while a 'conversation with himself'. From musing upon the compassionate service his own 'clean, well-lighted place' of work provides, he goes on to speak, on the general behalf, almost the definitive word of a man alone, without faith, yet possessed of an essentially religious awareness of God's previous dimensions. His adapta-tion of the Lord's Prayer, though theologically nihilistic, is not ethically so, but rather a register of his own seriousness of spirit.

What did he fear? It was not fear or dread. It was all a nothing and a man was nothing too. It was only that and light was all it needed and a certain cleanness and order. Some lived in it and never felt it but he knew it was all nada. . . .

Our nada who art in nada, nada be thy name. . . . Hail nothing full of nothing, nothing is with thee.

In his room he will lie awake till dawn. 'After all, he said to himself, it is probably only insomnia. Many must have it.' Yes, many; and yes, insomnia; each alone in his own night; but the physical description does not diminish the metaphysical plight. 'All I wanted to know was how to live in it', had said Jake Barnes. The waiter's 'clean, well-lighted place' is a kindness, something that helps people 'to live in it', with dignity.

'The Snows of Kilimanjaro', written some three years later, is a lesson not in living, but in dying. The dying man is a writer on safari in Kenya, whose leg after the most ironically slight of scratches turns gangrenous. On his slow death-bed, self-revealing and self-critical, the writer chastises himself, and indeed his wife, continuously for letting his talent be undermined by success and its effects—riches, oafish company, and too much alcohol; and his memories of all the experiences about which he will now never write permit Hemingway to indulge in those evocative vignettes of which he was always a master. But from first to last it is a story about dying, about facing death, which 'for years . . . had obsessed him', its approach and presence sensed with an almost medieval apprehension: 'He felt death come again. This time there was no rush. It was a puff, as of a wind that makes a candle flicker and a flame go tall', until 'it moved in on him so its weight was all upon his chest, and while it crouched there . . . he could not move.' The story is prefaced with a reference to Mount Kilimanjaro, whose

> western summit is called the Masai 'Ngàje Ngài', the House of God. Close to the western summit there is the dried and frozen carcass of a leopard. No one has explained what the leopard was seeking at that altitude.

It is towards that summit, 'great, high, and unbelievably white in the sun', that in his death-dream the writer flies, aspiring beyond his normal altitude in the realm of nothingness towards the House of God. But whether the House be God's or be deserted, whether the Lord's Prayer name Our Father or Nada, the dialogue is always between a man and, what it has to be called, his soul.

The three full-length novels that Hemingway was still to write all bear witness to what the writer in 'The Snows of Kilimanjaro' had admitted to be his obsession with death. All end or reach their climaxes with the death or impending death of the principal characters, figures as various as a small-time smuggler, an idealistic young guerrilla fighter, and a cynical middle-aged professional soldier. *Across the River and Into the Trees* (1950) closes with Colonel Cantwell, after a night of love and a day of duck-shooting, dying from the heart condition that has tracked and threatened him throughout. Cantwell is a representative Hemingway leading character, even if a rather coarse and unpleasant version, and as such he need not detain us here. The two earlier novels, however, offer the interesting difference of being consciously political in a way that his previous books had not been. *To Have and Have Not* (1937) is an emphatic protest against corruption, exploitation, political hypocrisy, and the immorality of gross inequality; while *For Whom the Bell Tolls* (1941) commemorates three days of a guerrilla action in the Spanish Civil War, on which Hemingway had reported as a passionate adherent of the Loyalist cause. Hemingway's basic politics were consistent with his individualism, which is to say that they were anarchic, libertarian, and humanist. 'I suppose I am an anarchist—but it takes a while to figure out', he had written in 1932 to John Dos Passos.[5] On such grounds, entirely to his credit and in contrast to a notorious number of his literary contemporaries, he had early on laid his unambiguous opposition to Italian Fascism[6] and his immediate hatred of Hitler.[7] But if it was 'natural' for a libertarian individualist to detest totalitarianism, it was not 'natural' for one such to take up left-wing collectivist politics. And it is from the resultant uncertainty as to political identities that the relative failure of *To Have and Have Not* stems. Harry Morgan, named after the pirate Henry Morgan, is precisely piratical, a swashbuckling individualist, given to private criminal enterprise. He dies an appropriate violent, heroic

death. What does not convince, though, what is not in character, is the swansong he utters while dying, the halting knell of
that individualism: 'One man alone ain't got. No man alone
now. No matter how a man alone ain't got no bloody chance.'
The words may fumble towards a historical truth, but they
have been learned in a politics lesson, rather than derived
from Harry Morgan. The character and his incipiently political
message have been separately conceived; and that absence of
conceptual integrity accounts also for the clumsy obtrusive-
ness of the methods whereby elsewhere in the novel injustice is
exposed. Hemingway's sentiments in this context are generous
and admirable; but it did not come easily to him to give those
sentiments a political cast. In fact, in the film made several
years later, Faulkner in his script, Hawks in his direction, and
Bogart in his starring role were between them, in being
unfaithful to *To Have and Have Not*, being more faithful than
Hemingway to himself.

  For Whom the Bell Tolls is a greater work altogether, albeit an
extraordinary combination of the exhilaratingly good and the
embarrassingly bad. Neither for the first time nor for the last it
is in the recreation of love that Hemingway goes astray. In the
depiction of the loss of love that leaves a man bereft he excels;
but in the description of lovers together he is ever liable to an
excessive, distorting sentimentality that infantilizes, demeans,
or renders ridiculous man and woman alike; never more so than
here, with Jordan's and Maria's brief affair.[8] Conversely, as in
A Farewell to Arms nearly all that has to do with war is excellently
done: the characterization of the members of the guerrilla
group; the comradeship, the hatred of enemies, the respect for
enemies, the bravery, the brutality, the self-transcendence, the
self-debasement. There are at least three permanently memorable narrative scenes: Pilar's tale of the murder of the Fascist
civic leaders, El Sordo's last stand on the hill-top, and the
mining and blowing up of the bridge. *For Whom the Bell Tolls* is a
story of men and women in action together, dependent upon
one another, fighting for a common cause; yet here again in its
final picture the light falls not upon that cause, upon history
and politics, but upon two lone individuals, both about to face
their deaths; upon Lieutenant Berrendo, the decent Fascist, 'his
thin face serious and grave', riding into Robert Jordan's range,

and upon Jordan, dying for the cause, yes, but also dying for himself, alone, with courage and honour. Beneath the new political clothes, it is the same man.

We are each of us alone, then, at home in nature when we can find our way there, but amongst others solitary individuals rather than members of a community; alive, we suffer, in body and mind; and, knowing that we will die, we dwell upon death. That is the human condition as it appeared to Hemingway, or as it appeared important to him. The ways he proposed of meeting or managing this fate were various and distinct, so that in different aspects his values may seem, loosely, stoic, heroic, Protestant, or hedonistic. Pleasure, sensuous pleasure—food, drink, and all kinds of physical activity—he conveys with a rare, discriminating vividness, especially in the early writings and in the retrospective *A Moveable Feast* where, aided by his recently rediscovered notes,[9] he shows a quite remarkable ability to recapture poignantly the look, smell and taste of things thirty and more years ago. If it is a world of pain, it is also one of pleasure, of visual beauties and tactile delights that ease our passage.

The North American Protestant in Hemingway, the country-man of Ben Franklin, is nowhere so evident as in his constant stress upon the importance of one's work, increasingly insistent perhaps as the spontaneous will to work diminished. What in *Green Hills of Africa* had been a passing reference to work as 'the only thing that always made you feel good' had become some fifteen years later for Thomas Hudson, in those adventures posthumously published as *Islands in the Stream*, an obsession rivalling that with death. Indeed, perhaps the pleasure too becomes part of this Protestant formation: one works hard so that one may play hard; and then one works hard again. Nevertheless, if work is to a great extent a moral safeguard against the devil's coming upon idle hands, it is also something less Protestant, more aesthetic, more pure, that leads towards the mastery of a craft or the perfection of those skills—of bullfighter, fisherman, hunter, and of writer—described throughout the writing in such attentive, admiring detail.

The principal element, though, in Hemingway's imaginative world, the quality with which in some form or other virtually all his best writing is concerned is courage: simply, courage. If life is intrinsically painful, and the prospect of death omnipresent, the act of living becomes by definition a test of courage. The courage required may be moral, or mental, or physical; it may be passive or active; it may be as ostensibly minimal as bearing it, with or without grinning, or it may be the stuff of awards for gallantry. The active exemplars include the bullfighters, boxers, hunters, soldiers, and guerrilla fighters, men and women: Pedro Romero; Manual Garcia; Jack Brennan; Wilson, the white hunter; Agustin; Pilar. The passive models cover a moral range from those who merely refuse self-deception (the abject William Campbell in 'A Pursuit Race', who knows 'they haven't got a cure for anything') to those who exhibit varying degrees of what Hemingway famously termed 'grace under pressure'. Some are with faith, like the priest in *A Farewell to Arms* or Anselmo who was 'a Christian. Something very rare in Catholic countries'; some without faith, like Count Greffi who 'had always expected to become devout ... but somehow it does not come', and the waiter of 'A Clean, Well-Lighted Place'; but all are seen to bear with grace—it is a matter of courage and a quality of the spirit—the pressures that fate exerts upon them.

The last and longest test of courage, beyond which there was really no need of further testing, was that undergone by the fisherman Santiago in *The Old Man and the Sea*, who after months of failing to catch anything wrestles day-long and night-long with the great marlin, only to have his magnificent fish devoured by sharks. Published in 1952, the long story proves a splendid exception to the otherwise poor or drastically uneven writing that Hemingway was doing at this time; and with its knowledge of mystery and its natural reverence ('Never have I seen a greater, or more beautiful, or a calmer or more noble thing than you, brother') it represents also a marvellous renewal after the morally and imaginatively dull record of competitive killing into which his previous saga of man and beast, *Green Hills of Africa*, had degenerated. *The Old Man and the Sea* is a story of skill, of all kinds of courage, of defeat in the flesh, of victory in the spirit, of pride humbled and self-respect earned, of suffering, and of final great peace of mind. It was the last fiction that he published.

The Old Man and the Sea is not a novel, but a long story, in its texture self-consciously and I think effectively poetic. The point has often been made, in one form or another, that Hemingway was essentially a poet rather than a novelist. Thus Harry Levin once expressed himself of the opinion that

> the qualities and defects of his writing are reconciled, if we merely remember that he was—and still is—a poet, that he is not a novelist by vocation . . . and that he is less concerned with human relations than with his own relationship to the universe—a concern which might have spontaneously flowered into poetry.[10]

And Wallace Stevens even went so far as to remark, admittedly in the casual space of a letter, that 'obviously he is a poet and I should say, offhand, the most significant of living poets, so far as the subject of EXTRAORDINARY ACTUALITY is concerned.'[11] Levin and Stevens may have different types of poet in mind, Levin's being more of a romantic lyrist, Stevens's more of an Imagist, but both perceptions are sharp and useful. Certainly in his attitude to language and the tools of his craft Hemingway was far closer to many poets, especially amongst his contemporaries, than he was to at least the more utilitarian of novelists. What is the famous diatribe against the rhetoric of war in *A Farewell to Arms*[12] but an emotionally charged, morally urgent elaboration upon Pound's Imagist dictate to 'go in fear of abstractions'? What is the lament in *Death in the Afternoon* that 'all our words from loose using have lost their edge'[13] but a sparse precursor of the passage in Eliot's 'Burnt Norton', where words 'slip, slide, perish,/ Decay with imprecision, will not stay in place,/ Will not stay still'? And in a letter to Owen Wister[14] about restoring the power of language what is his insistence that 'as it is spoken it should be written or it dies' but a version of Williams's call for a poetic 'word of mouth language . . . out of the mouths of Polish mothers'? Concentration, understatement, significant omission, antiphonal repetition and variation, austerity, verbal propriety: these are some of the technical devices or aesthetic values that he came to cherish, learned from others (Turgenev, Twain, Crane, and Conrad; Anderson, Stein, Ford, and Pound), but mastered for himself. With such literary priorities and with the priceless gift of his extraordinarily fine senses, especially of sight and taste, he developed an art capable of rendering outer and inner

worlds alike, not with miniscule detail or complexity, but with
startling, lucid simplicity. His achievements with language are
on a par and of a kind with the great modernist poets of his
generation.

In this short essay I have wished to praise Hemingway
rather than to bury him beneath a mound of his defects. For,
assuredly, his art had its limitations from the first; and, furthermore, he did not into middle and later life maintain regular,
assured command of his genius. Something went wrong; he
himself could feel it happening: 'Something happens to our
good writers at a certain age', he wrote in *Green Hills of
Africa*.[15] And as for his personal character, there are aspects,
some of which necessarily affect the art, which are at best
perplexing, at worst very disturbing. I feel bound here only to
acknowledge that he could be alarmingly cruel, and that this
cruelty could find expression not just in sudden, violent out-
bursts, but in betrayal of friendship, shocking ingratitude, and
prolonged meanness of heart, in protracted failure of the grace
he recognized and lauded. *A Moveable Feast*, for instance, is a
book by and large well thought of; it is often lively, brilliantly
clear, and very funny; but I find it fundamentally vitiated,
precisely in the simple terms here observed by his erstwhile
friend, Allen Tate, who incidentally is *not* maligned in the
book:

> I couldn't have known then that he was the complete son of a
> bitch who would later write about certain friends, all of them
> defenselessly dead, in *A Moveable Feast*.[16]

Let me leave that merely as a token of problems that would
have to be tackled in a longer study.

For here there is a simpler task, a happier duty, that of
reaffirming the predominant excellence of his art, and behind
that art the available greatness of spirit and, what is not often
enough said, his sheer intelligence, more vigorous than that of
many another more learned or more wordy. Pleasure and
delight, with the senses keen, he wrote about superbly well;
and their necessary correlatives, pain and grief; and death,
'the unescapable reality, the one thing any man may be sure

of: the only security[17]; and courage, heroism, dignity, nobility, words for qualities and levels of conduct without which life is impoverished and value perishes. Whether he be regarded as a man who knew God was not there, or whether as some sort of intermittently nominal Catholic, or whether as the man who had always 'believed in belief',[18] what is consistent, continual, and enduring in him is the religious man's concern for the soul and its state. He looked life and death in the face.[19]

NOTES

1. It is an extraordinary coincidence that the century's two most celebrated literary suicides, Hemingway and Hart Crane, were born on the same day, 21 July 1899, to mothers whose first name was Grace and to fathers whose first name was Clarence. The brief quotations from Hemingway's fiction in this essay are taken from the English editions published by Jonathan Cape.
2. *Green Hills of Africa* (London: Panther, 1977), p. 25.
3. See Carlos Baker, *Ernest Hemingway: A Life Story* (London: The Literary Guild, 1969), p. 529.
4. Ford is also caricatured in *The Sun Also Rises*, and both he and Stein are mercilessly depicted in *A Moveable Feast*.
5. Carlos Baker (ed.), *Ernest Hemingway: Selected Letters, 1917–1961* (London: Granada, 1981), p. 375.
6. See, for instance, the story 'Che Ti Dice La Patria', in *Men Without Women* of 1927.
7. 'I hate Hitler because he is working for one thing: war.' Letter to his mother-in-law as early as 16 October 1933. See *Selected Letters*, p. 398.
8. The relationship that Hemingway ultimately seems to wish to describe is one of an effectively incestuous closeness between a father and a daughter. For instance, in *Across the River and Into the Trees* Colonel Cantwell is not only more than thirty years older than Renata but also addresses her at times as 'daughter'. Hemingway himself had only sons, but liked to call younger women friends, such as Ava Gardner and Ingrid Bergman, 'daughter'.
9. In 1957, while staying at the Ritz in Paris, he discovered that two trunkfulls of notes had been gathering dust in the basement of the hotel for nearly thirty years. They were to form the basis of *A Moveable Feast*.
10. Harry Levin, 'Observations on the style of Ernest Hemingway', in Robert P. Weeks (ed.), *Hemingway: A Collection of Critical Essays* (Englewood Cliffs, N. J.: Prentice-Hall, 1962), p. 85.
11. Letter to Henry Church of 2 July 1942, in Holly Stevens (ed.), *Letters of Wallace Stevens* (London: Faber, 1966), pp. 411–12.

12. *A Farewell to Arms* (London: Penguin, 1935), pp. 143–44.
13. (London: Panther, 1977 edition), p. 68.
14. *Selected Letters*, op. cit., p. 301.
15. P. 24.
16. Allen Tate, *Memories and Essays* (Cheadle, Cheshire: Carcanet, 1976), p. 60. It was of course a posthumous publication. We are not to know how much Hemingway would have authorized.
17. *Death in the Afternoon*, op. cit., p. 234.
18. Baker, *Ernest Hemingway: A Life Story*, op. cit., p. 639.
19. After a concerted reading and rereading of virtually all Hemingway's published work, I have to admit to the unexciting judgement that conventional contemporary opinion about the relative merits of his work has it just about right. *Torrents of Spring* is of slight local interest to literary historians of the 1920s; *Green Hills of Africa, To Have and Have Not, Across the River and Into the Trees,* and the posthumous *Islands in the Stream,* which did not have his imprimatur, are poor work, though each with its fine moments; *Death in the Afternoon* and *A Moveable Feast* are flawed successes, *For Whom the Bell Tolls* a flawed triumph. The good books, though here again each with defects, for little in life or art is perfect, are *In Our Time,* considered as a loosely integrated sequence, *The Sun Also Rises, A Farewell to Arms,* and *The Old Man and the Sea,* which is almost as good as its immediate enthusiasts acclaimed it to be. He is at his best in the short story of various length, of which a handful of the finest must include: 'The Snows of Kilimanjaro', 'In Another Country', 'Big Two-Hearted River', 'The Short, Happy Life of Francis Macomber', and 'Hills Like White Elephants'. 'A Clean, Well-lighted Place' *is* perfect, a story, a prose-poem for the stage, requiring neither addition nor subtraction nor substitution; an exquisite miniature upon great matter.

12

Richard Wright's Inside Narratives

by A. ROBERT LEE

All my life had shaped me for realism, the naturalism of the modern novel, and I could not read enough of them.
—*Black Boy* (1945)[1]

I picked up a pencil and held it over a sheet of white paper, but my feelings stood in the way of my words. Well, I would wait, day and night, until I knew what I wanted to say. Humbly now, with no vaulting dream of achieving a vast unity, I wanted to try to build a bridge of words between me and the world outside, that world which was so distant and elusive that it seemed unreal.
—*American Hunger* (1977)[2]

1

Both these observations, each without doubt something of a flourish with which to round out his two Volumes of Autobiography, nonetheless serve their purpose well enough: they underscore how momentously Richard Wright regarded his call to a literary career. The first directs us less to the kind of fiction he himself would eventually write than to the liberating shock of recognition he experienced on reading the likes of H. L. Mencken and Theodore Dreiser and others of the first current of American literary realism. For in their different anatomies of America he saw not exactly the mirror of his own life—how could any of them have written with authority of a complex black Southern boyhood lived hard against the colour-line and under the permanent threat of white racist violence?—but human existence depicted as an oppressive power-web able to damage and often consume the individual.

The later observation belongs to Wright's 1930s Depression and Chicago years, the era of his vexed membership of and departure from the American Communist Party which together with his increasing disenchantment with America and subsequent F.B.I. and State Department harassment led on to his permanent European exile in 1947. His sense of elation on opting out of the Party's *dicta*, for all that it had helped him towards what then seemed a credible ideology of racelessness and anti-capitalism, almost exactly parallels the sense of self-possibility he reports in *Black Boy* on leaving the Dixie South for his own northwards migration. To 'build a bridge of words' between himself and America (and worlds beyond), for a veteran of Mississippi-style racial custom and a former C.P.U.S.A. activist, must indeed in the light of that background have seemed an unreal notion. For in claiming the right to use words to his own design Wright not only gave notice of his chosen path as a writer, he also affirmed that he intended nothing less than to take on and beat at its own game the white-run and proprietary world accustomed as if by ancient decree to doing the very defining of reality.

To emphasize Wright's passage into authorship—his belief in writing as a crucial liberative and existential rite—is, I hope, equally to imply a great deal about his fiction itself. For so committed a writer (and committed in a manner distinct from the customary Marxist and Sartrean senses) and for whom from the outset fiction clearly meant more than writing in any one single key, it must have been an irritatingly inadequate praise which on publication of *Native Son* (1940), the novel which most established his name, confidently pronounced him America's first 'Negro protest writer', its 'black Dreiser', the custodial voice of 'black anger'.[3] For though Wright rarely did other than assume a departure-point of deep abiding dissent, a personally endured bitter intimacy with American racial hypocrisies, this kind of phraseology, well-intended or not, ultimately proves unhelpful. It has locked his and a whole tradition of Afro-American writing into too reductive an opposition: white oppression as against black protest, a simplified dialectic in which black and white play out their predictable adversary racial roles. As in the cases of Ralph Ellison and James Baldwin after him, Wright recognized from the start that so easy a version of race and human ways would not take him or his reader very far. Some 'anger' might indeed get ventilated. Black grievances might or might not win a sympathetic hearing, especially where white liberal guilt was involved. But the fiction as such would get rendered down into something akin to. diagrammatic sociology, treatise or sermon rather than worlds taken from life yet transformingly re-imagined. Equally the real complexities of race—its elusive sexual and psychological components, the fine nuance and built-in taboos and patterns of offence and defence—given that Wright as a black writer could hardly not write out of his historic blackness simply would get by-passed.

Yet Wright's grasp of these complexities, and often in truth his own individual complexity, rarely won notice. Throughout the Depression years and even into the 1940s he was regularly taken to reflect the Communist Party view that Marxism pointed a way 'beyond race' and towards the holistic view of history he calls the 'vast unity' in *American Hunger*. Then, during the Eisenhower Tranquil '50s, as an expatriate in Paris and where read at all, he found himself castigated as some kind of literary dissident, an ungrateful black anti-American voice in league with an intellectual class still enamoured of Soviet Russia and unacceptably out of sorts with the nation's taste for the Cold War and its middle-America W.A.S.P. consensus. In turn, in the 1960s, having for years played Dean of the expatriate black colony in Paris, he was claimed by yet another image. The generation raised on Civil Rights and then marches like that into Selma and inner-city explosions and the rhetoric of Malcolm X and the Panthers seized on him as an exemplary spokesman for Black Power, an early standard-bearer of either-or black militancy. In this, too, his name was to be set off against assumedly acquiescent Native Sons like Ellison or Baldwin or pacifist Christian black leadership in the mould of Martin Luther King. None of these accounts, however convenient and understandable for their time, went near to meeting Wright's overall measure.

All of these versions of Wright, furthermore, to one degree or another, persist. His 'bridge of words', despite the massive debate about 'realism' from Zola onwards to today's Derridaism and post-Modern polemic, goes on being referred to some implied generic (or at least Dreiserian) standard of realism/naturalism. Nor has Wright won free of his slightly antiquarian Marxist armature, the mind forged on *New Masses* and 'scientific' history and Afro-America's equivalent of Mike Gold or John Reed. With Black Power and the 1960s came the Black Aesthetic view of Wright, the author of *Native Son* and volumes like *Twelve Million Black Voices* (1941) and *The Color Curtain* (1956) as the voice of a self-referential black culture, a domain of separatist black consciousness and value inaccessible to prying white eyes.[4] But though Wright himself nowhere argued for so exclusive a standard of judgement, the rediscovery in the 1960s of a usable black cultural past did help to relocate his work as a point both of contrast and continuity with the inter-war New Negro and Harlem Renaissance for which Alain Locke's anthology *The New Negro* (1925)[5] served as a manifesto. Even so, rarely did the proponents of the Black Aesthetic adequately confront Wright's own cultural eclecticism, the Southern-born Black Boy to be sure but also the author who acknowledged among other departure-points Heidegger and nineteenth-century European existentialism and a writerly line which lists Poe, Hawthorne, Kafka, Dostoyevsky and Melville among its luminaries. Nor did it meet Wright's many ambivalences about pan-Africanism and global notions of blackness, not to mention his own ambiguous position as a black guest-exile in still colonialist France. These different versions also tend to cross and overlap, one or another part truth taken for the whole. Oddly, the deceptive clarity of Wright's work has played its part here, its ease of access tempting the incautious into too ready a final version both of the man and his writing. For an author, certainly, almost taken by rote to lack the finish of, say, a Hemingway or Fitzgerald, or later an Ellison or Baldwin, Herman Melville's drily sage observation in *Moby-Dick* offers just the right cautionary note: 'I have ever found your plain things the knottiest of all.'[6]

2

Loosening Wright and his fiction from these interconnecting personal and racial myths becomes even more difficult in the light of the role he became called upon to play for other Afro-American writers. First, there has been the question of his 'school', the constellation which includes among its pre-eminent names Chester Himes, Ann Petry and Willard Motley, and at a slightly later remove, figures like William Gardner Smith, John O. Killens and John A. Williams. All of these, however markedly different in interests and manner, somehow have to be thought Wrightian realists, the composite literary voice of a black America writing stock 'Negro protest'. That Wright, for sure, whether during the Chicago and *New Masses* 1930s or as the presiding resident of the Paris black literary colony or as the subsequent Third World apologist, did exert an extraordinary influence does not have to be doubted. His style as a realist, too, obviously did make its impact. But to credit him with some coercive or patriarchal direction over the imagination of writers as insistently self-propelled as Chester Himes or Ann Petry amounts to serious distortion. Himes's relation with Wright, for example, especially as set out in his two-volume autobiography, *The Quality of Hurt* (1972) and *My Life of Absurdity* (1976), pays a far more complicated tribute to his fellow-exile—for like Baldwin he both loved and found himself frequently warring against Wright—than formula allusions to a Wrightian school anywhere near allows.

Wright's relationship with his supposed two principal 'sons', James Baldwin and Ralph Ellison, similarly tells an altogether more freighted story. Baldwin's two well-known essays, 'Many Thousands Gone' (1951) and 'Alas, Poor Richard' (1961), in all their stylish self-disaffiliation from Wright, need to be decoded as an act of the most especial intimacy, a freedom sought as much from Wright's strange hold on the white world's version of American blackness as from Wright himself.[7] Ellison, too, for his part, has given an equally complex account of his relationship with Wright. On the one hand, in 'Richard Wright's Blues' (1945) and his subsequent 'The World and the Jug' (1963), he speaks of simply 'stepping round' Wright, perhaps understandably the remark of the creator of so richly endowed a novel

as *Invisible Man* (1952).[8] Yet just as *Invisible Man* transforms for
its own purposes the many backward glances to Dostoyevsky,
Melville, Poe, Joyce, Malraux and the other figures Ellison has
mentioned in *Shadow and Act* (1964) and in several interviews as
influences (not to mention his echoing of Jazz and black
folklore), so it calls up Richard Wright also and in particular the
most powerful of his short stories, another adroitly subterranean
narrative of identity and revelation, 'The Man Who Lived
Underground' (1945).

The saga of Wright as assumed black literary touchstone
continues most dramatically into the 1960s in Eldridge
Cleaver's *Soul on Ice* (1968) where in 'Notes of a Native Son' he
uses the Wright of *Native Son* as he sees him—'the Richard
Wright [who] reigns supreme for his profound political,
economic, and social reference'—to berate James Baldwin as
the incarnation not only of sexual but political effeminatiza-
tion, ever willingly knee-bent to the white man in a damning
two-way sense. But Cleaver's admiration of Wright as the
tough heterosexual black warrior and condemnation of
Baldwin as castratus and the hater of his own blackness,
however eye-catching, also will not serve as anything like the
whole case. With just cause Cleaver might have been seeking a
mythology suited to the polemical needs of the Black Panther
challenge to America—the call to Afro-Americans to cease
being the compliant and all too literal prisoners of a history
begun in slavery and continued in the nation's ghettos and
penitentiaries—but a mythology indeed is what it was and not
one to capture the full human ambiguity of either Wright or
Baldwin.

From another angle there has been the Wright of John A.
Williams, both the fictive Harry Ames of Wright's major
racial-political thriller, *The Man Who Cried I Am* (1967), the
wise but sacrificial figure whose legacy is offered as one of
necessary total vigilance against destruction from white power
interests, and Wright the subject of a tender biography for
children, *The Most Native of Sons* (1970). Williams's depiction of
Ames as the victim of F.B.I. and C.I.A. machinations working
in some kind of harness with various white-supremacist groups
also points forward to the Wright Addison Gayle has revealed
in *Richard Wright: Ordeal of a Native Son* (1980), a piece of

excavation (however dully written) to complement Michael
Fabre's standard biography, *The Unfinished Quest of Richard
Wright* (1973). By gaining access to most of Wright's Government files under the Freedom of Information and Privacy Acts
of 1966 and 1974 Gayle shows how, in cold sober fact, Wright
did suffer from McCarthyist red-baiting and racist government
officialdom. The rumour still persists, indeed, in some Paris
and black circles, that his death did not come about by natural
causes. Gayle's account also yields another important significance; it was written by a leading Black Aesthetic critic and
assumes a stance towards Wright which suggests that only
another black American with the right 'blackness' of outlook
could understand Wright's place within an America directed
by its white police and Intelligence agencies.

Finally, and if it is not dutifully insisted that he wrote only
unembellished naturalism, the long shadow of Wright can
again be detected in an absolutely contemporary 'post-realist'
body of Afro-American fiction in which realism becomes
phantasmagorical and Bosch-like in its imagining. Among the
best and most symptomatic of this kind of work have to be
Chester Himes's pyrotechnic Coffin Ed/Gravedigger Jones
romans policiers first published in French as part of Gallimard's
Série Noire, in which Harlem becomes both a literal black world
and a magical shadow-territory shot through with violence
and *bizarrerie*. To these should be added the versatile pastiche
fiction of Ishmael Reed beginning from *The Free-Lance Pall-
bearers* (1967), William Melvin Kelley's highly Ellisonian *dem*
(1967), and novels like Hal Bennett's *Lord of the High Places*
(1970), Robert Deane Pharr's *S.R.O.* (1971), Cyrus Colter's
The Hippodrome (1973), and John Wideman's *The Lynchers*
(1973). In this legacy, not one always granted to Wright, the
implicit surreal ingredients of his own fiction become palpably
more central, realism turned inside out, absurdist and often
bitingly macabre and funny.

Given, thus, these extraordinary thickets which have enclosed
Wright and most likely still kept his true self just out of view—
whether the Richard he himself invents in *Black Boy* and
American Hunger (and deftly perpetuates in reportage like *Black
Power* (1954), *The Color Curtain* (1956) and *Pagan Spain* (1957)),
or the veteran of that intimidatory Mississippi and Arkansas

black upbringing, or on the evidence of his contribution to *The God that Failed* (1949) the half-in half-out Chicago Marxist, or the Greenwich Village and New York personality and shock author of *Native Son*, or still later the Paris expatriate and internationalist Third World advocate—it can hardly do harm to concentrate yet more attention on the subtlety of imagination actually at work in the fiction.

It may well be that Wright's fiction can no longer be read clear of his several legends or his impact on almost all subsequent Afro-American writing. Further, the turbulent politics of race, particularly as they evolved through the Civil Rights era and after, would seem to have claimed him as part of a black American pantheon which reaches well beyond things literary. Certainly for anyone still inclined to seek in Wright's fiction the unencumbered story-teller, it has become pretty well impossible not to be conscious of reading one or another 'Richard Wright', most of all the major forebear of contemporary black American literary narrative. In other words, Wright as mythic founder-figure and the giver of black-realist testament has settled like a dense blanket over the fiction, adding yet further layers of complexity to an achievement already in itself hedged with racial and political complication.

3

As Wright himself has been made over into legend, so to a disturbing degree has his fiction been imprisoned inside a set critical vocabulary. This agreed account continues to interpret him in terms of Dreiserian naturalism or Protest, albeit updated in some cases by Addison Gayle and others still anxious to evaluate according to Black Aesthetic writ.[9] Without denying Wright's inclination towards naturalism and the location of his stories within a solid contour of social reality, I want to underline just as much the somewhat different writer he himself hypostasized and nowhere more clearly than in his celebrated preface to *Native Son*, 'How Bigger Was Born'.[10] There, as in essays like 'The Literature of the Negro in the United States',[11] he insists on his equal inclination to see in black history not only a literal past scarred by oppression but a matchingly inward and emblematic drama, one remembered within the collective Afro-American psyche and in Blues and black oral tradition as much as in the punitive outer record of racial gains and defeats. The last paragraph of 'How Bigger Was Born' especially insists on this double inheritance:

> we have in the Negro the embodiment of a past tragic enough to appease the spiritual hunger of even a James; and we have in the oppression of the Negro a shadow athwart our national life dense and heavy enough to satisfy even the gloomy broodings of a Hawthorne. And if Poe were alive, he would not have to invent horror; horror would invent him.

In so claiming James, Hawthorne and Poe as *semblables* (again an essay like 'The Literature of the Negro in the United States' which avers that 'The Negro is America's metaphor' shows how conscious he was of *black* literary tradition), he points precisely to what the half-title of Melville's *Billy Budd* most helpfully calls 'inside narrative', that which for Wright is the inner other story being told under the outward guise of realism.

In this respect, the stories collected in *Uncle Tom's Children* (1938) and *Eight Men* (1961) offer especially useful points of illustration, each at once 'naturalist' yet at the same time parabular and imbued with recognizably deeper memories of racial encounter and phobia. The note I refer to is struck, for instance, in 'Big Boy Leaves Home', the first of the tales in *Uncle Tom's Children*, by the protagonist Big Boy when he says of the events which have left his friends Lester, Buck and Bobo dead and himself a terrified Northwards-bound fugitive from Dixie lynch law: 'It all seemed unreal now.' On the surface the story appears to offer a straight (if highly dramatic) episode of Southern racist violence, the account of four black boys whose swim at a Summer water hole leads on to death and flight. But the story's virtual every detail activates far more ancestral resonances from deep within Southern racial history, the rites whereby black manhood is killed or at least mutilated for its supposed desiring of white womanhood and in which 'the South' as sometimes in William Faulkner's mythical kingdom of Yoknapatawpha becomes both a bucolic river and pine-wood Heaven and a brute Inferno.

Told as a classical five-act sequence, the story opens with

the boys' banter, their snatches of black bawdy and the 'dozens' and the general rough-housing, all of which represent the marks of time spent as adolescence. The landscape of the woods, the 'cleared pasture' and the 'tangled vines' thus serve as actual landscape and as Nature's seeming stamp of approval. At the swimming hole, they encounter the first discord within this Summery boyhood harmony, the sign put up by Ol' Man Harvey, 'NO TRESPASSIN', its frank illiteracy at one with the intrusion of white property-ownership into natural free space. With the arrival of the white woman and her soldier lover, the story calls into play the South's even more familiar racial equation: Big Boy, 'black and naked'; a screaming belle; and the avenging white manfolk with blood on his lips after the first tussle with the gun vowing death to 'you black sonofa-bitch'.

Paradise thereby turns to nightmare, pleasure to pain. Big Boy flees after the death of Harvey's soldier son back to family and community (to the Bluesy chorus of his mother 'This is mo trouble, mo trouble') and then away again into hiding at the kilns to await his latterday Underground Railway escape in a truck owned by the emblematic Magnolia Express Company. Big Boy's journey down into this kiln-pocked Hell is heralded by 'six foot of snake', racism's devil serpent made incarnate, which he kills with his stick, even though he imagines in his Dantean hiding-place 'whole nests of them', each 'waiting tensely in coil'. His underground hole, like Fred Daniels' in 'The Man Who Lived Underground' and that of Ellison's unnamed narrator in *Invisible Man*, particularizes the larger historical hole into which Big Boy and his three friends and the black race in general have been cast since slavery. He thinks back across his benigner past of home, school, the train, the songs and 'long hot Summer days', the terrain of the twelve-string Blues guitar and the briar-patch. And against this deep, comforting place of memory he plays out in imagination his fantasy-revenge on the white race, would-be heroism of the kind he thinks will make headlines like 'NIGGER KILLS DOZENS OF MOB BEFO LYNCHED'. Yet even as he dreams, the posse hunts down and captures Bobo to the refrain of 'We'll hang ever nigger t a sour apple tree.' Bobo, in turn, burns to the chorus of 'LES GET SOURVINEERS' and 'HURRY UP N BURN

THE NIGGER FO IT RAINS!' As he dies, another black boy martyred to white hate, so Big Boy chokes the Cerberus-like dog belonging to his white pursuers, token redress for the butchery of his friend and yet also the necessary murder of his own prior innocence.

As he then makes his escape, his insides drawn 'into a tight knot', he senses rightly that the 'home' he is leaving is both his own corner of the South and the whole serried history which lies behind it and also the self which for him has now passed out of innocence into experience and been fashioned by the same 'horror' and 'shadow' which will mark his near-namesake Bigger Thomas. Big Boy, as it were, has internalized the historic penalty of being black and a sexual fantasy figure within the white American South. Wright's story thus operates on a number of double bases: it tells a latterday escape narrative to recall past nineteenth-century slave narratives, and it shows how each 'fugitive' black American carries on the pulse and deeply within the larger communal scars of racist brutality. Behind its surface, too, looms the memory of even older destruction, Biblical and also dynastic, Cain against Abel replayed as white against black. Wright deposits these layers of 'inside' meaning within the story's ostensible outer detail, whether the contrast of black and white, or Day and Night, or Nature as in turn kindly and hellish. To call a story like 'Big Boy Leaves Home' simply naturalistic leaves out its genuine command of tone, Wright's organizing pattern and cadence; in effect it leaves almost all the work still to be done.

Each of the other pieces in *Uncle Tom's Children*, even if one does not think them in equal measure successful, operates in similarly double manner. In 'Down by the River', true to the classic Blues from which Wright borrows his title, the ostensible story of a black drowning and white ingratitude for help given during a Southern flood encloses an inward parable of how the black protagonist—perhaps too obviously called Brother Mann—here, as so often under Southern auspices, is in every sense 'sold down the river' by unfair racial odds. As Mann drowns, the story describes his body as 'encased in a tight vase in a narrow black coffin that moved with him'. Such detail implies that this Flood doubles as the Flood of History itself, Southern-style, a murderous 'white' stream of time in which black skin has become the garment of death. Similarly, in 'Long Black Song', we again enter mythy Blues terrain as languidly Southern in atmosphere as the Georgia of Jean Toomer's *Cane* (1923), in which a black woman gets tricked into giving her sexual favours to a white salesman. Her husband, Silas, finally chooses to burn to death rather than be hanged cravenly for the revenge he enacts on the white order of things which has so cheated him. He follows 'the long river of blood', but for once a martyr of his own choosing and not of the system which both literally and figuratively has denied him (and black men before him) their rightful manhood. 'Fire and Cloud', a story again full of mythic association though weakened by Wright's too sentimental wish to envisage shared black-white resistance to racism, tells the story of an Uncle Tom preacher and black community leader who after a vicious beating comes to reject passive black Christianity in favour of implacable opposition to arbitrary white authority in his Southern small town. The beating itself, which Wright dramatizes powerfully as a Klan-style crucifixion, serves both as an instance of brutality and a rite of deepest inward liberation for the Reverend Taylor and the past standard he represents. The story also reflects Wright's own move from nominal Christianity into a more Marxist view of real salvation, change through solidarity.

In 'Bright and Morning Star', another of Wright's stories with a Marxist and inter-racial element (which appropriately was published as a separate piece in *New Masses* in May 1938), he sets the warm maternal presence of Aunt Sue, the black mother of two activist sons, against white Southern law-and-order thuggery. An' Sue, to give her her black name, represents Faulkner's Dilsey no longer available as black choric servant-figure for white people, but the black woman as fierce protectress of her own.[12] In shooting the stool-pigeon who has brought on the torture and death of her son Johnny Boy and thereby in turn bringing on her own death from the racist villainy about her, she becomes the very incarnation of the death of Uncle Tomism, or as the story puts matters 'the dead that never dies'. She becomes legend, the exemplary myth. Wright's language throughout works literally yet also iconically, whole phrases so pitched as to call up black Bible cadence and a

211

past racial history told and re-told to the point where it becomes parable. Typical is the following:

> But as she had grown older, a cold white mountain, the white folks and their laws, had swum into her vision and shattered her songs and their spells of peace.

The inside narrative of 'Bright and Morning Star' resides exactly in Wright's lexicon of 'cold white mountain', 'songs' and 'spells of peace', black pictographic community speech which belongs to the world of Blues and known deeply in the heart. Aunt Sue indeed dies in fact but lives on in myth.

In this respect, Wright wrote no better story than 'The Man Who Lived Underground', the centre-piece to *Eight Men*. Its journey-form rightly has won praise for how it calls up Dante's *Inferno* and Dostoyevsky's *Notes from Underground*, and for how, too, it cannily anticipates *Invisible Man* and LeRoi Jones/ Imamu Baraka's *Dutchman*. For in Fred Daniels's underground odyssey, Wright develops both a literal-seeming drama of escape—a manhunt no less—and a parable of the black American as at once underground man and yet also witness, at once forced into hiding his own true self yet able to see all. In descending via the manhole cover down into his underground, Daniels sees the America into which he has been born as a land of both plenty and waste, a nation which simultaneously offers and withholds its abundance. Each glimpse of this America he experiences as one previously denied access, a kind of black underworld trespasser or scavenger forced to live at the margins of or underneath the presumed white mainstream of the nation's history. Little wonder that his first sight is that of a glistening sewer rat, a rat also to anticipate that which Bigger Thomas kills at the beginning of *Native Son* and which prefigures his own rodent-like fate in the final police chase. Everything Daniels sees, and on occasion steals, Wright sets against the spirituals being sung by the black congregation, America's black history as carried by the historic power of its music and the story's touchstone against which to locate white reality.

As Daniels flees down into the sewer, he appears to step free of time itself and to become a traveller through all single versions of time. The story's questions ask: 'How long had he been down here? He did not know.' Plunged thus into a time beyond any one time, each thing he sees takes on a weight well in excess of the literal. He sees first the dead abandoned baby 'snagged by debris and half-submerged in water', a Blakean Innocent, eyes closed, fists clenched 'as though in protest', and its mouth 'gaped black in soundless cry'. Such mute human frailty links directly to Fred Daniels's own fate, his self also essentially still-born and an object of repudiation. As he 'tramps on', one particular black figure in history yet also the personification of all past black 'tramping', he next sees an embalmer at work, his 'establishment' ice-cold, white and diabolic. The embalmer's own 'throaty chuckle' underlines the point trenchantly, whiteness as Hell.

In turn, each subsequent encounter works in similar double manner, actual scenes yet far more, America and reality as parts of a coded, visionary landscape. The coal-bin conjures up not only literal fuel but the whole underground fire of black life itself. The movie-house and its flickering screen offers an analogy with Daniels's own miasmic perceptions of the world as seen from his black underground, life in truth seen as if on a cinema-reel. The fruit and vegetables he steals become almost painterly, food transposed from actual to surrealist nourishment as on a Dali or Impressionist canvas. Similarly, the jewels he takes glisten hypnotically in the dark, real plunder yet also Gatsbyesque fantasy wealth. Even the newspaper heading, 'HUNT NEGRO FOR MURDER', assumes an air of disjunctness, language as some foreign cryptogram which encodes reality to its own system. The same note applies in the Aladdin's Cave Fred makes of the stolen banknotes, and in his tentative first efforts to write out his name. In writing *freddanniels* and the other words he becomes the like of the first Cave-dwellers, a human presence obliged by history to begin again in the path towards finding his signature.

The world thus seen from the black underground both patently exists as fact yet equally as hallucination. Daniels himself resembles as much as anyone Melville's Bartleby, a fellow-prisoner of walls:

> What was the matter with him? Yes, he knew it . . . it was these walls; these crazy walls were filling him with a wild urge out into the dark sunshine above ground.

213

He is finally shot because the story he re-surfaces momentarily to tell cannot be credited by the police, any more than can be that of Ralph Ellison's narrator in *Invisible Man* or Baraka's Clay in *Dutchman*. Wright's naturalism again secretes inside narration, the elusive underground sediments of black American history. 'The Man Who Lived Underground' undoubtedly offers the best of *Eight Men*'s stories, yet each of the others (and especially 'The Man Who Was Almost a Man' and 'Man of All Work') operates to a decipherably similar doubleness of purpose. As so often Wright's surface functions as the equivocal outward show of the other narrative being told deep within.

4

These double purposes of Wright's fiction apply equally, if not more so, to his longer work. All five of his novels—*Lawd Today* (post. 1963), *Native Son* (1940), *The Outsider* (1953), *Savage Holiday* (1954) and *The Long Dream* (1958)—blend and interweave different skeins of narrative within the story ostensibly on offer. *Lawd Today*, to take Wright's probable first novel which ironically was not published at the time of writing because of its lack of a 'clear' Marxist orientation, outwardly tells a representative twenty-four-hour day in the life of Jake Jackson, black Chicago postal worker. Its lively surface detail has all to do with the Lincoln Day Holiday, Wright's informed sense of Chicago's South Side street and bar life, community dreams of magical Numbers fortunes, black talk and rap, down-home food and sexual opportunism. In other words, it maps black urban style, the energies of a major black city-within-a-city. At the same time, *Lawd Today* explores wholly more inward terrain, Jake Jackson as a man close to psychological split and collapse. The increasing hatred he shows his wife, the valetudinarian Lil, and his inability to keep rein on his temper, mark a man going steadily out of control. Jake in fact veers increasingly towards murderousness, the victim of a process which has locked him into that internalized ghetto Chester Himes once eloquently termed 'the prison of my mind'. Reality might apparently reside in a Chicago Lincoln Day Holiday with extracts from Roosevelt Firesides on the radio, 1930s popular songs and a busy scenario of commercial hustle. But for Jake, fissured, dangerous, reality also lies far more inward, in the realms of the beleaguered psyche which can erupt into violence at the barest provocation. *Lawd Today* uses its documentary format to depict history as both daytime reality and incipient interior nightmare.

The same, I would maintain, largely holds true of *Native Son*, for all its assumed status as a naturalist classic of a kind with Dreiser's *An American Tragedy* and Steinbeck's *The Grapes of Wrath*; it also is an 'inside' story and precisely as 'dense and heavy' and full of 'shadow' as Wright himself hoped it might be in 'How Bigger Was Born'. At the immediate level *Native Son* tells of the tenement upbringing of Bigger Thomas, his half-witting murder of his white patron's daughter, the subsequent disposal in the furnace of Mary Dalton's body and in turn his flight, the murder of his girl Bessie and his trial and defence as developed in the top-heavy dialectics of Mr. Max, the Jewish and Marxist lawyer. So much, to be sure, added to the 'realist' urban background of Chicago, half-locates Wright's novel: but it also leaves the fuller achievement of *Native Son* seriously unacknowledged.

It has been objected to *Native Son*, in part by James Baldwin, that it reads as though set in something of a historical vacuum, its principal characters unsatisfactorily one-dimensional and without sufficient human resonance.[13] To the extent that this is true, it suggests not so much weakness as the fact that Wright was attempting narrative markedly different from that assumed to be naturalistic; he was in fact as much writing his own version of the kind of narration he mentions as the line of Poe, Hawthorne and Dostoyevsky. The landscape of the novel, for instance, certainly proposes a real Chicago but also and in matching degree a Chicago of the mind and senses, the bleak outward urban landscape of *Native Son* as the correlative of Bigger's psyche. His violence, from the opening episode with the rat and his bullying of his poolhall friends through to the murder and incineration of Mary and his flight, takes its course as the expression of his turbulence within. It serves as his one form of self-articulation. *Native Son* thus should be read as exploring psychology and human personality in a manner as close to, say, Kafka, as to Dreiser or Steinbeck, the Chicago of the novel as much the expression of the displaced city pent

215

up inside Bigger as the Windy City of actuality. In arguing for
this more 'shadowed' reading of *Native Son*, three supporting
kinds of allusion must do duty for the novel's procedures as a
whole: they have to do with sight, with the image of Bigger as
rat, and with exactly the kind of city depicted in *Native Son*.

Not only 'The Man Who Lived Underground' but *Native
Son*, too, calls up *Invisible Man* in its handling of seeing and
sightlessness, typically in a passage like the following in which
Bigger considers the implication of having killed Mary:

> No, he did not have to hide behind a wall or a curtain now;
> he had a safer way of being safe, an easier way. What he had
> done last night had proved that. Jan was blind. Mary had been
> blind. Mr. Dalton had been blind. And Mrs. Dalton was blind;
> yes, blind in more ways than one. . . . Bigger felt that a lot of
> people were like Mrs. Dalton, blind. . . .

Just as Bigger's black world sees him one way—merely wayward if his hard-pressed mother is to be believed, a tough
street-companion according to his poolhall buddies, a lover in
Bessie's eyes—so, too, to the white world he is seen only
through part of his identity, as some preferred invention like
the recipient of Mr. Dalton's self-serving largesse, or the prole-
tarian black worker imagined by Mary and her lover Jan, or
Mr. Max's example of how 'scientific' history shapes the individual consciousness. Even the final chase scenes across run-
down wasteland Chicago against which he is silhouetted by
the police cross-lights show him only in part, the formulaic
rapist-murderer. Bigger's full human self, even at the end
probably ungrasped by the victim himself, lies locked inside
'the faint, wry bitter smile' he wears to his execution.[14]
Perhaps the true self lies teasingly present in the white cat
which watches him burn Mary's body (an episode to recall the
duplicitous intentions of stories like 'Ethan Brand' or 'The
Masque of the Red Death'), in part the emissary of the white
world which has hitherto so defined Bigger but just as
plausibly the rarest glimpse of his own fugitive and 'whited'
identity.

The rat killed by Bigger in the opening chapter also sets up
a motif which resonates throughout the novel. Its belly 'pulsed
with fear', its 'black beady eyes glittering', the rat points

forward to the figure Bigger himself will become, the part-real, part-fantasy denizen of a grotesque counter-Darwinian world in which human life—his own, Mary's, Bessie's—seems to evolve backwards into rodent predation and death. Whether in pursuit or the pursued, Bigger becomes damned either way, just as he victimizes others while doubling as both his own and society's victim. These inner meanings of the novel also lie behind Wright's three-part partition of 'Fear', 'Flight' and 'Fate', as much notations of *Native Son*'s parabular meanings as the apparent drama at the surface. Bigger's parting words to Mr. Max suggest that he has some first glimmerings of the process which has metamorphosized him into a human rodent, but he goes to his death still trapped by the predatory laws which he sought to repudiate by throwing the skillet at the rat in the opening chapter.

In 'How Bigger Was Born', Wright speaks of Chicago as 'huge, roaring, dirty, noisy, raw, stark, brutal', that is as the city of the historic stockyards, oppressive Summer humidity and the chill polar winds of the mid-Western Winter. He also speaks of Chicago as a city which has created 'centuries-long chasm[s] of emptiness' in figures like Bigger Thomas. *Native Son* depicts Chicago in just that way: as a literal instance of colour-line urban America but also as the more inward City of Dreadful Night, for Bigger both the world among whose tenements and on whose streets he has been raised and the city which he has internalized, one of violence and half understood impulses to revenge. To discern in *Native Son* only an urban-realist drama again evades the dimensions of the novel Wright himself knowingly calls 'the whole dark inner landscape of Bigger's mind'.

5

Though by no means disasters, both *The Outsider* and *Savage Holiday* go seriously adrift and for connected reasons. In the former, Wright cannot resist loading his story of Cross Damon as the black twentieth-century man of alienation *par excellence* with an accompanying (and intrusive) set of explanations about *angst* and the whole eclectic tradition of outsiderness. Not only does he actually name time and again founding figures like Heidegger and Kierkegaard, but he glosses Damon's different murders and assumptions of identity with allusions to Dread, Will, the legacy of the Absurd. To this end, too, he imports into the novel Damon's fellow outsider, the hunch-backed District Attorney Eli Houston, to whom it falls as it does to Mr. Max in *Native Son* to analyse the processes which have made Damon what he is, the perfect instance of the a-moral, alienated man of will. In *Savage Holiday*, Wright's touchstone becomes Freud, human personality in the form of Erskine Fowler, an ex-Insurance Man eased out of his job to make way for the boss's son and the victim of an almost absurd turn of events which results in the death of a neighbour's young boy. His own glaring sexual repression eventuates in murder, the stabbing of the boy's voluptuous mother whose easy sexual style torments Fowler. As in *The Outsider*, Wright can be lively, but more often he turns essayistic and tutorly. The failure of both books lies in the fact that Wright simply will not trust his own tale to do the work; whether the keystone is Existentialism or Freudianism, the inside narrative is made damagingly explicit. Wright's philosophical interest thereby throws the drama of his novels out of balance, their inside direction far too available from the outset.

Fortunately, though not without other faults, Wright's last novel *The Long Dream* (a sequel *Island of Hallucination* remains unpublished) shows no blemish of this kind. In part this most likely has to do with Wright's return to the materials he drew from so convincingly in *Black Boy*, the Deep South and its haunting memory as a place of origins. For the story *The Long Dream* tells, that of Fishbelly Tucker's childhood and passage into adult identity, Wright organizes without the directing hand which breaks into and flaws *The Outsider* and *Savage Holiday*. Indeed, the sheer full-plottedness of the novel could hardly have left too much scope for that kind of intrusion.

A major part of the novel's success lies in Wright's meticulous recreation of Fishbelly's childhood, at once the wholly individual childhood of a black boy in the South whose undertaker-father takes care to educate him as best he knows into the wiles needed to survive in the treacherous world of small-town Dixie, and at the same time a version of Black Childhood itself, the dynastic re-enactment of what it means

218

to be black, curious and permanently at risk from white authority. Fishbelly, from the first acquiring of his folk name (which Wright does marvellously) through to his first sexual awakenings, does learn from Tyree his father, but he also comes to know that his father's business exists on deals struck with the Chief of Police, Cantley, and that the town's tacit and demeaning lines of agreement have been arranged on the basis of white superiority and black inferiority. Further, Fishbelly perceives that his father, by running a Numbers racket and brothel, is also embalming his people figuratively just as he embalms them literally in his undertaking business. The chain of events which finally kill Tyree and lead to Fishbelly's jailing on a trumped-up sex charge involving a white woman thus again assume a double set of meanings. Fishbelly's story, in all its twists and detail, offers the chronicle of one life: but it also absorbs the ritual of black coming-of-age, the perception of what it is to be man and nigger, self and shadow.

Fishbelly's story undoubtedly plays off Richard Wright's own. And like the story Wright successfully fictionalized into *Black Boy* and *American Hunger*, it refracts through the one life the more collective story of black community as experienced in the American South. The impress of that South, its deeply inward story as well as literal geography and the past as shaped below the Mason-Dixon line, Fishbelly carries with him as he flees not as Big Boy and others to the Northern city but as Wright himself to Europe. Wright persuasively locates this double-memory in 'the locked regions' of Fishbelly's heart. The novel, too, rightly makes vivid use of dream and memory, forms of imagined life which work to deepen the impression of 'inside narrative' and which play against the 'actual' history being told at the surface. *The Long Dream*, then, offers the seeming literal history of Fishbelly, but as the title suggests and the last chapter makes explicit a history which is also 'dream' and 'nightmare'. Both stories lie within Fishbelly's mind, the South as at once the realm of literal phobias and outrage and his own troubled growth into adulthood and the matching other realm of all the 'shadows' which have settled within his personality.

In his Introduction to George Lamming's *In the Castle of My Skin* (1953), Wright explicitly calls attention to the ancestral racial layerings which have marked out black experience in the white West. He also implies how impossible it would be to render that experience to any single measure, be it that of Protest, or one or another version of naturalism, or even of Marxism or Existentialism or Freudianism. One observation in particular helps to locate the multiple reaches of his own fiction:

> the Negro of the Western world lives, in *one* life, *many* lifetimes.
> . . . The Negro, though born in the Western world, is not quite of it; due to policies of racial exclusion, his is the story of *two* cultures: the dying culture in which he happens to be born, and the culture into which he is trying to enter—a culture which has, for him, not quite yet come into being. . . . Such a story is, above all, a record of shifting, troubled feelings groping their way towards a future that frightens as much as it beckons.[15]

Such a story, we might want to say, amounts to exactly the inside narrative on offer in Richard Wright's fiction.

NOTES

1. Richard Wright, *Black Boy* (New York: Harper and Brothers, 1945), p. 274.
2. Richard Wright, *American Hunger* (New York: Harper & Row, 1977), p. 135.
3. A number of the reviews from which these phrases are taken are usefully reprinted in Richard Abcarian (ed.), *Richard Wright's 'Native Son': A Critical Handbook* (Belmont, California: Wadsworth, 1970).
4. See, for instance, Addison Gayle Jr. (ed.), *Black Expression* (New York: Weybright and Talley, 1969); Addison Gayle Jr. (ed.), *The Black Aesthetic* (New York: Doubleday and Company, 1971); Addison Gayle Jr., *The Way of the New World: The Black Novel in America* (New York: Anchor Press/Doubleday, 1975); Mercer Cook and Stephen E. Henderson, *The Militant Black Writer in Africa and the United States* (Madison: University of Wisconsin Press, 1969); Stephen Henderson, *Understanding the New Black Poetry* (New York: William Morrow and Company, 1973); George Kent, *Blackness and the Adventure of Western Culture* (Chicago: Third World Press, 1972); Hoyt Fuller's articles in *Black World* (formerly *Negro Digest*) and the Special Issue of *MidContinent American Studies Journal*, Fall, 1972, Vol. XI, No. 2. A useful retrospect on many of the issues raised during the Black Aesthetic controversy can be found in Marcus Cunliffe, 'Black Culture and White America', *Encounter* 34, January 1970. From another

angle see also Houston Baker, *The Journey Back: Issues in Black Literature and Criticism* (Chicago: University of Chicago Press, 1980).

5. Alain Locke (ed.), *The New Negro: An Interpretation* (New York: A. and C. Boni, 1925).

6. Herman Melville, *Moby-Dick*, Chapter 85.

7. 'Many Thousands Gone' first appeared in *Partisan Review* 18 (November–December 1951) and is reprinted in *Notes of a Native Son* (New York: Dial, 1955). 'Alas, Poor Richard', which incorporates 'Eight Men' (originally published as 'The Survival of Richard Wright', *The Reporter*, March 1961) and 'The Exile' (*Le Preuve*, February 1961) is reprinted in *Nobody Knows My Name* (New York: Dial, 1961).

8. 'Richard Wright's Blues' first appeared in *Antioch Review* 5 (Summer 1945) and is reprinted in *Shadow and Act* (New York: Random House, 1964). 'The World and the Jug', based on an exchange with Irving Howe ('The Writer and the Critic', *The New Leader*, February 1964, and 'A Rejoinder', *The New Leader*, December 1964) also appears in *Shadow and Act*.

9. See especially, Gayle, *The Way of the New World*, pp. 209–19.

10. 'How Bigger Was Born' first appeared in *Saturday Review*, 1 June 1940, 3–4, 17–20.

11. Chapter 3 in *White Man, Listen!* (New York: Doubleday, 1957).

12. Other portraits in Afro-American fiction which might be thought to continue this kind of portrait of the black woman include Merle Kinbona in Paule Marshall's *The Chosen Place, The Timeless People* (1969), Alice Walker's Ruth in *The Third Life of Grange Copeland* (1970) and Meridian Hill in *Meridian* (1976), Gayl Jones's Corregidora in *Corregidora* (1975) and Toni Cade Bambara's Velma Henry in *The Salt Eaters* (1980).

13. Especially in 'Many Thousands Gone'.

14. For a useful gloss on the scene, see Graham Clarke, 'Beyond Realism: Recent Black Fiction and the Language of "The Real Thing" ' in A. Robert Lee (ed.), *Black Fiction: New Studies in the Afro-American Novel Since 1945* (London: Vision Press, 1980), p. 220.

15. George Lamming, *In the Castle of My Skin* (New York: McGraw-Hill Book Company, 1945), p. vi.

13

Norman Mailer: The True Story of an American Writer

by JEAN RADFORD

Among students of the American novel, it is a truth universally acknowledged that Norman Mailer is a man in possession of much talent in want of achievement. Starting in 1948 as one kind of a writer, he developed into a stylistic chameleon (realist, allegorist, journalist), crossing generic border-lines (with essays, short-stories, criticism and the novel), raiding a number of ideological positions (marxist, existentialist, left conservative, Zen) and in the course of his progress losing and gaining more points in the critical 'Bimmler' than almost any other contemporary American novelist.

I want to suggest, first, that this intellectual and stylistic mobility is important not merely for American literature but for the future possibilities of the novel form; to suggest that Mailer's changing literary strategies are not simply expressive of his personal qualities as a writer, but are symptomatic of the social and aesthetic problems faced by *all* contemporary writers. The great divide between those novelists who have turned toward fantasy and fabulation on the one hand, and those preoccupied with 'faction' and non-fiction modes on the other, is now too striking to ignore. In the last year, the major literary prizes around the world reflect this division: the Nobel

222

Prize for literature going to Gabriel Garcia Marquez for his *One Hundred Years of Solitude* and in Britain the Booker Prize being awarded to Thomas Keneally's non-fiction novel *Schindler's Ark*. In this re-run of what some critics describe as the old antagonism between romance and realism (or, going further back, as the distinction between the 'true' and the 'real' made in Plato's *Republic*), Mailer's position astride this divide, his forays since the 1950s into journalism and 'non-Literary' discourse and his attempts to forge new connections for narrative form are both significant and valuable.

Secondly, I would argue that Mailer's recent work *The Executioner's Song* (1979), is not just a commercial interruption of the 'large social novel' about America which he has been promising for some fifteen years now, but is itself a major achievement and a partial realization of that project. In the account of the Utah murderer Gary Gilmore and his execution, he has assembled a new repertoire of literary devices through which he mounts a panoramic documentary on American culture. The montage of voices, produced from hundreds of interviews with those involved in the Gilmore case, has in effect released Mailer from the limitations of his personal voice and vision and provided him with a new means to address the contradictions and nuances of his world. Apart from the compulsive readability of this 1000-page fiction, *The Executioner's Song* is remarkable among his works for the almost complete absence of Mailer's personality; there is no authorial verdict on the events narrated, no distinctive Maileresque 'style' separable from the multitude of narrating voices. Mailer remains almost invisible, behind or beyond his handiwork, working in Joycean fashion with a very rich verbal palette and working, it seems to me, brilliantly. Not perhaps since *The Naked and the Dead* has he come as close to writing an epic on the American way of life.

Mailer started writing while still at Harvard in the early '40s and the influence of various '30s writers—Farrell, Dos Passos and Steinbeck—is evident in *The Naked and the Dead*. This novel in four parts describes the capture of a small island in the South Pacific from the Japanese in World War II: it offers a detailed realistic account of an Intelligence and Reconnaissance platoon from the initial landing, in combat, through a reconnaissance patrol to the conclusion and after-math of battle. Intercut with this narrative are the inter-chapter biographies of the platoon members, in a manner which recalls the techniques of *USA*. The debt is not merely a technical one either, since many of the ideas in the book are clearly continuous with the social vision of Dos Passos's trilogy. The patrol is used as a microcosm of American society, and the racial and sexual attitudes of the enlisted men with their power-hungry dreams are used to represent the corrup-tion of the American dream. The conversations between the neo-fascist General Cummings and his liberal Lieutenant, Hearn, dramatize the political alternatives which Mailer envisages for post-war America. The juxtaposition of the frag-mented physical ordeals of the private soldiers with Cum-mings's highly structured overall conception of the war, is itself one of the themes of the novel: the undemocratic nature of an army engaged in fighting against fascism.

Where the writing about combat is brisk and effective, and strongly reminiscent of Hemingway, the somewhat determinist presentation of character in the 'Time Machine' sections is a legacy of the naturalism of the '30s, which Mailer assumed along with the more experimental newsreel style of the social commentary. As he revealed in the *Paris Review* (1948) inter-view, the characters in *The Naked and the Dead* were carefully researched. He kept a long dossier on each man, had charts to show which characters had not yet had scenes with others, and used his sociological data methodically. It was for the 'social realism' of this large cast of characters that the arch-realist Georg Lukács was to hail Mailer as a contemporary realist in his *The Meaning of Contemporary Realism:*

> *The Naked and the Dead* marks a step forward from the trackless desert of abstractions towards a portrayal of the actual suffering of actual people during the Second World War. Arbitrary though much of the detail is, and retrograde though the author's subsequent development has been, the merits of that achieve-ment . . . should not be overlooked.[1]

Lukács's comment is typical of critics who see Mailer as a renegade realist; it not only fails to understand his subsequent achievements but actually misrepresents his first novel.

Mailer's own statement, in *Current Biography* (1948) is much more relevant:

> In the author's eyes *The Naked and the Dead* is not a realistic documentary; it is rather a 'symbolic' book of which the basic theme is the conflict between the beast and the seer in man.

The novel in fact operates in a mixture of narrative modes and is both realist and 'symbolic'. Although the realist/naturalist elements are dominant in *The Naked and the Dead*, the allegorizing impulse which was to prevail in his second novel *Barbary Shore* (1951) and later again in *An American Dream*, is present from the first. If Mailer's allegiance to 'the real' emerges in the characterization of Valsen, Polack, Minetti and the others, the reconnaissance trip and the assault on Mount Anaka become an allegorical quest in which the nature of man and man's relation to Nature are examined. The allegorical element is underpinned by the finding of the Japanese officer's diary which functions as a sub-text to the theme of the beast and the seer: 'I ask myself—WHY? I am born, I am to die. WHY? WHY? What is the meaning?'[2] Thus while the conflicts between Hearn and Cummings about the merits and demerits of different social systems represent the political, Mailer introduces another level—the existential questions—which pulls the mimetic description of character and event back toward the mythical-symbolic pole. It is this complex negotiation between the rival claims of myth and realism, *within* each of his novels and from one book to another, which makes his writing so resonant.

Abandoning the omniscient technique of *The Naked and the Dead*, Mailer in his next two novels shifts from third- to first-person narration. Although the thematic concerns of *The Naked and the Dead* are developed—in his treatment of the failure of the Russian Revolution to provide an alternative to the American Dream and the nature of Hollywood as the dream-factory of America—neither *Barbary Shore* nor *Deer Park* is as effective as a fictional treatment of these issues. In *Barbary Shore* the fictional world of the Brooklyn boarding-house and its inhabitants collapses into a chapter of political speech. The unifying motifs—the images of the revolution betrayed—cannot support the weight of Mailer's ideological argument.

Lovett, the first-person narrator and a writer who has lost his memory, is the surrogate for the writer who has rejected the borrowed authority of Mailer's composite voice in *The Naked and the Dead* and not yet found an alternative. The same difficulties with voice and point-of-view are evident in *The Deer Park*. The novel begins in the first-person, as Sergius O'Shaughnessy gives a prolonged introduction of himself, the setting and characters. Only in Part II does the main story-line begin and O'Shaughnessy recedes into a witness-narrator role. In the third part of the novel, the narrator's role and authority decrease still further—('I have the conceit I *know* what happened'). Here he is referring to the Eitel-Elena affair which is told in the third-person, although O'Shaughnessy's tone colours the presentation. In effect the point-of-view becomes that of a first-person narrator with omniscient powers but the uncertainties of the narrative method begin to tell on the novel. The psychological realism of Eitel's characterization is insufficiently integrated with Marion Faye's apocalyptic visions and Sergius's mystical view of Time as 'the connection of new circuits', and the fiction falters between these three centres of consciousness. It was however an important experiment for the writer struggling to find his own voice—as Mailer comments in *Advertisements for Myself*:

> . . . the style of the work lost its polish, became rough, and I can say real, because there was an abrupt and muscular body back of the voice now. It had been there all the time . . . but now I chipped away . . . I felt as if I was finally learning how to write. . . .[3]

The short stories, essays and articles published as *Advertisements for Myself* (1957) and *Presidential Papers* (1963) are part of that explosion in literary journalism which Tom Wolfe was later to call 'The New Journalism'.[4] In these essays Mailer brings all the resources of fiction to bear, working on his new 'muscular' style, experimenting with point-of-view strategies, stretching his language to include the kind of demotic American which he had previously kept within quotation marks. Where in *The Naked and the Dead* the literary and the colloquial divide into description and dialogue, the purple passages and the 'fuggin', here the two modes are brought together. *Advertisements*, like

Lowell's *Life Studies* published the same year, is a form of autobiography which tells the story of a writer and his struggle with available forms. It is also a reconnaissance trip by a writer who like the hero of the story 'The Man Who Studied Yoga' feels he can no longer employ the anonymous omniscient narrator of the classic realist text. When Sam Slovoda is asked by one of his friends why he has given up his projected novel, Sam says he cannot find a form. He does not want to write a realistic novel, he says, 'because reality is no longer realistic' (p. 166). Again, rather like Robert Lowell, Mailer was at this point reproached by some critics for narrowing his scope from the epic sweep of his early work to the confessional mode; but there is no real contraction evident in the range of his concerns. His problem is rather to devise new methods of addressing the 'non-realistic' realities of America, to construct a narrator within the fictional frame, with a voice large enough to carry his creator's ideas about the world to a reader 'changed utterly' from the reader of nineteenth-century realist fiction. This problem, clearly, is not peculiar to Norman Mailer. It is perhaps *the* most urgent and difficult task facing the twentieth-century novelist. Within the most realistic tales, the narrating subject is seemingly removed from the frame of action, a voice (as in *The Naked and the Dead*) charged only with the duties of representation, a presence that strives to appear solely as absence. Mailer's attempts to represent that 'absence', to acknowledge his own voice within the text and to give that narrating subject a fictional existence, found its most radical expression in *Armies of the Night*—but not before he had made an excursion into a rather different realm.

An American Dream (1965) which originally appeared in monthly instalments in *Esquire* magazine, marks a return to an older narrative tradition. It is a 'romance' which rather than aiming at minute fidelity to 'the real', in Hawthorne's words, presents 'truth under circumstances . . . of the writer's own choosing and creation'.[5] Stephen Rojack, Mailer's first-person narrator-hero, is an American pilgrim in quest of rebirth and regeneration in an allegorized but recognizably American setting. The novel opens with a reference to Jack Kennedy and closes with a 'phone-call to Marilyn Monroe and claims 'a certain latitude, both as to its fashion and material'[6] which relates it not merely to the 'ideal' dreamlike world of the fable but to the violent thrillers of American popular fiction. Whatever one thinks of Mailer's views about power and sexuality[7] this is a brilliant dramatization of them. The suspense and economy of the narrative-line, the range of characters, the use of classical myths and gothic atmosphere, are all highly effective. As a negotiation of traditional and popular forms, as a sustained structure of interlocking metaphors, *An American Dream* is one of Mailer's most controlled pieces of writing. It succeeds in almost every way that *Barbary Shore*, his earlier allegory, failed. The one question it does not resolve is the author's need to break away from the first-person mode of narration which he discusses in *Advertisements*:

> For six years I had been writing novels in the first-person . . . even though the third-person was more to my taste. Worse I seemed unable to create a narrator in the first-person who was not overdelicate, oversensitive, and painfully tender, which was an odd portrait to give because I was not delicate. . . . (p. 203)

Neither Rojack nor DJ, the first-person narrator of *Why Are We in Vietnam* (1967), can be called 'delicate' and with his audio-visual media hero, DJ, Mailer manages to expand his narrator's voice into a polyphonic, polymorphous choir of American speech. Like the singer Shago Martin in *An American Dream*, his voice is 'not intimate but Elizabethan, a chorus, dig?'.

It was not, however, until *The Armies of the Night* (1968), published exactly twenty years after his first novel, that Mailer moved back to third-person narration—and here it is a third-person with a difference. The authorial position is represented as neither the 'I' of his essay work, nor as an author-surrogate narrative persona like Rojack or DJ, but through the creation of a character called Norman Mailer. This simple device—calling his hero by the same name as the author whose name appears on the cover of the book—has several advantages: Mailer has a subjective vantage-point from which to expound his most pressing concerns, but at the same time the device forces a new distance into the expression of those ideas. He is able to write about the problems of America as he sees them with a new flexibility and irony, and the stridency which mars so many of his essays is absent here. The author's voice is neither excluded from the fictional frame, nor inflated to fill it, instead it is partially 'objectified' by Mailer writing in the third-person about 'Norman Mailer'. As an attempt to bridge the fiction-autobiography, novelist-reporter dichotomy which had dominated his writing for more than a decade, *The Armies of the Night* represents a major advance.

The sub-title 'History as a Novel—The Novel as History' indicates the nature of the undertaking: the attempt is to write both a history and a novel about the anti-Vietnam war march in Washington in October 1967—and in doing so to make certain points about the interrelationship between fictional and historical modes of writing. The first section ('History as a Novel') is in his own words 'nothing but a personal history which while written as a novel was to the best of the author's memory scrupulous to facts'. In the second section ('The Novel as History') Mailer uses a more 'historic' style to write what he calls a kind of 'collective novel' about the battle of the Pentagon. The point of cross-cutting between the terms 'novel' and 'history' in this way is presumably to subvert the traditional distinction between the novel—imaginative, subjective writing—and history—factual, objective writing; to argue that in so far as history is *written* (and not just *events*) it shares certain characteristics with other forms of writing. Mailer is not suggesting that nothing exists outside discourse (which would be a rejection of ontological realism and hence idealism) but that since we cannot know 'history' except through discourses about it, historical discourse has no more privileged a relation to 'the real' than does the novel. He thus moves freely between the novelistic and the historical modes, enriching his factual account with fictional techniques—as in the speech which he inserts into the mouth of the commanding officer in 'A Palette of Tactics':

> ... the point to keep in mind, troopers, is those are going to be American citizens out there expressing their Constitutional right to protest—that don't mean we're going to let them fart in our face—but the Constitution is a complex document with circular that is circulating sets of conditions—put it this way ... —they start trouble with us, they'll wish they hadn't left New York unless you get killed in the stampede of us to get them.[8]

Through this creative reconstruction, a device commonly used in classical histories, Mailer gives an 'interiority' to characters on the other side of the battle. The characters encountered by the protagonist—Lowell, Dwight Macdonald, the Marshall and the Nazi together with a host of students, demonstrators and jailbirds—are vividly presented. But to get beyond the limitations of Mailer-the-protagonist's point-of-view, to present a more inclusive 'historical' account, Mailer-the-writer invokes his authorial prerogative of omniscience. The point is neatly made: the historian is an omniscient narrator of 'collective novels'.

Like the Constitution, then, *The Armies of the Night* is 'a complex document'. It is a culminating point in the history of Mailer's literary career: another volume in the muted auto-biography of the writer which runs through his work, an essay at the big novel about America in war and peace, and further than this, it is a reaffirmation of the novel as a form and a philosophical justification of the 'novelistic' approach to experience. The exchange between Robert Lowell and Norman Mailer at a Washington party before the march is a dramatic prologue to this argument. When Lowell tells him he thinks him the best journalist in America, Mailer's retort is an affirmation—not just of Mailer—but of the role of the writer:

> 'Well, Cal,' said Mailer using Lowell's nickname for the first time, 'there are times when I think of myself as being the best writer in America'. (p. 22)

The choice of the word 'writer' (not novelist) is his assertion of the unity of his literary activity which takes in both fiction and journalism, and his refusal of the categories of 'artistic' and 'non-artistic' forms of writing. If *An American Dream* is a bid to combine the conventions of 'serious' allegory and popular fiction, *The Armies of the Night* makes the same attempt in relation to journalism and the novel. As Rojack confronts the need to make connections between the 'intellectuals' guild' and the 'horde of the mediocre and the mad' who, in his view, people the American continent, so the hero of *The Armies of the Night* defines his responsibility to connect 'the two halves of America . . . not coming together'. Both Rojack and 'Mailer' in the later book, are writers walking the parapet between the intellectual and the popular, and Mailer with his dream of making 'a revolution in the consciousness of our time' is too ambitious a writer to settle for a minority 'art' audience.

More than ten years after the Pulitzer prize-winning *Armies of the Night*, Mailer was awarded a second Pulitzer Prize for fiction for his 'true life story'[9] *The Executioner's Song* (1979). His work during this period continues the shift away from 'pure' fictionality in a series of engagements with popular culture— writings on sport, sexual and party politics, the space programme and the media. He uses this material, as he used the geographical and sociological descriptions in *The Naked and the Dead*, to pursue his existential questions about good and evil, the meaning of life and death. Despite some powerful short pieces like the essay entitled 'The King of the Hill', too often Mailer extrapolates from the detail of his material to make familiar generalizations about mystery, Dread and the technologizing of America. There is a repetitive quality about *The Fire on the Moon*, *The Prisoner of Sex* and *Marilyn* which suggests that this working-through of positions was becoming compulsive and his metaphorical flights a stylistic tic. There was also his failure to complete the big novel about America; Mailer was 800 pages into this new novel (since entitled 'Ancient Evenings' and reputedly set in Egypt) when he began to write the story of Gilmore.

Apart from the financial imperatives, the story—which in an interview he described as '. . . a found object . . . gold'[10]— offered him a chance to develop his interests in reincarnation, the experience of working-class America and the role of the media. It also promised a new and enlarged audience, new scope and a new hero—a figure very different from himself. Most importantly, perhaps, the wealth of documentary material provided a bedrock of detail which resisted recuperation and operated as a check on Mailer's generalizing habit:

> The more I worked, the more I began to feel I didn't have the right to generalize on the material. In the past, of course, I always have. I usually had more in me to say than proper material with which to express it, so that it was natural to overflow into essays. But at this point in my life, I thought, well, the people who have chosen to listen to what I've said have registered it, I've sort of used up my audience, and I thought,

well, I want another audience, I want those people who think I'm hard to read.[11]

It is this effort to reach and represent the popular—'the mediocre and the mad who listen to popular songs and act upon coincidence', as Rojack characterized them in *An American Dream*—which informs the narrative strategy of *The Executioner's Song*. Unlike Truman Capote in *In Cold Blood*, Mailer does not use his own voice or point-of-view on the events narrated. Instead, the tale of Gilmore's release from jail in April 1976 through to his execution in January 1977 is told almost entirely in the language and from the point-of-view of those involved with Gilmore during this period. Only the use of the third-person signals the presence of the narrator, indicating that the first-person pronouns of the recorded interviews have been transposed into the third-person—that 'I was six when I fell out of the apple tree' has become 'Brenda was six when she fell out of the apple tree.' Not only have the usual tags 'she said' or 'he said' been omitted, the narrator's voice is virtually effaced in favour of the diction, syntax and grammar of the original 'speakers' or interviewees.

One important consequence of this technique is that the vast cast of characters, from East and West, are present not simply as secondary figures whom the narrator 'objectifies' for the reader in his own voice, but to some extent retain their subject-positions in the discourse. Thus their perspective, their angle on Gilmore is not qualified or situated by the narrator's 'voice-over' but by the juxtaposition of accounts: of Brenda's with Nicole's, that of the family with that of police and prison officials, the psychiatrist's with the journalists and so on. Gilmore himself, as David Lodge noted,[12] is never used as a reflector of events. He is always the object of other characters' perceptions and when his actions are described by the narrator—for example in the two unwitnessed murder scenes—it is without any interiority. This different tactic has two effects: first it maintains the enigma of Gilmore's character, and second it reduces identification. His position as 'hero' is not endorsed by the adoption of his point-of-view—he is allowed to speak directly only through the letters and interviews which, since these appear in italics, are typographically marked off from the rest of the narrative.

The narrative organization which denies Gilmore any privileges with voice, also refuses the reader any privileged relation to an omniscient narrator of the kind Capote permits in his non-fiction fiction. Compare, for example, the description of the murderer's sister's house in *In Cold Blood* with the description of Nicole Barrett's house:

> The house, like the others on the slanting hillside street, was a conventional suburban ranch house, pleasant and commonplace. Mrs Johnson loved it; she was in love with the redwood panelling, the wall-to-wall carpeting, the picturewindows fore and aft, the view that the rear window provided—hills, a valley, then sky and ocean. And she was proud of the small back garden.

> Her little place was the oldest building on the block, and next to all those ranch bungalows lined up ... like pictures in supermarket magazines, the house looked as funky as a drawing in a fairy tale. It was kind of pale lavender stucco on the outside with Hershey-brown trim. ... In the backyard was a groovy old apple tree with a couple of rusty wires to hold the branches together. She loved it.[13]

Although both Capote and Mailer are using 'setting' for thematic purposes, and both descriptions depend, more or less, on the character's vocabulary and point-of-view, the degree of objectification is very different. In Capote's novel, the narrator who calls the house 'pleasant and commonplace' is clearly distinct (and distant) from the Mrs. Johnson who 'loved it'; in Mailer's description no such evaluative distance is present. This is noticeable not only in individual passages, or their use of setting, but in their presentation of the major characters. Both Capote and Mailer, for example, sketch their childhood histories, and include psychiatric reports on their subjects, but whereas Capote's text gives a certain authority[14] to the psychological explanation for the murders, Mailer not merely refuses to give the 'professional' report on Gilmore any more status than any other point-of-view, he positions the psychiatric commentaries within a medical-legal debate on Gilmore's sanity so that they themselves become objects of scrutiny.[15] Within *Executioner's Song* there is no single authoritative voice or consensus of views, and certainly no voice from the 'intellectual's guild' to give the reader a guided tour of middle-America, directing and explaining, instead, using a form of 'free indirect speech' Mailer ensures that it is the voices themselves ('an Elizabethan chorus, dig?') that are foregrounded.

Read as a play for many voices, it is not just another non-fiction novel about a murderer, but a novel about the state of the nation—or rather about the state of the nation's language. *The Executioner's Song* is therefore 'about' Gary Gilmore only in the sense that Joyce's *Ulysses* is 'about' 16 June 1904 and the sub-titles of two halves of the book 'Western Voices' and 'Eastern Voices' direct us toward this kind of reading.

'Western Voices', the first half, presents the smalltown thief and murderer who in Mailer's words 'was quintessentially American and yet worthy of Dostoevsky', and tells how he falls in love with a girl 'who is a bona-fide American heroine'.[16] The latest in a long line of Mailer's homicidal heroes, Gilmore is heroic not for the way he lives but in the manner of his death. For he is the beast who begins to 'grow' (Mailer's word) into a seer when he chooses to die for his immortal soul rather than damage it further by serving another life sentence in prison in the West. His girlfriend, Nicole, is a feminine counterpart, self-destructive where Gilmore is destructive; her similarity to Mailer's other sexually 'wasted' waifs clearly establishes her as a bona-fide Mailer heroine—like Cherry and Marilyn, a victim who suffers, but this time survives her man. Not merely does Mailer not generalize about his material as he does—disastrously I think—in *Marilyn*, the effect of the fictional strategy (her presentation in 'free indirect speech') is such that there is less sexual objectification than with almost any other Mailer heroine since Elena Esposito of *Deer Park*. By allowing her to, as it were, 'speak for herself' the text effectively distances itself from the sexual objectification it describes. This is another of the complex effects produced by Mailer's narrative strategy.

The second half of *The Executioner's Song*, entitled 'Eastern Voices', in a sense continues the story of Gilmore—his imprisonment, refusal to appeal against sentence, and his eventual execution. But it tells another story of how an enterprising, unscrupulous writer called Larry Schiller—of some talent if small achievement—collected the material for a book on Gary Gilmore. The means whereby Schiller negotiated with Gilmore, his relations and lawyers, his interview techniques and sub-contractual relations with other agents and reporters, as well as his personal life, are then recounted— again from various points-of-view. Almost all of Mailer's novels have contained a figure of the writer (Hearn in *Naked*, Lovett in *Barbary Shore*, Sergius and Eitel in *Deer Park*, Rojack in *Dream*, DJ in *Why* and Mailer himself in *Armies of the Night*) and the second half of *The Executioner's Song* continues the saga of the writer and his conditions of existence in a commercial, media-ridden world. Further, the second half of the novel in effect lays bare the devices whereby the first half—Gilmore's story—has been constructed. It partially 'deconstructs' that story by narrating the story of the writer, Schiller, behind whom, as the direct heir to his labours, stands—none other— Norman Mailer! (A fuller 'deconstruction' would have to include the tale of the two-and-a-half years that *he* spent writing *The Executioner's Song* but, as it is, that story is split off into the Afterword to the main text.) In addition, certain passages in *The Executioner's Song* ironically allude to these processes and problems in writing; when for example Mailer presents Barry Farrell, a writer subcontracted by Schiller to conduct an interview with Gilmore, he raises the whole question of authorship:

> It looked to Farrell as if Gilmore was now setting out to present the particular view of himself he wanted people to keep. In that sense he was being his own writer. It was fascinating to Barry. He was being given the Gilmore canon, good self-respecting convict canon. (p. 793)

The intricacies of narrative form—the question of who is doing what to whom in the writing and reading of fiction—are playfully put before the reader here. In *The Executioner's Song*, as in all his earlier writings, we can read the 'true-life story' of an American novelist and his struggle to find the best possible form.

Too serious a writer to play nineteenth-century 'artist' with the novel, Mailer broke with conventional realism after his very first full-length work. The sequence of experiments which followed represent his belief that 'preserving one's artistic identity is not nearly so important . . . as finding a new attack on the elusive nature of reality' that 'primarily, one's style is only a tool to use on a dig'.[17] Mailer's achievement is not just the individual novels, considerable though many of these are, but the use to which he has put his talent. He has attempted to take the novel out of its canonized existence—the good self-respecting 'art' canon—back into relation with other forms of writing, in the firm belief that only an alliance between the different literary practices—journalism, autobiography, history etc.—will safeguard the novel-form from the assaults of the non-literary mass-media forms which in the twentieth century dominate Western culture. He has thus proved a radical not merely in his politics, but in the sense that he has tried to return to the roots of the novel. For, according to one formulation,

> The novel develops from the lineage of non-fictitious narrative forms—the letter, the journal, the memoir or biography, the chronicle or history; it develops, so to speak, out of documents.[18]

Mailer's non-fiction novel draws precisely on these sources and *The Executioner's Song* is in my view an achievement which suggests that he has the talent, and the stamina, to go forward from there.

NOTES

1. Georg Lukács, *The Meaning of Contemporary Realism*, translated by John and Necke Mander (London: Merlin Press, 1963), p. 90.
2. *The Naked and the Dead* (London: André Deutsch, 1960), p. 189.
3. *Advertisements for Myself* (London: André Deutsch, 1957), p. 203.
4. See Tom Wolfe, *The New Journalism* (London: Picador, 1975).
5. Nathaniel Hawthorne, Preface to *The House of the Seven Gables*.
6. Ibid.
7. See my *Norman Mailer: A Critical Study* (London: Macmillan, 1975), Chapter 4, for a discussion of Mailer's sexual politics.
8. *The Armies of the Night* (London: Weidenfeld and Nicolson, 1968), p. 257.
9. *The Executioner's Song* (London: Hutchinson, 1979), p. 1053.
10. John W. Aldridge, Interview with Norman Mailer, *Partisan Review* 47 (1980), 174–82.
11. Ibid.

12. David Lodge, 'From a View to Death', *Times Literary Supplement*, 11 January 1980.
13. Truman Capote, *In Cold Blood* (London: Hamish Hamilton, 1966), p. 180; *Executioner's Song*, p. 72.
14. *In Cold Blood*, p. 302.
15. As Mailer confesses in the Afterword (p. 1052), the placing of the psychiatrists' interviews was one of his 'creations'.
16. *Partisan Review* interview.
17. Ibid.
18. Rene Wellek and Austin Warren, *The Theory of Literature* (London: Penguin, 1973), p. 216.

Notes on Contributors

JOSEPH ALLARD teaches literature and art at the University of Essex. He has published a number of essays on American painting, prose, and poetry and on music theory, and is one of the organizers of the Essex Festival of Contemporary Arts.

HAROLD BEAVER, editor of Melville's *Redburn, Moby-Dick* and *Billy Budd, Sailor and Other Stories* for the Penguin English Library, is Professor of American literature at the University of Amsterdam. A collection of cultural and critical essays, *The Great American Masquerade*, is forthcoming.

HERBIE BUTTERFIELD is Reader in Literature at the University of Essex. He is the author of a book on Hart Crane, a monograph on Robinson Jeffers, and numerous essays and shorter pieces on American poets and prose-writers. He is also editing a volume in the Critical Studies series on American poets.

ROBERT CLARK is a lecturer in English and American literature at the University of East Anglia. His *History, Ideology, and Myth: Classic American Fiction in its Social Context, 1823–1852* is soon to be published by Macmillan.

RICHARD GRAY, the editor of this volume, is Reader in Literature at the University of Essex. He has edited two anthologies of American poetry and a collection of essays on Robert Penn Warren. He is also the author of *The Literature of Memory: Modern Writers of the American South* as well as essays on American poetry and fiction.

A. ROBERT LEE teaches American literature at the University of Kent. He has edited an edition of *Moby Dick* and (in the Critical Studies series) collections of essays on black fiction, Hawthorne, and Hemingway. Among his other publications are articles on Melville, George Eliot, Chester Himes, Robert Penn Warren, Mark Twain, and a pamphlet on black fiction since Wright.

JIM PHILIP was educated at Cambridge and Sussex Universities. He has also been a Visiting Fellow at the University of Pennsylvania. He lectures at Essex University on modern English and American literature, and has published extensively in both these fields.

JEAN RADFORD is the author of *Norman Mailer: A Critical Study* and teaches English and American literature at Hatfield Polytechnic. She has written a number of articles on critical theory and is currently researching a book on women and narrative.

ALLAN GARDNER SMITH is Chairman of American Studies at the University of East Anglia. He has published a book on early American psychology and fiction and articles on Poe, Twain, Melville, Wharton, and Crane. He is at present completing a study of Hawthorne to be published by Croom Helm.

CHARLES SWANN lectures in the Department of American Studies at the University of Keele. He has published on Scott, Galt, Hawthorne, Eliot, Mark Rutherford, and Stephen Crane. He is at present engaged in a study of English literature 1830–80.

BRIAN WAY was Senior Lecturer in English at the University College of Swansea. He was the author of a short study of *Moby Dick* and *F. Scott Fitzgerald and the Art of Social Fiction* as well as of numerous articles and reviews, mainly on the American novel.

Index

Index